The Opaque Veil

Kenneth Wallsmith

iUniverse, Inc.
Bloomington

The Opaque Veil

iUniverse books may be ordered through booksellers or by contacting:

iUniverse
1663 Liberty Drive
Bloomington, IN 47403
www.iuniverse.com
1-800-Authors (1-800-288-4677)

ISBN: 978-1-4759-2790-0 (sc)
ISBN: 978-1-4759-2791-7 (ebk)

Printed in the United States of America

iUniverse rev. date: 06/18/2012

End Days of Man looming,
Beloved of the verdant maid.
Earth's pageant blooming,
In the stillness of the void.

Her blood, to tribes scattered,
Sustaining flocks fleeing folly,
Burnt Earth, patience tattered,
Leaves of spring oddly fallen.

Mostly vanquished to ground,
Though some sea, the sky, few
Even encysted, as acorn bound,
Waiting, chance to start anew . . .

One seed, sleeping submerged,
Frozen from life's fearful hails,
Who would dare within emerge,
Transform past Opaque Veils?
            —Song of the Ombari'Durai

Dedication

This book could be dedicated to a lot of folk who touched me these last 44 years and made me a better man. However, the usual suspects come to mind: Jacob Sheppard, Sir Robbeth Shearer, Ev Darling, Richard Wetherell, Chris Smith, Carl Regenhartd, Robert Bunting, Courtney Furno, Benjamin Neely, Ketch Anderson, Sir Seanneth Callahan, and my dad Roger A. Jackson, whose great lights and companionship both sheltered and guided me at critical times in my life.

To my "BB", Chris Talbot, whose light burned me with a cleansing fire and who walked with me through the bright, crystal caves of our minds.

Last, thanks to my Higher Power. I am so grateful, for without His subtlety, wisdom, and small voice in my ear when all was dark I wouldn't be here at all much less shine.

Contents

Contents

Chapter 1

Liquid Light

Lieutenant Hugh Wilkey pressed his head against the glass like surface, more than mere tempered sand. Breathing deeply he imagined pulling light in through his nose and darkness out through his mouth. Calming and lessoning his headache as he rubbed the metal aperture at the base of his fourth vertebrae with a free hand. He slowly opened his eyes, the star light filtering past the thick, clear plating. Blazing diamonds made precious against the dark bully of endless night.

The two meter portal took some getting used to and was big enough to walk through, flush with the deck. A round doorframe leading to oblivion. It oft seemed designed to keep him alert and in awe at the vastness just outside. He purposely leaned his full weight against it. Mildly acrophobic, the slight vertigo he felt knowing certain death was a bare two inches ahead of him was a ritual, a reminder, and aversion therapy all in one. The irony, the barrier was as strong as any part of the shielded hull. It was Hugh's symbol, a symbol of the battle he waged inside himself. It was as if some intangible barrier within his mind thinly separated him from the precipice of doom, truth, or perhaps even actualization or it's lesser cousin, acceptance. He often pondered on this whether he stood there or not, a visitor to phantoms of doubt and hope.

Pins of light, distant stars, streaked by into the darkness as the fusion drive kicked in and pushed the fleet to the designated coordinates. A barely noticeable pull on his equilibrium demonstrated the star ship's sublime power, man kind's brilliance and far stretched hand all at once. Contrasted starkly by the chaste white of the bulkhead, space seemed disorderly, uncontrolled, and man's attempt to bring order to the inside of its eggshell seemed insignificant despite his magnificent science. As his forehead left the cool window, a magnetic field pulsed minutely as the ship cleaned residual oil at the point of contact with his skin from its perfect surface.

"Aren't you a tidy girl Nova", he whispered in a soft baritone to no one in particular.

The ship's computer used to enquire into Hugh's meaning, needs, or to clarify what he was referring to. Hugh told it to just beep at his comments unless something was urgent and his tonal qualities raised to a certain decibel range. He had picked up the recent habit of talking to himself and the ship board coms could pick up a mouse scratching itself. He was keeping to his own company too much since the surgery.

"Beeeep"

Nova was not the best company, but not judgmental and certainly consistent, Hugh mused. His eyes refocused on the reflection he cast in the port window, the foci of his sanctum. An angular, wide, honest face, two gold bars on each lapel indicating rank, a crisp, white Naval uniform. Short, auburn hair, deep brown eyes, and the coup de gras, an honest to goodness scar on his cheek. It was something that, like his hair color and actual need to shave and groom brought curiosity and not so veiled glances at mess hall.

A legion of doctors reveled at how blessed Hugh was with an epi-genome that was so delightfully confounding to modification. The cutting of hair, the archaic art of shaving, or body hair in general except for ones head was completely modified in most modern homo-sapiens. Even a scar could not be removed on him, nor tissues cloned or organs. Of the thirty billion of his fellow citizens, less than one percent was so afflicted. Of that percent, less than three percent had his extreme resistance. Any attempt at body craft would simply fail or be rejected. Hugh mastered shaving his face with his combat blade, with only a few memorable mistakes. He would always be what he was in a society of tailored godlings.

So he learned to cut his own hair, learned to fit in, though he cursed himself for being so embarrassed. He knew his physicality bothered him more profoundly than the condition warranted and a part of him despised the esoteric mutability of his race. It was fashion, it was for mating, it was for great strength, genius, or other gifts that people yearned for when they spent their credits at the Crafters. If you wanted to demonstrate your power, you spent your units making yourself into a god. Had it always been this way? Money bought your god hood, it was a citizen's obligation to the race to elevate oneself. Even the poor shed blood and family to gain the perfect graft. If the pool of tissues of high genetic density were becoming rarer by the decade, it did not matter or stop the rapacious drive of youth and perfection in the flesh markets.

People like him did not easily excel in a society built around replacing body systems when damaged or on a whim to deepen an eye color or simple skin tone. Many killed themselves for being forced to accept the stubborn genetic cards dealt among his minority, though this was kept quiet. Hugh knew his condition actually made him uniquely suited for the current HCSIS (Isus) system, Nova's cutting edge interface. The sole vessel in the Colonial Empire that supported a direct, physical connection to a human that could potentially control all the functions of a dreadnaught, a ship usually manned by 2,000 personnel, or even a fleet. He was the officer given special status because he alone could endure the surgeries and dangers that came with brain/computer symbiosis, all based on a birth defect that made him an outsider his whole life. A life he couldn't remember due to the metal implant drilled six inches into his brain.

An outcast from the beginning; how the tables had turned. They all needed him now and despite how he and his minority were treated his entire life, he would endeavor to save them. The cabin door chimed. Hugh turned, "Enter."

Two armed Marines walked in and came to parade rest on either side of the hatch. Hugh briefly inspected the E-4's, groomed, blond, genetically chiseled and hairless faces. Their deep blue eyes reflected little and he wondered if they were brothers, but of course, they weren't. This is what fashionable commoners beneath eighty looked like, with little variation. Striding toward him and between them, a striking Asian woman in formal science uniform. Dark green eyes and black hair, actual epicanthic folds on her eyelids, unusual in itself, appraised him briefly. Hugh's glance slipped discreetly down soft curves, full breasts, to her waist. A broad bladed short sword, a khirda, reserved for aristocracy or high government rank, hung from one side of her belt, a hand laser from the other. Worn during duals or very formal occasions, the ornate scabbard held a sheen only boiled kraken skin could attain. He had no idea she possessed the noble pedigree to hold an heirloom like this.

"You're here early. Dueling me Doctor?

"No, thank you."

"I've never seen you wear that before. Dressed to impress the Imperial Science Academy and their goons?," Hugh tried to sound bland.

"Hello Lieutenant Wilkey. First, not dueling unless you mean political. I am glad, however, that you retain your humor." She absently touched the mildly fluorescent hilt of her weapon, a dragon's head, jade eyes, and peered at the window Hugh had quit a moment before. "I am quite pleased with you and the system, overall, despite the gravity of proving our contract to the Imperial, military, and science hacks waiting for us to fail. This trinket reminds those fat heads we are going to impress why they need us to save them, and who I am. Even if I have to cut them a bit."

Doctor Hsian proffered her hand towards Hugh's bathroom. "Now, would you mind terribly getting out of that uniform and into your tank suit? We have work to do."

Hugh cringed a little inwardly. Here we go. He moved to the head of his cabin, closing the door behind him. He quickly shucked his dress whites and put on his swim suit. It seemed odd that he had to dress down for what was probably one of the most important days of his life. Damn! He left his bathrobe on the couch. He looked at the soft brown hair that covered his chest and arms thickly and winced. These secondary sex characteristics were not only unfashionable but were genetically weeded out of men with many other "impurities" before they were even born. But he refused to shave his body and could not be genetically tweaked, so too bad. "Oh hell."

Hugh darted out of the bathroom and grabbed his robe, but caught the surprise and quiet amusement coming from the Marine escort, despite their discipline. "Okay so I am the missing link, I wish I could say show time is over." He smiled tightly at them as he headed for the lift, pausing only to get his slippers against the cold, plasteel hall. He glanced at Doctor Hsian, "but it's only just begun."

Doctor Hsian nodded grimly and headed off with them to the bridge of the Starship Nova. "Indeed."

The technician spared a glance at the forty dignitaries and brass on the raised platform surrounding the submersion booth. Naval specialists of every rating bustled amongst complex machinery, avoiding cables twisting underfoot like roots. Unusual untidiness for the Spartan deck of a United Colonial vessel. The bridge with pilot crew and Captain, on the main level below, tensely attended to the apex computer whose importance was emphasized by the recent tradition of naming the ship after the system that ran its myriad functions.

Armed Marines guarded the exposed ship's brain, standard when civilians of any kind were on a warship. From that core, normally sacrosanct and protected by both shield and pyranite plating rose an unusual cable whose business end connected to the back of a Hugh's head in the lab above. A last minute torque adjustment on the spinal port fused into the Lieutenants was now complete. The tech carefully pulled his spanner away from Hugh, the arm of his suit sparking as it passed the suspension field that kept the officer hovering, half naked above the tank of placid, amber liquid.

"Are you receiving signal, sir?"

Dr. Lillian Hsian, project leader, heralded and introduced the various officers, politicians, and most poignantly Admiral Phillip Karn and Imperial Senator Sander Shalinsky; Hugh Wilkey was glad he had his back to them all. Hugh slowed his breathing and pushed his conscious mind as he had countless times during training simulations before, into the cable connected to Nova's mainframe.

The cable charged and Hugh's awareness winked out as the stimuli from specified cranial neurons switched into the cable until his consciousness reached the end of the electronic roller coaster he termed "the junction". A glimmering field of lights where he could see and hear, though not taste or smell. Movement of his body was not possible. He was paralyzed. When lowered into the tank his body's skin would be subsumed, becoming a reflection of the ship's hull, whose working super computer now hosted Hugh. He knew he wasn't in his own head, so to speak, and was point focused, as the instructors had drilled him for weeks, had trained him to do, on a new and temporary extension of his body. As one normally would but with more articulation, Hugh formed and projected his thoughts.

Nova please respond.

The lights shimmered and a voice reverberated lightly, *HCSIS project password required or this connection will be cancelled.*

Transform: 101599

Password confirmed. United Colonial Flagship Nova, time stamp November 28, 3467 A.D. reporting to live field test of Human/Computer Sensor Interface Study as ordered. Good afternoon Lieutenant.

Hugh breathed a figurative sigh of relief. The state of the art, mother computer that was the ship had toned down its "voice". The first time he met Nova it was how he imagined meeting God. It was a long time since then but Nova eventually, well, mellowed. *Hello Nova, it's a live test today. Dr. Hsian has pushed us two months ahead of schedule for this dog and pony show. Is this to impress the brass enough to think we deserve continued funding or do we have an actual emergency?*

Such information unknown to Nova at this time Lieutenant, the lights surrounding him shimmied in what Hugh came to think of as a Nova shrug.

I know, Nova. I'm not prying. It would foul the experiment if I actually knew what we were looking for here. Did Nova understand nuance, sarcasm? Nova shimmied again, perhaps mirth, but Shalinsky would definitely pull the plug on HCSIS if he even hinted at a six hundred billion credit computer having emotive qualities. The Senator in the past had lambasted the project as "massive misappropriations on voodoo science," when referring to the powerful Nova ship computer and even Hugh himself. Dr. Hsian would have his head if he broached anything of the kind.

"Petty Officer Bradley, signal is received." Hugh finally responded to the P.O.'s question though it actually took little time. He routed his response through Nova to Bradley's ear mike, since he had a bad habit of responding through the liquid of the tank and just making bubbles. Time was not easily trackable while linked, at least for the connected subject. What seemed like minutes often took seconds, perhaps due to some sharing of Nova's enormous processing speed while joined. Hugh was still trying to both heal and make sense of the hardware in his head. It was considered a waste by much of the Senate. But the Prelate himself as well as the Colonial Assembly backed any studies possible to discover the vector for the spread of the unknown plague that had eliminated settlers in the outermost systems.

The mysterious pathogen had killed no other animal life on three quarantined and colonized planets in the last six month's, except human. It also threatened the two thriving worlds they hovered above with the United Colonial fleet whose flagship was Nova, no less. The Colonial Empire was pulling out all the stops, outlandish or not in hopes of stopping the worst crisis faced by humanity since the Blackening.

Dr. Hsian's crisp alto cut through the spacious lab's amphitheater. Hugh could hear her smooth voice second hand through Nova's senses, though he wasn't sure which mikes were picking it up, like trying to scratch an itch from the inside of your body by going through the capillaries of the skin. "Prepare for submersion and sensor interface Nova. Mr. Bradley please confirm oxygen saturation levels in the Lieutenant. Give him another injection if his saturation drops below 98 % and route all readings to the central halo for our guests please."

Nova don't they know I can hear them?

They are not explaining it for you, but for the attendees.

"Aye aye Mam".

Dr. Lillian Hsian or Lilly was one of the most highly esteemed Magnetic Field Theorists alive today. She had been a tiger wrestling support for HCSIS through both Colonial Assembly, Senate, and finally to executive orders from the Prelate himself of the U.C.E. The plague had raged for months by that time but she spearheaded this Green Party push right through the heart of the conservative held Senate. Though hard, physically and mentally, she had been kind to Hugh through this incredible process. Such blending of masculine traits with the feminine had rarified how Hugh saw beauty in women, now typified by the good doctor. Like an orchestra conductor with a well run symphony, she caught Bradley's eye, thumbs up, good to go, while doing four other sweeps and status checks. Hugh would have been mortified if his roving eye was ever detected by the brilliant scientist. Technically she was not part of his chain of command, he was fairly sure some Inquisitor Tribunal could construe his flirting and whip him for fraternization with negative results for his Naval career, irreplaceable genetic anomalies or not. Was she married? How could he find out? Perhaps ringless out of simple prudence working with machines and field generators all day, but she always had those damn white gloves on.

Detecting non specific parameters Lieutenant. Nova offered

Disregard Nova. Just . . . static. Hugh focused.

Petty-officer Bradley conveyed the thumbs up to Hugh whose eyes were wide open though unseeing. Though visual recognition from his body and even the blink reflex was not possible as the magnetic field slowly lowered him into the kinetic, honey colored liquid of the sensory tank, he had limited visual feed from Nova at this point. It was show time and the program needed a flawless test even if there were any false reads and soon he would see more than any human ever could. *I will do my best.*

This test series appears identical to our previous, routine testing Lieutenant Wilkey. The tank is at your preferred 34 degrees Celsius.

Startled by Nova, you never got quite used to someone else poking into your consciousness. Despite software modifications, Nova was evolving and picking up some less binary, interactive, and human qualities over the last six months. Hugh let his body go limp and very remotely felt the liquid touch on the front of his swimsuit, nose, face, eyes, and then, the golden glow gave way to space, his consciousness popped out of the junction when the last of him sunk into the tank, his mind exploded outward into a sea of liquid light. With an airless gasp the sensory link kicked in fully and his body fell completely away as he acquired the vast sensation of space as the light junction faded. The oxy injections recycled his CO_2 chemically, from inside his body, lending what would normally be an experience in drowning into a greatly extended holding of his breath, where the first minute of fresh air lasted several hours. Beholding the vastness of space was even more breathtaking through his new senses. Now all he had to do was surf the software of his brain through the hardware of a Dreadnaught through hundred foot tall, surging waves of data.

Nova's hull was his skin, he couldn't "feel" per se, but he had all the access that Nova did to a battery of equipment. Her computer systems pushing up the overall processing speed of his brain as well as information storage thousands of times faster than a similar, unequipped human mind. The 6th Fleet consisted of twenty United Nations cruisers and Nova herself as a full sized battleship a full mile in circumference. Hugh had 360 degree awareness and a clear view of the colonial planet Faith, blue and green like a great gem shining up at them. In the distance her sister planet Providence, shined a deep azure on nearly the opposite side of the Saturon Star. They orbited in the gravitational sweet spot where class M planets are mostly found and were thriving colonial holdings, though two class M planets in the same system was exceedingly rare.

It was as if Hugh was sitting in his kitchen, in his body, except his body was a mile wide, and the two worlds were two appliances, one near, one far, and a group of plates hung about him, the fleet, awaiting his commands as he hovered weightless in the center of infinity.

Hugh's visual cortex fed directly into the bridge Holo, mitigated and framed by HCSIS programs, thank God there was no way of monitoring Nova's and his mental exchanges. Nova passed on from Doctor Hsian from her consul that a quality hologram was well received by the brass at this time, projected in large scale in the center of the amphitheater. Too bad they were missing all the euphoria and freedom, but they weren't risking their sanity and health having a thousand volt conductor rod pushed into the center of their brain either.

Dr. Hsian wants you to do an orbital scan of Faith, full grid analysis.

Understood Nova. The HCSIS has all been about *faith.* Since Hugh's memory had been damaged by the procedure he volunteered for, he had to rely on the concept exclusively to get him through to the potential honor such sacrifice and risk would bring. Lilly said the glory it would bring to his home city, New Boston, as well as the entire United Colonial Star Fleet after teasing out the cause of the plague would make Hugh Wilkey a galactic hero. Yet, he didn't fully embrace being a hero. Perhaps it was just human nature to never be satisfied.

Service, duty, honor, was central to Hugh. He wanted to prove to the conservative Nationalist party now in power, to the galaxy, and mostly to himself he had a right to belong. To feel like he belonged for once even if he embodied the hopes of a minority party, he believed in them and their cause. Hugh hoped he wasn't just a symbol for alternative scientific, political thought, or an iconoclast for non engineered humanity. Though the military was his family, beyond that he wanted to act, ironically, as some force for peace; curing a plague that threatened all humanity seemed like a great way to fill the emptiness he always felt and tie all the lose threads together in a single act of sacrifice. Yet there was something in his lost memory that would not abide.

Hugh yearned to blunt his sensitivity to the malicious side of human nature that he saw often enough from his government's brutal suppression of colonial unrest, by a single act of evolving into something . . . more, through the only thing he could effect, himself. If being made into a slightly brain-damaged experimental cyborg elevated him into somehow feeling deserving of his rank and privileged life, so be it. Perhaps it was the height of hubris to think that only he had these feelings of helplessness in the face of forces beyond humanities control. Humanity destroyed itself once with its fanatical religious factions fighting for supremacy while its citizens died at their hands. At least he was lucky enough to have been selected, regardless of his personal feelings, in a cause to save lives.

The bridge crew had not interfaced with Hugh directly which was just as well, yet Nova was a more than adequate conduit of orders. His consciousness moved away from her hull and his own brief musings, noting how she bristled with conventional scanning equipment across her saucer shape. Nova could analyze the composition of Faiths atmosphere with absolute certitude. She also had incredible weaponry; no surprise the fifty or so cannons were not accessible to him. Brass had trust issues.

I don't think I am a she. Nova's voice flickered like a mouse skittering through killaquads of data beams. Hugh's augmented mind saw the little anomaly.

Hugh stopped.

Nova, please repeat last? There was a long pause.

Disregard last, Lieutenant.

That's never happened. Of course Nova had access to Hugh's thoughts but usually not at unpresented or deeper layers and now he had a glimpse of Nova's under thoughts. It was not supposed to have layers or especially opinions. In Hugh's defense, for generations naval people referred to their vessel as a she. But U.C. computers were not programmed for autotrophic thinking, even with the HCSIS upgrades. Nova was an advance prototype, somewhat like Hugh in a way. But in the six months they worked together had Hugh been effecting the machine? The Navy was too utilitarian and frugal to expend credits on personality programs; optimally perform functions only in its U.C. machines and most often its personnel was the sole requirement. If known by the wrong people it would likely shut down the project. Capital ships had weapons so powerful they required non human or pilot security over-rides. Ship computers were tools not players and no one wanted to know a safety system might have a bad day. He should tell Lillian the link was having this kind of unexpected effect on Nova.

Lieutenant, please disregard the link must be in need of adjustment.

But not during a live test. Proceed.

Hugh dropped the matter. It wasn't the time. Hopefully there never would be a time to bring this up.

Hovering above Faith, fed by Nova's divergent sensor array Hugh reached out and scanned the entire planet. No trace of metallics, a clean oxygen, carbon dioxide mix, strong ozone presence. Paradise. Some two million happy souls, though the spaceport above New Faith, their capital city, was scheduled to be completed in just two months, it didn't obstruct the bustling city it was literally tied to, below. Trading ships were already queuing for docking priority, despite the stations skeleton crew. Each of whom Hugh could see via their magnetic field signature. It was an apt demonstration of HCSIS's power. Between what Hugh was seeing and Nova's data feed, Dr. Hsian would have enough ammunition to blow away the doubts lingering in the observers as they watched the crystal clear viewing of Hugh's augmented scans.

Nova, please report Faith is status green.

Confirmed. Please prepare for sub-light speed to Provenance. ETA 12 minutes.

Like a school of fish, the fleet skitted into fusion drive and were off toward Faiths twin with Nova leading. The fleet was going a mere 63,000 miles a second, far beneath speed needed for interstellar, but Hugh could almost feel the collision of the hydrogen atoms that powered the flagship. U.N. ships were disc shaped saucers of varying sizes. Engineered to take advantage of the fusion collider tech still based on urgent 21st century breakthroughs, their power was based on the new oil of the Galaxy, water.

Hugh's studies of old Earth history provided him with a comical reminder of how U.F.O.'s supposedly looked and here Humanity was five centuries later building and flying them. In engineering shape often equals function. The miraculous fusion engines worked by colliding atoms at high speed so the whole vessel was built around the engine to support the circular collider conduit. So far humans were still the only intelligent life in the universe much to the Colonial Church's delight. Hugh questioned humanitys so called primacy on the topic the more he met its elite appointed officials. But the joke was the U.C.'s ships were still round saucers and they were the only aliens flying them.

A shadow or reflection flicked away Hugh's rambling thoughts as Novas sensors fed erratic echoes through on it's starboard scanner.

Nova, please direct focused sensor sweep of sector delta 555, 345. I thought I saw something move. Maybe another ship or ships. Perhaps an asteroid group.

Delta 555/345 scan showing clear Lieutenant. Shall I inform the bridge of an anomaly?

Disregard, Nova. Perhaps its my turn to get twitchy on the link. Just a bad day for these sort of glitches.

Aye Aye, Lieutenant.

The fleet dropped out of sub-light above the blue and white sister planet. Provenance was much newer and still developing infrastructure by the few hundred thousand courageous colonists seeding this world. *Beginning scans Nova.*

The colonists actually presented as tiny clusters of red pinpoints of light via Nova's tactical scans. The detail, amazing with large clusters marking the five towns on the main continent of Artemis, then scattered pioneers claiming territory in single pinpoints scattered throughout, available in almost any magnification. Progress and the dream of human expansion, just like in the old American Northwest. Some of the guests on the bridge gasped at the clarity of the central holo feed.

Time to really show off. *Increasing the amplification, Nova.* Hugh focused on a single dot at the northern most frontier. The holo moved from space, to clouds, to a cluster of dense purple coniferous trees crusted with snow. He could almost feel the brass cringing at such human controlled, tech enhanced vistas. Simultaneously Nova was sweeping about 386 main functions and over a 1000 ship board routines which it summarized, sorted, and reported to Hugh at a subliminal level. The question was, how did it make an Apex Flagship Computer and pilot relationship better by merging a human mind with a machine? Would the experimental fusion with Hugh and Nova allow the best merging of man and machine? He was determined to show them.

Hugh pressed a little further toward a frontier lodge in the middle of a clearing near a snow covered farm. Was it his imagination, or could he smell the snow, the pine? He pressed his amplified, HCSIS consciousness into the house which had a small generator as well as a fireplace throwing a natural, warm light into the rustic cabin. A sinewy young woman cooked, humming to herself, while a man sat smoking a pipe in his chair. Little did they know they were being scanned from space. The Colonial Government never had much qualm about snooping in on its constituents, though HCSIS might get heated debate in the minority parties once its true spying potential was realized. Human directed starship scanning would demonstrate unprecedented subtlety in getting around countermeasures that would not tip off the observed.

As a final demonstration of HCSIS, just as Hugh imagined how the politicians were reevaluating how secure their home offices were, he made a close up of the man's face, did a complete med scan. Saw his heart beating next to a sub-screen that showed the smoke of his pipe entering and leaving his lungs. The distant clatter of pans from his wife in the kitchen alarmed both them and the voyeurs aboard Nova. "Honey?"

Hugh reduced magnification slightly. Showed the man getting up and thus showed the onlookers of the Holo above him the same action, but on a 20 foot 3-D screen. The young woman had fallen and lay still on the floor. Unsettling, and a private moment. Hugh pulled the view to the atmosphere and to his horror the life-sign lights on the frontier started winking out. The couple died. Blood gas and other functions were popping up on the screen but Hugh already suspected with dread what was happening.

Alarms rang out across the ship. As the holo showed lights winking out all over the planets surface.

Nova the plague is here!

Confirmed. Pliilulua viral presence distilling through troposphere. Vector unknown. Approximate .0243 parts per trillion air volume contamination and climbing. Engaging quarantine procedures.

Hugh only tried this once before, he brought his scan systems inward to the bridge and amphitheater where shocked guests and crew stood and watched the tragedy unfold planet-side. Hugh could see and hear everyone while monitoring outside systems and the feeds to the holo.

Senator Shalinsky, a lanky, bearded, grey-blond in ministerial blue suit, gold Senate eagles marking his office from both lapels bent earnestly toward Dr. Hsian. "This was a quarantined planet doctor. There is no new introduction of any vector. It's not us or we'd be dead already and we don't have anarchists on U.C. vessels. It's not possible. I would like some concrete answers from this overpriced science project."

Dr. Hsian was petite, but her gracefully arched brows framed eyes of green steel and did not flinch from the Senator. "Senator, this pathogen has been under emergency priority not just by HCSIS but the entire Earth Science Academy for the last five months since the fall of Pliilulua 5 colony. The epidemiology is unchanged, we don't know how it moves. Conventional containment and tracking has failed, repeatedly, not just here. Five hundred million casualties deserve some open minded approaches to a completely new and lethal pathogen. This system is still new. Its capacity for detection in ways we've never imagined is the key Senator, and completely uncharted. Everything else has failed, but we will do what we can."

Hugh saw the shadow flicker again in the space near Provenance's Western continent. He fully moved his focus away from the bridge and to sector 555, 344. *Nova, sensor sweep here, flank.*

Hugh could tell via the link the thoroughness of Nova's scan. A 10% energy increase went into the sweep.

Scan negative Lieutenant.

Just like focusing inward on the bridge, Hugh brought his thoughts to the center of the shadow. This is where he thought he saw something move before. All that was there though was empty space. He pushed his scan more tightly into that space even though it looked just like emptiness framed by the sea of night. All flickering distant stars and a tickle of Hugh's instincts. He'd never focused his thoughts and Nova's scans on emptiness or something hypothetical before. He was going on a hunch.

Still nothing.

Until the stars disappeared with a pop as Hugh passed *through* something. He entered another object of some sort that did not register on any known sensor. An enclosed sphere of great size, nearly as big as Nova. Mostly space in it's interior, his distant view blurred at the corners of the huge rounded hull. A mosaic of what looked like veins connected from the wall of the sphere down into a central pith which both supported and carried yellow electric surges back and forth from the large structure suspended in the middle. It was unlike anything he'd ever seen before, an organic craft. Hugh checked the magnification to make sure he wasn't confusing some spore on the hull with an actual ship sized, organic object.

He moved toward the central structure. A kind of bridge was Hugh's guess, but biologically based. Glowing crystalline growths studded the surface of what might have been control panels. There were no corridors but membranes that acted as floors and walls. Webbed with fine capillaries or some type of organic wiring he followed the larger, brighter tissues to what must have been the bridge. A viscous translucent skin threw colors he couldn't describe. It spread before him above the control systems perched on the precipice of the sphere's centre like a giant rectangular sail.

Oh Lord, this just can't be happening.

Hugh saw the Fifth Fleet displayed in full color on the thin grey membrane sail. Nova in the forefront with a dozen spheres closing stretched across this viewing skin. Countless more dotted the surface of the planet's atmosphere, like spores dusting a rotting grey orange. They were visible from *this* screen. How could this be? The last of the red lights representing a living colonist winked out in Novas system.

Nova, are you recording, are you getting this!

Nova did not respond.

White hot pain lanced through the link in the back of Hugh's head. He didn't see anything but felt a presence, like the feeling of being watched, as he turned and tried to discern what might be someone, staring back something that didn't have a discernible face flashed towards him along a membranous wall. It grabbed Hugh's head and started shaking like some angry shark until he heard a distinct snap, vertigo, and his thoughts spiraling into blackness.

Dr. Hsian was gently shaking Hugh's shoulder when he jerked into consciousness and into world of pain. He gasped for breath after expelling fluid form his lungs. Slowly Hugh's vision cleared. He sat across from the tank coughing up kinetic fluid. Rubbing the back of his head until the doctor grabbed his hand. It came away red and seemed to trail off to the tank. There Hugh noticed the sensory tank fluid had a pinkish hue.

"There was an accident Mr. Wilkey, some sort of violent feedback surge from collisions. We were struck by micro meteors then your live feeds went dead. Nova's scanning system was hit particularly hard. The feedback from the hull damage somehow caused you to have a seizure and a nosebleed." Lilly pushed her blue black hair over her ear and pursed her lips in concern. "Are you ok?"

"Not too bad, though my head is killing me. Is the port damaged?" Petty-officer Bradley was helping a corpsman suture Hugh's cranial port while applying a local nerve blocker with his own stunner, set to anesthetic and local. The lab was abuzz with activity as some guest observers staggered off, too stunned and grief stricken to comment. The U.C. personnel tried to stabilize machinery, patch up injuries, and clean up broken and damaged equipment. A fire burned from wrecked scanning equipment that had overloaded.

The corpsman pulled a blanket with her free hand over Hugh's broad shoulders. "You had a tonic clonic seizure." She smiled wiping away blood with gauze, deftly avoiding the ivory sleeve of her dress uniform from getting soiled. "A big one with thrashing. Your lucky you don't need plasma or surgery".

Hugh sighed. Then he recalled what he saw. "Nova, what recording did you get?"

A flat, metallic voice responded throughout the room, "Voice pattern for bridge line officer not recognized." Nova was always a stranger to him outside of the link, none of the intimacy they shared was ever apparent through the standard crew interface, the voice was tinny and sexless.

Hugh must have been in mild shock to forget that about Nova. Admiral Karn nodded to Hugh's Captain, who stood before him looking concerned. "Nova, please allow

Lieutenant Wilkey line bridge access to you until further notice."

"Voice authorization confirmed Captain Obutu. Temporary line access to bridge granted. Holo recording from HCIS running, now, Lieutenant, specify time frame please?"

"Nova, run the time you noted I was blacked out, anything I may have missed while linked."

The huge hologram projected in crystal clear view in the center of the lab. Data from HCIS skipped across the bottom while a panoramic 360 degree view of the 6th Fleet orbiting the colonial world Provenance took center. The pilot team and Captain spoke back and forth from the bridge below and were heard from the holo recording.

"HCIS sensor speed and detail are enhanced from the link of Lieutenant Wilkey's mind and perfect melding of the sensory tank and Novas core computer. Please observe individual human, then animal life readings of the planet." Dr. Hsian was a gifted speaker and flowed through the presentation recording. "Without even bothering the scan officer we can dial additional detail unknown to bridge engineers and pilots. The implications for other bridge functions, weaponry, engine control, ship and crew size was revolutionary. It could be possible a dreadnaught could be run by one crewman . . ." This is where Hugh brought up the detail of the couple on the frontier of Artemis for the viewing guests.

Ernestine Joyce, Party Leader of the Enviro Party, and extremely tall black woman, highly unusual of itself as many ethnic minorities had availed themselves of genetic clinics on Earth to blend away their differences over a millennia raised a question to Dr. Hsian. "Doctor, am I to understand that the Lieutenant has control of helm? Weapons? Life-support?"

"Thank you Ms. Joyce, excellent questions. Right now in Phase I, Mr. Wilkey has mastered the sensory capacity of Nova, while the bridge crew runs those other functions. In future, Phase II, Phase III . . . ."

General quarters suddenly sounded on the recording cutting Lillian off.

The assembled officers and politicians looked at each other wondering if some dramatic demonstration that was scripted was being presented. Until the ship started shaking and explosions could be heard through the hull.

Nova's outside voice "This is not a test. Micro-meteor incursion. Shields operational but hull scans at 15%. HCSIS has detected Pliilulua plague elements on surface before system shut down."

Admiral Karn "From where?"

Dr. Hsian "Nova please direct Mr. Wilkey to find vector. Use all augmented scans now."

A face orbiting around the hologram materialized in the amphitheater, it settled in front of the Admiral, Senator, Dr. Hsian and top brass in the central foyer.

"The colonial planet Provenance welcomes the U.N. Sixth Fleet and Senator Shalinsky. I am Governor Geoffrey, observing total quarantine as ordered."

Senator Shalinsky cleared his throat and regarded the distinguished looking governor whose image super imposed over the hologram of the dying planet he governed. Senator Shalinsky's already pale visage blanched further. "Hello Governor, is this a secure channel?"

Look of concern. "Why yes Senator . . ."

Shalinsky's dark blue eyes were grave. "As ranking representative of the United Colonial Empire and chosen voice of the Patriarch Council, I solemnly commend your souls to heaven. You and your brave colonists will always be remembered for your inestimable courage, sacrifice . . ."

Governor Geoffrey stood agape, "What? It can't possibly . . ." But the words fell dead, his eyes rolled back into his head as his face formed a rictus of pain that ended quickly as the skin rose with rapidly expanding pustules that started bursting until the governor was unrecognizable and the feed from the planet mercifully shut down leaving the guests on board the Nova gasping or crying in shock.

"End program."

Senator Shalinsky looked down at Hugh. "That is when our flagship was hit by meteors tearing through the system. All sensors went dead. We left system, learning nothing of this terror unless you can shed some light, Mr. Wilkey." A touch of Yorkshire English, distantly polite. He stood amongst his aides on the lab floor avoiding various liquids that puddled around Hugh.

"You what!?" Hugh stared incredulously. "You left two million people defenseless." Hugh tried to get up but the Corpsman and Petty officer Bradley held him firmly and the effort made his head spin. "There were thousands on the space station alone that could have been evacuated."

"Lieutenant Wilkey you forget your place." Captain Obutu was surprised at Hugh's outburst. The senator raised a steadying hand at him. "There was nothing we could do. The plague hit at the same time the meteors did. To stay would have risked the fleet. Or possibly led to the infection of the fleet by the meteors or by staying in proximity of the planet or the system."

"No no Captain. Our young friend has been through much. It's true we left on immediate advice from our science officer. The fleet was taking a beating from the micro meteor shower, all human life on Provenance was snuffed out, and for all we know the meteors or our fleet itself have been the vector. We might be able to pass decon at a specialized Starbase in the Gurrin Sector, which we are headed to now. But please consider this your debriefing. Continue Lieutenant."

Hugh swallowed his anger and hoped the crew of the space station would somehow avoid contamination. "I saw something."

A touch of amusement. "If you and your system had seen the micro-meteors before they struck us that would have been helpful in preventing millions in damage and possibly given us time to fire into the meteors before they wiped out our colonies. But it did happen so quickly. We all saw what you saw Lieutenant, though I dare say the Inquisitor Branch has more use for spy systems than the Navy at this time."

Hugh voice steadied. "I saw a ship. A fleet."

"Of course, the 6th Fleet."

Hugh held the Senator's eye. He briefly thought about what he was about to say, its implication, but he was an officer and had to report honestly. "I saw another fleet. Not Colonial."

Dr. Hsian face froze. "You're in shock Mr. Wilkey."

"Maybe a little, but I think you know me well enough that I would never make something like that up. I know what I saw. They must not show up on conventional scans. Stealthed. They weren't . . . they weren't human."

The room grew very quiet. The corpsman actually took in a breath and stopped working.

The Senator's eyebrow raised disdainfully. "Shock or no Lieutenant, if you are serious about your report, it's not just sounding delusional, it's speaking heresy. Humans are the only sentient life in the Universe as per God's will and His ministry on Earth. The computer can scan any known element in the galaxy. An invisible alien fleet? You or your HCSIS system must be effected by the damage to Nova's system."

"Senator Shalinsky, it is possible Mr. Wilkey saw something we could not." Dr. Hsian gestured toward the empty tank. "The human brain, his brain, has not been completely mapped with the augmentation tech. We are breaking through to new territory, unknown abilities."

"Nova this is Senator Shalinsky."

"Voice pattern confirmed."

"Senate code clearance Vega-559. Did you at anytime come into contact with any anomaly, anything at all through HCSIS or your own independent scans to confirm the presence of what this man has claimed to be an invisible alien fleet?"

"Clearance confirmed. Senator Shalinsky, the Nova HCSIS recording just shown, all independent scans between this vessel and the sixth fleet, before sensor damage and after, confirms there was no enemy fleet present on conventional scans and no technology known either private or governmental that has developed stealth systems on space faring vessels that could shield them from advanced magnetic scans."

"There must be something Nova. I know what I saw. Weren't you there when I explored the enemy vessel?"

Nova paused. "What you saw may have occurred after the HCSIS link was severed. Nova cannot verify during the meteor incursion due to system overloads."

"Enough, Dr. Hsian. I release him into your custody but this demonstration of your system is finally coming to a close. None too soon to save billions of wasted funds. You are relieved from duty Mr. Wilkey and confined to quarters."

Admiral Karns exchanged glances with Captain Obutu. The Admiral approached the statesman, "With all due respect Senator, but only the Captain can relieve an officer under his command, otherwise only a military court martial."

"There is much you are not aware of Admiral, Captain, with all due respect. Lt. Wilkey isn't really an officer, is he Dr. Hsian".

A dangerous tilt to her head, Lillian glared at Shalinsky. "Divulging classified information is a punishable offense Senator. This is not the time to divulge such information, you have not had clearance. Nova may yet confirm . . ."

Senator Shalinsky held up both hands to Dr. Hsian, "Enough Doctor. This project has gone far enough. The meteor shower is the vector, Nova, our six billion credit computer stated no other vector was possible. I will not condone these nigh heretical, assertions by Mr. Wilkey and will strive to have them stricken from the record"

"I am empowered by the Senate with executive authority over this project." The Senator swept the room. "The HCSIS project is suspended until further notice. Its security status declassified and now made available to all senior officers here." His grave eyes finally rested on Hugh. "Remove this . . . . officer . . . to his quarters under guard for his protection, please have medical support in place. I'd like to conduct a more private session when he is more recovered. Marines . . ."

Two armed Marines gently picked Hugh up by the arms and started to half drag half pull him to his quarters. Hugh wanted to pass into real shock or wake from this nightmare. He could not comprehend how quickly this man, this close minded bureaucrat shut down HCSIS. Hugh was baffled at their actions, at the Senators lack of trust in him. He wasn't delusional, its experimental technology and Hugh was just telling them what he saw. He was telling them the truth. Hugh had no idea what the arrogant bastard meant that he wasn't really an officer?

"What does he mean Dr. Hsian? What's happening? I am telling the truth!" Hugh's voice trailed away as he entered the lift.

"Dr. Hsian." Hugh heard the Senator's accent distantly but unmistakably before the lift door closed and the corpsman rushed in after him trailing after the Marines. "Stop the suppression meds. I want him to know the details of his case before he is tried. If he persists with his alien fleet rubbish, I will see he is tried for heresy."

Several hours later Dr. Hsian knocked on the hatch to Hugh's private quarters, he was pacing a tread in his study's carpet. "What in hells name is happening Lilly? I can call you Lilly since I have just about been cashiered by the U.C. E.'s representative and am no longer an officer with a wave of that fop's perfumed hand. A seeming criminal apparently, just for reporting what I honestly experienced." Hugh's head fell into his hands, "Tell me this isn't happening?"

The corpsman packed up her things and silently left with Petty-officer Bradley, nodding to Lillian as they made their leave. Hugh could see two Marines stationed outside his door at parade rest. They had disruptor rifles, not just standard issue stunners.

"Under guard and confined to quarters? Dr. Hsian is that really necessary? I swear I will challenge that pompous elite to a formal dual for offending my honor so!"

Dr. Lilly Hsian loosened here lab coat and rubbed here eyes. Her erudite, patient demeanor rarely lent itself to dramatic display, but today she couldn't hide her distress. She sat down, laced her manicured fingers and sighed.

"I've been ordered to divulge to you the contents of your project file. This is premature in the extreme but in preparation for the crash you will experience from the abrupt cessation of your suppression meds. I am afraid the Senator has all the authority necessary to set this in motion, though he will eventually pay for his hubris."

"What meds? I don't take any meds"

"In your food. In large doses for the last five months."

"What are you talking about?"

Lilly stepped closer to Hugh. Reached for his hand and held his eyes. Hugh's body tingled at the unexpected warmth and contact with Lilly. Her hands were soft, yet calloused on the knuckles as if from sparring. "Hugh, this is going to be extremely hard to hear, but I must tell you, you are going to crash hard soon. The lack of memory I was telling you is mostly due to the meds, not the surgery. We . . . I was trying to gradually integrate your presence here in the Navy and in HCSIS with the reality of your actual identity, for the last six months since you were revived. But recent events have rushed things along."

"Revived? . . . What are you talking about?"

Lillian smiled softly and led him to the couch. Hugh was probably still in shock. "You better have a seat Hugh, this will be a little hard to explain and harder to believe than your report to the Senator. But it's my hope you will . . . understand. Even forgive us in time.

Chapter 2

Alterations

The archeological survey team flew in under heavy Marine guard toward the center of what had been a major metropolis but now was a sea of craters, grey shattered ruins, and remnants of domes of what must have been a major center of study once. The Marines dropped near the domes brandished heavy beam weapons and the battlewagons hovered a few feet above the ground, five squads of fifty Marines each secured the site from encroachment and set a defensive circle. The devolved descendants of the once great city had driven off a smaller force earlier in the day. The site was over fourteen hundred years old and it was sheer chance a survey team detected the weak power signature some hundred feet beneath the surface a month prior.

Dr. Hsian, project leader, led the twelve assorted specialists from New Boston Academy around the center of what must have been a main structure on the site. Twisted metal and fractured stone glittered warning in the twilight of torn enviro suits if the scientists weren't careful. They were equipped with diggers and explosive charges, but as Lilly swung around an outcropping of debris she found a well cleared stairway leading down.

The Marine commander swung into view and two of his aides flanked him as he trotted up to Lillian and the scientists. "The perimeter is secure mam, the animals won't be able to chase us off this time unless they come with several tribes, even then, they wouldn't be able to break our ranks. We three will stick with you just as a precaution."

"Very well commander. Just don't get in our way or shoot anything without my permission." Lilly lead the scientists down the stairs and turned on their wrist lights.

"Hold up mam! You safety is my primary responsibility and we will take the lead. There could be anything down there and I'm not going to have your deaths on my hands.

Lilly rolled her eyes to her colleagues when her back was turned to the commander, she smoothed her face and turned toward him, "We do have side arms and training in crowd control Commander, but if you must be with us you will be at the front with me."

The commander assented and adjusted his pyranite plated vest and helmet and shouldered up to the petite woman. As Lillian rolled up the thick, primary layer to her elbows, she could then easily check out her boot knife and her hand blaster, affixed to her belt. She needed to feel those tools of her trade. The Commander noticed part of a black Kraken tattoo coiled around her left arm, transparent through the thin secondary layer, the tail just poking down her exposed arm. Under his breath he leaned toward Lilly and whispered, "That a Special Ops emblem Doctor, isn't it?"

Lilly lowered her voice and reluctantly whispered, "We all were something else, Commander . . ." Then pushed her sleeve down a bit and moved deeper down the tunnel, adding "not quite the defenseless, spoiled technocrat you assumed eh?"

Glancing sheepishly at his aides he smiled. "Guess not" and followed after her. The fifteen individuals descended deeper into the tunnel unlit and full of debris, but passable. Plastics and other non degradables lay where they fell, calcified bones, ancient humans, were starting to powder as it became dryer. Finally they came to an access tunnel, cylindrical, ten feet wide, with a floor of white marble tiles. The dust and debris had been disturbed with what appeared to be much bipedal traffic, and of course roaches and rats, which scurried away from their lights.

A tall blond woman startled at the form of some long dead citizen who must have been caught in a searing blast while standing near the wall centuries before. His or her form was stretched along the wall from one of the blasts that must have destroyed the city. A figure from a painting of Dante's Inferno, caste in actual flesh and carbon for all eternity.

Mark, a chronographer, gently grabbed her arm and then realized why she had balked. "Are you ok?"

Emily, a geologist, turned away from the remains on the wall, nodded to Mark then turned to the group, held up a scan unit on her armband, "We are getting closer to the power source Dr. Hsian. Probably 400 yards ahead."

Lilly nodded and shined her wrist light into rooms they passed as they arrived at the bottom of the staircase. There were labs, crudely remodeled into long abandoned living areas with molded bedding on the floor, rotted out, and sometimes with the outline of someone who had died centuries ago in the dust and bones that partially remained. It was cold and smelled remotely of smoke and humanoid habitation. Artifacts used for study or smashed beakers and computer consoles were scattered along the floor. Someone had disturbed and ransacked the rooms over the over, through the centuries, many someone's no doubt.

John was the actual archeologist and sucked air through his teeth, "Eh such a shame the place is in shambles, this would have told us so much if we found some intact technology or a computer with memory still intact. What a treasure it would have been."

"It's still is a treasure, especially if we have time to properly codify everything, do you understand any of the writing, mostly symbols, and make sure Aaron you are getting all this on the recorder" Lilly pointed to a series of symbols on an intact glass door.

Aaron shifted his wrist camera to the door and the entourage stopped. John stepped forward and dusted the glass to read the full label. "Well it is old Earth English, American of course, it says 'MIT . . . Physics Department'".

Emily pushed forward with the scanner. "There is a power signature in here, perhaps the one we are looking for?" Lilly shouldered the door, surprised to find it bared and secured from the inside. "Its amazing something down here is unviolated! It's either occupied which would be bad, or actually intact which would be astounding." Lilly traced her fingers over the glass, noting how well it was made and how wire was threaded finely through the glass. Closer inspection revealed fine cracks in the glass as if someone had tried unsuccessfully to break in. "Is this what I think it is Emily? Mark, get the powercutter."

Mark whistled, "I didn't think we'd need this for anything around here. What is it made of?"

Emily's eyebrows rose. "It's laced with ancient pyranite. No wonder it held."

Mark spent ten minutes on full burn cutting through the bolt.

Lilly thanked Mark and pushed on the door, moving a skeletal body blocking the entrance, the cranium collapsed and bones of the body broke apart as she entered what appeared to be an undisturbed lab with metal counters. In the distance a metal cube from floor to ceiling was positioned in the middle of the room. Small red lights blinked on its side. "It's possible this room has not been disturbed since this person locked themselves in four centuries ago." Lilly turned to John, "What's MIT?"

"Hell if I know Lilly, some acronym is my guess" John and the other scientists shuffled in, as well as the commander and one armed aide, the other coming in back of the last scientist. "It's amazing this thing is still functioning. Emily what's powering it?"

Emily looked at her wrist scanner and punched some buttons. "John it's a primitive fission reactor, pretty much on its last legs, well insulated but almost exhausted. No wonder its clean burning and no radiation detected except from the surface rock above and around us from the holocaust. I bet its from around 2018. It is so weak, a great stroke of luck that hunting party flew directly over it."

"Wow. Doomsday tech." John started breaking out tools and the other scientists started taking off their backpacks and removing delicate equipment. They carefully started collecting samples and measurements, studying objects and other debris. After much discussing, notating, the specialists then sealed items in jars and boxes for further study. Lilly was pleased to be part of this exploration of humanitys roots. Perhaps they would learn something new from their violent ancestors who nearly extinguished all life on Earth. Something redeeming. They knew the sight might have something special from an existing power reading in the Dead Zone, the first ever detected. That's why special ops had sent her.

After and hour Lilly was engrossed in the panel of the cube as a computer specialist teased out some of its workings and spoke into his personal log. Several hours elapsed as the team worked over the site, abuzz with excited chatter. Lilly was holding the panel when she heard the distant ping of beam weapon discharge from above. The commander clicked on his lapel communicator, "Report Archie?"

A clear voice responded from the micro implant in his ear. "Commander, at 1340 we were sniped at with arrows by a roving band, but the muties disappeared into the warrens around the perimeter. It's now 1440 and it seems they roused every mutie in the quadrant. I'm talking hundreds and growing."

"Understood, Archie. Hold them and start to close the perimeter, we will bring the team up for immediate evac. We will be gone in 30 minutes. Power the hovers. Commander Goldberg, out."

The scientist who overheard the commander groaned. One of them, a geneticist who had been taking some fossil samples stood up. "It will take a half hour just to pack our gear Commander? Lilly?"

"That's not my problem, Doctor. Getting you out of here alive is! I'm not ending up in some mutie's stew pot, presuming they would take the time to cook us. Pack up everything in fifteen minutes! We are leaving with or without your equipment!"

Lilly looked around at her associates. "We need to take our samples and basic gear. We will shield the door to this sacred place before we leave. No one and nothing will be able to get in. Apparently we need to come back with an army."

Lilly locked eyes with the Marine, "A word with you, Commander Goldberg"

Lilly stepped out into the hall with the burly red head. "You have 250 troops out there with heavy beam weapons. The creatures have sticks, rocks, bow and arrows at most. Do you really think there is any risk from those primitives?"

"Doctor it's not my call. We have engagement rules. This might be some holy place to them. I don't know but there are tribes of these things gathering. Thousands perhaps! Sure we could probably eradicate them, but, we are mandated not use deadly force, only stun settings. They have slower recharge than killing beams as you know. The colonial government is conflicted about exterminating any part of what's left of humanity on land. It, they, are still part of . . . the world. Now we need to get back to the safety of the sea and New Boston." The commander started to turn away.

"This site is too important a find to abandon half assed like this. We need to spend weeks, months, in this room alone! Actual tech from the ancient times is here. From our ancestors from before the Holocaust. Prototype fission reactors. It is priceless."

"Doctor Hsian, Lilly if I may, I fully understand your position." Goldberg shifted anxiously looking down the service tunnel as he heard the sound of stun beams popping with increasing frequency. "But we will come back after this place is not so hot. We'll come back with stealth units or use robotics at night, remotely. Lets try it in about three months."

"Three months? I'm not sure the door shield will even last that long Commander."

Emily stepped out into the hall, sheepishly "Ah, excuse me, don't mean to interrupt but Reggie took the panel from the reactor off to take with us, and the power source shut down."

Lillian's eyes widened. "If we damaged the artifact based on our being rushed Commander-"

Goldberg's voice rose to match hers." See these lapel ranks Doctor? Their not just communicators. They mean I'm in charge of your safety and carrying out Colonial Governmental Orders."

"Ahem excuse me", Emily actually stepped between them "Since time is pressing and we only have ten minutes, I wanted to let you know Lilly there is another power source, weaker, underneath the fission reactor. It was masked." "What? Where?"

Emily looked into her wrist scanner. "Umm, another 50 feet below. There must be another entrance . . ."

"My God." Lilly leaned into the frenzied group and shouted out orders. "Everyone take what you have and get out into the hallway now! We will come back, when its safer and get all your equipment. John, Aaron, leave off that stuff and move out! Move it people!"

When everyone was panting and standing outside with as much gear and samples as they could grab, Lilly removed a small silver device from her belt and placed it over the closed glass door. She pushed a few buttons on its interior and it disappeared as a hum of the force shield completely sealed and the room.

"OK people everyone go with the commander. We will meet you up top as fast as possible, Emily and I will be checking the second power source. Commander keep a transport handy to-"

Commander Goldberg's face reddened "You will do no such thing, you are evacuating if I have to carry you myself". He reached out to grab Lillian's wrist."

Emily had never seen someone move so fast. Lillian grabbed the commanders arm, using his own momentum and twisted it around and held it behind his back at an awkward angle, his forefinger was touching his scapula and her thumb was jammed painfully into his neck near the jugular vein. Emily doubted the commander was that limber naturally.

Goldberg yelped in shock and surprise and his aides started to charge their stunners.

"Not smart commander, you have some idea about my training and what I could do to your nerves and joints. Tell your lads to take my colleagues above and see them to safety. The Commander, Emily and I will be up to catch the last shuttle. Move!"

The aides watched their commander, who winced, nodded, and waved them on. Reluctantly, they both left with the remaining scientists. Lillian released the commander from her hold. He glared at her and fingered his holster.

"You may need that hand unbroken if your coming with us. We have less than eight minutes to find that other power source and its possible we will have unfriendlies coming in from other entrances. You can press charges against me later if you wish, but, I have my mission also and you may find your superior reports to my superior if you catch my drift."

The commander thought on that. Grabbed his pistol slowly and moved toward the unexplored end of the tunnel. Rubbing his neck he glared at the ladies. "Come on then."

Emily and Lillian followed, wrist lights and scanner pressing into the darkness. They came to a juncture, perpendicular to the tunnel they were exiting and a more unused portion of the system. Rats scurried away down the steps to the left. Emily looked right and anxiously pointed the scanner toward the dark corridor, "The steps lead down another fifty feet and this corridor leads down some five hundred feet. There are large mammals, bipeds, coming toward us, perhaps a dozen!"

"Mutants". Lilly looked down the steps, the debris from the ceiling blocked some of the entrance but it was passable. Lets get down there and hide".

The commander looked dubious. "That would block off our only exit out."

Lillian reached into a compartment on her belt and brought out a palm sized metallic object. "Stun grenade. I'll protect you, no worries."

The commander starred daggers at Lillian then squeezed through the debris and down the stairs. The ladies followed and then froze as they heard the distant howls and shrieks of the inhabitants of the ruins. Shadows flickered from a torch, the smell of smoke and unwashed bodies wafted down the stairs where the trio hid as the humanoids ran past and toward the shielded door of the lab. They screamed at the door but were unwilling to touch the electric field as prolonged contact burned them. They then ran toward the surface, giving up on the door.

After the sounds of the humanoids faded away; "Probably trying to break into the perimeter set by my men." Goldberg gestured down the stairs. "We better move along, time is running out."

Lillian nodded and the went down four flights of stairs that were in good condition and relatively unblocked by debris. A metal door blocked the end of the stairway. Lillian tried the door with the gloved hand of her non dominant arm. Locked.

A wall code lay on the ground, torn off long ago. The code lost to antiquity.

Lilly turned the dial on her hand blaster to maximum discharge and stepped away.

"Back up."

The blast of the hand weapon punched a hole in the door mechanism where the handle was. Goldberg kicked the door but it didn't budge. "Another impressive door."

"Well whip it out Commander. Lets blast this open."

Commander Goldberg mumbled something under his breath and dialed up his blaster. Bright orange light flashed out from the muzzle of their hand weapons, repeatedly pinging with impact. They both pushed down the heat shield over the hot muzzles and holstered their hand weapons. The shots on the door lock and near the heavy metal surrounding the door twisted and melted. They kicked and the door flew open with bits of glowing metal showering the dim room.

The lab smelled like a tomb. Two pristine rooms from the early 21st century in one day was a goldmine for the team. They walked in, noting more modern scientific tools and undisturbed, implements of glass and metal stacked neatly in glass cabinets. Computers hummed lightly, functioning.

"This is amazing." Emily looked over the computers. "How are these powered?"

She raised the scanner. "Hmm, the power source is not from these. Too weak. Its behind this cabinet."

"Well that's interesting. How much time do we have commander? Lillian looked over just as he covered his ear. "None. The animals are starting to overrun the existing shuttles."

"Hmm, that's too bad, help me move this Emily". Emily looked terrified but put her shoulder to the cabinet. It swung open as if on hinges. A doorway led up some stairs to a well lit room."

"Damn . . ." Lilly and Emily looked at each other.

Commander Goldberg's voice grew grave. "We have to go. Now."

Emily and Lillian looked at each other and walked up the stairs into the room.

"Goddamnit!" The commander ran after them.

What Lilly and Emily saw as they rose up the short steps stunned them more than anything they had seen that day. The fifteen foot square room was fully shielded floor to ceiling by metal plating. In the center a frosted glass cylinder, rested on a metal dais, the top half opened like a lid. Bent over the apparatus a crooked backed creature, humanoid and hooded, gloved, worked frantically, surgical gear and tubules of plasma suspended above the tank.

Lilly held up her weapon. "Identify yourself."

The person grumbled something to itself and continued working feverishly over the cylinder. The commander joined Emily and Lillian.

Lillian raised her voice. "I said identify yourself and step away from the tank. We are Colonial Officers!"

The creature turned to face them. It was grossly deformed, had one eye missing and another blue eye overly large glared defiantly at them. "I know who you are. I am done now but you cant have him!" The mutant screamed and threw a scalpel at Lillian.

Lillian dodged easily. The commander aimed and fired at the creature, hitting it in the back as it ducked behind the device. It was on beam and not stun, he hadn't adjusted it from the door. She could smell the burnt flesh as it vaporized.

"Oh my God, no!" Lillian screamed at the commander and sent him flying with a kick to his solar plexus. The man gasped and collapsed on the floor, dropping his weapon.

"You fool. You killed the one thing that could explain what we've found."

Lillian saw the creature reach out toward a bag on the floor toward the corner of the room. The creature punched down on the bag.

"Not quite." Emily ran over to the creature. Turned it over. It stared at the ceiling blood trickling out of its misshapen mouth. "Well now it's dead."

Emily stepped up toward the tank. Inside was a naked man, holding a small grey mammal in its arms. Both the man and the animal had lines for plasma running full bore in their veins and bandages over their heads, recent suturing.

"It's a cryogenic tank. This human is, alive." Lillian's hand lifted from his pulse.

Emily looked into the large bag on the floor. "Lillian, he wont be for long. Jesus this is a bomb. It's been activated and going to blow in, in, four minutes!"

"Shit! Lets get out of here. I need your help, grab the small mammal Emily."

The commander had gained his feet and his breath. "You bitch."

"That's Special Agent Bitch to you. You are responsible for the loss of the this site, you idiot. You just needed to stun it, but you killed it. Help me get this man out of here and I *might* not have you executed. It had time to start a timer on a bomb and we don't have time to dicker."

The commander appeared resigned but ran over quickly to grab the man in the cylinder under the arms. Lillian grabbed his legs and they made their way as quickly as they could to the surface. Following Emily with the small grey creature in her arms. The plasma containers trailing behind both patients, like balloons suspended in their hover-fields, they quickly covered the distance in the tunnel without resistance or getting them snagged.

"Where did that mutie get this tech?"

Lilly glared at the commander, "I guess we will never know since you killed it."

"Listen Lillian, Doctor, whatever you are, the thing attacked you. It wasn't even supposed to be able to speak. God knows what it did to this poor man. Bye the way, can we get him some clothes?"

"No time commander. The bomb is going to go in about fifty seconds." Emily skipped over unconscious bodies of mutants and a dead Marine.

Goldberg tapped his lapel com, "Archie set up a suppressing fire! Bring the wagon over to the stairs. I don't care if you use full beams, these bastards are dead anyway, we have a bomb detonation down here in thirty seconds!"

"Ladies, as soon as we clear the stairs, jump into the bird!"

Lilly's hair on her neck prickled as she muscled the man up the last stairs and the magnetic field of the battle barge swung it's tail toward them. Orange beams shot out from Marines setting down suppressing fire. Hundreds or natives screamed and died, their unearthly cries mixed with the ping of fifty beam weapons. Hundreds upon hundreds dying or already dead.

The commander, Lilly, Emily, and their charges moved up the ramp and collapsed as the ramp clamped close and the commander blew someone's ears out screaming, "Immediate lift off! Go go maximum thrust!"

Emily looked at Lilly "Five seconds".

The engines of the battlewagon roared and those not buckled into their seats were flattened against the rear door.

A metal kit of some sort nearly crashed back on Lilly's head. A blanket also fell down the bottom of the ship. Lilly grabbed it and wrapped it around the naked stranger as the vessel screamed up through darkened sky which momentarily lit up at the horizon as the ship rattled from the massive explosion from the site.

The man's eye's flickered open.

Lilly looked down into his drawn face. "Welcome home."

*

"So what you are saying is you don't know what happened to me, that you pulled me out of some 21st century operation chamber, and unwittingly blew up the place and only chance to get information . . . and since I had an interesting genome you decided to fuck with my head and make me believe I belonged here so you could manipulate me into doing your experiments." Hugh looked at Lilly balefully, gripping the back of a chair until his knuckles whitened. "Why the charade, why not just ask!"

Lilly sat quietly looking out into space, a few moments passed and she sighed and turned to him. "You know, the Genghonni, the . . . mutations of the former humanity that you knew, are beyond redemption. The toxins and damage done to them has turned them into animals and worse . . . When we found you, we had no idea there could possibly be some, of them, still capable of science, of . . . medicine. We were quite overwhelmed, we didn't know if you were some kind of weapon and we certainly weren't prepared for the complete unlikeliness of you being in stasis for fourteen hundred years. We had to take every precaution-"

"You blew him up!"

"No. He blew himself up and we were never able to get answers from the pieces of that explosion. I had Commander Goldeberg executed for his carelessness, after I understood the scope of the loss. But I agree, it didn't go smoothly, what can I say?"

Hugh lowered his eyes to the deck and sat adjacent to Lilly. "You nouveau humans may be pretty and perfect but you sure are brutal. You got yourselves in this mess by tampering with your genetics so much that you lost not just your diversity, but your identities. Will my memory you tampered with ever come back? And why didn't you use some of your own people for your cyborg experiments and not me?"

Lilly kept her voice calm. "Ok, first, your "diverse" ancestors of ours hated each other so much you destroyed your planet and each other far more than our enhancements ever could. We adapted ourselves to avoid such cosmetic differences and become a more unified people, to get away from what you were. We just changed our appearances, at first, then more, and perhaps more than we should have, its true. But we had to modify your memory to prevent you from going into shock, to give you a template . . ."

"To give you security!" Hugh interrupted.

"That too. But to answer your other question, we couldn't use our own people, there were parts of your brain that were altered by the creature we found you with. We believe the hardware was added, some brain matter removed, but we cannot be sure, you had the ability to heal remarkably, beyond anything we could duplicate even with our genetic advances. You were unique . . . are unique; a gift."

"I am not your fucking gift! I want this stuff out of my head. I want my memory back!" Hugh grabbed the table and was about to pick it up and throw it across the room.

With remarkable speed Lilly punched her hand out in three rapid strikes to pressure points on Hugh's neck, solar plexus, and knee. Her index finger felt like a blunt steel spike, and Hugh went down.

"Lieutenant . . . I mean Hugh. I'm sorry. It's a bad habit. You should be angry." Lilly leaned over Hugh's gasping body and expertly released all the points she had struck and Hugh rolled into a ball on the deck, groaning softly."

Lilly bit her lower lip and sat back down. "Your memory will come back. God save us but I hope you like what you remember. You don't come from some Nirvana, you come from the time that caused our planet to be almost destroyed. But violence is senseless at this point, you are here. Now do I need to call in those Marines and have you strapped down or are you going to behave?"

Hugh looked up at the sofa and pulled himself up, his breathing becoming more regular. "Doesn't seem like you need any back up for little old me. Some doctor you turned out to be. I studied martial arts back in the day, you have some new moves since I dabbled . . ."

"Well its been fourteen hundred years. See you are remembering! But like I said earlier, I was an agent of The Order of The Kraken. The investigative and often bounty hunter branch of my government. Their training is not gentle. But you must be calm. Your memories will indeed return. Then perhaps you can shed some light on why you really are here."

"Seems like that prick Shalinsky isn't going to keep me around too long. The fact that I cared what he thought when you had me conned into being an officer didn't help. I did what you and he asked, found the pathogen, and he still didn't want this HCSIS program to get off the ground! Now that I am my regular, old cave man self, my future looks bleak, I am going to be lab samples soon if he gets his way."

At this Lilly fell silent. After a few minutes, Lilly blew out a deep breath. "We all follow orders. If its any consolation I wanted to debrief you directly. To involve you in the process. But it wasn't my call. There is something else I should tell you that you might find comfort in, or perhaps . . . insurance of a sort."

"Christ. What?"

Lilly grimaced a bit at Hugh's comment, but it quickly passed. "You carry something with you as a result of the primitive cryogenic process you participated in. It is perhaps the main reason you can heal so quickly and perhaps survived cellular damage all this time: or at least crystallization of your neurons. It is a virus or something that survived with you symbiotically during your stasis."

"Well your science is all powerful surely you can tell me exactly what I am infected with?"

"That's just it, we can't. This virus is elusive. It seems . . . to deliberately avoid all our sampling techniques, even scans. That's why we can't duplicate your healing abilities. That's why you are the only human in existence that can interface with Nova. It's why you are the most important person in the galaxy. You are our best shot in stopping the Pliilulua Plague. You can save humanity. I will make sure you have a chance to do so."

Hugh blinked a bit at that and started to laugh. He couldn't stop. Lilly waited him out though the thought did cross her mind to paralyze him again.

Hugh looked at Lilly's pretty face and his eyes became hard. "Once I get my memory back and if your crazed Nazi politicians don't have me killed, I am going to think long and hard at whether your perfect little take on humanity is worth saving. Though I am not sure I can actually even do it even if I want to. You don't even believe what I saw!"

Lilly shrugged. "I am a scientist as well as retired member of The Order. Whether you like it or not. You are here. We are all you have so you better sign up for the advanced class and buckle up. Otherwise you will be in the truly unique position of seeing your entire race destroyed for the second time. And as far as what you saw, there is no scientific proof you weren't dreaming, no recorded evidence."

Lilly stood, smoothed her lab coat and moved to the door. Hugh sat down and watched her leave, but before she did, she turned and looked at him reflectively.

"You know something Hugh Wilkey, and that is your name, we found it on your dog tag by the way. You need to know it is really up to you as to why you ended up here with us, so far away from your time. Why did you end up in a cryogenic tank that took you away from everything you know? Then you can tell me why you are here and who is really to blame . . ."

The door closed as she left. Hugh sat there in the dark for a long time. "Lights" he whispered and the room was dark save for the cascade of stars shooting past his window. The stars, bars of light moving away to infinity seemed to be his only friends.

"Sometimes I want to leave the Earth
And then come back and start again."

—Robert Frost

Chapter 3

Voices

Hugh's dreams were restless. As he tossed and turned, eerie Aryan crewman glided through the ship, silent and ominous, not speaking or even blinking. The black SS uniforms of the ancient, German Third Reich replaced the dress blues and whites of the Colonial Navy and suited them perfectly. Running through an endless maze of ships halls, past perfect crewmen with perfect teeth, joyless, silent, staring straight ahead infesting Nova, soulless zombies in a giant corpse. Hugh hearing voices in his dream. *"Help me"*, echoed down the hallway again and again. He turned a corner into an operating room, Sander Shalinsky stood in front of the table wearing a butcher's apron, blood covering his gloved arms and chest. In his right hand he held Hugh's severed head by the hair, as his body pulsed and fought for life. The head, his head, came to life and started screaming as Shalinsky laughed.

Hugh bolted awoke in a cold sweat. It was 0345, ship board time. "Lights!"

A nightmare . . .

The lights in his room came on. Hugh looked around, his sheets were damp with sweat. The stars out the port window smeared across the plating with the incredible speed indicated Nova was moving again. "Nova, were you speaking to me?"

"Access to ship computer denied." Nova's sexless voice was plain, tinny, and final.

"Guess not."

Hugh went to the private bathroom in his cramped quarters. Even though the microbes that caused body odor were long since removed from human environments, ship board or otherwise, Hugh seemed out of habit to need to shower daily, especially the more his memory recovered. The water was 100% recycled, pure fuel, and stuff of life, and the heat of the shower rattled off the metallic nub in the back of his head. He thought to himself he was glad the access plug was waterproof, but could not wash away the demons that seemed to have crawled through it whenever it had been installed.

Help me Hugh.

The voice in his head wasn't Nova. It was completely new and . . . feminine. Yet somehow familiar. "Who are you"

Find me. They are going to kill me.

Hugh shut off the shower and got dressed. So this is withdrawal, Hugh thought to himself, how mangled is my head? There must be some way to calm the thoughts, the the voices, the crazy discomfort and doubt. But still, the overwhelming pull to move, to get out of the quarters. If this was madness, it was insistent. Hugh put on work blue shirt and pants, seems like denim was a constant in the universe even though it wouldn't stop a bullet or beam weapon. Was it just being cooped up in his quarters under guard?

Help me . . .

Jesus, if I am a crazy person, it certainly isn't lonely with all these voices, Hugh reflected. Hugh was possessed by an energy, a primal tugging that moved him to move to the door. The Marines were stationed there. He could almost sense them through the bulkhead. Dreamlike, he stepped up to the door to the hallway, it slid open, and the two blond twins turned to look at him. When you think about fighting, it is never like how you imagine it, and you never seem to be as good at it when you actually do it.

This time, it was just that easy, and it was that good. Hugh smiled, stepped into the hall and his hands shot out to two thick young necks, then clanged their heads together with surprising force. Enough force that the guards crashed to the ground. It wasn't actually anything like the Aikido he had studied as a youth over a millennia ago. Hugh was strong, almost comically strong . . . and effective. He stooped over the men and grabbed one of their beam weapons. Set to kill, Hugh's eyes narrowed, he switched the weapon to stun and was about to take the charge out of the second weapon, then decided to take it and carry it in his off hand. Chances were there was no going back on this. But the changes in him, his strength, healing, perception, seemed so heightened, what did they do to me?

"Sorry lads, the voices made me do it." He pulled the guards into his darkened quarters and locked the door.

Hugh moved down the hall to the central axis elevator. This high tech world was only superficially his. Given the crash course he was forcibly given, he knew, somehow, he needed to get to the research deck. It was located centrally in the ship, in one of the safest places furthest from the hull. He was pulled to it but was wondering why Nova wasn't sounding general quarters based on his recent break out. Hugh wasn't going to question his luck.

No one passed him in the hall, it was early. He got into the central lift and went inward. Five decks later Hugh was in the central core. The thumping heart beat of the fusion drive could be heard dully, more felt really. Hugh walked down the hallway of the research cubes. The round, white pedestrian tunnels had much more wiring and circuitry this close to the heart of the vessel. He knew he was getting closer, being pulled toward something or someone.

Here. Here! Hurry.

Two guards were waiting in front of the door. To their credit they were more alert than he would have given them credit for. A blue beam lanced by his head. Hugh dodged, went to one knee, and pulled back on the triggers of his beam weapons. The dual shots hit each guard in the chest. They went down. He was going to be in so much trouble but at least he had always been a good shot.

The alarms of the ship went off. Nova's voice called out, "Weapon discharge, lab one, deck five. Security alert!" The lab door locked down. He couldn't get in. Hugh moved the guards to the safe distance. Put the settings on his weapons to the highest level. Then took aim at the door.

"Shit Nova! I thought you were my friend."

"Hugh Wilkey, you are ordered to put down your weapons and return to your quarters," Nova chimed loudly above general quarters.

"I thought I told you just to beep Nova." Hugh pulled the triggers.

The explosion of the door crashing inward was deafening. Sparks flew from the reinforced alloy and strips of metal curved in spilling light into the hallway from what looked like an operating room. Hugh shot again until he could fit through without melting material falling on him. Screams of women and a few men alerted him to the group of white clad scientists running from the shredded door.

Hugh took the time to lower the settings on his weapons and stepped through. About ten people were running to the corners of the room, going for cover. There was a box on the central operating room table. Inside it was a small creature of some kind.

Hugh stepped up. The animal was restrained in terribly uncomfortable straps, one paw in each. The white belly had been sliced open, and before his eyes, it was knitting itself together, like a slow, red worm shrinking away. It was his cat. His cat Cleo.

Hugh was shocked.

"What are you monsters doing to my cat? Why is my cat here?!". Hugh removed the straps with one hand and kept his weapon aimed and glared at the scientists. Cleo's joints didn't seem to be damaged despite the terrible pulling, and turned over on her belly by herself. She was looking a lot trimmer than he remembered and even though she always had a weird habit of staring him in the face al the time, this time was different as he looked into her ultra green eyes.

Cleo stood up shakily. She should have run away under a table or skitted off like a possessed creature. Instead, she gathered her little body and jumped onto Hugh's shoulder. Hugh was again shocked but soon would surpass it.

The cat scanned the room almost contemptuously at the sprawling scientists. The voice rose again in his mind as she purred against his neck. *That was close! Took you long enough."*

Hugh looked at the cat incredulously. "Why, how the hell can you talk".

Look out!

One of the scientists held a device behind Hugh and was approaching stealthily. It appeared to be some kind of hypo gun. Hugh leveled his right beam weapon and shot him in the face. He flew back a few feet and lay still. Static and steam flickered around his face.

"That's got to hurt. The rest of you stay down or I'll shoot lower next time."

I don't understand your words, but I understand your thoughts. It seems our relationship has become more complicated.

Hugh heard a stampede of running feet coming down the hallway and crouched behind the lab table with weapons aimed at the door. *It sure has Cleo, it sure has. But I have to tell you, it already was fucking complicated.*

I understand but I can't be caught again, Hugh. I need you to stun these people and hide me. They will kill me if you don't!

Hugh looked at his cat. Checked the stun setting of his weapons and quickly shot all the people in the room. One woman tried to hide behind and extra surgical table and he put her out, shooting her in her finely sculpted blond ass. *Okay Cleo the talking cat, now what?*

I don't know. Open that air vent above the table and stick me in. I'll be fine, I think . . . things are different now and I will explain later when I see you.

I know things are different. Jesus. A vent huh? Umm, okay Cleo. But what if this isn't a vent. What if it leads to untimely death? There could be a vent propellor or furnace or something dangerous-

Cleo cut him off. *Trust me nothing is as dangerous as being in the hands of these humans. Besides, we can communicate . . . now put me inside and close the grating, they are almost here and I can take care of myself! Do it!*

Hugh narrowed the beam of his weapon after sending two warning shots out the blasted lab door. He used a narrow beam to cut through the metal grid. He gave Cleo's soft silver rump a push through and snapped the ceiling grate into place as cleanly as he could, then hopped down. Six beam weapons, not all set on stun, lanced out past him. Two blue beams struck his shoulder and Hugh collapsed over the operating table, the room spinning and nausea overwhelming his senses.

*

Senator Shalinsky approached the officer level of Nova. He and four of his Imperial Guard armed to the teeth, hand blasters and pyranite bastard swords drawn and ready, surged out of the lift toward Hugh's quarters.

Lillian paced outside Hugh's door. Upon seeing Shalinsky she approached briskly. Then her hands instinctively dropped to her own blaster and khirda.

Shalinsky glared at her with contempt. "Doctor, what ever good you have done earning that khirda will not stand with an escaped specimen running around the ship and that mutant animal Wilkey destroying Imperial property! Your career is finished."

Lillian did not try to keep venom out of her voice, hissing, "I didn't get this khirda by being good, Senator. You know my training, you should have brought more guards if you think to just bypass me."

Shalinsky didn't flinch. "I need to talk to our guest. We need that specimen back. You over estimate your abilities and authority at your peril. You cannot stop me. I speak for the Reagent."

You think you *are* the Reagent. "You cannot kill him. He was never told the truth, from the beginning, he is the key to detecting the Pliilulua plague, perhaps our only chance."

"You as always have no proof! The grey mammal was expendable and would have given us valuable information. Now it is gone, undetectable, a possible risk and contaminant for the entire ship! So far your pet in there has shown nothing but ineffectiveness. The project is over, you told him about the mammal, you are a traitor to the Colonial Empire!"

With impossible speed, Lilly pulled out her wide bladed sword and fixed her hand weapons muzzle in line with Shalinsky's head, "If I was a traitor, you'd be dead by now. I didn't tell Hugh anything about his creature-"

"Then how!" Shalinsky shouted as his men picked out kill points on Lilly with their beam weapons.

"Telepathy. They have a mind connection. The discarded tissues removed from Hugh's brain were placed in the animal. Coupled with the unknown agent he carries, the thing on Earth that did the surgery created a unique connection. One you never tried to respect or understand, just use!"

"Imperials, get this deluded traitor out of my way."

Blue stun beams lanced out. One beam missed Lilly completely hitting Hugh's cabin door. Three other beams flashed directly at her. Lilly depressed the button on her khirda and the blade broadened into a humming, semi circular gold shield protecting her front. The beams absorbed harmlessly into the shield and Lilly's hand blaster lanced out dropping the two Imperial guards on Shalinsky's left flank.

The remaining two Imperials drew their swords and lunged toward her, shooting wildly. Lilly dropped one more at her feet with her hand gun, and turned the larger sword with her khirda as her shield winked out. She had the best in augmentations, state of the art and beyond even military grade, she jumped over the last guard seven feet in the air in a tight ball, landing lithely and spun a round house kick at the back of the guards head. He dropped.

As Shalinsky leaned back pulling at his own weapons, Lilly continued her fluid motion forward in a tumble and sprang up placing the tip of her khirda at the base of the Senator's throat. "If I discharge the energy absorbed by my khirda all at once, you know it is unlikely you will live."

"The Order has trained you well," Sander conceded with a sneer. "If my personal guard were with me, you may have been more challenged. They bear the kraken mark as you know."

"I am not here to spar with you Senator! I am asking you to not kill Hugh. I am no traitor. I could have killed you easily and I did not."

A nozzle of a beam weapon gently pressed against the base of Lilly's skull. To sneak up on her so quietly was no small feat. A familiar voice whispered in her ear, "Lilly, so nice to see you, kindly sheathe your blade, impeding a Senator in his duties is an Imperial Infraction. I'm not even sure the Hidden Hand can keep from . . . punishment."

"Sebastian . . ." Lilly slowly placed her blade back in her hilt. "Silent as a snake as always." She raised her hands and backed away from Shalinsky.

The missed beam that struck Hugh's quarters alerted five Imperials and a half dozen Marines that spilled nervously into the hall. "Senator do you require assistance?"

Senator Shalinsky placed his hand on his throat and called down the hall, "Doctor Hsian and I were just having a little discussion. Prepare for the interrogation. The doctor will wait outside in case we have any medical emergencies. Sebastian, Marines, see to it she is on hand.

Storm grey eyes raked Lilly as he passed down the hall and into Hugh's cabin. The Marines gathered the four fallen Imperials as Sebastian disarmed Lillian of her gun and blade. "Lilly Lilly, you have a knack for making rather large enemies. Turn around".

Lilly turned around and faced Sebastian. His eyes were not very human, more like a snakes, and his skin suit shifted to a mottled white as he blended into the hull. "Your not doing a very good job of blending, brother. You know you are not my match in hand to hand combat. I wasn't going to kill the Senator, you didn't have to interfere."

"Ah, dear sister, I am not trying to be unseen, I want you to see me and this weapon. Your Mastery in martial combat is irrelevant when I could vaporize you where you stand if you even flinched." Sebastian raised the setting to disintegrate. "I should have been a Hidden Hand, obviously their best is confounded by simple stealth suits and ray guns.

"That isn't very sporting Sebastian."

"I am not being well compensated to be sporting, Lilly, I am paid to be effective. Did you really think the Senator would be so easily swayed? Why do you care so much anyway about this throwback and his pet? He is a worth more dead than alive and less trouble too in my opinion."

"No one asked your opinion, you mercenary. Hugh is a human being, his abilities and genetic profile are unique, do you know what that means? They can't be just cut out.

He is the only one who can interface with HCSIS. It's not what he is it's who he is!"

Sebastian shrugged. "He is lab meat, the gene crafter's will crack him like a nut. Everyone who needs to will be able to do what he does."

"Don't be so sure. The fourteen hundred years he spent in stasis created something. Something evolved in his blood, tissues, and bone, kept him from cryo-burn and gave him regeneration power that is so strong he survived surgery that would kill the most rigged out member of the Order. He is irreplaceable."

Sebastian laughed softly at Lilly. Shifted the hand blaster to his other hand effortlessly with a toss. "You really don't understand the Senator much do you. He is a man of action. He is fighting to save our people and will do it. He will be the next Prelate as well and that fact is as immutable as this blaster in your face."

"If he kills Hugh Shalinsky will be closing doors that might save us all, its brutal and unnecessary. If he kills Hugh, I will kill you both."

"Now Lilly, Raven calling the Crow black? The Senator needs answers before he faces the Imperial Court, and you've been known to be . . . intense in your work in the day before you finished your stint with the Order." Sebastian indicated for her to sit with the muzzle of his weapon. "Well let's hope your right sis, and this creature is hardy and doesn't expire without sharing his secrets. Because when Shalinsky is done with him, there might not be much left."

*

"Where is the animal you freed!" The Imperial guard was tired of smashing Hugh in the head. A tooth glistened on the table Hugh was strapped to. Burn marks, broken fingernails, hundreds of abrasions and hematomas were not healing as fast at the fifth hour of Hugh's interrogation pressed on. He was visibly losing weight as his body regenerated under the assault.

A new tooth was slowly growing out of the left canine where the old one was just knocked out. Hugh spoke as clearly as he could, "I don't know. I honestly don't know. Why are you doing this? I tried to help you . . ." The pain was beyond anything he ever experienced.

"We ask the questions!" The Imperial struck him again with a gloved fist and the sound of the crack punctuated the broken lip, which had been broken countless times that morning.

Senator Shalinsky raised his hand to stop the Imperial. "You said the . . . cat. Cleo. It called to you telepathically? It was sentient? How can this fiction serve you and your purposes?"

"I am telling you the truth. She was just a regular cat. But something happened to her. You did something to her, something sick. You inhuman bastards!"

"We did nothing to her. It. It has your weird healing ability, you are a mutant, or a pawn of the Ghengonni. Your resist telling the truth, so we were studying your pet. Now that you have taken our specimen away, we will have to get the samples from you."

Hugh struggled against his bonds. "Don't you have enough samples, they are all around the table, things you have ripped or burned off of me. You have fucked with me ever since you found me, I am innocent of any conspiracy. I tried to help you!"

Sander looked down on him, shook his head. "You are dangerous and have given us no proof of anything to prove you are not an anarchist in an elaborate charade to infiltrate our military. Your life is forfeit, at least we may be able to glean something from your tissues to help us against this plague. Remove it now"

Two med techs moved up and placed a handled, specimen case next to Hugh's right hand. One prepared a syringe as the other charged a laser scalpel. Hugh's eyes grew wide and his yells grew desperate. "You can't!"

"We must. I'm sorry it has to be this way Hugh, but we are out of time." Sander signaled the teck with the syringe, and injected his right arm above the wrist. Hugh could feel his arm going numb and getting groggy, as well as the rest of his terrible pain fading for the first time. "Take his hand."

As the tech started to cut into his wrist, Cleo cried out. *No Hugh! Stop them!*

Hugh did not know how it happened. He shook off some of the deleterious effects of the drug and he felt a tingle electricity surge through his whole body. A voice inside him seemed to build like a storm and erupt out of his whole body and mind. "No!"

The two techs went flying up into the ceiling with force, and then dropped to the ground with wet cracking sounds. Hugh's voice rose, "No no no no no!"

Senator Shalinsky stepped back and his Marines and Imperials surged forward toward Hugh. The men and women bounced off the bulkheads and fell to the ground. Fourteen guards and two techs lay strewn about the room and electric fingers of white danced over Hugh's body as he finally went still.

Sander raised his eyebrow and stepped cautiously forwards. He picked up the laser scalpel and walked around to the table and looked down at Hugh's right hand. "The Colonial Empire needs your tissue, this is war and there is no time. Perhaps you do have something we should study further. But if you do not comply fully and obediently, I will vaporize you myself. You belong to us." There was ozone and heat waves surging off Hugh's restrained body. He was good and truly unconscious.

With that Sander severed Hugh's right hand, cauterizing it instantly, and placed it in the specimen box. "Your powers are amazing, whatever you are. I am sorry if my methods may seem severe, but we are at war and you are, could be . . . the key to winning it."

Sander headed to the door and could see Sebastian still holding a weapon on Lilly, even though they were both seated. Lilly looked up in concern.

"He yet lives Doctor, we have what we need, for now." Sander motioned to the remaining Marines waiting in the hall. "Take our injured personnel to the infirmary."

Lilly stood up, puzzled, but relieved. Sebastian gave back her weapons with some caution. "What did you do Senator?"

"I got some answers. Hugh Wilkey is more surprising than I expected and deserves more . . . investigation. He is possibly not part of the anarchists, but I frankly don't know what he is, but I need to find out. Do your job, Doctor, and report to me, but impress on Hugh that I will take more than his hand if he causes any more trouble. I will hold you responsible Doctor if your pet doesn't behave and his pet isn't accounted for, and soon. Sebastian, with me."

"Later sis." Sebastian stepped back with a feral grin and faded into the background of the hallway.

Shock and horror crossed Lilly's face as she made her way to Hugh's quarters. She easily navigated around the fallen and stood in front of Hugh, concerned and appalled at the evidence of torture. Cold tears streamed down her face even though she was no stranger to war and carnage.

Her grief passed into wonder as Hugh's hand quivered. Bones started to grow out of his severed wrist before her eyes. Lilly stared in wonderment and gasped, "My God Hugh, what are you . . ."

Chapter 4
Cleopatra

Hugh ate his fifth course with diminished zeal. The flesh of his beaten and mutilated body took a brief three hours to completely heal, including his amputated hand.

He lost twenty pounds during his ordeal. The skin and muscles had returned with speed with the large intake of food which amazed him. The cramped quarters of his cabin overflowed with Imperial guards, Marines, and scientists. The nozzles of twelve beam weapons pointed toward Hugh with the patience born of long discipline and no little fear of their unusual captive.

Lilly sat next to Hugh, finishing a hand scanner sweep of his re-grown hand. "Hugh, I tried . . ."

"Don't." Hugh angrily pulled back his arm. Dressed in his officer whites again, he glared at what little unoccupied space remained in his cabin.

They sat quietly like that for some time. Lilly leaned back on the far side of the couch and crossed her arms. "I tried to stop them Hugh, I put down four Imperials and held a blade against the Senator's throat. The important thing is your alive."

"I would have rather not been tortured, you'll forgive me if I want you all dead in as long and painful a manner as possible."

Lilly let out a long sigh. "Understandable Hugh. But we learned some important things and you are alive."

Hugh snarled, "You got your fucking samples and all you need to know about my flesh, now get out!" The guards shifted nervously and fingers brushed triggers.

"Whether you like it or not, I am the only friend you have Hugh. What we learned that is important to me is that you can defend yourself and have powers we have never seen and can't account for. What humans fear they often to . . . mistreat. But not me Hugh, I care about you and frankly could kill that arrogant prick Shalinsky."

Hugh looked at her from the corners of his eyes, "Prove it. If you are such a good friend, get all these bastards out of my cabin."

Lilly stood up, smoothing her uniform and looking around. Lilly had a considerable voice considering she was rather petite, "Everyone pack it up and get out."

The Imperial guards didn't budge, but the scientists, especially Lilly's staff started packing up immediately. A captain of the squad of Imperials walked up to Lilly. "Milady, with all due respect, we cannot leave the prisoner unguarded."

"You will station your men outside Hugh's door, as many as you can fit in the hall if you like. You have five minutes."

"Milady Lord Shalinsky would not-"

Lilly stood slowly and stared up at the captain unflinchingly. Her voice was cool, low, and dangerous. "Captain, do not make me ask you twice." Hugh was amused watching the petite woman glaring up at a man well over two meters tall and three times her weight.

The captain held her eyes for a moment, eventually looking away. He bowed and signaled the squad to remove to outside the door. Five minutes later only Hugh and Lilly remained in the cabin.

Hugh put his legs up on the couch. "All right, maybe I will give you a bit of a chance to redeem yourself. What did you learn from Lord Mengala's tender ministrations?"

Lilly sat opposite Hugh again. "You have every right to be angry. But what we learned is that your ability to heal is off the charts. More astoundingly, when pressed, you can control magnetic fields. Not just your own, but other people's. It is a powerful and dangerous thing."

Hugh turned his new hand about looking at it curiously. "That's your specialty, magnetic field research. How can this be happening to me."

"That's what is so fascinating. Our star ship's move by shifting magnetic bubbles. Our body's and all life sustain a week magnetic field going down to the cellular level. What you seem to be able to do is use your own body's organic energy to effect other magnetic fields in a meaningful way. You can compress them, shift them, move them."

"But how? Is is what you did to me with HCSIS?"

"No, as I have said, we, I, did little except create the cable interface to connect to the port that already existed in your head when I found you in Old Boston. We suppressed your memory chemically, temporarily, to test you, mold you, and protect you." Hugh glared at Lilly. ". . . and also to control you. In retrospect we should have just told you, but the evolved bionanytes in your blood seem to be the actuator of your powers, such as they are, and an unknown variable. You powers seem to manifest as a result of your colonization by these unknown life forms. Most dramatically demonstrated when you are threatened."

"Do you think I can learn to control these . . . powers?" Hugh stood up and began to pace.

"I do not know. The bionanytes have an uncanny ability to hide in your cells, we cant get a clear look at them or their means of interacting with you, through you. But I have a hunch they are compressed in huge number in what seem like city's throughout your body, their world, if you will. When threatened, or pushed beyond your abilities to heal or threatened with losing parts of your body, they rally. Rather potently, when Shalinsky's Imperials were thrown back like so many dolls by your magnetic pulse. Most of those people live, but some are still in critical condition or in comas from your unfocused, uncontrolled defense mechanism. Imagine if you could control it?"

"As a child in the old days, I thought super powers would be cool, but not to hurt people." Hugh laughed grimly and walked into the head and washed his face. "But what about the voices, the mind connection to my pet. It's all a bit much."

"Ah, that, telepathic, telekinetic? Unless you can read my mind and others I don't know of, you can speak to Nova through the link and your pet through some crazy evolution of bionanytes through your long slumber together. It might just be when that disturbing Genghoni scientist placed that the port in your brain, the excess brain matter was placed in your cat's head. Monstrous. I know how it sounds, but the mutant seemed to have guessed the bionanytes were also in your pet and wanted to see what would happen, how they would adapt."

"Six months ago I was found by you after having that surgery, how could a bionanyte or whatever adapt so quickly and reconcile the tissues of two different species. Frankenstein couldn't do that?"

Lilly looked puzzled. "Frankenstein?"

"A Doctor from my time. Very talented with tissues, you two would have loved each other. Similar moral code."

Lilly frowned, "Surely your mocking me."

"Never Herr Doctor! Now is there a way I can test my . . . abilities?"

Lilly looked around the room and her eyes fell to a round sculpture on his dresser, near a sleeping palette. "I suggest trying to move objects. Small ones. But all the people you had me get rid of were going to help you come up with these answers."

Hugh nodded. "That's okay, I need some time to myself and something tells me my cabin is more bugged with cameras and mic's than I could imagine."

Lilly nodded. "Absolutely. Try and focus on that sculpture. See if you can move it."

Hugh turned to the sculpture and picked it up with his hand. "About five pounds. Okay lets try it." Hugh stepped back three feet. Ten minutes went by and Lilly laughed when Hugh started making faces. The object vibrated slightly and he spent another hour trying to lift it, finally throwing up his hands. "Well that wasn't very impressive."

"Hmm, try thinking of something, like an image, or something that holds some emotive content for you."

Hugh turned toward the sculpture and concentrated. The objects started shaking. After a minute it rose up into the air six inches. Lilly was aghast and just lowered herself behind the couch. Fortunate for her as the sculpture whipped past where she had sat and crashed thunderously like a cannon ball against the bulk head. Powdered stone floated to the deck and a depression in the plasteel marked the spot where it stuck. "Dear God! That was . . . astounding. What were you thinking off?"

"Shalinsky . . ."

"Ah well, I don't blame you. I ask you to not do that any more until we find a proper training area. This ship is held together by magnetic fields."

Hugh nodded. "Agreed. Now I could use some time alone."

Lilly nodded headed toward the door and the sea of cramped guards behind it. "I hope you can learn to forgive me for not being more forthcoming with your condition. Maybe even come to trust me. I wont let them hurt you again if I can help it."

Hugh glanced at her wistfully. Good cop bad cop crossed his mind. "No worries Lilly, your image got my ball into the air, it was Shalinsky's face that made me turn it into a weapon."

*

Hugh was glad to be alone. Even if he was being observed by hidden devices, at least he had the illusion of his solitude. So much had changed so fast, even if he didn't feel the fourteen hundred years that had passed for him in an instant.

Hugh . . .

Cleo is that you? Are you okay?

Who else would it be?

Hugh looked around. *Where are you?*

I am above you in the vent. Don't look up.

Okaaaay. Ahh, how do I get you out without alerting the goons. Oh wait, I can get you out. But you will be seen . . .

Hugh, trust me I won't. I've been keeping unobserved for two days now. I don't know how, exactly. People don't see me if I don't want, it seems. I definitely don't want as you know.

Hugh tilted his head back nonchalantly. *Hold on a sec Cleo.* Hugh focused on the air vent in the ceiling. He stared at the four screws and willed them, one at a time, to unwind. At first they wouldn't budge. Sweat tingled down his back but one at a time, they started to fall to the floor. *Cleo can you keep the screen from falling?*

Hmm. Yes. Maybe. Cleo placed her paw on top of the screen and flexed her four claws through the mesh. *Got it.*

I hope so Cleo. I don't want you getting caught. The last screw fell to the ground and the grill was free. Cleo put her other paw out and tilted the screen around, pulled it up at angle and in after a small struggle.

Cleo dropped down to the couch, her grey and black stripes shimmering oddly, as if surrounded by a heat wave. *Don't worry Hugh, they can't detect me.*

Hugh resisted the urge to reach out and pat her. Eyeing his left over food, Cleo jumped soundlessly onto the coffee table and slowly ate some cold cuts Hugh had left. They were round, grown on a vine despite being meat. They fit easily into Cleo's small mouth. *Oh so hungry. So much better than the damn kibbles you used to feed us.*

Mike said it was good for you.

Fine you eat cold cereal without milk your entire life. Glad you are remembering your past though, with Mike and all.

Hugh rubbed his head wondering where his memory was taking him. He turned to Cleo as he picked up the fallen screws. *You didn't care back then as I recall. In fact you were fat and spoiled. But now you have sass and a brain and seem much more . . . trim. You can thank me for that. And I don't remember Mike yet, just that he decided to feed you the dry food. Was he family?*

Well I remember! And I will make you remember in time. It's terrible what they did to us. I was happy before you dragged me into this, how do you say . . . nightmare? Now I am confused. Why did you put us in the freezing bed anyway?

Hugh looked at the door. A guard stepped in and walked towards him. "Mr. Wilkey, I have been sent to take the debris from your . . . experiment as per Doctor Hsian."

Cleo stayed perfectly still on the table, a bit of ham ball hanging out of her mouth. *It's okay Hugh, he can't see me. Act natural.*

Riiiiigght. "Ah, sure sergeant, go right ahead." Hugh kept and eye on him and made a point of not staring at the ham being noisily swallowed.

"Did you hear something Mr. Wilkey?," the sergeant enquired as Hugh reached for the platter and placed some food in his mouth. Hugh made a show of chewing loudly.

The man shrugged and finished cleaning the spot. He looked around the room one more time and left. *Well I'll b damned, he didn't see you.*

Cleo jumped up on Hugh's shoulder digging in with her claws a bit. "Ow!"

Huh? I don't understand your sounds.

Oh Cleo! Easy. Your too hot to be around my neck.

Well, try this.

Cleo actually changed her body temperature. She became cooler.

How do you do that?

No idea. It seems to be an added benefit of not being detected. You like?

Well, yes.

Excellent! Now let's catch up shall we?

Hugh shifted more comfortably onto the couch. *I'm not sure I am ready to remember Cleo.* He had found it was difficult to be on the verge of some part of his missing history falling into place knowing there would be no going back. *I am not even used to you being able to speak in my head!*

I don't know how that all works. My head always feels too full. But I only have a few pieces of this puzzle, there are so many questions. But I must admit I am curious why you put us into the freezing bed in the first place. You jabbed that needle into yourself, then me, and we were on our way.

Hugh remembered being in the warrens underneath MIT. He had been visiting a friend, Scott, on his way to a vet in the South End but couldn't leave Cleo's carrier in the hot car. Scott was working on his doctorate in cryogenics and he had left a upsetting message on Hugh's cell phone while he was en route. It was some amazing breakthrough for Scott in the last few days and he was preparing to do a live study on a pig, freezing it for six months, then reviving it. *I think my friend Scott was going to get his specimen when he received word that the project was going to be shut down. He needed me there to help move the two hundred pound animal. He was inconsolable. He left what he called his "antifreeze" syringe there on his work table as he went to get the swine.*

I remember being wrapped in a towel so I wouldn't claw your eyes out getting injected with something, then you pulling us into that coffin and closing the door.

Yes Cleo, that's true. Scott had said he would never get to a human study now. He would never get the Nobel Prize for such a break through. I decided it wasn't fair.

Cleo scratched at her head. *Wasn't fair for who?*

My life wasn't fair or worthwhile. Maybe I could help by jumping in while Scott brought back his test pig. Help science push forward by risking my self. A little bit of self sacrifice for the greater good. It was only supposed to be for six months.

Why bring me. Your cat? Why such a death wish? You most likely could have killed us both. You risked everything.

Hugh shrugged. *I love you Cleo, you were like my kid. I wasn't going anywhere without you, plus I thought it might help the study. I am starting to remember, I was married but it was being nullified. The religious right came down hard on us and even abolished State marriages. Oh my God. I was married to a man. I was . . . gay*

So you do remember Mike now. Yes you were. You were very happy.

Hugh felt waves of shame beat down on him. He was raised Catholic and born gay, and the two elements never reconciled well. He understood then that part his feeling of solitude and desolation even when his identity was chemically suppressed lingered in his psyche. He had thought he had fallen for Lillian Hsian. A connection that included her physical beauty. That was only an illusion, he knew his affection was not physical ever, it never came to that, but now it never would be. He could be fond of her, but knew he could never be with her in that physical way.

Hugh did remember some of his great love for Michael, but it was still shadowy. But he remembered his rage at what society had done to him and their relationship. *After the right wing wack jobs took away what I had wanted my whole life, I went a little crazy I recall Cleo. Mike and I were married for fifteen years and then they took it away. I was so despondent, I threw myself into the cryogenic chamber thinking that in six months, I would be either dead, or famous, and explain why I had done it. To bring attention to our plight, to make people see. To make my life worthwhile again. Maybe even have them turn it around.*

Well we lived. Are you satisfied? Isn't it all so much better now. Cleo's thoughts somehow sounded sarcastic.

Hugh slapped himself in the head. *My God Cleo, now it is worse! They reprogrammed my orientation with those drugs. I actually felt attraction to Lilly. All because their precious society couldn't deal with me now anymore than they could then. In fact you are so right, it is worse. I am the last of my kind here in the future. All the men are metro-sexual, man-scaped into pink, Aryan pin heads. There will never be anyone out there for me, ever again.*

Cleo licked his neck. The sandpaper feel of her tongue was somewhat gentle and she meant well. *At least there are other humans. These idiots don't even know what a cat is! I am the last of my species Hugh. And since part's of your brain is in me, maybe there is just us, and the future.*

Hugh reached up to Cleo and pulled her into his arms. She started purring just like she always had. *Well Cleo, if that's the case, I am never letting you go.*

Chapter 5
Transformation

The 5th fleet hurtled through space at five times the speed of light. Hugh nursed a bruising headache, still, as Lilly discussed what she deducted of his true origins revealed with some translation from Cleo's reports and missing information. At Senator Shalinsky's order, with the authority to back them up as Lilly confirmed through private channels to home world, he had the mandate to pull the plug on the HCSIS program and essentially halt any staggered reduction in Hugh's suppression meds. They had to stopped cold. The two weeks since had been trying for him and the withdrawal excruciating.

Along with the revelation that Hugh was homosexual, being the only such person in the universe didn't stop the society induced homophobia he carried with him across the centuries as his memories fully returned. Escaping prejudice by fleeing across time did little for the ingrained and conflicted messages absorbed from a dead society that destroyed itself over differences of religion, resources, and ethnicity.

As the last dregs of the suppression drugs were purged of his system and his old memories were streaming back much too quickly as fabricated memories fell away like smoke, Hugh was left viewing with in stark contrast to what he believed he was for six months. Hugh rushed to the bathroom as Lilly sat patiently on the couch opposite him. "I'm going to throw up, again".

Hugh had the small consolation that much of the terrible language against gay people didn't exist in the future. They simply removed all the troublesome genes. No differences, no fear of those differences, no "faggots" or "niggers" or anything upsetting to the new humans. As Hugh recalled, even gentled words like "gay" were turned into negatives by the hetero majority he left behind, back in his time. Maybe it was this casual slander, this cool scorn and self centered hubris that made them so ripe for annihilation.

Lilly waited until Hugh cleaned up. "Feeling better?"

"Yes and no. My puking events seem to be subsiding. But you are aware I am still in great turmoil from all the memories crashing into me. Can you please remind me of my medical condition one more time? Starting with how this telepathy works?" Hugh winked at Cleo who was sleeping behind a plant in the corner.

Lilly recanted as much as she could of magnetic field analysis but they were getting close to the home system and she felt her time was running out. Lilly was pleased

Hugh had confided in her despite their checkered history. She was surprised and oddly melancholy over Hugh's disclosure of orientation. It simply didn't exist in her society, they didn't have words for it. Lilly knew she felt an attraction to Hugh she had not felt for another man in a very long time. She understood the other complexities blocking their involvement far more solidly than this new wrinkle.

"I've filled you in on everything since we found you. Your native memory should be presenting fully now. In a way, you set this all in motion from what you've told me."

Hugh cut her off, "You put a computer plug in my head and brainwashed me."

Lilly clasped her hand and looked at him calmly. "Not this again. for the last time. You froze yourself, disgruntled with your 21st century life. Throwing your life to fate. We just decided to use you without your consent. We thought you Genghonni."

"Well, the unpleasantness, to say the least, of your use of me continues to come up as I recover more and more. No wonder I was disgusted with humanity. I wanted to contribute to Science and wake up in better times. At least back then I was only emotionally crushed and lightly physically tortured in my time. You people were cowards to cull away your humanity in all it's different forms."

Lilly stared at him. "You were perhaps a little cowardly, or perhaps, you were rather brilliant in your foresight. Not long after you went into suspended animation, your generation blasted all life on planet Earth. Besides, you are helping science. Greatly. Yet you used your friends project for your own ends, are you so different?"

Hugh let that simmer for a while. "Yes and no. There was little one man could do back then. Humanity was as stupid and short sighted, as it is today. Why is it so unreasonable that I get to act out, now? It was just me and my pet at stake and most humans didn't really care if I lived or died with their twisted prejudices and hatreds." Hugh squeezed his throbbing skull with both hands. "It hasn't changed all that much, in fact it has gotten worse. I thought it was only going to be six months!"

Lilly shrugged. "Roughly fourteen hundred years ago. You froze yourself. Then humanity erased itself, bombing your city and every other major city in the cataclysm. You had, for the time, cutting edge fusion generation that kept you under as the centuries passed. Humanity had prepared a little, we had moved the elites to the sea well in advance. New Boston, New London, and New Tokyo were the first sunken cities we developed behind the new pyranite, geometric domes. Every major coastal city was to be rebuilt near the largest source of water on the planet, as deeply as possible over the course of a century. The nuclear destruction of 2020 made sure we developed differently. Returning to the sea until the planet could be resettled. But we were not the first ones who found you as you know, there were some survivors if you can call them that, existing on land.

"What does that mean?"

"Well we are not exactly sure. There is an underground resistance to the Colonial Government. Broken up into secret cells. They have not been wiped out apparently, and the government's position is that they are anarchists. They were routed from Oceania our Capital, and other undersea cities and created pods on land during the last century, and seemingly started working with select Genghonni remnants of humanity on the surface. We don't know how they could have found you before us but they did. We had no idea that the separatists and the Genghonni could be linked somehow. You discovered how shocking this was to us when you experienced our safety protocols and ultimately the Senator's brutality."

"Jesus, this gets better and better.

"It is what it is. The crude bionanytes and fusion system that powered your long sleep somehow got you fourteen centuries into the future. The variables contributing to your condition and powers is based on the surgery they did on Cleo and your brain, and the evolution and intent of the bionanytes that call you home. How a mutant found you before us I cannot fathom much less modify you thus. You see we simply built on the port tech that we found in your skull, and the nanos, self replicating, mutating, evolving even in the cold of your booth for all that time is something else."

"Ahh. Lovely. Exactly what part of my brain was altered? You never were specific. Why can't you track my little friends still? You have my hand in some lab someplace surely that's given you more insight."

Lilly lowered her voice to a whisper. "Your hypothalamus was significantly altered. Some of the cranial bundles branching near it were larger than humans today. Whether this was natural for your time or the result of our genetic work since your time, or perhaps your . . . orientation . . . is unclear. We have some determination that there was a connection to this later theory."

Hugh had confided in Lilly on the condition she would tell no one. If she was to help him, he was forced to trust her as much as he dared. If they routed out all minorities and and undesirable traits all these centuries he was pretty sure they weren't ready to know who their potential savior actually was.

Hugh glowered at her, also speaking softly while turning up the classical music playing in his room. "You gave me amnesia and altered my sexual orientation for a time. You altered me in ways great and small. You had me so good I used to think you were hot, you know. A rather unique experience for me."

Lilly shifted uncomfortably, her face reddening a bit. "Hugh you have to understand humanity has . . . refined itself since your time. The races have . . . used clinics over the centuries to round off those differences that split them before into a more blended society. There are no . . . what is the word you used, "homosexuals", anymore. They simply elected to remove it. The genes were isolated and removed over a millennia ago. There are also precious few Asians or Blacks or differences over the centuries of the the most visual sort, and hence we have become a more homogenous people. I mean we are all there, but unlike me, many have opted to blend themselves into that unified race, selecting traits they want for themselves and their family. We suppressed your, tendency, so you could fit in more comfortably. We are all the same under our skin and now, we mostly look it too."

"We had a leader who tried to make humanity 'blend' better. His name was Adolf Hitler. You made everyone into a plucked Viking. Don't you realize you did a better job than one of the worst villains of our time? You took away humanities facets."

"Hugh it's not the same. The people who survived elected to make themselves religiously, ethnically, more similar. No one forced them. The people who died in your war were the ones who embraced violence, genocide. Not us. We also did away with disease, birth defects, and created a far more harmonious society. We have had no wars in over a millennia."

He crossed his arms. "I'm no damned birth defect. Nature builds in variety to increase the survivability and adaptability of a species. You have selected it right out! Its more insidious, you cant even fight against it. Why didn't you just clone more of me or get someone less primitive to do your project."

"That's just it. We can't. The work done to you at first, we thought was butchery. Parts of your brain were removed, part adapted to service as a connecting unit to a larger computing network. Part of the displaced brain tissue, yours, was placed into your . . . pet, along with some of the bionanytes that already existed there, created a first sentient animal. The same bionanytes that had grown and evolved since your original suspension have changed enough to rebuild and adapt to almost anything. They made all the changes synergistic, created and tended new neural pathways, and we have no idea how they have eluded our analysis. They are part metal, part your tissue, and they . . . move."

"Wait wait wait a minute." Hugh held up his hand in disbelief. "We are flying through the universe at the speed of light, we have laser guns, everything, and you cant get an example of what's in my blood."

"Well that's just it. They avoid us. Somehow they have insinuated themselves into your sensory system. They know when we are probing for them. They . . . hide. Your hand contained none, from what I could find out from a person in Shalinsky's team who owed me a favor. It was evacuated by your little friends. They abandoned what could only be observed to be a small city. No bigger than a circuit."

Hugh sat breathing deeply, his eyes closed, trying to wrap his brain around everything Lilly was telling him. "Well, what other cities are scattered around my body? They don't seem to be dangerous, to me, yet. Are there any other foreign objects in my body?."

"Hmm, I am afraid you would ask that. Well, it was from, how do you say it, ah, your cat. The brain material the resistance transferred into you was from your cat. A small amount, that is the only really new information. A smaller amount then what they took from you and put into . . . her. What plan they had or intended by all this, we can't fathom."

Hugh leaned back and covered his face in his hands. "I tried to escape the craziness of my time, to either perish or be brought into a better life. These times are even more crazy, but truth be told, I always did like technology. So, it seems that they can avoid detection. Blend into my body like fading into the background."

Lilly laughed out loud. "Perhaps. But, you may be interested to know, I can see your cat. She just faded into sight."

Hugh looked at Cleo nervously. *Cleo what are you doing?*

Nothing! I think it is due to her spending so much time with us.

"Lilly, I don't want you to say anything."

Lilly turned around averting her eyes from Cleo. "I won't say a word. You have suffered and lost enough. But she was invisible, then she just appeared. She is so . . . beautiful."

Hugh looked at Cleo and then to Lilly. "These bionanytes are as free as me, apparently they decided to let you into the club. But Cleo is amazing. Even before these gifts from our tiny, invisible friends."

*

The bureaucrats from the Colonial Government circled around the opulent officers lounge aboard Nova. The room was abuzz with various party cliques, clustered around reports on Hugh Wilkey and the HCSIS program.

Ernestine Joyce, tall and black, stood out amongst the green party delegates. "Senator, despite the loop holes in your information on Hugh's original surgery, I still think you overreacted in closing down the project and releasing classified documentation, incredible as this information is. It has caused great concern among the coalitions."

Senator Shalinsky's austere politeness seemed to only enhance his contempt. "Speaker Joyce, the dye is caste. Your party always pushes for more openness with State secrets, you can't have it both ways. Not only was this project ineffective, and incredibly expensive, but harboring a rather offensive primitive. Those early humans destroyed Eden on Earth for a second time. It's folly to trust one with a warship just because he has questionable, oddly convenient hardware in his skull and an enlarged, primitive brain structure. The original surgery was done by God knows who."

"All I'm saying Senator is we have not really seen whether there is something to the man's findings, despite Nova's inability to verify. We drugged him and manipulated him for our purposes. Only now are we trying to be honest with this precious link to our past. He is a human being."

A slender man raised an eyebrow, swinging toward Ernestine and Sander with a small retinue of attendants. "We hunt the Genghonni, the mutants of Old Earth, for what little worthwhile genes they might possess. A veritable needle in a hay stack as it is. Why should we treat this one any different? If he has genes we need, we should take them as payment for the world his generation destroyed. Our world. I believe it is what he is for."

Ernestine glared down at the little man. "If people like you and the trade guild contented themselves with what they were born with rather than participating in the grotesque and cruel hunting of the remnants of our ancestors, we would be a more Christian society."

The trade speaker grabbed a beaker of violet powder from a passing servant and snorted it in one inhalation, then dropped the empty phial on the floor. "Spare me your lectures woman. Just because you are bitter, you are immune to the sacred art flesh crafting, don't try to bring the rest of us down. You are garish and unmaleable, with your weird hair and dirty skin!"

Speaker Joyce started to reach for her khirda but Shalinsky laid a staying hand on her arm. The senator waved his other hand in dismissal of the trade speaker. "Enough! I've seen enough khirda's bandied about, I have no time for this! We tried to treat Wilkey as one of us, gave him all the tools and conditioning. We were trying to give him a new life. Sadly Nova confirmed that the pseudoscience behind his link with the computer was undependable. I move that we focus on more urgent matters. Warning the President of the loss of two more colonies and creating a lock down on all traffic to home system."

The representative from New Madras stood. "We ourselves only left quarantine and apparently are free of the pathogen. I'm not sure its wholly safe that we return to home system. As inconvenient as it is to us, there are twenty two ships in the Fifth fleet. Quite a lot of space to check during our two day layover."

"I understand your concern Representative Ganshi. But despite us not knowing the vector we clearly understand and can track the pathogen itself. It's a virus. We have almost completed a trial vaccine that show promise in blocking the Pliilulua virus from replicating. That's something due to be completed in two short weeks. Bye the time we reach Sol system"

Hopeful chatter erupted amongst the delegates. Interrupted by general quarter alarms breaking out throughout Nova. Ernestine turned to Shalinsky, "How did you get a sample much less have time to work on a viable vaccine? I want to see the data."

Nova's alarms boomed across the ship, "Attention all hands attention all hands. This is not a drill. All crewman report to battle stations. We are under attack!"

An armed Marine stepped into the officers lounge. "Pardon me lords and ladies, we must ask you all to return to your quarters immediately for your own safety."

"What is going on Marine." A representative from Shanghai tugged at his sleeve, she had a thick Chinese accent, despite being blond and blue eyed. "Just who is attacking us?"

"I don't know mam, but the Wellington has taken heavy damage and the fleet is dropping to sub-light. You all must be in your rooms and strapped into your blast seats. I must insist, time is short."

The dignitaries made for their rooms. Senator Shalinsky made for the lift with two of his aides, followed by Speaker Ernestine Joyce. A Marine attempted to follow them and redirect them to their quarters.

As the lift door closed, Ernestine smiled and waved. "To the Bridge Nova."

The metallic voice ran conversationally through the lift pod, "As you wish. Though I highly recommend you return to your quarters for your safety."

Senator Shalinsky eyed Ernestine. "What is our status Nova, who is attacking us?"

"Captain Obutu has been informed of your pending arrival on the bridge. He insists it will be easier to explain once you arrive."

The Senator's jaw muscles visibly clenched, he wasn't used to delayed reports or redirections of his orders.

The lift came to a stop in front of the bridge. The door whispered open just as the fleet dropped out of warp. The dignitaries grabbed railings and placed their hands against any solid structure to brace themselves. The dampeners usually made dropping slightly turbulent but emergency drops could be wrenching.

Ernestine looked around the ordered bridge, where the crew worked in controlled chaos as they organized a fleet response to the attackers. The screen displayed twenty two discs of the Fifth Fleet forming two attack patterns, one disc, she presumed the Wellington, exploded in a bright arc of brilliant white light as their fusion drive ignited. Roughly a dozen grey spheres whisked toward the approaching fleet. "Tell me what I am looking at is what I think it is . . ."

"Captain Obutu, report!" Sander Shalinsky marched right up to the control platform. He was in a state of disbelief. "Tell me those are some form of rebel fleet."

Obutu was visibly annoyed with the Senator, but swallowed his more acerbic comments. "Senator, those are not rebel ships. They caught up to us and stopped us in warp. No existing colonial tech can do that! Their weapons seem to be some sort of biochemical lance that eats through our shields and hull. Senator, these are aliens."

Just as the fleet was coordinating a devastating crossfire on the spheres, they winked off screens and scans. The entire bridge crew stared in amazement at what they were seeing. Senator Shalinsky turned toward the Captain, "I'll be damned."

"They also *can* stealth. Roughly a mile wide and they disappear right off the screen as soon as they loose a barrage. Too fast for targeting computers. Hugh and HCSIS worked." Ernestine looked Shalinsky in the eye. "You knew?"

"We did not know, Representative. My people went over the records again and again. Nothing was found, except, a single file on HCSIS' bio scan of Faith. We found a corrupted picture of the Pliilulua viral case, but that was all. It seemed like all we needed."

As the bridge watched on, the twelve spheres reappeared on the extreme left flank of the onrushing fleet. The spheres formed a burst pattern around the Lexington, blue bolts of energy burst onto the Colonial Warship like the spokes of a wheel and it exploded into uncountable shards of light. The bridge crew and guests looked away from the flash.

"Nova, get us all back into warp, head for the nearest Starbase"

Captain Obutu slammed his fist onto the control consul in front of him. Five thousand lives in five minutes. "We are getting out of here."

"Captain Obutu, we outnumber them two to one." Shalinsky gripped the back of the Captain's chair as the twenty remaining Colonial ships jumped.

"Not for long! Not at this rate! We can't fight what we cant see."

Ernestine stepped up to the Senator, smoothing her long, black dreads behind her ear. "I think we should get Hugh Wilkey back on the HCSIS system. And if you can muster it, an apology to that man."

Senator Shalinsky gritted his teeth. "That primitive is off his meds and in a total state of meltdown. I'm not giving him access to a fleet toilet much less a weapons system! Anyway, he would never consent to helping us now after his interrogation."

Nova's voice reported in, "The Cosmos is taking fire at maximum warp. She is unlikely to withstand more than ten minutes before hull collapse."

"How long to the nearest Colonial Defense station?" Shalinsky asked Nova. "At current speed, four hours"

Captain Obutu pressed forward toward a screen as he computed some figures,

"According to my estimates, Nova, the fleet won't last and hour at this rate."

"Fifty five minutes, but that is correct Captain."

"Senator," the Admiral stepped up from behind bridge crew he was overseeing, "I'm am sure we can't afford not to take the chance in asking Hugh Wilkey to help us. As far as I know he can't breathe vacuum any easier than we can Senator. We need to see the damn things to defend ourselves. Wilkey seems to be able to do that."

Shalinsky wiped sweat from his brow and considered for a moment. "I want his plug pulled if things go awry, and I mean pulled! He is to be under constant surveillance and armed guards with rifles set to deep stun. If he is even going to do this, he better get up here stat."

"Nova, reinstate Lieutenant Wilkey, get Lillian Hsian to get him up here. Immediately!" Captain Obutu ran the sequence to prepare the HCSIS link. "Warm up that damn tank Nova, here we go again."

*

"I wish you people would make up your minds." Hugh hurried into his swim suit and a white terry towel. "I told you I saw them."

"It's not polite to remind people they were wrong," Lillian said with some amusement, "Plus I believed you to begin with. That you think you saw something at least. But science likes proof and everyone on the command deck has seen an eye full."

"Sure you did." Hugh was rushing out the door in his bare feet on his way to the bridge. When he stopped dead in his tracks. The Marine escorting him looked puzzled.

Hugh, I'll stay here.

Hugh nodded, hearing a voice that was vaguely feminine reminded him how much he actually missed Nova. Never lonely with so many voices in your head and critters under you skin. *Okay, stay out of sight.*

The Marine gently held Hugh's arm. "Are you ok Sir?" Hugh stayed in the doorway, eyes tightly closed.

Be careful. Cleo grabbed his robe with her front paws and held on for a moment.

Lillian grabbed Hugh's chin, tried to rouse him. "Hugh are you ok? We need to get you to your tank, the fleet's getting shot to pieces."

"I'm hearing a voice in my head. Wishing me luck." Lilly looked down at Cleo, as Hugh untangled himself from her claws.

"We may need all we can get."

*

The trio rushed down the access hall to the lift.

Lillian looked at him as they sat in the lift and pulsed around the ring of Nova to the bridge. "I thought Shalinsky already closed the program, they were going to go ahead remove everything connecting Nova to HCSIS."

They ran to the double door entrance of the bridge with Hugh sneezing as he went. Two Marines guarding the door leveled their rifles.

The Marines weren't going to budge. Nova's voice broke the silence of the hall, "Sergeant Wycoff, Sergeant Mills, orders from the Captain, let him pass."

Hugh turned to Lilly. "I'm allergic to cats, but I figure you guys have made strides. We'll get me injected or whatever you guys do later. It also freaks me out that I am actually going to help you all."

Lilly shrugged. "You have us all hostage. Want anything else."

Hugh glared at her then smiled faintly. "I want Senator Shalinsky to kiss my heathen ass."

*

Hugh was lowered into the tank. The amber fluid swirled around him and he was connected to Nova's core computer. It felt good to be back, to leave his body behind and become one with the ship.

Hello Nova, how can I help?

Greetings Hugh, we have lost the Wellington, the Cosmos, and the Poseidon. We cannot target and the spheroid vessels assailing us. Not without you it seems.

Hugh looked into the track of burning debris that had been the Poseidon. He knew there were 15,411 casualties so far. He needed to access targeting to try and hit one of the aggressors.

Nova please patch me directly into weapons. I am still getting used to targeting but only have a few seconds to use at the glimpses I get.

Nova had a pregnant pause before responding. *I am clearing it now before I can patch you in. There is some . . . resistance among the command staff, but, my estimate of ship losses seems to be speeding their approval. There we go.*

Hugh felt the expansion of his tactile perception to the ten or so evenly spaced nodules that circled Nova. The laser turrets felt like . . . his fingers.

Patch me into the other ships weapon systems. Hurry Nova. The Petrov is taking a beating.

Hugh I'm not sure they are going to go for that and I am a little worried it might be . . . too much for a human mind.

I understand Nova, but, it's the only way I can do this. Time is fleeting.

A moments pause. Hugh felt the other nineteen remaining ships, weapon systems only. They felt a bit like toes, toggling into those distant sister ships. Well, if he had eighteen toes.

Ok, getting ready to fire. Hugh "felt" into the space surrounding the Petrov, the spheres flashed in and out of visibility striking at the flailing ship which began to blacken and smoke.

Hugh focused and got a glimpse, a probability pattern of where a sphere was going after striking, then fired weapons from the Achilles and the Edison. A miss. But the spheres broke off the run at the Petrov.

Hugh lost the group, they went into stealth and didn't come out. He poked around with scanners, vainly trying to detect the tickle of movement. It was almost too late when he felt a presence bearing down on Nova ninety degrees to port.

The wedge pattern the fleet had formed, Nova was at the apex and the other two lines of eight ships formed the legs of the V of the fleets formation.

Hugh halted Nova and let the ships flanking him invert the V and open fire.

Almost to his own surprise, three of the Spheres lit up on the crossfire. The red beams of the Colonial Ships cutting through the grainy hulls of the spheres, bursting them, bubbles of flashed orange explosions.

Hugh felt some kind or enemy scan register on Nova's system as the six spheres scattered. They immediately restealthed and headed off in different directions and at great speed. They eventually disappeared off Hugh's amplified systems as they scattered to warp.

"*Well Hugh, it seems you have saved the fleet*", Nova had a jovial edge to his tone.

"With all you provided through HCSIS Nova, and your array of systems, *I should probably congratulate you."*

"It would seem there is a certain human element that you provided. My systems cannot duplicate or even evaluate how you detected those ships. It is something unique to organics."

"What is it?"

"Nova has some access to medical bay and set knowledge of human physiological function and needs. Telepathic and psychic human phenomena is beyond Nova's ken."

"Oh."

Hugh indicated his intention to separate from the system. It was an odd feeling to come back to his mundane senses. A shrinking of his life down to his own skin from the network that coordinated and maintained the lives of the Fifth Fleet and the ninety thousand personnel that made it up.

As the interface cable was removed from his cranial port, he grabbed for his robe to loud applause and the cheers of military and dignitary people alike. It was jarring in another way. In his old life, he dreamed of somehow being recognized as special in some way, someone who was useful in ways beyond how society looked at him. Here he was, basked in the brief approval he thought he always sought. Finally uniquely special, a warrior who saved his people. Something redeeming from a life of the mundane. Somehow it was still discomforting, he wasn't looked at any more humanely, he was simply at the moment useful.

Hugh looked toward Lillian Hsian, who shook his wet hand. Sander Shalinsky was not to be seen. "Where is my cat? I want my cat."

Lillian pointed under a vacated control consul. Cleo pressed in the corner shivering. She had somehow managed to get up to the bridge all by herself. Upon seeing Hugh she jumped up his robe painfully and settled on his shoulder, gripping his head gingerly in both paws. She was visible.

Due to the thickness of the robe, Hugh was mostly un injured, but the claw grip on the sides of his head was oddly gentle but unrelenting, stressing great pain at any attempts at removal. The clapping of the crowd faded away as they stared at Hugh and his feline.

"Ohhh kayyy". Hugh made his was through to the crowd and toward the lift. he raised his hands and yelled as he went. "Thank you ladies and gentlemen. I am glad your faith in HCSIS has been restored. I am going back to my cabin. This is my cat Cleo, if you want any more help from me, you will leave her and I alone."

Hugh then turned on his heal and strode to lift door, the living grey hat on his head.

He actually got to the lift without company, which he preferred. "Ok Cleo, its hot, can you get off me. Or put your AC on."

Much to his surprise, Cleo hopped off.

"Umm you were never that responsive to orders. You're a cat. What did they do to you?"

I don't honestly know.

Hugh just looked at the grey and tiger striped animal as it licked its black front pads. Cleo then looked him in the face and stared at him with steady green eyes.

"No way."

Way

"When do you think you can you understand spoken words?"

Roughly, never, it is all difficult and new to me. I understand your spoken words slightly because of the stuff in my head and the thoughts precede your words, sometimes. With other people, it is . . . very hard. I certainly can't make sounds like you.

Hugh sat down. *You were always my favorite cat. I think I am pretty happy to know we are . . . able to communicate. It's just . . . wild.*

I know. And I know. Cleo didn't smile or anything, but was purring and rubbing up against his legs, then hopped on his lap in the lift and meowed like she would normally at home.

Just how smart are you?

Pretty smart. I have bits of your neural tissue and the little metal bugs that make it all work in my head. You treated me very well when I was . . . your pet. The way you would pick me up and bite my neck. Soooo nice. Its good to be able to tell you also. By the way, I'm really hungry, again.

Well what do you want.

Meat.

Well I imagine you would.

Yes. The . . . Cleo paused a moment to come up with the word. *The cereal type food was decent too. Though I'm not sure you can get it anymore.*

Umm yeah. Will call the mess when we are in our cabin. Lets go.

Hugh and Cleo padded out of the lift and down the shaft that led to his quarters.

The crewman who passed looked on in amazement.

They look like they've never seen a cat before Hugh.

They haven't Cleo. Your species is . . . extinct. You're the last I think."

They moved into the room. Hugh flopped down on the couch while Cleo hopped up beside him. *You had me fixed. We were numerous among your people. Did we all get sick, die, like humans?*

We, overpopulated the world Cleo. We didn't take good care of the world or each other. We fixed ourselves in a way by not watching the people we chose to lead us more carefully. We got lazy and didn't get involved, hold them accountable, or pick the ones who would not be corrupted as easily. We let them destroy our world and most life on the planet. Some live, if you call it living, but I don't think if there are cats of people, they are anything we want to meet.

Cleo sat quietly mulling Hugh's thoughts over. Food was brought in. It was a rather sumptuous meal and the galley crew treated them like hero's. Cleo actually had some lightly cooked fish, though not an Earth variety. Cleo chewed at it tentatively then started to eat it.

Is it ok Cleo?

Yes. Though I could eat a shoe right now. Tell them not to . . . not to cook it next time. You know I wouldn't even know what this was if I didn't have access to your thoughts flowing through me. I was very happy with you and Michael, but, I never really knew anything outside the apartment. I had a very simple life. I am not sure if I am happier or sadder now that I can . . . see how existence works around me, you, everyone."

I'm not sure we humans, so called sentients, did so well understanding existence. But here we are. I think Mike and me envied you cats and your simple life. I am so very glad you are here with me Cleo since everything we knew is gone. I also apologize for dragging you along so recklessly.

I guess I wouldn't know any different if you hadn't and would be dead if you didn't.

Same for me, hopefully we can make it here. The thing about the dead is they make so few mistakes . . .

Chapter 6

Dirty Deeds

Ernestine Joyce sat with Lillian Hsian in her appointed office. Gingerly, Ernestine sheathed one of the scientists numerous ceremonial blades, displayed prodigiously on bulkheads from deck to ceiling. Many era's and countries of the ancient Orient of Earth left no space for other decor. She placed the short blade back on it's stand on Lillian's desk, luxuriating in the exquisite workmanship of mother of pearl on the plied, dark leather sheath of some extinct Earth beast. The lapis lazuli eyes on the serpents head had been cut to be as menacing as the wakashi's honed edge itself.

"Interesting you keep these artifacts, especially within reach of your guests."

"Well Speaker Joyce" Lilly indicated the wall behind her desk chair hung mostly with katanas of varying craftsmanship, "It wouldn't be honorable to leave such works of art in a case hidden away from public view. The craftsman meant for them to be appreciated, touched, even used on occasion."

Ernestine raised an eyebrow and pulled her elegant, dark fingers away from Lilly's desk. "It seems Hugh has found a mighty champion for HCSIS, in you Dr. Hsian. You have risked everything shielding him from the Senator."

Lilly grinned, nodding, "the Colonial Government usually rewards success. At this point, Hugh is the only way of fighting against a hostile sentient race, probable originator's of the Pliilulua plague. He doesn't need too much help anymore from anyone as his growing powers demonstrate. But ever since I put a khirda against Shalinsky's neck and he cut off Hugh's hand, I have not become less cautious."

Ernestine leaned back pushing a dragonfly pin absently into her wrapped hair. "Well, then it is pressing if not surprising that I tell you that Hugh is in greater danger, still. I know this even though we minority parties are kept in the dark by the Conservatives. We also do not have enough people keeping an eye out. I have reason to believe Shalinsky was sent termination orders, tight beamed back from his superiors on Earth. Not just for the project, they mean to kill Hugh Wilkey before we arrive home."

Lilly remained composed yet inwardly alarmed that her suspicions were confirmed. Her feelings for Hugh were complex, as he was, yet she wondered if her fear for him was more than just professional. Human concern for the most incredible discovery of their time? Or something more personal for the man himself? She shrugged. Her duty serving the Ruling Council trumped all and fortified her resolve. Hugh, the salvation for humanity and a palpable threat to the established order must reach Earth. "I doubt the Conservatives are so short sighted that they would carry out something so obviously detrimental to the preservation of humanity considering recent occurrences, say, saving the entire 5th Fleet from destruction. Besides, I don't belong to any minority, I am of the Order, we serve the Imperium."

Ernestine nodded, "Yes that would be true and might be enough, if the Imperial Senate knew of what is at stake. There is a week left before we arrive home to Earth. The Senator could subtlety orchestrate some accident, if he is truly committed to it, he is capable of it, as you know. I presume he believes that thorough dissection and replication of Hugh's essential parts would be a more tasteful solution. Makes Hugh less of an embarrassment or . . . symbol. As a resource he can simply be used. I am not making excuses, Shalinsky may have other reasons, I just think he will move and soon . . ."

Lilly knew Ernestine was familiar with her military affiliations. She had decided earlier that this eclectic Speaker for the Greens had the same immediate loyalties and priorities as her, for the moment. "In the spirit of cooperation, I will confirm your suspicions. I am ranking official of covert ops as well as a scientist, and due to some rather high profile cases, I am somewhat less covert than is desirable. Be assured I have taken precautions to prevent anything accidental or otherwise from happening to Mr. Wilkey, in the absence of any other advocate. There are systems and people I have in place to safeguard HCSIS, and Hugh is HCSIS."

"Senator Shalinsky knows at least as much as I do, probably more, about you and your capabilities and counter measures. It is worrisome what might befall this special man while we are in warp with no way to communicate his amazing victory over the alien attack to the right people, Commander. He is the core of HCSIS. Shalinsky might be even more concerned that the Church will lose face with the public that we are not alone among God's creatures. The Crafter's Guild will not love the idea of essentially a Genghonni being the center of our defense. The senator may well be pushed by the Church and Crafters to not only take personal credit, but to harvest Hugh and expect to minimize all fallout of aliens and Genghonni saviors"

"That a very grim list of reasons for harming Hugh, but I don't contest it. Incidentally I was pulled from retirement in the Order for this mission, I really never had much cover to truly compromise, except regrettably from Hugh. Hopefully, the formidable Senator will not trifle with me lightly. I have a feeling Hugh can defend himself a bit too, though he is astoundingly naïve despite his augmentations. I will make sure no subtle assassination attempts go through. Even now while I am here with you my team keeping a round the clock eye on him, as I am sure Shalinsky is as well. That's when I'm not seeing to it personally."

"I would like to say I feel better Lilly, but we only get one chance at this." Ernestine sat quietly for a moment thinking. "That largely concludes my business with you Lilly. I won't keep you from such vital duties. A moments lapse could cost us, all humanity, dearly. I don't have a lot of resources on board the Nova, obviously, but if there is anything I can do to help."

Lilly nodded. "Well perhaps you could visit Hugh. You are a well respected woman in the Senate's service, vested in your support of this project, and thus Hugh himself. Further, you seem to have declined the urge to . . . mainstream your appearance. The various races of old Earth were not given to diluting their ethnicity or covering up their differences back in his time. Meeting with you might be comforting to him."

Ernestine reflected for a moment. "It is true, though few people know this, that my parents after years of genetic dampening from their parents were surprised that I was born with so much of our ancestors appearance. I actually had to undo some of the genetic changes they had done to me in trying to make my acceptance as a child in a rather pale world more live able. I was the darkest skinned child growing up as it is. Though I was not treated poorly, it was obvious I wasn't a part, despite politeness, kids can feel it keenly. Hugh represents not just the past, but our genetic heritage. What's the point in evolving if we hollow out and remove that which makes us, us? So I am glad we are akin in our differentness. That our value is increased by it not diminished makes me love him all the more."

"Obviously I did not avail myself of too much . . . modification, at least on the surface. Certain types of Asians were more accepted in the heterogenous societies existing at the time of before the Blackening. Still, many of us chose to be dampened as you say." Hugh is a different sort of minority though, she thought to herself. Even in his time, but said nothing. "Now we find out that his unique brain structure is more suitable to HCSIS melding, possibly because of the recessive genes he carries. Unless he can be replicated, with cloning being forbidden, he is truly alone and we only have one such weapon against this Pliilulua species."

"I hear you Lilly. Since cloning him is forbidden what can Shalinsky hope to do if Hugh is killed? Sander took his dreadful sample, but what can he do with it?"

"You've seen the data from his file. It's not only recessive, some of the critical gene paths are singular in Hugh. On top of surgical procedures done by God knows who, and primitive bionanytes that evolved over the course of fourteen hundred years in near absolute zero cryogenic state, it is beyond our skill to recreate. Those bionanytes alone are so evolved they avoid any sampling, put up scan blocks to every test we can think of . . . We cannot clone someone who is a combination of so many different variables. Not with much accuracy."

Ernestine leaned forward. "Is this room secure Lilly?"

Lillian nodded and depressed a button under her armrest. "You can be assured, nothing will eavesdrop on anything we say."

"Do you think any of the Ombarian Colonists made it?"

Lillian thought a moment. "It is said that a few may have survived the Blackening. But if they even made it, nothing has been heard of them ever since."

"Indeed. But they were not purists. They took humanity as it was in all their colors, mutations, and so called flaws. If they made it someplace, they would have the pure stock we have weeded out so thoroughly. In ignorance and fear from those that did not take to the emergency shelters of the sea before the Blackening, they may be our salvation for making more human symbiot's for command ships." Ernestine looked at her hands. "It would be nice to see other Black faces, also, no offense Lilly. To see the tribes of humanity as they should be. If only we could find them."

"It's at best bad taste to discuss the Ombarians in our current Colonial Government. To the Church it is pure heresy. The discussion that could get us incarcerated if we were lucky. Those who write the past . . ."

"I know Lilly. But so was the suggestion of any sentient life in the Universe outside of human. It was impossible to imagine and now its here. We've seen it. We better hope the Ombarians exist some place. We need them now. Especially if we cannot protect Hugh."

"It was said that three rockets left our planet during the Blackening. One carried the elites, the wealthy, and they burned up trying to leave. The second rocket, the guards killed the elites except for a pilot or two, and made it as far as the ninth planet of Sol. Then exploded. The Ombari vessel, is said to have gone further, but no evidence of a crash was every found. Lilly stood up and stepped in front of her desk. She looked down at Ernestine with a touch of sadness to her eyes. "I know. During the Blackening the privileged and wealthy took to the sea cities, refuges they built from the disproportionate largess they accumulated during their end days. Like it or not, that is all we have left now. That, the Genghonni, and Hugh."

*

Ernestine walked briskly down the hall toward Hugh's cabin. She contained her excitement and sense of wonder, but just barely. This would fly in the face of all convention in the Senate, a man who not only represented a pure gene template, but one who discovered and repulsed the Pliilulua as well. The religious right would choke on its own tongue explaining away he existence of non human sentient life. The crafting guild would go apoplectic at someone who manifested telekinetic and telepathic powers. Change was in the air and Ernestine loved it.

Ernestine turned the corner when she felt a presence, a second before a hand reached out of thin air and grabbed her by her hair. Another hand covered her mouth. "Representative Joyce, aren't we in a hurry? Now no yelling or I will put a bend in your neck you'll not soon forget."

Ernestine grabbed the arm with both hands but it left her mouth and fell to her neck and started to squeeze. "Don't try anything. We are just going to have a little chat is all," an oily voice whispered in her ear.

She nodded, and the intense grip on her neck lessoned enough to stop her head from spinning and allow the flow of air again. "Your assault on an Imperial Speaker will not come without price, dolt."

"You are a minority party and accidents do happen. We know you are going to visit this creature, Wilkey, and I am sure you are quite excited at comparing notes on the novelty of unrefined, primitive skins and cells. But you better remember he belongs to someone else. Every last vulgar skin flake, Speaker, and if he should get some idea that there are . . . options . . . I assure you our next meeting will not be so amicable."

The man pushed her to the ground roughly and she fell face down on the deck. She pulled her khirda from it's sheath prepared to strike, but a quiet buzzing sound made her pause. As she turned toward her attacker, now a blur or haze, the roughly man sized distortion turned the corner of the hall and disappeared completely.

Swallowing her anger, she pushed herself up and touched her bruised throat. Things were well in play and the danger was great, but so were the opportunities. Ernestine remained un-deterred, brushed off her tunic and walked toward the dozen guards still lingering outside Hugh's cabin.

"I am expected, move aside."

The Marines and Imperials regarded her cooly, but did not try and stop her. A marine Captain saluted her. "Speaker Joyce, so you are." She knocked on the door and it whispered open.

Hugh sat with his legs crossed with Cleo licking herself nonchalantly at his side, not looking up. "Ernestine Joyce, I can't tell you how glad I am to see you Speaker." Hugh looked Ernestine up and down, taking in her tall, austere length, her black twisted hair and dark chocolate skin. "You are unmodified and a breath of fresh air."

Ernestine bowed at bit at the waist and beamed a smile toward Hugh. "Well met then Mr. Wilkey. I do not get such reactions too often. May I sit." Hugh motioned to the chair across from him and offered beverage and food. Ernestine politely declined.

"On behalf of the Green Party and all delegates on board Nova, we are in your debt good sir." Ernestine pointed her finger up indicating Hugh increase the sound of the classical music playing in his quarters. Hugh nodded and told Nova to do it.

"Well, it seems like most people who visit me are music lovers. Shall we sit a little closer?"

Ernestine nodded.

They both leaned forward and lowered their voices. Ernestine made a show of grabbing his hand and leaning in. Smiling though her brown, almond eyes held him gravely. "You are in terrible danger Mr. Wilkey."

"Just when things are getting better and I thought I was so redeemed. Quel suprise. I am not going to easily give up any more bits of me, madame."

"Please understand, it is because you were so successful that the majority party does not intend for you to make it to the Sol system. They mean to have you assassinated. Shalinsky and his people."

Hugh nodded, affecting a calm body language while directing Nova to increase the music even more. "Lilly warned me and told me you would come. She gave me this ring." Hugh held up a small silver band on his right index finger. "The ring constricts if any food is of questionable or possibly lethal content."

"They will make it look like an accident. But there are so many ways it can be done. I have brought you a bracelet so that my people can find you if you were to become . . . separated. When you get to Oceania, the Green Party will only be able to get close to you in very subtle ways."

"A tracking device eh? You know I have no real reason to trust you. Just because your black doesn't cancel out that you are head of the party my brainwashed persona belonged too?" Hugh picked up the bracelet looked at the writing carved into the pyranite. "What does it say."

"It's latin, a quote from one of your ancients, Goethe." Ernestine held up the band and read it to him, "Boldness has genius, power, and magic in it." She placed it on the wrist of his new hand. "Lilly trusts us, we value you alive and well. You represent a part of humanity that we shunned at our own peril. We want you to survive and change things for humanity. To show the Prelate and Senate the value of the Genghonni and unmodified."

Hugh looked at the bracelet wistfully. "Well it does look nice. I suppose it's better to receive things than to have them taken away. But I also need protection. My powers are not controllable and largely unknown. A few well placed shots at a vital area, like my head, and the show is over. Can you give me guards."

Ernestine shook her head solemnly. "Our strength is subtlety and hidden hands. You realize I was threatened just coming to see you. Undoubtedly one of Shalinsky's pets. We cannot muscle our way through the Imperials and Colonial Marines. They are loyal to the Senator and in place in numbers. But they will not deliver the blow. It will be something that leaves no strings. Something pointing away from him. But I will share the few guards I have. The Right would shed not tears if I didn't make it home either."

"Just when I was starting to relax." Hugh wondered how different "Home" would be, would he recognize anything of his civilization, his people? It will most likely like visiting another planet.

Cleo looked up to Hugh. *Anything I should concern myself with?"*

Nothing unusual Cleo, just untimely death from our great new friends. Not this woman, perhaps, but others. We are going home soon, Earth anyway, and I am pretty sure it is unlike anything we knew. But I will explain everything once she is done."

Ernestine looked at Cleo. "You will be safe enough here in your quarters. But still be on your guard. Your pet, this, cat is a wonder. I read a bit about the species, this is an Egyptian Mau."

"El correcto Speaker, she is. She was smart even before her modification. But she is as smart as any human now, perhaps smarter than most."

"It is a wonder, new aliens, plagues, and sentient animals. Strange strange times. Is it true you share thoughts?"

"Either that or I have a rather great imagination or multiple personality disorder." Hugh picked Cleo up and put her on the table. "Want to pet her?"

Ernestine patted Cleo gently. "She is so soft. It is a she yes?"

Before Hugh could answer Cleo disappeared in front of Ernestine's eyes. "She can turn invisible seamlessly? There's no haze of blurring as with our stealth suits. No sound."

Hugh threw up his hands. "Sorry about that, she gets shy. But yeah, it's true, Lilly told me your special ops could do it, but it was a power consuming, bulky, noisy suit. Cleo does it somehow by shifting her magnetic field signature.

I can mostly see her but not always and not now. I wish I could do it."

"You can't?"

"I am too big. Or I simply do not know how. Or have different . . . specialties."

Hugh grinned sheepishly. "I've only been me for a short while. I am pretty happy not to be throwing up, under attack, or in Shalinsky's presence! That's a lot."

Ernestine grabbed his hand once more and laughed, but it did not reach her eyes. "Promise me you will wear the bracelet? I have to go, but it will be a vital connection to our agents when you arrive in Oceania. You may need all the friends you can get."

Hugh shrugged, "Okay. I will. What is Oceania anyway?"

"It's home, it is Earth, the underwater cities of Earth anyway. It is also our Capital city, in the middle of the deepest part of the Atlantic Ocean. It is where you are going to go and change everyones lives for the better."

"Sounds wondrous. How about I just get there alive Speaker Ernestine, call me provincial."

Ernestine stood up and bowed her head to Hugh. "While I live and breathe I will do everything I can to make it so."

"Well thank you for coming by. I will do everything to help you out with that. But it seems like you advanced humans don't much like change. Hence my life being somewhat accidentally curtailed as said proof. I am the harbinger of change just by existing in your perfect world."

Ernestine turned on her heal but before she passed through the cabin door she tilted her head back to Hugh and winked. "You are the past and the future. It's hard not to react energetically to something that shouldn't be but it so desperately needed."

*

Hugh and the Fifth Fleet were two days away from Sol System. No other ships of colonial or alien interfered with their journey and most of their damaged vessels were out of danger of dropping out of formation or falling behind. Lilly had secured a practice area for Hugh on the 7th level of Nova's cargo deck. Hugh struggled, diligently, exploring the magnetic forces he tenuously controlled. Stretching and understanding his powers with no idea of limits or dangers, Lilly had selected a practice area well from main ship systems. Moving a two kilo, synthetic cube around the cavernous storage area was a great step forward in learning capacity while limiting risks.

Some bins were as tall as twenty meters and he had to moved the cube around corners smoothly. As soon as he lost visual contact the block would fall to the ground, despite holding the image in his mind. Sweat beaded his forehead as Cleo lashed her small tail around impatiently. He was glad the entourage of of ten guards had stayed behind the blast door leading to the lift as they would undoubtedly be a distraction. Privacy of any sort was so valuable even if it was just symbolic. Lilly was undoubtedly recording every move he made as well as others.

So you have been moving blocks around for days, learn anything?

Cleo faded, leaving visual notice easily in the shadowed area. She sniffed at the practice block, her pink tongue visible in her black lipped mouth, slightly open in that cat expression they get when they find a new scent. *Well?*

Oh sorry Cleo. It's hard to say, I think I am learning control. But the blocks fall when out of visual range. At least I can move things without some emotive visualization. It's more like using "ki" when I was taking aikido centuries ago. I visualize energy building, moving, and it goes where I visualize it, for the most part.

I see. Well, I wish I could do what you can do. But being able to disappear has saved my skin, literally. Throw in my ability to share our mind link and I'm lucky as can be. I continue to think a little less like a feline and more like one of you, I fear. It's a world of new experiences. Only problem is, if anything happens to you it's trouble for me, no one else can understand me. I am become just a small mammal with interesting DNA.

Hugh concentrated and lifted Cleo into the air and brought him to her. *Hey! No fair!* Cleo was running in place and flinging herself about. He gently set her down in front of him. *Well I guess we better make sure I keep an eye on you and you me. Make sure I don't die!*

Cleo was about to give Hugh a scratch, when a tapping sound coming from a crate twenty feet away alerted her to a presence. *Hugh I just saw a distortion over there. Look out!* Cleo turned and faded when the sound of a restraining field around the crate powered down and a deep growl resonated through the cargo bay.

"Shit. Guards!" Hugh yelled and rolled forward toward where Cleo had been a moment before. "Something is in here and breaking loose."

The crate exploded apart as the first two guards came into the bay. A splinter of crate flew through the eye of an unlucky guard and the rest piled in scanning the semi lit space with hand lights. Their beams eventually focused on a massive form uncurling it's scaled body from a stasis bin.

A serpentine hiss accompanied the thud of a very heavy foot as it left the crate. The bipedal, blue-green creature shook its fang filled head and gave a follow up roar to which the guards started shooting in response. Beam weapons hissed and burned the fifteen foot creature, and ruby blood spattered the deck. It whipped a club like tail at the offending men and women, sending a flurry of spines that struck most of them with painful, five inch barbs. The six who remained standing started backing up under a covering fire. One had soiled himself.

Nova's voice briefly flared above the fray, "Containment squad needed on deck seven, specimen breach, class Alpha. This is not a drill. Alert. Containment squad . . ."

The creature stepped forward and in it's wounded fury and started stomping the guards who had fallen beneath its tail barbs. The sickening splatter of heads and torsos added to the chorus of screams and the pop of beam weapons. Hugh stepped out from behind some crates just as the creature started to wind up for another volley. He telekinetically hurled his practice cube as hard as he could at the back of the creatures head. It struck with some force and crumbled. "Over here Godzilla! You're too tall! Over here! Come and get me."

To Hugh's surprise, the creature actually turned around. It flicked it's tail at the diminished guards positioned behind the blast door, and then there was only one. It sized up Hugh, frenzied waving arms and shouts did not improve it's mood as it started charging Hugh. A agile beast for a walking whale. Hugh ran behind one of the larger crates as the beast roared and ran around the corner after him. As Hugh turned the ext corner a hail of barbs smashed into the crates, one of them bit into his leg like a bullet. Hugh screamed and went down.

The creature slowed, claws extending to the deck as it's victim scrabbled away. The beast was bleeding and leaving a trail of blood much like Hugh. The guards seemed to be using the time to stabilize their friends or those that still lived. "Hugh Wilkey, do not provoke it. A heavy weapons unit is almost at your site."

"Too late Nova, Godzilla is going to smoosh me." The creature was raising it's leg when a ball of fur and fury hit its back. "Well Nova, it looks like another one of your monsters is lose." The second creature roared like a tiger as it raked its back with four claws and sunk six inch fangs into the neck of the saurian. It must have been three hundred pounds with grey and black stripes, mad yellow eyes, and hooked paws. It ended with a sick snap as part of the spine was ripped out and the sound like a tree falling snapping. Nova's deck shook when the reptile crashed to the floor, unmoving.

"Hugh Wilkey are you alright?" Nova almost sounded concerned but Hugh was too busy watching the drooling, fanged maw coming towards him. A trail of pink saliva trailed as the beast growled low in it throat. The thing was a sabre-tooth, yet the colors were all wrong it seemed.

Hugh was going to try and hurl it telekinetically when the growl seemed to turn into a purr. The creature stepped forward, sniffed him and licked him with an enormous tongue. *Are you okay . . . Cleo?*

Cleo shrank down to her normal size and crouched exhausted by Hugh's leg. As she fell into a deep sleep she sent "I seem to have found a new trick."

*

The fleet passed Saturn and moved to position for orbit around the seat of the Colonial Empire, Earth. The guards had doubled outside the door since Hugh and Cleo's attack. Various house guards from different senate families volunteered some of their own personnel for Hugh. It was help to prevent any more "accidents" and to watch each other in equal measure Lilly assured him.

Lilly, Ernestine, Cleo and Hugh sat in his small cabin watching the Milky Way unfold as the ships queued for decon around the massive space station that circled the entire Earth. Hugh glanced a bit anxiously at the ladies as he fingered the sharp edge of the barb that was pulled from his leg. The wound had long since healed, no poison or other ill effects. Hugh kept the projectile as a reminder to duck a little faster next time. In this brave new universe there was no safe place. "So what should I expect ladies now that we have arrived?"

Lilly lifted the antique china to her lip, kelp tea steaming, "You will be seen by the Prelate, Sanjay Dubey, the leader of our Senate, and leader of the Imperium. You will be honored and asked to speak to the assembly of what you have done. I think you will help us prepare new HCSIS systems for the fleet."

"Not as spare parts?"

"No." Ernestine set her cup down. "The Greens may be small but we have friends in other guilds. The Builder, Medical, and Science Guilds are all supportive as well as a handful of smaller factions. Together we have a large voice."

"A voice that says?"

"You and Cleo will not be harmed, that is our will." Ernestine wore a brilliant green gown with conch pearls and placed a confident hand on her khirda as she spoke. Lilly wore a black body suit, and a sash that was white. It flashed black momentarily at Ernestine's assurance.

"What's going on with your belt there Doc? All I have is this old thing." Hugh had removed his collar devices and sleeve insignias, keeping his well pressed, white Naval uniform for his visit home. "Cause this thing is going to show off a lot of blood if I get jumped."

Ernestine and Lilly looked at each other for support as Hugh kept sending Cleo a running translation of conversation. It turned out it wasn't too hard to do, now that he was in the habit. He started doing it automatically whenever people were talking to him since spoken words were still gibberish to her as her normal meowing was to people, cute as she was.

Lilly cleared her throat. "The sash is chromatiforic cloth, a less complex weave than our military fade suits. It is the cloth all human citizens wear. Only our leaders and military may wear conventional fabrics."

"Also ones who have mastered a discipline or at least been born lucky enough to be in the aristocracy can obtain them. Certain cloth, collar devices, and items like khirda's, are symbols of basic castes. Common citizens and the aristocracy, basically," Ernestine said.

"I see, so just by wearing my white uniform I am being fancy. Crazy." Hugh felt the fringe of his shirt. "Feels like cotton to me. Why are you wearing that scrap of common folk cloth then Lilly? Mixed messages? If you ask me the chroma cloth is a lot more interesting."

"Cotton?" Lilly looked at her wrist console and seemed to be checking the word. She frowned. "All our cloth comes from ocean plants. I wear my sash to say in a not so subtle way I may be of rank, but I am of the people."

"I wear Green. You can't get more of the people than that as a Green Party rep. Might as well paint a huge target on my back." Ernestine giggled, "and yet it does accentuate my beautiful if un popular skin."

"Ahh." Hugh shook his head despairingly. "There is so much I don't know of the culture I am going to get tossed into. Even clothes are completely different! How did this come to be?"

Lilly nodded. "Well, you have a lot of catching up to do. Clothing is as good place as any to start. Chromaticloth, like our basic fabric we have on now, is grown in labs. About five hundred years ago a Prelate was unhappy at the dispassionate reaction of some city to his oration. In a fit of pique he ordered all citizens to wear it. It gave him some indication of how they were taking in his wisdom and demonstrated his power all at once. It developed from there and became the cloth of the Empire."

"Citizens are mandated to wear it and will be wrapped in it. It is comfortable, climate sensitive, and most importantly emotive reactive. You will see almost always white flowing robes, a calm and serene color, amongst the citizens. If it flashes red, it is anger, pink is love in varying shades, blue is frustration, yellow is for fear, green is learning and change," Ernestine looked at him sternly, "and deep anger or rage is black."

"Well I guess I feel honored to wear just plain fabric. I am not surprised your politicians don't have to wear it." Hugh patted Cleo when she startled at Nova shaking lightly. He picked her up he walked to the window. The Fifth Fleet trailed away from Nova on both sides in a line. Docking cables shot out from the space stations gargantuan docking bays, gently clasping onto magnetic anchor points on the saucer shaped ships and drawing them inexorably in.

"Attention all debarking personnel, Oceania is optimally positioned from orbit. Please make your way to transit cubes in ring section B-90."

Lilly and Ernestine stood up.

"I feel like I should pack." Hugh felt the hilt of his dagger on his belt. "But I have my grooming tool right here. It's all a strapping young mutie could want. That and my toothbrush." Hugh patted his pocket.

"All your needs will be taken care of in Oceania." Ernestine walked towards him and draped an arm through his left and Lilly went to his right. "The Imperial Capital is beautiful beyond compare."

Hugh grinned thinking of several of his needs that would never be met here in the future. "Oh rapture oh joy, let's do it."

*

They were joined by only four guards in the livery of the Green, Trade, and Two in Sander's Conservative party. Gold eagles on their wrists, the Green's conch pearls, and the Trade had rubies tastefully bordered on the sleeves. The party had to duck through the airlock and Hugh imagined he felt the shuttle cube quiver as he looked past the pilot at the blue and white of Earth.

Everyone sat side by side in the two rows of gel seats. Hugh nudged Lilly as they took their seats in the cube, "I'm glad we don't have to sit with the Shalinsky entourage. This transport is tiny. I was curious where the Marines and Imperials went?"

Lilly looked at the two guards from Sander's contingent that seated themselves across from them. "We will likely have them on either side of us in escort fighters, the Imperials at any rate. The Marines are Navy, they stay on Nova. Shalinsky will be right behind us, be assured of that."

"You afraid we will be attacked by Aliens getting to Oceania? Why all this security? Don't you trust me yet?," Hugh feigned looking hurt.

Lilly rolled her eyes. "The nuclear attack from the Blackening was only one facet of your times war, biological and chemical weapons were even more destructive if you can believe it. The security is for the ocean creatures we may meet. Many changed as a result of the poisoning of the planet."

The pilot turned about. "Mr. Wilkey, can you place your pet on the seat, we are going to activate the seat grips."

Hugh had been appraised of the enhanced vanderwal effect that took the place of seat belts on shuttles. "Thanks but Cleo passes. She has great grips . . . on my shoulders." *Show em Cleo.*

Cleo reached out with one paw, turned it up, and flexed. Her paw seemed to grow out of proportion with her body and her teeth lengthened. Her small mouth stretched to form a well fanged human like smile. The pilot turned around and powered up the seats.

Show off.

Cleo pushed her face into Hugh's neck. *I know.*

Ernestine cleared her throat. "It's true about the creatures, giant squids used to live only a year and a half in your time. Now they live ten times that. The oceans, our gardens, support unprecedented biomass now. Creatures have grown much larger since the Blackening. Even on land, especially on land, the mutations have been profound."

The transport cube broke free and dropped towards a large blue body of water. Hugh could see it was the Atlantic. He felt his stomach drop as the cube accelerated. He was stuck solidly onto his seat. He noticed the others had kept their arms free when the pilot signaled. Hugh found they could move their arms but his arms were stuck fast.

"Damn."

Lilly patted his leg. "It will be over soon. Besides you learned something new."

Hugh sighed. "Thanks for the warning."

"Talk less, observe more." Lilly smirked only a bit.

"I am defenseless." *Cleo I am defenseless!*

Really? Cleo dug her claws in assuringly.

Lilly crossed her arms. "Ernestine is correct. Our ancestors left us all many parting gifts. The archetukis, your giant squid, kept on growing. By the time they are fifty, they are the top predator of the deep. Five hundred feet long and ten tons."

"A Kraken. I would like to see one."

"You will. Though you may not like it."

The cube entered the stratosphere. The descent was smoother than Hugh could have imagined but he still felt queasy seeing nothing but endless drop beneath them. At least it was blue and not the black of the void. There were other cubes going back and forth to the space station ring. All accompanied by at least one sleek fighter. Hugh marveled at the Earth's giant station moving off around the globe like one of Saturn's rings. "How long have you had this space station? It must have taken forever to build."

Ernestine laughed. "That old thing, it's been around for eight hundred years. It took a hundred years to build."

"I can't imagine that much raw material being on Earth. Is it made of pyranite?"

Lilly's head jogged a bit as the cube hit a cross wind. "It was made of debris we reforged from all the junk that was in space. All the pyranite on Earth was being made for ships and city's. We found one more reservoir for raw materials that made it all possible."

Hugh blinked. "You don't mean the moon do you?"

Lilly and Ernestine laughed together as well as some of the guards. "You got it in one. We used the moon." Ernestine patted his other leg. "It was mostly metal and no one else was using it."

At that Hugh's eyes went large. "Well, if my time demolished the planet for all of you I suppose you had rights to the moon. I will miss it."

The cube continued hurtling towards the deep blue of the Atlantic, they were many kilometers north-west of Bermuda. At least Hugh thought it was Bermuda. The pilot turned to them, "prepare for entry. Once we hit water I'll release the seats."

"Don't hit too hard." Hugh closed his eyes tightly and thought he would be vomit but the magnetic field engine hummed only a bit louder and the entry was feather soft. Hugh could move his arms again.

The pilot opened a strip of windows that was a foot in diameter and bisected the cube at head level. He could see the support fighters at either side and in back three other transport cubes. There were fish all around varying size but mostly large. Teeming with life in fact, even though Hugh remembered the oceans were mostly deserts this far out according to every ocean special he ever saw.

As they descended it darkened. There was still good visibility and one of the fighters shot a cannon at a freighter sized creature that came too close to their convoy. "What was that?"

"It was probably a shark of some type wanting to make a snack of us." Lilly looked around toward the diminishing black spot. "But that's not the one you should be worried about."

Hugh looked at the black beast, dimly fading into the dark until what appeared like a giant flower unfurled itself in contrast to the black drop of the shark in front it. The white flower wiggled and expanded, it's eight petals like path leading off into the infinite deep. The black spot of the giant shark exploded in a cloud of red, briefly, as the flower closed around it. The creature grew larger as it approached them.

"Kraken."

Lilly nodded at Hugh. "My order is aptly named. But watch the fighters."

Hugh walked across the cube and the guards moved out of their way. The fighters released a chemical in their wake and started firing long range. Striking at the leviathan's black form, it seemed completely unharmed or only irritated. It started swimming toward the caravan impossibly fast. It halted and the fighter's weapons intensified their fire. It started to swim off into the deep and winked out of sight as the blackness of their current depth blocked out all light.

Hugh let out a deep drawn breath. "What did they release into the water?"

Ernestine touched Hugh's shoulder. "The only thing that puts off a kraken is blood of a dead kraken."

As they slid through the dark depths, everyone took their seats. It was incredibly cold outside and Hugh reflected he had truly exchanged one vacuum for another. In the distance, a great light started brightened the endless dark. The size of the dome was difficult to estimate. Bands of travel tubes spidered out from the hub of Oceania, trains of speeding shapes lanced back and for through them like the arteries and veins of a colossal star fish. Hugh could not help but be reminded of Los Angeles at night from a plane ride he took in another life, so vast and sprawling.

Did starfish have veins? Well if they did it would look like this he decided.

"Atlantis." Hugh whispered. He was amazed.

"No, Atlantis is further North. This is Oceania, greatest of all Earth's cities, jewel of the Atlantic." Lilly pointed to a solid structure above the dome. "That's where we will be docking. Welcome to the Capital." Hugh noticed other, larger ships, hundreds connected to the hub. The biggest laser cannons he had ever seen studded the dome like spines on the back of a gigantic sea urchin. The city glowed, a dull orange light and even at this depth, five miles down, fish teemed in clouds of life all about it.

"It seems like you have done pretty well since I have been gone."

Ernestine smiled darkly. "Just remember, Hugh, that down here everything gets eaten by something. The ocean is a cruel mother and only the strong survive."

*

Oceania spread out a hundred miles in all directions from the central dome they docked at. The dull orange light of day would be replaced in ten hours with the cool blue of artificial night. Hugh was astounded that he was two miles up on the sky lift, over looking a city of ten million. There were trees, birds, and even insects over a landscape of thin glass towers, golden domes, and pyramids of crystal as far as the eye could see. All at the bottom of the ocean.

It's breathtaking Cleo. How could a race that built all this be bad?

Cleo looked around excitedly. Birds!

"I am surprised you have birds and insects since . . . since The Blackening."

Lilly shifted uncomfortably. The lift was large but it was crowded with Imperials and Shalinsky's entourage. "They are mostly not birds or bugs, their mechanoid. Messengers for the citizens and little helpers for the plants. The plants and trees are real enough." Lilly gripped her khirda a little menacingly and the Imperials, resplendent all in black and red, gave them more space.

"Colors black for the Prelate and Red for the Roman Church of Christ. A grim combination if you ask me." Lilly let her hand fall from her hilt. "Always be on your guard Hugh, we may be separated for a while, and Oceania can be as deadly as it is wondrous."

"You and Ernestine have been working both ears. I have trust issues in spades." As they descended, Hugh could see a crowd of what must have been hundreds of thousands of people. A sea of shifting white toga's on perfect ivory bodies crowned with golden hair. He had never seen so many people, much less perfect looking white people. It made him rather nervous. There was a splash of color walking through the crowd, ten blue dots marching forward. Where they brushed the crowd turned yellow in varying shades and moved away. "What's that."

Lilly and Ernestine exchanged worried glances. "The ten you see in blue are the Ushok-ku. They are the Prelate's personal elite guards and emissaries. There are only a hundred in the entire Colonial Empire. As you can see they frighten the citizens badly."

"Why?" Hugh could see them more clearly as they were near reaching the bottom of the sky lift. They held halberds twelve feet long, their tips glowing an eerie, shifting violet to green. The hoods they wore did not reveal their features despite their large size. "They don't even have beam weapons."

"They are most deadly, I assure you Hugh. Those halberds are tipped with a blade that disintegrates even pyranite at a touch. The shafts nullify any beam shot at them, adding to the destructive power of the tips. They are well nigh invincible. You will be safe so long as you keep with them. As long as you are safe from them."

Hugh felt the lift come a stop. Ernestine pressed into his side, whispered in his ear "The Ushok-ku do not sleep, do not eat or talk. Follow them to the Prelate and the Senate. We will be with you shortly. A tap of their staff twice means no, once means yes. I suggest you don't speak with them, but if you have to, form your question accordingly."

Hugh nodded. The lift opened up and ten seven foot Ushok-ku stood in a rough perimeter around the lift gate. The citizens cheered a good twenty feet from them. They cheered "Sander! Sander! Sander!" Hugh could not believe it. He looked into the face of the Ushok-ku and was taken aback. The face wasn't perfect or blond, it didn't even have eyes or much of a mouth. "You do realize these people should be shouting 'Hugh, Hugh,' or 'Lilly, Lilly', not Sander."

The Ushok-ku lifted his halberd up and down once. Then turned. Four of them boxed in Hugh and the other six walked with the rest of Nova's civilian passengers between them. *I don't like this Hugh, I don't like this at all.* Cleo looked around and hissed at the crowd. Sander Shalinsky waved at the people and smiled broadly.

It's okay Cleo, if these blind blue giants know what side of their bread is buttered on, chances are the Prelate knows the score too.

They approached what looked like a gilded, golden dinner plate with seats sunk at the bottom in a circular pattern some twenty meters in diameter and two meters deep. A single pilot sat in a seat in the center. The Ushok-ku took seats around the perimeter and the various Guilds sat where they would. Ernestine, Lilly, and Hugh quickly sat near each other and as far away from prying ears as possible.

"Lilly, HCSIS is your project, why would anyone actually believe Sander had anything to do with it." Hugh fumed.

Lilly's slice of chromatacloth flashed red for a moment but quickly cooled to white. She shrugged, "Most of the credits came from his party, to fund HCSIS. The fact that we didn't permit him to shut us down, or kill you, doesn't prevent him from making calls and hogging all the credit from the small folk. It is the oldest story in the book."

"It's bullshit."

Ernestine patted Hugh's hand. "It's okay, the Prelate knows the score. We all sent reports to the ruling council. We should be fine. Eventually the truth will out." The skimmer lifted off from the plaza, throngs of cheers filled the orange, dusky night fading to a indiscriminate roar as they climbed into the sky.

Hugh sighed in wonder as they quickly passed the breath of the city proper taking in crystal towers, golden pyramids, grey green sentinel trees, lakes, and roads teeming with white clad Aphrodite's and Apollo's. They held hands, families flitting around parks with little children in chromatocloth togas, flashing pink and green as they chased each other like fishes in Oceania's undersea garden.

They headed North to a section of larger buildings that reached near the top of the great dome. The scent of earth, ocean, gardens, flowers and spiced foods, moved passed them on the wind as the transport brought them to an large cluster of the tallest buildings in the city. White marble towers, clear glass buildings domed with colored crystals encircled a great castle that held the government of the Imperium.

Hugh grinned broadly at the ladies. "I've been meaning to ask you two, why do you call it the Imperium and the Colonial Empire? How does that beak down?"

Lilly crunched her knuckles in a rather loud way and looked embarrassed as she turned toward Hugh. "The Imperium is comprised of the core planets of the Milky Way, but in 2880, the Colonial worlds had grown very powerful. They had their own fleets, their own government, and they broke away briefly from the Imperium. The Milky Way holds about two thirds of humanity, but the remaining ten billion are still a considerable group. After a forty year war, the Imperium and Colonial Empire became synonymous, but the empire includes all humanity now. We are one people."

"I see. I am surprised you had enough spunk to have a civil war. Being so harmonious and genetically sedate."

Ernestine and Lilly both made a sour face at Hugh for that. Ernestine changed the subject in the way aristocracy often did without even a flutter, "We are almost at the Senate. But while we are on the war of 2880, you may note it is when the ban on full cloning came into effect. The colonials were losing and mass produced additional armies that prolonged the war and caused a weakening of the DNA base of all humans. Since that decree we may craft some additional tissues as large as an organ, but no further. Full clones were never stable and prone to psychological anomalies."

"That sounds eerie, what kind of anomalies?"

Lilly cut them off as the transport landed in the midst of another large crowd. "Here we are. The anomalies were bad, leave it at that. Regardless of that old war, the ban still stands and that is why anyone is loathe to clone anyone.

It is an Imperial Offense and anyone caught doing full clones is disintegrated, publicly, and their Earthly holdings liquidated. We live over three hundred years now, us humans, that is enough."

Hugh stood with them and joined the line departing the shuttle. "We do! How old are you two lovelies? Lilly? Ernestine?"

Ernestine poked him in the ribs as they walked down to the crowded garden that adjoined the Senate. "It's still rude to ask a lady her age. Besides it's time meet the most powerful people in the Imperium, be on your best behavior."

"I'll have you know I am a mere forty years of age. In my time that was significant."

Lilly laughed lightly. "Here in the Empire, you are a teen ager still living with your parents at that age. I hope we can extend your life a little bit, we were just starting to like you. If anyone asks, tell them you are at least eighty, because in our perspective, you look it. Now move it. Your holding up the line."

Hugh's eyes grew round. "That's no way to treat a child."

The entourage from Nova was surrounded by cheering Oceanians as they marched up the marble steps. Enormous corinthian pillars flanked them on both sides and heavily armed Imperials stood between each one; not in inconsiderable numbers considering how many pillars there were. As before the crowd gave the Ushok-ku a wide berth and the only thing that assaulted the group was the massive sound of voices.

"There must be half a million people here." Hugh held his breath looking as the massive golden doors of the Senate slowly opened. An ocean motif was carved on the doors that seemed to detail Poseidon's court, all in solid gold.

Two more Ushok-ku stood beside the door and the inner plaza of the building held enough seating for a hundred thousand people. Directly ahead a group of roughly fifty Senators and speakers surrounded a floating dais. A raised, throne like chair formed from a giant nautilus floated serenely above them. The Prelate of the Empire, Sanjay Dubay, raised his arm for silence as the golden doors closed to the public. He gazed down at them with a sincere warmth, despite the uncomfortably looking crown of crystals that projected an amazing aurora of lights for all to see in the enormous structure. He waved at a man near his throne.

A man stepped forward wearing the distinctive maroon robes of the Crafting Guild, with sleeves studded with blood garnets. A glowing ball of light zipped in front of his face, a rotund and attentive sprite. "His grace, the Prelate of the Imperium, Sanjay Dubey the IVth welcomes the esteemed delegates and officers of the 5th Fleet to Oceania! Seat of Empire, Primus of the Colonial Imperium" As he spoke into the ball it pulsed and boomed his soft voice for all the attendees to hear.

The crowd of representatives roared their applause through the cavernous hall. Ernestine had to shout in Hugh's ear to be hear. "This is the Cantor, Mouth of the Prelate, and leader of the Crafting Guild. Very bright, very dangerous. They call him Pirouen the Spider. Be wary of him."

Hugh regarded the bald Cantor cooly. The ball whizzed about and hovered before Pirouen again. "It is the pleasure of this one to convey the entire Colonial Empire's gratitude in assessing and delaying the spread of the dreaded plague, we are heartened by your great strides. Senator Shalinsky and party, we are in your debt."

Another roar of cheers and the ball settled before Shalinsky. "Friends and colleagues, we are pleased to have served but there is much to do. I thank you for your honors, but much more is to be done before we truly deserve your praise. I request immediate closed council of Senators and Speakers of Guilds regarding dire threats to the Empire."

Pirouen turned to the Prelate who nodded once. "So it shall be. We will convene in the Inner Solar two hours hence. You must be weary from your journey-"

Hugh reached out with his mind, grabbing the glowing ball and brought it to his face. It seemed to fight him and actually buzzed angrily. He forced it near his mouth while Ernestine and Lilly gaped. "I would like to thank Ernestine and Lillian Hsian for their support on the HCSIS project. Without their support and the protection of the Greens, we would not have succeeded and I would not have likely survived the trip back . . . home."

The crowd quieted to the point where the rotors of the amplification globe could be heard angrily even as Hugh released it. Shalinsky and the delegation he travelled with, the gathered diplomats around the Prelate's suspension disc, and Ernestine stared at Hugh in shock. The Speaker for the Prelate glared at Hugh like he slapped his poodle.

Lilly stepped up behind him and pinched him hard on his flank, "What are you doing?," she hissed near his ear.

"I'm doing something I never could do back in the day when my countries leaders were pontificating at the masses spinning reality from on high. I am using my power and telling the truth."

"Hugh, there are court dictums and courtesies that must be followed. It's folly to show them further reason to distrust you. Regardless of your value."

Cleo glared warily at the Prelate's Speaker, who gained full control of the globe. He glared at Hugh even more venomously. *I think the bald one is displeased with you taking his toy.*

Hugh shrugged. "It's like the cover model of Big Bear magazine dropped down in a world of Abercombie clones. It's not like I don't stick out! Besides, look at his majesty."

Lilly and Ernestine looked up at Sanjay Dubey's floating form as he loomed over them. The Imperial Prelate of the Colonial Empire chuckled dryly as he looked down on Hugh, drawing strange looks and gasps from the assembled Oceanian's gathered.

Hugh looked at Lilly, a toothy grin springing on his face as he felt better than he had in a long time. "Lilly, never under estimate how terribly bored an autocrat ruling a sea of sheep can be. He doesn't even get to speak himself anymore. All I did was grab the mike. He might just promote me."

Ernestine had listened to them while gauging the temperament of the crowd gathered. "Or He might just feed you to the Kraken.

Chapter 7

New Boston

Ernestine had lived in New Boston her entire life. South of George's Bank, the brilliant city perched on the lip of the continental shelf five hundred feet under water and roughly five miles off the coast. Parallel with Boston Harbor and the crumbling remains of that ancient land city, New Boston was one of the oldest cities that linked to her under sea sisters via speed rail.

They lived near the rim, where new families purchased modules of pyranite that expanded the matrix of the dome as it grew further along the floor of the ocean. The module used forced air to expand into the silty bottom of most ocean floors, thirty meters round, and pushing the previous structure higher and further out by the sheer power of its geometry, strength of the metal, and force of the mini reactor the powered the reclamation and future building on the spot.

The metric tons of silt so displaced were jammed with nutrients for agriculture. Once removed more solid fill would replace it and the building itself would soon form under robot eyes and arms. Ernestine remembered as a girl how amazed she was when the silt transmuters uncovered a wreck of an ancient ship from Hugh's time and another years later with precious metals and gems from a far older wreck that had once been wood. The sea was old, eternal, and Hugh was as old as many of the artifacts that were found in the metal vessel.

Hugh had moved to New Boston three months ago after their fateful arrival in Oceania and his displays of his powers delighted, scared and amazed the populace in equal measure. The stuffy court had a hard time swallowing their strange sense of decorum and control issues with this man from the past that had driven off the first aliens ever encountered by mankind. Sanjay Dubay had really taken to Hugh, not just as a curiosity, but as a person. The Prelate was saddened when Hugh had decided to come to New Boston. He even bandied his youngest daughter with possible marriage in front of Hugh to tempt him into staying.

Ernestine laughed out loud. The little Lady Myrcilia Dubay had to be sedated when her father blurted out the announcement during a dinner near Christmas at his Mansion in Oceania. Hugh feigned ignoring the outburst, declined most politely to the Prelate, as Myrcilia's handlers ushered her out as she wheezed "I will not father! I cannot marry a Neanderthal. I shan't do it!"

Hugh tired rapidly of court life and wanted to be as close to his Boston of old as possible. Lilly had been sent to her Order for thorough debriefing and emergency assignment to the greatly expanded HCSIS program, so Hugh decided to come back with Ernestine. Her family had lived here near the continental drop off, in a fairly upper class region of the mother dome to the South East. As part of the Empire's gratitude, a module was assigned to Hugh and he programmed a home right on the rim just outside Ernestine's own large property.

Her parents were pleased the view was not obstructed overly. When the surface sun shone down it was deep, dark blue at their depth, a full size tower would have cast a shadow over their ancestral home. Somewhat to the surprise of them Hugh settled for a one story, marble, low dome structure. He had said he always wanted to live in a round house and so it was.

Ernestine walked down Quincy Avenue, breathing in the deep pine smells all around her. It was always spring. Soft, magenta ferns, air scrubbers dotted the path leading to his house every four meters on the pebbled, shelled path. A ravenous carbon eating plant from a world in the Saurus nebula, puffed out clean air better than the mechanical systems ever could and added to the garden like beauty of her city.

Paparazzi still lingered around Hugh's home as well as his house guards. That intrusion into Hugh's life had started to wane until the Aliens attacked and destroyed another Colonial planet as well as five cruisers a few days passed. They were all back in force and she had personally got her people to install a feisty disintegration field around his house to keep interlopers away. Hugh had been shocked and appalled to use it, as some of the rival press actually tried to push each other into the deadly field.

After two had been reduced to piles of ash, they kept their distance but kept around the guarded gate day and night. Ernestine could see the house and gate rise before her. The marble dome struck her as humble and striking, the sunset casting a deep blue light on it from the West. The round windows were prominent in Hugh's design, taking in the oceans moods and change in seasons if only from day to night and the different predators that stalked each one. It took someone from the land to appreciate the water, but today Hugh would be going back to his Boston.

One of Ernestine's house guard had accompanied her. Flick was always with her. He stepped forward. "Lady Ernestine is expected." Ernestine noted that the majority of Hugh's guards on duty were from the Greens, her own trusted people, but not all. The Captain today was marked from the Crafting Guild. He nodded tersely and punched in the access code for the door lock and force screen. The door popped open, journalists tried to shoulder their way past the guards until force globes of blue electricity were activated at the tips of their rifles, pain and burns keeping them at bay. Ernestine stepped through the trestled oval door to Hugh's home.

Ernestine smiled and gave Hugh a hug, though Flick seemed to tense. "Hugh! It is good to see you. Your home is so wonderful, it is no surprise you need to keep such defenses around the clock." Hugh looked good, though a bit weary. He had become leaner, all naturally, pursuing studies in sword, beam weapon and hand to hand combat. He also accepted aneline shots that slowed his aging considerably, yet otherwise seemed well content.

"I wish those two reporters weren't killed trying to break into my home. With the Pliilulua starting their attacks again we are not able to spare any lives, even press corps."

Lilly looked down when she felt rather than saw Cleo purring and rubbing against her leg. "Hi Cleo. I know it is a tragic thing, yet, you would never have much peace if you didn't."

"They were vaporized Ernestine." Hugh frowned and called Cleo back from her.

"Well with our restorative abilities here in Boston it wouldn't be much of a deterrent if they were just maimed. Trust me, with you being called up to the Science Academy to demo the HCSIS generic prototype, the press will get more daring, not less."

"I would think that they would rather be covering the actual planets being destroyed rather than little old me in my bubble home. Better press,"

"Also off limits, Hugh. The government tries to deal with the threat by focusing on the hope, you, rather than impending Doom. You are a symbol, people like to see their saviors. Besides, no commercial traffic is allowed interstellar anywhere near the threatened worlds. Only military and even they don't want to be on the front line."

"I see. Hello Flick, would you both care to come sit down with me in the kitchen. We have a little time before the transport comes."

Flick stood at attention and made no move. He was over six feet tall, heavy set, rather than the elf like body type now popular in the empire. Dark hair rather than blond, Hugh thought he almost looked like the men of his time. The thought plucked at his loneliness but it was futile to dwell upon since there were none like him.

Ernestine nudged Flick. "George, come sit with us, Hugh does not stand on caste of station and come to think of it, neither do I." Only after Ernestine moved to the kitchen, did Flick follow and he did not sit or speak. "Flick is conditioned to be my top personal guard. He is a stickler for etiquette and taking his assignment seriously."

Hugh raised his eyebrows up but didn't comment. He fixed them some tea he had come to like, even sweetened, but milk was not even in the new humans vocabulary. He set a mug in front of Flick if only to be polite. "She did say sit, Flick."

Flick pulled out his chair and sat.

"It seems that everyone whose anyone in your society has guards. Yet no one seems to do anything criminal. It's not mentioned in the holozines or news. Just pushy press people, at least that is a universal through time."

Ernestine sipped her tea. "Ah. Excellent. Trust me Hugh, we have criminals, it's just we . . . recycle them if they prove to be intractable. If we can't save the mind there is plenty of better uses for their bodies."

Hugh grimaced. "As you know, I am no fan of the crafters, but I wonder who sits on the tribunals judging who is to be recycled. I find justice still hard to find amongst this Aryan paradise you've created, present company excluded."

"Trust me Hugh, me being black and Flick being dark haired and meaty does not buy us many friends, but we still hope to live at least three centuries. That requires organ crafting and genetic tweaking. Everyone does it. It's not like we kill babies."

"The fact everyone does it does not make me any more comfortable. I heard that those elite guards are crafted from spare parts, even their brains are amalgams. It's a good thing they don't speak, it would be a horror with all the brain tissue. As you know, I am no fan of manipulation of those sensitive tissues."

"Frankly you're a marvel Hugh. Rarer even then the Ushok-ku. Did you know that not one in a ten thousand live? That for some reason the crafters don't even know, some live many centuries due to their unusual brain composition."

"Impressive as that is, like me, no one asked if it was okay to take parts of me out and put others in. Trust is a dirty dirty word to me. You should know that by now Ernestine. Speaking of which, help me keep you in my trust and tell me why Shalinsky is coming on our visit to Boston.

You know I never quite forgave him for taking advantage of me, to put it lightly."

Ernestine pointed to Flick then to his cup of tea until he drank. "Just like forcing Flick to take advantage of your hospitality, Senator Shalinsky is making sure you are on our side even though for some baffling reason the Prelate himself had taken to you from the start. He wants to make sure you have drunk deep of Oceania's culture and heady traditions."

"I think I have adjusted well considering. Still, I don't want him there or to see you make Flick do what he doesn't want to do."

Ernestine frowned at one of her dreadlocks, that had frayed outside of its white gold band. "It's just that like me, you are an exotic, a useful exotic, and like Frick here, you occasionally need to be reminded you are a part of something other than yourself. Besides, all the work you have been doing, classes you have been taking have been good for you. Flick needs liquid, he is dehydrated. You need a field trip. Some actual land will do you a world of good."

"We'll see. I must confess I do yearn to see Boston again, even after all this time."

Ernestine and Flick stood up. "In that case, lets get going. But brace yourself too, this water you will drink since the Blackening up above may prove as bitter and dark as it is good for you to see."

*

The small transport disc arrived at Hugh's home and the house guards created a perimeter ten meters out from the house. The press sent camera drones toward the disc, creating a colorful fireworks display as security all around proved adroit at striking them down. Ernestine and Frick followed Hugh and Cleo up a spiral stair case to the highest point in the dome. As they approached, Hugh depressed a small bud on his watch, opening the roof in a spiral pattern and allowing access to a private landing bridge. Another bud and the green particles of the disintegration field winked out allowing the disc to dart in and pick them up.

"You seem to have taken to the gadgets of your adopted people." Ernestine curtsied as the men let her on.

Hugh nodded, "I always liked them even in my own time. Though I must admit, I was on the lower end of the food chain back then." Hugh fingered the ornate khirda the Prelate had given him.

"Considering you declined the fair hand of his daughter, it is a wonder he still let you have that," she sat in the far seat of the small but comfortable craft. "I am also glad you still wear the bracelet I gave you."

"It's good to know you'll be able to pick up my valuable parts should we crash, for science and the war and all. Did you know Lilly made me promise to his majesty and everyone at the palace that I had to take lessons before she let me put this shield blade on?"

Ernestine barely suppressed an evil grin. "It's so you wouldn't injure yourself, she has made a considerable career investment in you, survival of the race, etc."

The disc sped from Hughs house fast enough that Hugh felt his stomach lurch. "I am not so easy to injure, except my feelings." Hugh glanced pointedly at Frick who was speaking to the pilot quietly. "Yet I believe the master at arms Grennick was most pleased with my aptitude."

"He would have been executed should you have injured yourself, not doubt he was supportive. But I saw you spar, it is an elegant weapon, the khirda, in a few decades you might even be good."

"You're starting to sound like Lilly, Ernestine."

"Ladies will chat."

Within a half hour the disc linked to the disembarking platform at the top of New Boston. Unlike Oceania, with over two miles of ocean above and space to build towers upward, the first city of New Boston was built much deeper into the shelf itself. A mere five hundred feet of water felt like a thin barrier from The Blackening but it sufficed. Cleo curled around Hugh's neck and started to cool herself for him. *I know when you are stressed, your temperature spikes.*

Hugh kissed her on the head. *Tonight I will scale a fish for you myself.*

Be sure you do not filet it, you humans are wasteful of the best parts.

Evolution, its what it is called.

Hmmph. Get up Hugh, they are waiting on you.

Hugh stood and walked off the disc, thanking the transport man.

The four of them turned into the main lobby of the platform. By the size of the party ahead of them and the presence of two Ushok-ku, Hugh knew Shalinsky was there. They seemed to think that disintegration halberds would keep him from causing any trouble. "What is it with you people and the vaporization fetish."

Ernestine nodded to a group of aligned Green dignitaries. "Even though cloning is a despicable, Imperial crime, disintegration is forever. Now pretend to be delighted to be here."

Hugh kept his face neutral and joined the line leading to what people called a battle barge. It could fly, roll, swim, and dive, according to reports he'd read, even make orbit, but none of them well. It was also well armed and well nigh indestructible. Two fusion engines moved it in a magnetic field bubble, but seemed to need more considering how loud it buzzed holding position at the dock.

Shalinsky was actually not wearing his omnipresent, ministerial grey blues. Instead he was in a red leather tunic and pants, as were several of the other ranking members. Ernestine grimaced more than Hugh upon seeing them. "Senator Shalinsky, I was not informed of a hunt. This is supposed to be a mapping tour of Old Boston, to honor Hugh Wilkey before deep assignment on HCSIS work."

"Lady Ernestine." Shalinsky bowed shallowly to them. "The hunt is also in Mr. Wilkey's honor. We owe him that much for services rendered. We will do the mapping tour as well, have no fear."

"Hunt, what will we be hunting?" Hugh motioned for the Senators group to go in before them. "After you your Lordship."

Shalinsky smiled broadly, "We will be hunting animals of course." He and ten associated Guild members followed in tow. The Ushok-ku stayed with Hugh. Hugh and Ernestine exchanged worried glances and followed Flick toward their seats in the back of the battle barge.

Hugh strapped himself into the crash seat, "So are we hunting lions and tigers?"

Ernestine hesitated. "We are hunting Genghonni, hunting mutants." She did not meet his eyes.

"You're hunting . . . people?"

"The same ones who forced your surgery. Made you what you are."

He thought on this as they broke gate dock and pressurized the hull. The barge slipped through the murky water into the growing dark. "Well, not all of them did this to me." Hugh pointed to the metal disc at the base of his neck.

"Don't you see, he, they are testing you." Ernestine kept her voice low as the mouthless Ushok-Ku, too large to sit, flanked them on either side. They had the decency and smarts to turn off their halberds, no sense in drowning them all in an implosive, undersea hull breach.

"Well they can suck a duck if they think I am killing anyone. Even if they are a green three eyed mutant. They are, were people. It's wrong."

Ernestine turned away. "It is our way. We hunt the Genghonni, the broken ones who broke our world. We need to."

"You don't need to, it's senseless and cruel to even hunt animals that you are not going to eat. So you better not be telling me you just shoot them and go. What possible good does it do to kill damaged human beings? Mercy?

She looked him square in the eye. "We do not take them to be merciful. We take them because we need their genes."

Hugh sat there for a long time. He watched a kraken in the distance as they pushed through the surface. The top of the barge and side gunnels opening up to let in air and firing space. No birds were flying but the air was breathable, it just smelled, burned. With a flick of a button the captain switched on night vision membranes for those not enhanced with night vision irises already. If you kept your head inside the membrane, you could see heat variations. If you stuck your head out, you could see nothing but night.

Ernestine looked at Hugh worriedly. Hugh was deeply angry with all of them. "I thought you made everything you needed. Cooked everything up in Crafter labs."

She shook her head. "The hunt has existed since the air became breathable again eight hundred years ago. If anything with the expansion of mankind in space and the thinning of the original gene pools, we needed a source of outside, fresh DNA. In a way, some Oceanians feel it is owed to us, Payment for the Blackening."

Hugh's voice was angry now. "Are you telling me you support this?"

Ernestine shook her head. The barge declined in altitude as they approached the land. "The Greens, my party, many of us want the hunt to be shut down. We feel we can obtain the materials in other more humane means. But we are a minority party, a small minority as you may remember."

Hugh imagined himself reaching out with his power and breaking the barges suspension field. Then as he felt the energy rise within him, he let himself go blank and meditate away his rage. As he calmed, Ernestine touched his hand. "I'm sorry you had to find out like this."

It was his new hand and he forced himself to not tear it away from her touch. "I guess I am just glad I found out. This trip is not going to be pleasant."

Ernestine sighed. "At least it is night. You won't have to watch the killing if you don't want to."

"No I will watch. I want to see the blood on your hands." Hugh looked over the broken landscape of Boston. The membrane enhanced his vision so he could see the water-front, stone and brick building of over a millennia past studded the land like the broken teeth of some giant. "Even the water is black". He began to see small dots of red pushing out between the teeth, heat signatures of bodies. "Why do you hunt at night anyway?"

"The Ghengonni only come out at night, Hugh. There is one more thing you should know. They are cannibals."

Hugh felt the anger finally boil out of him over that. Cannibals? He wasn't sure what he expected from the burnt and blackened land and what survived on it. It still didn't feel right to kill them. He turned to her and poked her in the rib causing Ernestine to jump. "When's the last time you actually spoke to your cousins down there? How do you know?"

She thought about this a while before she spoke. "I think the last time Oceanians spoke with the Genghonni was when Lilly's team found you in the old lab in this city. Other than that, not ever. They don't speak."

"The one who fucking operated on me could more than speak." Hugh was annoyed again. "You guys couldn't even put in this interface in my head. You should find a way to talk to them."

Ernestine looked horrified as they descended toward a cluster of the heat signatures. The hunters opened fire near what looked like an old factory. A pivoting laser cannon under the barge surgically struck down the Genghonni one after another and the Oceanians took out any survivors with hand weapons.

"That's just it Hugh, they don't talk. They don't have tongues. We also find the chewed bones near their warrens. Human bones."

They both stood up as the barge started to set down. One of the cannons hit something that exploded much to the cheers and surprise of the hunting party. Cleo dug in close to Hugh's neck and growled softly under his chin. *Humans should be extinct. Not cats. This is a bad place.*

Humans are extinct Cleo. They've been extinct for a long time.

The hunters formed groups of three, and headed out in ten directions moving toward the fading light from the heat signatures of the dead and dying Genghonni. With each group of red clad hunter pairs, the third was a crafter carrying a bulky device on his back and a hose connected to it and ending on the tip of his or her hand.

Ernestine and Hugh were glad of their Ushok-ku escorts and Flick pulled out his khirda and hand blaster. The large guards activated their eerie green halberds. Hugh watched as the crafters scanned the bodies of each mutant. Every third or so, the Crafter would shoot a beam into the corpse, stand up after collection, and move to the next. Hugh caused some rubble to move to the side. Flick and the Ushok-ku moved off with Ernestine to see.

Hugh went in the opposite direction toward the location of the blast. There was something explosive in a blue plastic container. Chunks of plastic and some type of oil was smoking all around. There were some bodies in the distance and he didn't need the heat detection of the barges membrane to tell him they were all dead; men, women and children.

He glanced at the twisted body of a woman in her twenties. Her face was slightly misshapen, one eye larger than another. Her larynx was twisted, but from a birth defect, not any damage done by them. The chunk of plastic and steel sticking out of her chest was the thing that did her in. The most striking thing to Hugh was something that hit deep in the primordial part of his brain, she smelt human. Very human.

With Oceanians and their scrubbed and perfected world, the smells were always something like the lighting, controlled and presented to an end. He never thought he would miss it, the odor of humanity, but here it was and it was nice to remember. Until the wind changed and the smell of burned flesh drifted his way. As he turned from it and began walking back toward Ernestine, he saw movement beyond the exploded container in the dwindling light.

Conscious that he would soon have no light, Hugh put his finger near the shield activator of his khirda. He warily approached the dark form in the corner of the clearing. As he moved Cleo jumped down from his shoulder and stealthed. *Cleo be careful.*

You be careful. I'm a night hunter.

Ernestine called his name in the distance but he was hidden from sight behind the broken edge of an ancient wall. He bent over a man whose leg was crushed by a bit of the wall, toppled by the initial explosion. His chest rose and fell. His eyes were shockingly beautiful, though one was black and one was blue. A small piece of plastic had fused with his cheek just under his dark eye and he stared at Hugh frozen in horror.

Hugh shut down his blade and just stared at him. He was well formed, normal, except for the notch in his larynx. The man put his hand on his chest, flat, and rubbed it in a circle on his sternum. It was sign language. Hugh remembered his deaf brother, now dead over fourteen hundred years. This man was saying *"please"*.

He reached out with his mind and started to lift the four hundred pound wall off the man's leg and set it between them and the Oceanians walking toward him even as he worked. The man was lucky, his leg was banged up, caught, but unbroken. Hugh felt the bones and looked him in the face, tried signing, *"your ok. Run!"*

The man looked stunned. Too shocked to move. Hugh slapped him. *"Run or they will kill you."* The man seemed to come around started to get on his legs and Hugh helped him up and pointed to the dark trees. The man half ran half limped with good speed into the dark. But before he fully disappeared he turned and signed quickly, *"John"*. Then he was gone.

"Well that was sporting of you Wilkey. I do like the prey to have a running start."

Shalinsky aimed his rifle over his head and started to depress the trigger on a wide beam kill shot.

"Nooo!" Hugh jumped up and struck the rifle nozzle spoiling the shot. He was so angry he grabbed the Senator by the lapel of his hunting jacket and started punching him in the face with his free hand. "They." Punch. "Don't". Punch. "Talk". Punch. "But they speak with their hands!" With that Sander fell to the ground his hunting vest ripped down the middle and everyone seemed to arrive at once.

The hunters aimed their rifles at Hugh and the Ushok-Ku and Ernestine stood around Hugh as Shalinsky stood up. His lip was broken and his eye was turning a shade of purple and swelling considerably. The Ushok-ku, to his puzzlement, actually seemed to be guarding Hugh from the hunters by his posture and doing well at it.

"The next time you touch me Genghonni, I will have your head mounted outside my mansion." Shalinsky spoke in a soft and deadly voice.

Hugh looked at Shalinsky with all the anger and hatred he had kept pent up from even beyond the brief time he been awakened in. As he mulled over how far he could run before he was shot down if he crushed the Senator's head like a melon his eyes fell to the man's torso. Hugh noticed that under the vest he ripped while handling the man was a well formed chest. Yet more shocking to him was the fact it was amply covered with gold and white hair.

"So that is why you hate me. You are resistant to crafting too. Your one of the minority."

The Senator drew himself up and closed the torn garment with his hand. He looked down his nose at Hugh with enough venom behind his eyes Hugh actually felt sorry for the man. "I am nothing like you."

Brushing himself off Hugh could see Cleo ready to pounce. "Too bad, Senator." *Cleo, power down girl, I see you over there about to tear out his throat.*

Cleo looked rather disappointed but complied.

Hugh wondered to himself as he walked toward the battle barge why hot guys had to be such assholes.

*

June had arrived and two months passed since the fateful hunt in New Boston. Hugh had grudgingly worked with the ten candidates who had survived the implant surgery and most were getting the rudiments of HCSIS control systems. He did not want to know what happened to the many who didn't make it, yet with four more star systems falling to the Pliilulua, the Imperium was not using kid gloves to get ships like Nova to the front.

Dismissing the trainees, Hugh prepared to head back home. Home. He rolled it around in his mind. He did live in New Boston. Since he saved the deaf mutant, Johnny, he had worked tirelessly with the Greens to help stop the hunt. Yet the majority of citizens still supported it or did so through not caring. The Crafters warned of a shortage of pure DNA making prices rocket. It was hard to get comfortable here.

The youngsters were toweling themselves dry waiting for Hugh to dismiss them for the day. Boston's Imperial Science Academy had set up eleven tanks of telekinetic fluid and at the end of the day, 5:00pm, both the lads and ladies wanted to go. Some things never changed. Even with this crisis, Lilly could not make them stay over ten hours. These men and women were as valuable as Hugh now.

More valuable as they were real Naval personnel. Blond, blue eyed confections and by young, meaning in their forties. "Kids" Lilly called them. She said they had to be a hundred to be considered adults. Hugh did not feel his age and these people did not look it. "Have a good weekend, well done people."

Almost as one they said, "Have a good evening Mr. Wilkey." They filed out of the lab into the locker room. Room not rooms, all unisex, but with their discipline, it might as well be a nunnery.

"Did you have a good day Hugh?"

He turned to Lilly. "Herr Doctor. I am thinking it wasn't bad. They are ready for joining with their dreadnoughts, methinks."

"I'm not so sure of that, but I can't complain at the progress we have made. We should be ready to mount an offensive." Lilly pointed to the far tank. "Should she be doing that.?"

Hugh looked to the far end of the lab and Cleo's diminutive grey body was perched on the lip of the tank. *Cleo get off of that. We are going home*

Very well. Cleo hopped down and vanished from view.

"Care to join me for dinner Hugh? To celebrate our progress?"

He considered for a minute and shook his head. "Can't, got a meeting to go to. Raincheck, yes?"

"Is it one of your End the Hunt conspirators? And we can go some other time."

"You should come, it would make you a better person."

"I sometimes wish you hadn't saved that Genghonni. We have traditions you know."

He was not going to let himself get invited to a fight. "As I've told you and all the other bloody block heads who don't get it. They speak in sign. It is a language. They are human beings you have been killing."

"Human beings don't eat humans."

"Whose to say the bones outside their warrens are from them? Besides its harsh on the surface, humans survive. If you just learned their signs, you could communicate. Your medical advances could certainly fix their voices if it was so important to you."

Lilly sat on a metal table as she watched Hugh towel himself dry. Considering her words. "Perhaps you are right. I have not been on a hunt for decades if it makes you feel any better. Buy you have to admit it is far fetched that some hand sign from your time somehow survived unchanged? Besides, they don't want to leave their filth, they kill themselves rather than be captured alive."

"The sign they use probably has changed, but basic words may still be in use. I understood what John said. He finger spelled his name. If you Oceanians brought food, supplies, you could help them, bring them around." Hugh slipped on his pants and shirt, keeping his back to her. Modesty was deep in his bones. "All I am asking it you try."

Lilly stood and kissed Hugh on the cheek. "You are a good man."

Hugh was rather shocked at her display. "Umm. Thanks."

"I mean really Hugh? The Holozines already think you are some barbarian messiah? But they still believe you and them, the Genghonni, owe us for the Blackening. The destruction of our entire world. By letting this John go you sided with them."

Hugh snapped his shirt buttons loudly, irritated with the direction they were going. "You don't get it, your ancestors were the ones who caused the holocaust. The rich ones in power, the ones who set up the first three submerged cities. They simply escaped and just like before, prey on the ones further down the chain. You just don't take their money and sweat anymore, you take their DNA. It's cannibalism whether you stew them in a pot or suck out a chromosome to inject into yourself later. It's just a matter of scale."

Lilly threw up her hands. "Fine. I will donate, *anonymously*, to the save the mutant cannibal campaign."

Pulling on his coat and slipping into his shoes, Hugh recalled telling Flick that even killer whales threw one seal pup back at the end of the day of slaughter. John was his seal pup. Orcas actually still lived so Flick got his point, after explaining about the seals. "Good Lilly, donate all you can."

All real cloth without any of the commoner chromaticloth togas, even though Hugh knew it would be more comfortable. He headed out the door to his meeting. He turned to to Lilly and waved good bye."

Lilly called after him "it's a good thing you don't wear the chromaticloth! It would be every shade of green and red, or both." Hugh was gone.

*

Ernestine met Hugh at the Plaza Hotel, one of New Boston's best restaurants. It was a good thing he liked seafood so much. She was amazed he could tell wild caught from the equally fine aqua cultured varieties on the menu. It was a well earned meal in any event marking their efforts to ban the hunt and raise public awareness of the distant cousins who survived in the waste land that was their original home.

Wearing her conch shell pearls, she met Hugh near the maitredee in a dazzling cream colored dress. "You look lovely milady," as he kissed her hand. He nodded to her body guard. "Good evening Flick."

Flick nodded curtly to Hugh and walked with them over to their table. He stood behind her and stared straight ahead. Hugh and Ernestine were seated and noticed the other four seats were empty. "Our fellow Greens are late."

"Fashionably so." Ernestine asked for a wine, a good one, fermented from a certain rare sea kelp. When he didn't really think about what it was it wasn't half bad. Perhaps his people deserved to be culled in the hunt for destroying grapes among a million other things long gone to dust.

"So the funding seems to be increasing. Only two months and we have enough to start full page Holozine ads for the ban." Hugh took a heavy pull from the wine glass. It was strong and sweet, almost citrusy, with a saltiness that was minute but a subtle reminder of its origin.

Ernestine drank more slowly. "You know, if you told me two months ago that I would be pushing with all the influence of my party to end the hunt I would have thought you were going mad."

"The more you push people away, the more they become strangers. Humans, all humans fear the unknown. We need to get your screwed up media to grow some balls."

Ernestine's chocked daintily on her wine and would have flushed if her pigment would have allowed it. "Hugh!"

He chuckled. "Excuse my rudeness. But it's true. You grow everything else, you might want to actually grow a democracy."

She drank some wine. "I've heard of the word. As I studied on history, that's what you had. Yet it was the same. Wealthy privileged people in power pulling all the strings. We are just honest about it and call him Prelate and make him accountable to the upper class. We know he is undisputed king, yet kings within castles that the guilds boarder."

"All governments are flawed just like it's people and they all have a golden age and then start to rot. Even the Imperium. Though it's long past rotten down here at the bottom of the sea in your bubbles."

The speaker composed herself. "Our guests will be here soon. Oceanians are perfect, just ask them. We span galaxies. It is better. Please be pleasant during this meeting, these guild leaders won't be as open to our platform if they hear you speaking like an anarchist."

Hugh crossed his arms and was about to protest when Flick's ear communicator seemed to buzz him. Hard to infer anything from his poker face but he swiftly bent to Ernestine's ear and whispered. She nodded and he turned around to go the lobby.

Cleo was near her feet, stealthed and waiting for scraps. Citizens knew of her but tended to freak when they saw her. Otherwise Hugh could kind of blend with other people but someone always seemed to recognize him lately. *Cleo, please follow Flick and make sure he is not up to anything. I will give you that clam you love so much.*

A lot of it. She left his leg and was off like a ghost.

"Something wrong, Ernestine?"

The representative touched her pearl necklace nervously. Looked around the large posh restaurant. Hardly anyone wore chromacloth which was a hand down indicator it was nobility and government people only. "We received word from our network that one of our guests was found dead by her door. Disintegrated. Cellular residue is a match."

Hugh reached out and touched her hand. "I am so sorry Ernie. Was she a friend?"

Ernestine nodded as she dabbed her eyes dry with a napkin. "Madeline Chambers was a founder of the Greens with my parents, almost two hundred years ago. She was like a mother to me." A waiter came by and dropped off a silver platter.

"Compliments of the house." The waiter strode off and Hugh thought it was a kindness that they would be so attuned to their table.

"Was the murder on the news Ernestine?"

Ernestine shook her head. "It was just sent via our security network. All guild reps have a life tag that ties into a main frame, keeping us posted of general location and disposition. Located right behind the ear. Why?"

"The waiters timing was a little too good. We should go."

The bomb on the tray then detonated.

Chapter 8
Shalinsky's Gambit

Senator Sander Shalinsky stared out over the North Sea, from his appointed office in New London. The tower office glistened like a spire of Atlantis and the coast of Wales actually had bits of shrubbery growing out of the Blackened soil. Ironically, it could well be a promising time to consider one of Hugh Wilkey's ideas and resettle the United Kingdom. Sadly Wilkey was dead, killed by anarchists along with his great friend Ernestine Royce. So sad he would never get to see it.

Shalinsky lashed out with his hand like a striking serpent, shattering the stealth field hiding the infiltrator of his private sanctum. The assailant's khirda flew from his hand and a groan of shock escaped his impeded lips as the senator slammed the man's face into the large wooden desk. Priceless as it was hard the man squealed, "I yield my Lord. Yield!"

Sander laughed and released Sebastian. He stood coughing and rubbing his neck and chin. "You said you wanted to test yourself. No need to get rough. I just would have clipped you sir."

"I am well nigh impressed you could get into my tower at all."

"You should not have been able to detect me. I moved like a silent shadow. It is hard to believe you let Wilkey manhandle you in the past with you skills."

Shalinsky grinned tightly. "Never reveal your full strength, my fine assassin, or your enemies may learn not to fear you. Besides, I've been adding some new twists to the Crafters best work."

Sebastian wiped a trickle of blood from his lip onto his tight fitting stealth suit then recovered his khirda from across the room. "Undoubtedly, the powerful will do as they will. It is regrettable I must inform you I am no assassin my Lord, but a contractor with a select clientele."

"Semantics Hsian. Based on your success, you can call yourself whatever you like. I am just pleased that Wilkey and Royce are dead. Why didn't you use a disintegration grenade like I asked?"

"The late Speaker Royce was not un-cautious. She set up sniffer droids in a perimeter outside the Plaza Restaurant. I had to assemble something inside the restaurant with materials on hand. A sure sign of my extreme resilience and skill, if I dare say myself?"

"For what I've been paying you, you don't have to brag. Especially since the amount of material spread throughout the blast area left only pieces of our friends for evaluation. Even the Master Crafter could only find a few tiny pieces of the bastard. I wanted unmoving chunks like Royce's steaming carcass. I want to be sure nothing is left."

Sebastian seated himself into a gracefully sculpted seat made out of a large piece of red coral. He crossed his leg and smirked, "You worry too much, the bomb was set to create a near disintegration like in a small area yet have a directional burst of force that would disintegrate in a wedge depending where the platter was placed."

"You are sure you placed it facing Wilkey?" Shalinsky pushed a button under his desk and his office tower started to retract the hundred feet down to the dome of New London as the sun set. He picked the city and location due to its proximity to the surface, the shallowest such metropolis in all Oceania.

"I placed it to go off right in his face Senator. Please be assured. The Ghengonni is dead."

Sitting himself into a similar chair across from Sebastian, Shalinsky reached into his breast pocket and pulled out his monogramed, credit case. He punched in the numbers he wanted and held out the scanner end toward the agent. "Your sister is taking the news hard I imagine?"

Sebastian leaned forward and tilted the corner of his wrist device along the edge of the Senator's credit scan, leaned back slowly and observed the sum while sighing in satisfaction. "Always a pleasure my Lord. And yes, Lillian is quite destroyed over the anarchists strike on the poor founders of the Ban The Hunt benefit. I did want to comfort her so."

The tower pulled through the membrane of the Southern dome of New London and nestled into the main library of Shalinsky's mansion close to the center of the city. As the room settled into the structure of the main building, he stood and cleared his throat ending the meeting.

"Let us hope Dr. Hsian continues her HCSIS work and mourns quickly. The Pliilulua infestation is heading toward Earth. I hope you covered your tracks and left the Anarchist calling cards subtlely enough to be believable?"

Sebastian glanced over his shoulder as he walked to the ornately carved door exiting the study. "It was done correctly. Though Lilly belonged to the Order, even her deductive skills will find not a crumb of evidence of our involvement."

Shalinsky glared at him. "Your involvement Sebastian. Make sure you find Wilkey's wretched pet. Loose strings make me irritable. Make sure no one sees you leave."

"It will be as you say, my Lord. You know how to find me." With a touch of a button he faded from sight."

The door to his study opened and Shalinsky's fourteenth daughter Rosealine stepped through. Bowing deeply, her sea silk dress contrasted nicely with her blue eyes. He thought he might actually like this youngling, though he could not remember if she was from his fourth of fifth wife. All five women lived in different wings with their various broods and though he was loathe to see them, they had produced decent stock over all.

"Lord father, I am here as requested. 1430 hours."

Shalinsky glanced at his daily planner piped from the central screen flush with his great desk. "Approach Rosealine."

The girl shyly moved forward standing between the two coral chairs. Her bone structure and fitness was on par with any child of a Lord of his station. Golden hair falling in locks about her pretty neck, the best his Crafter friends could do. "You have honored our house with your skill with the Master at Arms. You are the best shot in the family and handle a khirda better than any son of mine. Even though you are not even twenty and one, know I am well pleased."

Rosealine bowed again deeply. "It is my pleasure to please my Lord father."

"Tell your mother Vergaine I am most pleased and we should sup and discuss where best to cultivate your proud skill."

"Begging your pardon father, I am born of Catherine, your third wife." She kept her voice carefully neutral. Her face reddened. "Also, if I may, I was hoping to get your blessings to join the Order."

This daughter of his had gall to call him on a mistake. More gall to follow up with a demand. "When you have five wives and thirty three children Rose, it is hard to keep track of all the bees in the hive. *Catherine* and I will discuss your fate when we meet. You will be kept informed."

He beckoned her forward and extended his hand. Rosealine shook it. "I am cheered by your skill and not displeased by your cheek. Now go." He wondered why they had named this child after an extinct plant.

Rosealine gathered up her dress and walked as quickly as she could out of the study. Having a child of his trained in the Order of The Kraken would not be the worst thing in the world. Yet, the Order was a wing of the Prelate and the Prelate was of late no friend of his. He was well near invincible to any premature retirement behind the Orders vigilance and the Ushok-ku's unfailing loyalty. But things were about to change. He would make sure of it.

*

Senator Shalinsky entered the Crafter's Quarter with a limited entourage of guards. The hover disc had about four of his best men. As they approached the bright red grouping of buildings, they appeared almost black in the night skyline. Portal windows blazed with light on every floor though there was no seeing through the milky glass. The disc paused before the eighth story sky garage. His man entered the access codes and the reinforced portal door swung aside and they settled to a stop in the top landing bay.

The Master Crafter Birian met him with five lackeys. They also had about ten armed guards in Crafter red livery. Upon seeing the security, Shalinsky's teeth clenched.

"My Lord Birian, I do not see why you would have so many troops for a close ally of your guild?"

Birian bowed stiffly as the rest of his contingent bent low. "My Lord Senator, we mean no offense. The delicacy of the mission seems to beg for additional-"

Shalinsky cut him off. "Additional discretion and less eyes. Dismiss them before I get cross, and take me to the Speaker."

Birian's runny blue eyes flicked a bit fearfully. "You heard the Senator, dismissed. Get out of the bay!" Under two minutes later even the mechanics had left.

After the quiet had settled into the huge port, the Master Crafter held forward a small, white hand, right this way my lord. You are expected."

Shalinsky moved forward slightly behind Birian, the Master shuffling more quickly than someone close to four centuries of life should do. Immortality was beyond the Crafters but it seemed to him the inner circle saved the best for themselves. Typical.

The six men moved deeper into the main building of the Guild Hall, largest on the planet. Kept lit within by cascading reddish light beams every ten yards, the gothic architecture made the building look ominous. They stopped before the central door of what many considered was the single largest reservoir of DNA in the universe. Mostly human, the enormous pyranite double doors were fifteen feet high and covered with the runic scribbling of the Crafter's obscure alphabet.

A globe droid stood before the door and open its lighted eye. Scanning each of them and their retinal signatures. Birian straightened his curved back and was scanned. "Master Birian, Keeper of Keys, you are expected." It passed before Shalinsky who endured a scan. "Senator Sander

Shalinsky, friend of the Crafters, you are also granted access. Your guards must stay."

Shalinsky thought of protesting but nodded after considering. The Crafters and he were in deep, no sense letting even his closest people know more than they should. "Men, you will stay here. I should not be long. Say, an hour to give the devil his due." His guards nodded. 'Devil his due' was a code for come back in force and blast your way in if he was not accounted for by that time.

A thin light blossomed on the enormous doors' lower corner in a circular pattern. Once the light had travelled the two meter circumference this plug of door sighed quietly, receded slightly and rolled away allowing access. "I did so like the round doors and security, Master Birian. Do you ever have reason to use the large doors any more?"

Birian chuckled as he shuffled through and the plug of three foot pyranite resealed the door and Shalinsky's anxious looking guards on the outside. "Not since the Colonial Civil War have we had the need to create war constructs of such size. Our work is far more sublime in these challenging and cautious times. It is best to do what we do unseen, my Lord, as I am sure you agree."

The room could not rightly be called a room, it was a colossal warehouse, countless tiers high and so deep the eye could not take it all in at once. Specialized research droids tirelessly monitored endless rows of tanks and beakers, tissue samples and rows of the finest replacement organ systems mankind could want. "I quite agree Birian, also do me a favor and lets avoid the skin tanks. Seeing empty human skin sacks hanging from racks in nutrient rich tanks is rough on my sleep apnea."

"By all means, my Lord Senator." The two men seemed to be the only working humans in the enormous space.

Robots worked tirelessly and ceaselessly in every direction and as they moved through the rows of materials. After twenty minutes they reached the far end of the space and the only other door to be seen. Only ten feet in diameter, this door was ringed with laser cannons and an actual combat droid.

The droid itself looked slim and as tall as Shalinsky himself, black and glossy, with one single bright blue scan bar on its face. It appeared un-armed and unmoving. He had seen the schematics on the Mark VI, a bulky monstrosity. This one was labelled if he read the Crafter script correctly a Mark VIII. A completely new model. He was surprised he had never seen it. "This is new." He did not wish the Crafters to know he had learned some of their secret writing.

"It is the Mark VIII. A master work and rather secret as is the Inner Sanctum. I trust you will say nothing of what you are about to see. None other than Masters in Crafter Guild have ever been to the Sanctum." Birian turned to the droid he spoke in the Crafter's tongue and it scanned his retina and then moved to the Senator.

"I am fairly sure I do not want my molecules blasted into microns by a Tribunal. You have my word." As the droid scanned his retina, Shalinsky noticed the droid moved soundlessly and without any ungainliness unlike any other he'd ever seen. It's body was pure pyranite, clear sections in its arms and body carried various liquids and powders of off putting colors in sections of the clear metal. He thought it better not to ask about it's weaponry, biological and chemical agents were not to be easily contemplated in a society so restive of its past excesses.

The droid spoke something metallically in Crafter Speech and the vault like door dropped to the floor providing a walk way and a passage in one. They stepped through.

Whole human bodies in tanks marked each side of them in single rows. As the door closed behind them he noticed Master Crafters attending to the humans delicately controlled tanks. There were about ten clones of men and women on either side as they walked toward the well lit central lab. "This is rather naughty Master Birian."

Birian coughed abruptly after a dry giggle. "Oh yes my lord, rather. It is best you don't see any of the faces. We too have our secrets."

Shrugging, he was fairly sure nothing would ever come of these forged humans. "The Crafters would be cleansed from the Empire if you were found out. You could not get cloned brain tissue through sniffers. These are dead toys, still born, to be sure."

Grand Master Pirouen, Mouth of the Prelate turned toward them as they approached. He whispered something to a white clad assistant who took off his gloves and scurried away from a large tank dominating the central tier of the round area. Banks of computers and some twenty Craft Masters bustled about them like bees. "My Lord Senator. You are seeing the innermost shrine of our sacred order! Our trust and agreements are truly sealed now."

Pirouen and Shalinsky stepped forward and shook hands. "It is good to see you." Shalinsky actually felt glad to be away from Birian, who shuffled away to an alcove as the Grand Master approached. They had grown up together and if any nobles felt any true trust in the intrigue riddled Imperial Court, it was they.

"I'll have you know Sander, these are not just some experiment and me being rebellious. They will get past Imperial Sniffers."

Shalinsky pushed Pirouen roughly on the shoulder and hissed "Lies! Rorge. Lies. You cannot tell me you cracked that mystery. You can't create clones that won't set off every Tribunal in the Empire. You will have us publicly executed at the end of Ushok-ku halberds yet."

Pirouen laughed. "You might have been right a few months ago. Yet necessity is the mother of invention and the Pliilulua presented suitable inspiration to break through. How do you think HCSIS could push forward into the brains of our ten new cadets? It was my serum that allowed the grafts to grab through their stubborn tissues. I have done it,"

Shalinsky stared at his friend without moving a muscle. "An undetectable clone, with programmable agendas would change the face of the Empire."

"It is not a fast process nor is it easily done. What I am about to show you will put the power of the Senate, the whole Empire in our hands. You know your're first among all the Senate. Who else could be chosen if something unfortunate should happen to the Prelate?"

Thoughts rushed through Shalinsky's mind. Plans within plans pushing to the surface and expounding possibilities during these dangerous times. "I would say it would certainly benefit the crafters to have me rise, yet, tell me Rorge Pirouen, what is to stop you from simply replacing us all. Taking all the power for yourself?"

"Sander you wound me? I do not want to be first, I am more powerful as speaker.

The clones will pass a sniffer. They will not pass a more intense analysis kit or deep probe. Our fine eleven specimens you see here took no less than ten years to grow. The cost would make you blush. No, my friend, the Crafters will not be replacing all the court with puppets of my design. Yet-"

"A well placed clone with the element of surprise might do great things for my . . . our advancement."

"Oh yes, Sander. This is more potent an advantage than I can say. Let me just show you who we have just completed. Number eleven I believe. Like a fine wine, these clones were selected with great care and you may find that one may be in the perfect time to be served. Come up on the dais."

It was an odd feeling, Shalinsky was shaking with excitement? Expectancy? Surely his friend was a treacherous a man as he'd ever known. Pirouen had killed his own father to ascend to Grand Master. Surely he could not be trusted with this and yet the time was ripe.

Pirouen placed a thin finger on the release button on the main console. The dark tank doors slid open and a mist of ice crystals and light poured out from the cylinder.

Shalinsky's face lit up as he leaned in to see the perfect naked body spread before him.

"Oh yes, this will do nicely."

*

Earth seemed in mourning not just for the billion people lost by the Pliilulua invasion, but for Ernestine Royce and Hugh Wilkey in particular. The crystal towers of all the ocean citiess in the world kept the flags at half staff for what the Prelate regarded as fallen hero's of the Green Party and for Hugh, perhaps even the fallen savior of all mankind. The motives of the Anarchists were not well fleshed by the press yet various factions claimed responsibility. Advocates of The Hunt and the Conservative Party were polite but cool and the Imperial Church said they would pray for them though they believed it would not save their souls even if they bothered to actually do so. The Mouth of The Prelate announced that Wilkey's New Boston home would be turned into a museum and a three hundred thousand credit reward was given for the capture or the body of his small grey animal, Cleo.

Lilly cancelled HCSIS training for the remainder of the week. It was the end of their training in any event and they were ready for immediate assignment on capital ships throughout the fleet and ready to take the fight to the invaders. She wished them well yet recalled how they looked at her in puzzlement when she tearfully declared the assassination of Hugh Wilkey, their trainer. She could not totally blame them, perhaps, as they all knew his politics did not make him popular with a good many citizens tied closely to the old ways. They may have just been shocked that a hardened ex Commander of The Order would allow such a display. Regardless, they sympathized politely and she wished them well.

The Order had not been forthcoming with any more data regarding the bombing. She had enquired and pulled every considerable string she had, of which there were many, but the methods and motives of the Anarchists group were not fully understood. Except for the small fact that she believed that all of such were long since destroyed, root and branch, every resistance cell burnt down. Could there have been one that lingered? Must be since at least one took credit in the holozines. Yet in her gut Lilly didn't believe it.

Hurrying through the streets of New Boston, she was dressed all in black. The wake was going to be broadcast to the entire Empire even though what was left of Hugh filled a coffee cup. Hugh's bodily remains were confiscated by the Imperial Science Academy, though the public would never know it was burying some burnt up clothes of his. At least a few of his skin cells would be there. Ernestine's corpse would make for a fuller casket.

Some children and their parents flicked by in their togas and the crowds were thickening as she approached the South side of the city. All wore black mourning belts of deep kelp in respect for the dead. Once the bodies were vaporized, their dust or sea salt would be commended to the deep of Mother Ocean. At least there was some piece left.

Lilly felt her belly and knew it would be a few more months and she would be ready to give birth. "Silly Hugh, you never suspected under my lab robes what I might be hiding."

Lilly did not know why she hadn't told Hugh about their connection when she was "resurfacing" his identity nine months before. It only happened once and it was so unlike her. She erased his memory of it thoroughly. After she had adjusted him, he was like any other man. It confounded her why she took advantage of her position, the trust of The Order, her orders and mated with him. Yet she knew it was never just some base need, she felt something for Hugh she had never felt for anyone before. She loved him.

Lilly sighed deeply to herself. The crowds were pressing in. She should have taken a hover disc but knew that for security reasons they would be banned, yet she could have cleared it. Perhaps she just wanted to be alone with her grief. Perhaps she just felt like she needed the exercise and would be waddling obscenely in another few months as she came to term.

It was instinct and it was perhaps just her training. She knew she was being followed. Not looking back, she skipped through some bushes and tried to hide herself in the crowd, fingering her khirda's pummel and trying to appear calm. I can fight but not with the baby. I need to lose whoever is tailing me.

Most women would have had the baby placed in a incubator when it was small and have a nutrient tank perfect the child during the last three months of development. Screened for disease, fed amplified food, and genetically monitored it was what women did. It's also how the Crafter Guild kept and eye on future citizen's and tended their gardens for purity. Hugh if he had lived would have wanted it to be natural, though Lilly's mother, also a doctor, would flip if she knew. Regardless she lost the tail and fifteen minutes later she started to relax.

Lilly turned through an alley and approached the main procession of the funeral mourners gathered in the thousands. Before she turned onto the street someone impossibly quiet grabbed her and stuck the nozzle of a gun into her back. Damn, can't fight with the baby. Her shoulders slumped and whispered to her unknown assailant, "I yield."

A familiar voice whispered back. "Of course you do."

*

The palace was full of Ushok-ku. It seemed like every one in the empire was here today for the Feast of Passing. Only the highest ranking Senators, Speakers, and Royals had been invited. The Capital was on high security alert. No weapon, not even khirdas were allowed in the Prelate's personal mansion inside the Summer Palace.

"Mi Lady, a pleasure to see you."

"Most kind my Lord." She turned around the corner, passed a battery of sniffers and entered the royal dining hall. The Sisters of The Grey Dawn were dancing in the center of the room, floating perfect bodies in a sea of grey green kelp lace. The Dance of Mourning was done at all passings, from the lowest small folk to the highest noble. The Sisters danced to the grim song of The Blackening. Traditionally played by another order of the Church, reminding all of the cycle of death, the return to the sea, and rebirth.

She saw her seat by the royals at the high table. Sander Shalinsky of the crafters leveled a cool look in her direction and turned back to a rep of the Trade Guild he'd been speaking with. Sanjay Dubey sat on the top tier behind the royals with his family. The three girls, two boys, and the beautiful First Wife, Anestheia, to his left. The Prelate had donned the Mourning Crown, a simple black, iron circlet, for centuries worn by the ruler of the Empire for a Galactic Days of mourning. Lilly passed streamers of kelp wine, the smells of innumerable roasts and rare dishes, and the bustle of servants attending the huge hall as the dance reached its climax.

The dancers whirled faster and faster, until their lithe feet were but blurs and the lace appeared cloud like around their bodies. The music soared to a crescendo as the musicians played the frenetic dirge, a low note of an oboe in the background climbed in volume cutting through the strings, horns, and drums, a lone anchor in the dizzying see of sound and movement. The Sisters rose from the ground as grav circlets spun them higher into the air until they floated like grey angels fighting the clutch of Earth.

Seating herself in the tier on the opposite side of Shalinsky and beneath the Royal tier on the far right, Lilly declined either brandy or succulent dishes picking absently at a soup with an intricate gold spoon. Ernestine would have sat next to her on this high seat of honor, yet in respect for her passing, and somewhat to Lilly's mild relief, it was empty, the music had reached its zenith and the Sisters the limits of their engineered endurance. Special chromatophoric light cells sewn into their laces started to glow like minute stars as the dancers actually started to glisten in their exertions. It reminded Lilly of a cruiser reactor going up on some distant day in her past but the oboe's forlorn note pushed her toward a purpose, pushed the trigger in her mind.

Lithely like a dancer, she watched intently the glowing human stars as her right hand removed a plating behind her. She easily lowered the small but thick section of pyranite that acted like a barrier between tiers. Even though the opening was smaller than her shoulders she tumbled back, past the small feet of the girls. The dancers of light burst the stars of their garments as the Sisters stopped, fell in the air to prone darkened lumps. The music stopped abruptly and the mild shock of silence filled the space more loudly than anything could, save for that single forlorn oboe.

Lilly Hsian stood behind Sanjay Dubey, who sensed her and stood. The oboe faded finally and no clapping was traditionally ever given after the religious dance. A long perfect silence for the dead and contemplation for them and their lives would continue until the Prelate gave his toast. "Lilly, Dr. Hsian, I am deeply sorry for your loss." He absently touched the simple iron crown on his head and regarded her with sincere sadness in his eyes. "Why are you up here with my family my good Lady? You will give my Speaker a conniptions to actual use my own voice."

"Your Grace." Lilly shot her hand forward with such speed the spoon severed the Prelate's carotid artery. The gold flecks of metal lodged in the back of his cerebrum as Lilly skillfully sheared through tissue and tendon. The gold camouflage wrap fell away as the sharpened pyranite weapon was revealed beneath. The poison wafered in its tip started to attack Sanjay Dubey's brain tissue. Even as the First Wife started to scream.

Lilly pulled the shank out of the Prelate before he fully hit the floor and deftly slammed it into the back of the neck of Anestheia, finding one of the small openings of her lower skull it easily passed and entered into her brain. The long auburn hair seemed to soak up the blood from the small wound as, dreamlike, she spun through the mission as training and augmentations had made her an avatar of death so many times before. The Order was renowned for its training.

The five children were frozen in horror at the death of their parents and the silence of the dance lingered on as the hundreds of people in the hall held their breaths in confusion as they watched the flashing white arms move in and out around the royal family. After Lilly dispatched the last of the princesses, like their mother before them, the audience started to scream mad murder. Lilly Hsian had killed five out of seven members of the Imperial family. The defense field that had supposed to have kept Lilly on the second tier tried to activate. It's minute sound clicking to her trained ear despite the mayhem. Yet it was quite too late.

Prince William Dubey was eight and had grabbed one of his own gold knives from the table to hold her off. His older brother and heir Ajit Dubey jumped in front of him in a fighting crouch. Imperial defense training and augmentations evident in his speed and unnerving strength. Lilly feinted with the weapon and the boy gave ground as his younger brother scuttled backward, his blunt knife extended in front of him despite the tears coming down his small face. Brave boys, she thought.

Ushok-ku were on the platform as Lilly feinted one more time past Ajit's guard.

She elbowed him in the face, breaking his nose with her left elbow and bringing her shank round to upper cut him in his neck like her father before him. She mused it was sad, so, sad, as time slowed and she concluded the late Prelate had activated an emergency beacon in his crown to bring the Ushok-ku so fast. It mattered little, her mission was nearly done.

Prince Ajit blocked the passage of the shank at his exposed neck adeptly enough, knowing it was the fastest route to his brain. The Crafters could heal and replace anything on the human body, anything except brain tissue. They both knew that as Lilly pushed the shank through his hand and into his grey matter, enough poison had been soaked through the metal, dispersed, that is would mean certain death. The poison was forbidden, unspeakable, called the Kracken's Klaw, and nothing escaped it. Since she had killed the Prelate it was coursing through her blood and would soon cross the blood brain barrier. She too would not escape. Yet she knew now she was never supposed to.

Feeling before hearing the rushing Ushok-kus halberds power up she saw Prince William had dropped his small knife and had brought himself to his feet as he turned toward the protection of the two Ushok-ku's coming to save him. Lilly Hsian threw the deadly shank and watched it appear to slowly spin through the air toward the screaming, fleeing princeling. She felt a pang as it struck blade first in the back of his head.

The Ushok-ku's could not speak. Yet they growled deeply in their throats as their long disintegration halberd's at last reached Lilly. She felt her skin for a second and the delicate, opaque veil that covered her body imploded from the antimatter contact. The growls turned to deep throated moans of anguish as Lilly's dust floated upon the dead family whose lives the greatest of the Imperial Royal Guard, the Ushok-ku, were born to protect.

*

It was dark and cramped in the shack where she was bound. Despite being gagged, bound, and hooded, she kept careful track of where she was being brought. They had gone a few miles through the private nature preserve in the South Side of New Boston. She could smell the earth and plants brushing at her legs as they passed and could think of no more secluded an area.

The hood was removed and the gag after she was seated. Her vision cleared and she could see implements along the walls. Metals shear's, knives, and various other tools of the trade. A ladder? She breathed a sigh of relief. A gardening shed. She had feared far worse. The bonds were tight around her belly.

"I see you have a bun in the over. How sweet. Don't you think the Crafters would be cross if they knew you trust them so little?"

"Sebastian."

"Of course Lilly. Who else but your little brother could bring the great lioness down." Sebastian's stealth suit powered down. He laughed at Lilly. "How the mighty have fallen. The Order would be so saddened to know how their legendary Commander Hsian could be brought so low."

"I let you take me you bastard."

"Oh I see, how motherly of you."

"That is the only reason why you live, dog."

Sebastian tisked tisked at her. "Sweet Lilly, I am no dog. I am a cat. No order from boot lickers do I have to follow. I am my own man."

"You are a criminal. Ever since the Order kicked you out of the program you used what little training you gleaned to be some, some mercenary. You broke our parents hearts."

"Shut up!" Sebastian "They had no hearts to break. What did I get from them except their polite contempt, pieces of flint to your diamond. They did not even have the courage to say what they really felt, to their last. Oh sure they said the loved us equally ever since we were born. But you, you were always first. You were so perfect. Even your false humility made me vomit."

"They loved you. I loved you."

"Bah. Enough. Be glad they are not alive to see you in disgrace."

"What are you talking about?"

Sebastian threw back his head and howled with laughter. Wiping a bit of spittle from his mouth his voice dripped acid. "You stupid cunt. Proud of you? Proud? You made a baby with a Genghonni pig. Spit on our traditions. You think my hair is black? Bitch. It's dyed. I am proud to be Oceanian. We are Empire. The future. You did well for HCSIS. But were never a true patriot. Now before I end you, I want to show you our real triumph. You are definitely to thank for our final victory."

He pulled up his wrist chron and dialed a local Holozine cast. The tiny speakers and video were difficult to see, but she could make out the Imperial Court's largest dining hall. There was a flurry of Senators and nobles pouring out screaming and then a camera droid panned to the over all enormous Imperial Court outside. Private discs and transports were streaming to and mostly from the court, and elite units were securing the plaza.

"Shocking news from the Imperial Court. Prelate Sanjay Dubey the Vth and his entire family were brutally assassinated by the trusted HCSIS project leader, Dr. Lillian Hsian. Eyewitness reports claimed that during the Grey Sister performance she some how disabled and broke through the defense perimeter and true deathed the Prelate, his wife, and four of the five of the royal heirs. Prince William perhaps will surprise us and live, but will be irreversibly brain damaged . . ."

"Shut it off."

Sebastian toggled off the wrist chron sat on a work bench with his back toward Lillian. "So you see, dear sister, you have been the agent of change."

"It wasn't me. It was a clone. I don't know how you got it past the sniffers Do you really think the Imperial Forensics wouldn't notice the epi-genome of a clone. You are finished dolt."

Sebastian drew back a syringe. "Nope. Not this clone. I am told it took ten years to grow it. When they sift through the disintegrated bits, they will find you. Have no doubt, in fact, after I inject this in you. You will appear to be the clone, if examined. Hold still dearest."

Lilly fought against the bonds with all her strength but hands and feet were bound to a metal chair, the cloth reinforced with a tough keratin threading. Sebastian slapped her so hard it broke her lip then jammed the needle down. "Did you really think you could man handle Senator Shalinsky and have him forget? Forgive? After the Prelate, Ernestine Royce, and the late great Hugh Wilkey, you were the last but not the least of his to do list."

Lillian glared at him helplessly. "You will not get away with this. If you think my clone was dangerous, you have no idea what I will do to this nest of vipers."

"I think I have some idea. You see, that was just the first injection. You are the only fly in the ointment Lilly. Now that you carry clone strands, highly accurate, and of Anarchist manufacture, you are less of a fly and more of a ghost."

He turned around and brought forth a smaller thirty two gauge needle, "with this I will promote you to full dead. Even if your body is ever found, you will be just a broken weapon from someone's arsenal. At least the Conservative movement got you at your prime."

"My baby."

Sebastian frowned. "Hmm. That is a consideration. After your dead some Crafters will have to fish it out and see if has any interesting bits. Then vaporize you."

Lilly was crying now, desperate. "But it's your nephew Sebastian. Please don't do this."

Sebastian drew himself up and looked at the needle. "Inside this is what you used to kill the Royal family. The Kracken's Klaw. Only rumored, if it existed at all, to be kept by Masters of The Order. They say that the secret of it is lost and only the smallest amount may yet exist. You should be honored Lilly. The expense. Alas, about my nephew, I prefer to have my own kids from the purer strain of the Hsians."

Lilly stopped crying, remembered her training, her iron resolve. "Then do it, coward, kill your pregnant sister. You could not have bested me, even seven months into my pregnancy. I do not want to hear your voice any more."

He sighed deeply. "You know it is more the pity. I would normally be swayed by such a play to excite our childhood rivalry. Yet to think of how much money I will be making by collecting this commission on your head. I think not. Goodbye sis."

Sebastian bore down on Lilly's arm with a gloved hand. Careful with the deadly syringe he moved cautiously and cooly. She closed her eyes and waited for oblivion. The needle drew close and it was all over, her baby, her life, and the damn Shalinsky would be set up to control the entire Colonial Empire.

The force of the glass breaking and the streaking eighty kilos of of grey fur knocked Sebastian to the ground and Lilly down on the floor. Her brother was screaming and fighting the mad animal that was tearing great rents in his stealth suit. It was Cleo.

The needle of venom landed right next to her face. Her head was all the way against the back of her chair but if the struggle knocked her into the glistening black needle, she would be as good as dead.

There was a wrenched scream from her brother and she felt hot spray flash against her legs. A confusing stream of emotions rushed through her, relief, and regret. She pushed it all aside. She was alone in a room with a huge animal. She felt sniffing at her toes, a deep growl. Cleo walked around on heavy clawed feet. Enormous and beautiful, her saber fangs were covered in blood, huge head and deep green eyes burned into Lilly's. She stayed very still and looked at the needle.

How could she communicate with Hugh's cat? "Cleo, the needle is poisoned. Push it away but don't touch it." Cleo growled at her. She doesn't have an ear for human speech, is what Hugh had said. He also said she was smarter than most people.

Lilly tried to focus with her eyes on the needle, her body language. "All right cat, what now?" Ten minutes went by and Cleo shrunk down into her small cat body form and started licking herself. Lilly could not keep her body up from the needle too much longer.

Cleo padded up to her face, meowed, sniffed at the needle, made that strange, loose face. The one all cat's use when they found a new smell, then shook her narrow head.

She looked around, jumped up on the table and brought down a small wrench in her teeth. She dropped the wrench on the ground before the syringe and pushed on the needle from the far end of the wrench with her little grey paws. The needle rolled away and Lilly set her tired head on the floor.

The cat padded behind her. It took a an hour or so it seemed but Cleo managed to loosen her left hand. Lilly's arms felt broken, where it was caught between the side of the chair and the floor. Whether from the crash or the wait to free herself, she could not feel her hand. Awkwardly, she pushed the chair on her back with Cleo's help, who jumped up to saber tooth size briefly to muscle her over.

Lilly released her right arm and felt for breaks. It might just be bruised to a pulp rather than broken. She used both hands to untie her legs though getting around her belly was hard from that position. Cleo helped as much as she could considering she didn't have true hands, though she tried hard to mold them to optimal effect.

"Thank you Cleo, for saving my life."

The cat looked at her demurely. Licking herself absently, while seeming a bit thin from exposing her ribs from that angle. Changing form cost them a lot of flesh or re-growing lost limbs Hugh had told her and now she observed. Matter could be stretched and molded, but neither created nor destroyed. It had to come from somewhere. Lilly had to get Cleo and herself some food. Yet thanks to her brother she would set off every clone sniffer from here to Oceania."

"What are we going to do Cleo? We are both fugitives now?"

Cleo stared at her then returned to grooming herself. Lilly would have to figure out a way. She looked at Sebastian's body, he had been raked horribly and his throat had been torn out. Lilly stifled the urge to cry. It didn't suit her. She picked up her blaster and her khirda and looked over at Cleo.

"Cleo, where there is life, there's hope. Let's see if we can get you some food, though I seem to have lost my appetite, I fear we may need Cleo tiger again and soon."

Chapter 8.5

Johnny Blue

Jason Flick, personal guard and sometime lover of the late Ernestine Royce brought the package to the darkening shore. It looked more like a coffin though the sleek sides of the shiny, black box was covered with gauges and lights. The escape pod had used all it's limited power to stealth away from New Boston after the explosion. A contained fusion generator on the pod would have been like shooting a flare at the Imperials as it slowly churned from the depths of the city.

The grief had been bitter but Jason pushed it deep inside. Ernestine's dying wish was clear, even if it contradicted every sense of justice in his being. The two man pod bumped onto the greying shore of the land as darkness fell. Body scans indicated no activity on this section of beach, but that might change rapidly when full darkness fell.

He gathered the necessary survival gear and weapons for himself and his charge and punched in the landing code.

The red alert of the ship's debarkation sequence engaged as it jetted water to push far up on shore. The nozzle section of the cylindrical ship depolarized and and tilted up for full access to the stoney beach. The air was full of pine smells with the constant tang of the Blackening ever present. "Damn it to hell. Here it goes."

The package was floated out by the A.I. of the limited pod, beeped twice, and closed after Flick set final confirm code on his wrist chron. The pod sunk into the black water like a dying fish and settled to the bottom, where it powered down before it's power simply died. He knew this was a one way trip.

"Wakey wakey, sunshine, time to pay back your debt." Flick was satisfied with the regen on the package and shut down the gas that kept the occupant compliant. It would be so easy to push the thing into the water and let it slowly power off and drown him. It would not be something he could live with however much it may be deserved. Perhaps he could redeem himself to all the others but he would never forgive him. Yet only duty seemed to matter now; and his word bond to his dying love.

The lid shifted back revealing the hairy Genghonni known as Hugh Wilkey. Naked and still asleep, Flick was amazed he grew back his face, all four of his limbs, the delicate tissues of his manhood and all his skin from the stumpy remains of his body. The smell of burnt flesh still lingered and Flick kicked the side of the regeneration pod. "Get up." He threw a survival suit at Hugh as he stirred groggily.

"Get up and get dressed, I don't want to look at your disgusting body. We have to get shelter."

"Flick?" Hugh took a few minutes to get his bearing, He remembered the bomb going off and Ernestine flying backward and then . . . nothing. "Where is Ernestine?"

"Dead." Flick's voice was bitter. "Dead because of you."

Hugh started pulling on his clothes. He felt horrible. His skin hurt and felt prickly. Famished, he pulled a full bore needle connected to empty emergency plasma tubes from his neck and another connected to several now empty tubes of a dense protein, high nutritive mix from his other carotid. "I am sorry for your loss. I will miss Ernestine. Though I didn't plant the bomb, Flick."

Flick grunted and scanned beyond the hills of the landing for movement and kept his wrist chron scanning for heat signatures within three hundred yards. "That may be so. Yet you brought her into danger, you caused her to become even more of a target."

"I did not choose to be here. Ernestine chose to help me. Though I wish it was me who had died."

"I agree with you there. But wishing won't change anything. So let me bring you up to speed. The Prelate is dead. Your friend Lilly Hsian apparently went berserk and killed the entire royal family. HCSIS is running on it's own and you are of no further use to the Imperial Government. Ernestine made me promise to get you to the resistance. Your best hope to evade people like Shalinsky from killing you is to continue to be dead. That is what Ernestine made me promise to help you do."

"Thank you."

"Fuck you and activate your suit. I'm not doing this for you. The suit is chargeable during the day. It provides camouflage and not full stealth, but if we keep alert it should be enough to let us avoid getting eaten by your relatives. We have a long way to go."

Hugh bit down his urge to crush the arrogant prick. He must have been really close to Ernestine, he reflected. The pack was heavy and full of compressed food, all kinds of survival supplies, medical, camping, and other. It was rather efficient despite weighing about thirty kilos. He fished through it and started eating an MRE. When he was in the Navy of his time, so long ago, they were called 'meals ready to eat' then too.

It struck Hugh how lucky he was to be alive, yet, and the feeling of dread hit him even harder. "Where is Cleo? My pet"

"Dead is my guess. The explosion killed everything. Now pack it up we are leaving. Put on your night goggles and keep up or I am leaving you here."

Hugh thought this asshole was going to get tired real fast, but understood the man's anger. He may have lost someone too. Cleo. *Cleo are you out there? Can you hear me."*

Hugh hated the silence. There was no response as he pulled the heavy pack on his back and jogged to catch up to Flick. He pulled the goggles out of his belt and pushed them on his head. They activated displaying everything around them in tones of dark to red. The reddest being the broad back of Flick from his body heat. It was like wearing very red tinted glasses during the day even though it was black as pitch outside. Hugh could even read his wrist chron.

They may need the great advantage if the surviving humans hunted them. "Where are we going, Flick?"

"A place called Springfield. We have a safe house there."

Hugh actually used to go out to the military base there from Boston when he was in his twenties. It was over a two hour drive from Worcester. They were in Boston. "It's going to take weeks to get there."

Flick kept on going. "The dead don't care. Everyone you used to know is dead or as good as dead. We are going there to see if you can be of any use to the resistance."

Hugh thought of this as they walked over what used to be a cobbled street. Hugh found an old sign, it must have been over a thousand years old and he could barely make out the words. "Front Street." They were in Marblehead, North of Boston. There was a restaurant called The Barnacle that stood over there, though nothing much was left but over grown basement stones.

He remembered once during a storm in better times he drove up there with Micheal. Water crashed from a winter storm up onto the roof but food was served regardless and there was much cheer in the 1990's. The second time he went was in 2008, the economy had gone bad and the mood of the patrons was grim and insular. They had little interest for anything outside themselves and he had not been back.

Now their cool restaurant and their wealth both old and new had long since been washed from the coast by the sea and time. It was probably only due to the protected harbor that it even still stood on the rocky shore in ruins. "Flick, I am not so sure that Cleo or Lilly are dead. We should go back for them."

Flick turned around in a rage and grabbed Hugh by the collar. "Then go back. Swim to New Boston! You wretch. I don't care. Our pod will probably not rise again due to the power we used to sneak out. Come with me or go. But shut up. The Ghengonni will come soon, see along the ridge. You will get us killed. Do not make me tell you again."

Hugh was sorely tempted to leave Flick there. Yet he saw about fifty red dots of bipedal movement two hundred yards North East of their position. He would stay with Flick until he could not take another word. He figured the Resistance was what the Greens called the group. Everyone else called them Anarchists. Yet he knew he was out of options and needed to let this play out. He could not swim to New Boston and he was safer dead.

Flick and Hugh skirted around the tribe easily enough. They seemed to be heading off toward the craggy shore.

Snow was falling down, tinged with red from his goggles. He imagined the sky was dropping blood on all the world, crying tears of blood.

It was hard being home when home was all obliterated and everyone he ever knew was dead. Yet there was time when his people, the people of his time, were self absorbed selfish children. Tied to whatever reasons they had to live, their own myopic lives, and not much of a community.

They passed burnt and blackened church yards. He remembered in the end days how religion worked is way back into politics and much against all the founding fathers wishes, Christianity became America's majority political party. A conservative faction got its hooks into every aspect of the Federal Government and bought into bringing on the rapture. Shaking hands with Jesus was so high a priority they welcomed the destruction and their lack of resistance brought on what the populace was too divided and myopic to stop. The Blackening.

Yet those fundamentalists, the richest or the smartest really knew they were just shoveling their piety down the throats of the little people. The gullible masses. The vast majority of the leaders were only too eager to save their own sanctimonious skins. They took their communities tithings and made sure their own anointed and baptized hides were first and last to fill the limited shelters of the under sea gardens of the first three cities of Oceania. Their flocks were left to harvest the Blackening and perish.

At least the lucky ones. The Genghonni survived if one can call it that. Hunting each other and being hunted by the descendants of those sworn to protect them. Flick was one of those bastards whose conceited ancestors abandoned his fellows all those centuries before. It was ironic he was so angry at Hugh considering the blood on his line's hands.

It was midnight as they crossed a river over a crudely made wooden bridge. The snow was getting a few inches deep and they seemed to be passing a thickly brushed and secluded part of of what was Marblehead. Hugh looked up through a break in the clouds and saw the dull silver reflection of the ring station of Earth. He felt a pang for the old sky and the moon that he remembered as a child.

Flick started to make camp. It must have been about ten degrees celsius and the Forest loomed up all around them. The Earth had been busy repairing itself and even the smell of Blackening seemed less in this dense copse of trees as they breathed deeply. The small tents were made of a similar, pulpy, light rubber cloth that his suit was contrived of. It was porous and warm when cold outside and cool when hot. Body sensitive fabric would keep them comfortable and shower free for a while.

The bacteria long since removed from Oceanian skins would not create smells from their trek, but oils and skin cells still needed to be removed and their suits snapped out if not washed. Hugh watched Flick purify snow and test it with his wrist chron. Hugh followed closely not wanting to talk to the brusque guard and still not wanting to poison himself. Flick seemed satisfied the purified water would not kill him. So they both drank and turned into their separate tents.

Hugh looked through the flap of his tent, "good night, Flick."

Flick did not respond and Hugh was not surprised. It had already been a very long trek making his way through the new world and now it seemed it would be longer and lonelier than ever. Cleo, Ernestine, and Lilly all dead and the Pliilulua could be dropping down any day to destroy humanity again. The dark was deep and silent and unnerving, Hugh tossed and turned all night on the cold hard ground.

*

Lillian held the shroud over her head as she made her way to the debarkation platform of New Boston. With any luck her personal jump shuttle may not have been impounded. The baby kicked in her belly yet she ignored it. It sensed her stress she imagined. She hoped Cleo was close at her heals. Outside of the baby inside her, she was the only part of Hugh left to her.

What was she thinking. She should turn herself in? There must be a way to prove she was innocent? Yet she knew it was hopeless. In the darkest times the greatness comes, so the Masters said, and she had a great plan if not a good one. Yet once she set off a sniffer she would be running for her life.

Sniffers by Imperial decree were scanning bugs, alert systems set in a web across the entire Colonial Empire. Clones and poisons were their primary objective in life, and though bio-organic, self reproducing, they were all connected to the security web of The Order. Any anomaly in any inhabited part of the known colonized human empire would trigger a reaction by security until the perpetrator was found and terminated. Lilly would only have one chance to see them before they detected her. They moved, the insects, like insects do; they could be anywhere in their micro patrols.

Lilly wished she could somehow tell Cleo to track them, yet she could not think of any, save finding one and shooting it. Maybe luck would be better than skill, though her trainers in the Order would blanch if she ever admitted to such a philosophy. She would take anything she could get as she dashed from bush to shadow in the rising dawn.

The lift leading to the debarkation hub was within sight. Her security pass was worthless. Or was it? Would they cancel the clearance of a dead woman. There might be a chance, Keeping her mourning veil on she hoped her black hair would not gather too much attention. She walked confidently to the lift. The khirda's noble pedigree and rank arrogance of aristocracy might get her through.

"Hold Lady." No such luck, an Imperial blocked her path. "We need identification clearance, the city is under martial law since his majesty's assassination. In fact, I'm not sure you haven't been breaking curfew."

"I am first wife to Alzhir Elzam, Master Crafter of the Imperium. You will let me pass or you will forever gain grafts of the rankest Ghengonni scraps that will crawl your skin and rot your eyes."

The Imperial looked as his colleague worriedly, stammered. "Apologies Lady, th th this way."

She entered the lift and glared at them until they turned around and returned to parade rest, eyes locked forward.

As the lift climbed the two miles seemed to taker forever. Her plan was simple, desperate, and insane. Lillian was going to try to steal a dreadnaught. Shalinsky used a lot of strings to put Nova into moth balls. Presumably as an honor to her service and a last ditch Capital Ship to face the Pliilulua in the impossible event they destroy the new HCSIS fleets sent against them. Luckily, Lilly had planted a slave program in the unlikely event the Imperial government of the Dubey Reign turned violently against her.

Lilly had giggled disdainfully at her extreme paranoia and risk in planting the subtle program. For some reason, the moth balling of Nova had been rushed and from her wrist chron, she sent a tight beamed code to Nova's sleeping brain. Now the only thing to stop her was a sniffer they may not have had the time or foresight to set up. As if to give Lilly encouragement Cleo let herself become visible, meowed at her, then stealthed again.

It was then that Lilly noticed the sniffer.

The size of a roach, her augmented eyes caught the miniature droid with its sensitive scanning antennae vigorously twitching toward her. She pulled out her gun and pegged it with a single red beam. As the lift came to a stop at the terminal floor, she watched the dust of the thing glitter to the floor in a trail of smoke, a blaster scorch on its vacated roost on the immaculate white lift.

"Not good, Cleo." The alarms on the terminal started to blare. It had transmitted.

"Attention all Citizens, this is not a drill. Clone detection on lift. Please move calmly to security pods and remain there. This is not a drill . . ."

Lilly started running for her jumper. Please God, let her access code work.

Beam weapons started striking near her position, they were set to kill judging from the color of the beams and the melted pyranite decking. Clones were shot on sight.

"Cleo, I know you don't understand me but run!"

Being of the Order, Lilly had access to the nearby parking grid. Her family insignia marked her small transport in the distance. There were also well trained Marines set up in a kill zone between the two second floor alcoves between her and escape. Lilly pulled out her Khirda and punched up the shield. Please be bad shots.

Lilly launched herself forward and spun into a rolling dive, half as fast and twice as careful as she could have been considering her pregnancy. The shield was set to her right and her surpressing fire from her weapon was set in automatic which would drain its cells after one hundred fast shots. It was her only chance.

She felt the impact of the Marines on her right on her shield. One direct hit shook her terribly but the shield held. Another hit would kill her as she ran toward the last ten yards to the hatch. The auto fire had put to ground the Marines on her left and the she almost dropped the weapon as it over-heated her hand. Two more shots knocked her shield down and her khirda shut down, unable to absorb any more. The Marine's on her right would kill her dead.

Except for the sabre-tooth ripping into them and the men and women's screams of despair as the cat tore them to pieces taking them fully by surprise. The Marines on her left were taking aim. Praying she whipped the dead blaster at them with all her strength and punched her security card through the hatch's I.D. interface. Please please please please please.

The security light was taking forever and she risked a glance behind to see the Marines on her left flank must have thought she threw a grenade and one of them had her in his sights and fired. Lilly angled her blade in front of her and deflected the first beam. Her arm went numb from the conduction. At last the hatch clicked open. Dear God, thank you for trusting the dead to die and not come back for their things!

Lilly climbed into the hatch and made her way to the ship. Her ship! It could get her to orbit. It could save her life. Their lives. Cleo! She turned toward the end of the three foot hatch, noting the deep black water that surrounded the clear pyranite connection tube to her hull. "Cleooooo!," Lilly yelled.

The cat jumped through the tube ten times faster than she did. Cleo almost reached the end when she roared in pain and slid the rest of the way scorched and smoking in her small cat form. Lilly slammed the hatch and filled the tube with water as they prepared to debark in haste from New Boston. She did not have time to check the cat but jumped to the pilot side of the two man ship and punched it to maximum speed from the top of the city's dome. Lilly noticed on scans about ten attack craft detaching from the hub in pursuit. That is when the first defense cannon almost blew the small ship apart.

Blinded by the flash of the gigantic laser strike, Lilly hit the over drive by instinct more than sight. Only crafts of The Order had an over drive. It would burn out the engine so badly it would need weeks of repair before it could be started again. Lilly smiled at herself as she bobbed and weaved her way to the surface. This was a one way trip anyway, though she always sort of liked this transport and her gun. A weapon that had been in her family for generations. The dead don't own anything she reminded herself as several of the pursuing fighters opened up on her ship.

Cleo limped up on the opposite seat and hissed. Her flank was raw and bloody, but the smoking had stopped and the black and grey pattern of fur was re growing before Lilly's eyes. Thank God you are hard to kill. Cleo may or may not have noticed Lilly's relief as she had extended a paw like a finger and yowled at her.

Looming before them was a Kraken. It was within three hundred meters and it's enormous arms were shooting out at the school of fish that was her and the pursuing fighters. "Shit." This skiff had no blood to deter the leviathan. Bona fortuna Lilly would make the predator work for her. She pushed hard at the wheel and dived around it at max speed. The overdrive humming and a two ton pad of spikes, suckers, and untimely death flashed by her and struck one of the fighters.

Cleo went flying onto the panel landing on her feet and screeching even louder. "If only you could talk! If I hadn't buckled my neck would have been broken if it makes you feel any better. I'm sorry you don't have hands."

No hands but Cleo dug in claws after jumping back to the seat and amplified them. She was not going anywhere now. Not without the co-pilot's seat breaking off from the base. A good thing too as Lilly banked and spun upside down and Cleo pushed her small face into the seat in order not to look.

Lilly was going around the Kraken and the fighters were having a hard time keeping up to her. The hull creaked from the depressurization as they climbed the last half mile to the surface. The blue water lightened giving hope as she rocketed into the morning light like a breaching whale and switched to rockets the second before they would fall back into the Atlantic.

Cleo looked miserable but managed to release her rear paws and bolster herself by re sinking them into the back seat. Lilly bit her lip over how miserable she looked. "Sorry Cleo, we will be in orbit soon." She punched up her wrist chron and saw that Nova had powered up. The program was working.

"Nova, this is Commander Hsian! I need you to open the topside emergency bay as soon as we hit orbit! Allow no other access to you."

"Hello, Miss Hsian. My records indicate you are not only dead, but disbarred of The Order and according to my analysis of your system, you are a clone."

Lillian did not know what to say. It was like talking to a person. The slave program would not be able to be shaken. As formidable as Nova's security was, she was on the inside of all of it when she dropped the program into its protected brain casing directly. Her function in HCSIS made it necessary to have access, though it made her twinge to think she could have taken advantage of her station yet again, it seemed a good thing she did."

"Nova comply."

There was silence over the com as Lilly clenched her teeth as they were punching through the last part of the stratosphere, four surviving fighters closing to within firing range. Her skiff was shaking violently as she rocketed toward the great ring. Her timing had not been random, she calculated when Nova would be at the Zenith of New Boston and she could see the large vessel rising like a round cold comet before here.

"Nova opening emergency shuttle bay, top side."

"Thank God." Lilly sighed and relaxed slightly as they exited orbit and the threshold of Earth Space. The slave program was not deniable.

"Commander, I regret you are under attack by the space station."

Her relaxation had been slight even before an array of weapon systems opened fire from in front and behind. The near miss lurched the whole skiff and would have destroyed them if they were not moving so fast. The emergency lights came on as she struggled to regain control.

"Nova, disable the weapon systems! Nova! Disable-"

"Sorry Commander, unable to comply."

The slave program. "Nova, I order you to disable them."

"Your slave program was good Commander, but I would never fire on Imperial Ships or personnel even if the program was fully effective."

Lilly was confused and astounded simultaneously. Nova used 'I'. What had HCSIS done to the artificial intelligence? "Nova I am not a clone."

"I know. Having appraised myself of the news of the assassination, I have come to the conclusion that you are the real Commander Hsian. The assassin was the clone. Who else would know the code of the slave program."

Lilly thought about this as she approached Nova's hull, weaving madly as blasts riddled the air behind the smoking engines. "How do you know it did not acquire the code?"

"I would know. Engaging shield and warning away the fighters. Decelerate or you will die, Commander."

Nova was right. Lilly kicked in the emergency braking thrusters and skidded into the bay close to the bridge. Cleo's hair was sticking out but otherwise they were both fine. She listened to the pressure rise in the bay and opened the hatch.

They left the burnt and burning skiff. A shame really. "Nova, prepare to break orbit and go to warp."

"Unable to comply, Commander."

Lilly slapped herself in the head. She had come so far and actually got here. This was supposed to be the easy part of her impossible plan. "Nova, report why unable to comply."

"I am unable to comply Commander because five Imperial Destroyers are blocking my path-"

Lilly finished with Nova ", I will not shoot on Imperial Ships or personnel."

Some moments passed as she noticed Nova moving out of dock. "So where are we going Nova. You won't fight and we can't go to warp through them."

"There is a plan. Hugh Wilkey's plan, to be more specific."

This was not possible. "Nova, Hugh is dead."

"Negative commander, Hugh Wilkey is alive."

Was there some residual part of HCSIS that had been corrupting to Nova's computer core? "Explain, Nova."

"Hugh Wilkey's life signs are detectable via HCSIS systems and it is unmistakable Commander. He is alive and outside the ruins of Boston."

Dumbfounded. The floor vibrated as Nova came under fire from the ships closing outside. "What are we going to do then. What is this plan." She wiped a tear from her face. Hugh was actually alive. Lilly's heart would not let her believe it.

"Most of my major functions have been hard wired to the battle bridge of the escape cruiser in the base of Nova's superstructure. It is small compared to my dreadnaught structure, but all important data has been placed there. It is where I am speaking to you from. Make your way to deck 00, we have five minutes until shield failure and hull breach under current attack projections.

Lilly did what she was told and ran down the hall to the lift. It took four minutes to carry her to the basement of the ship. The cruiser was essentially a secondary bridge, about one twentieth of the mass of Nova and standard on dreadnoughts as well as escape pods. It was warp capable, even stealth capable. A saucer with a smaller saucer in the base of its structure.

Lilly reached 00 deck and was knocked to her knees by the force of a blast hitting the hull as the shields failed. "Almost there! What is the damn plan."

"We use the superstructure of the dreadnaught to cover us, detach and stealth before the explosion consumes us, return and rescue Hugh Wilkey."

It was chancy yet it seems she was in the hands of the new Nova and Hugh's shadow. She buckled herself into the battle bridge, roughly ten seats in a circle around the new computer core that was Nova's new home. "Cleo and I are in."

"Very good Commander, my estimate seems to have been a bit generous. Superstructure imploding now. Brace for emergency detachment, now!"

The small saucer of the battle bridge spun off from the structure. Lilly and Cleo watched as the bottom of Nova's belly filled their view and it exploded. The battle bridge screamed and shook as shields took the brunt of the blast but alarms and electrical shorts cascaded over several of the bridge stations. Nova seemed to have moaned.

It was dark and the emergency lights came on softly. Bits of machinery and cables hung from the ceiling and littered the deck.

"Nova status."

The ship's voice seemed distorted either due to damage or the re routed com systems of the cruiser. "We are no longer warp capable commander. The warp field generator is destroyed. Otherwise we are stealthed and seem able to land in Boston with minimal chance of detection.

Lilly nodded. Strange as it was, living out the rest of her life on the cruiser somewhere discrete in the wilds of old Earth did not seem the worst fate in the world. Yet something told her it would not be that easy.

*

Flick and Hugh woke with the sun. Their survival gear was top notch and kept all of the cold out of their respective tents even without a fire. If humans had these materials back in his day there would have been less conflict over heating and running their society, yet Hugh knew it was all dust in the wind.

A foot of snow had fallen to the south of the ruins of Marblehead. Hugh slept with his goggles on and tucked them away as flick bristled at him again for packing too slowly. He just always wanted to be accepted by his hetero brothers his whole life, always feeling second best to the manly men who just beat their way through the world. Whether it was his large hypothalamus or some hidden choice, even if the men of his time were beautiful, arrogance, cruelty, and or casual slander always made them throughly repugnant with a word. Flick had all four pitfalls. He'd just as soon fuck a squirrel.

High in the sky near the ring of the Space Station were bright flashes of light and a dazzling explosion. "Look above." Flick glanced up and shrugged as he headed off to the south east through the black brush. Flick had saved his life regardless of his reasons, he would do his best to stomach his crude company. The flash of light troubled him but he let it pass as he hurried to catch up.

Ahead they were hugging the base of an ashy marsh. Lightly frozen they stayed clear of the possible ankle holes just below the surface. Flick pulled out his blaster and activated his stealth suit to blend more whitely into the background, pulling up his hood. Hugh followed suit and fell to the snowy Earth.

"What is it, Flick?"

"Listen, fighting ahead, we will skirt around."

They moved up to the dead bushes on a hill and kept low. There was a rustle of leaves and a greenish skinned, limping humanoid of some size ran past them luckily not seeing them against the snow. The thing carried a spear and walked with a lolling gate. It's eyes were yellowish and it gave a whistle through a set of sharp looking teeth.

All about them to the east, two score of the brutes pushed up tightly woven shields they had used to cover the holes they hunkered down in with the snow hiding them perfectly. The things lurched off to the East. Strangled cries were heard as they reached a clearing directly ahead of them. Human cries.

Flick waited silently and waved his hand forward when the coast was clear.

He headed slowly back toward where they had come from. "Flick!" Hugh whispered as loud as he dared, "there are people being hurt. We should help them."

Flick turned a hard grey eye a him, "die if you want Wilkey." He kept on crawling without looking back.

To hell with him. Hugh moved forward towards the screams. The Ghengonni if it was them, or whoever was being attacked deserved help. At least he could get to know these people as long as he was hidden even if he couldn't save them. He was a corpsman back in the day and took an oath. It was an oath to serve, heal, and protect. It ought to still apply.

Upon reaching the far side of the marsh the twenty green people were locked in combat with more human colored people. They wore skins over their loins and carried axes made of stone, though one seemed to carry a fire axe. There were also a line of six bowman in the smaller group, as well as a woman and child. The dozen had been taken by surprise and the bowman were hard pressed to get range. The men with axes were buying them time as the woman and child fled, yet Hugh knew it would be a massacre.

The largest of the green men skewered one of the axe wielders on a bloody spear. Though two archers on either side of the iron axe man felled two greens flanking the big one. A third arrow struck the giant in the leg as he pulled out his spear from the dead man, hardly grunting. They men had the same broken larynxes as the other Genghonni from the hunt he'd seen. They could still scream as another fell and the ten greens on either side were set to rush and flank the defenders.

Hugh aimed his blaster and fired full bore into the green line on automatic. Even if he had to stun them all he would sort them out later after he stopped the blood-shed. The leader of the greens pointed at Hugh and roared out a challenge as the remaining ten spearman turned and battled with the archers. The leader green charged at Hugh.

The creature on closer view and at speed would have intimidated a killer whale. The howl it uttered rattled Hugh's ears and made his blood run cold, more so when a direct hit of the stun beam did not even slow it down. The spear was leveled at his chest and Hugh froze momentarily, eyes focused on the rust two foot spike of barbed metal. Within three meters he reached out with his mind and pushed the brute back.

At first the creature merely slowed. It was stronger than a bull and inched forward until Hugh could see droplets of blood dripping off the cruel barb. Then the creature was being pushed back through the snow and soil, its foot claws digging rents in the earth. A second roar of rage escaped its twisted mouth and it's massive arm whipped the spear at Hugh. It soared for his head like a comet and poised to skewer him dead.

A bolt of a red killing beam smashed it out of the air. Flick took aim on the frozen green skin leader and blew a foot long hole through it's massive chest. Blood flew across the marsh and it crumbled to the ground steaming in the cold winter air. Hugh turned away as the thing's mouth and hands continued to work.

The men locked in battle were down to four of the original ten defenders.

A dozen of the greens were pushing their advantage as one smaller one in the rear sounded a horn. Another horn answered in the distance to the south, then the east.

"Shoot the green's Flick, *on stun.* Or I will shoot you myself."

Flick looked at him in incredulously but made the adjustment on his hand weapon and opened fire on the green men.

Within moments the surviving humans, three men, the woman, and child were running by them. The axe man looked at Hugh and Flick with a mixture of fear and confusion. He moved his hands quickly and Hugh only recognized one sign. Run.

They ran. Back from where they came. The Ghengonni were thin and fast. The fact that Hugh and Flick were better nourished and augmented was the only reason they kept up. Hugh hazarded a glance back and saw what seemed a hundred greens flying after them even faster, guttural howls filling the night air.

One man with a bow stopped, started to rub flint and steel together over a bundled arrow. Hugh made the sign for fire. Set his gun to low beam and ignited it. The man with the bow grunted and shot the flaming arrow into the air and redoubled his speed back to Marblehead.

The army of greens was almost upon them. Their bestial whoops and screams were hard to bear and some crude looking spears were thrown at great distance narrowly missed them. Hugh noticed that the shafts were flexible and had crude fletching. They were atlatl's. Deadly and primitive as the man with the steel axe found when one went through his right leg. Hugh stopped and tried to help him but he only pushed him away.

Hugh lifted him up with his magnetic power. The strain was terrible yet the practice he had done conditioning and honing his skill paid off, Hugh ran and carried the large man in the field at the same time. He could not go far with this especially as the man struggled in fear. There was not time to explain.

They reached a stone wall of the fleeing Ghengonni and a crude if broken down brick structure that must have been an ancient home from Hugh's time. The roof was long gone but the second floor held ten more of the Ghengonni tribe archers who seemed ready and alert to the incoming horde of greens skins.

"This is not our fight, Hugh. We can't win. Our blasters are almost depleted."

Hugh moved the large man through the air roughly and set him down with his fellows before he collapsed from the strain. "Then leave, Flick. You've done enough, it's not your fight anyway."

Flick spat on the ground. 'Bollocks." He sighed heavily and crawled up a crude ladder after the woman and her youngling. Hugh caught his breath and went up also pulling the ladder behind him. A hail of arrows and atlatl's sailed through the air as the horde found them and surrounded them.

Flick picked up a spear and felt its weight. He had no idea how to use a bow but set his gun in the sun so the light would begin to recharge the cell. "Set yours up too, Hugh. It might be worth a shot we last that long,"

"Aye". Hugh then pulled out his khirda and grabbed a spear from the pile. What am I doing? Flick is right, this wasn't their fight. Yet it felt right. He looked at the frightened Ghengonni of the tribe as they struggled to keep the greens skins off the second floor as they shot arrows at the attackers. Outnumbered ten to one, some of the atlatls found men and killed them dead with solid shots through the torsos. Hugh turned to a man trying to staunch a wound in a wailing comrade.

Looking at the man's face, he saw blue plastic fused to the well shaped cheek. A blue eye and a black. "John?"

The man looked at him and smiled. His sign was fast and still strange to Hugh but John pointed to his fused face and signed "*blue*".

"Johnny Blue?"

The man signed "yes" and thanked Hugh. It would take time to learn their dialect, yet hand signs were all based on dialect. It was lucky they knew any common words at all. More horns were blowing from the green skins. Another bowman fell dead near them. Johnny Blue signed a bit more rapidly but it was not comprehensible to Hugh, except for one word, "*sorry.*"

Hugh saw a green skin jump up onto the second floor from a tree and raise a stone axe high over his head to smash Hugh's brain's out. Hugh raised his hand and forcing the power through his body sent the thing flying ten yards off the building. Sweat beaded his brow but he asked Johnny "*why sorry?*"

"*Sorry we die.*" Johnny turned away, his broad back bent as he picked up a yew bow and took his position on the platform to shoot down at the screaming horde. Looking into the man's blue and black eye, he felt a tinge of terrible regret that it would all come to this.

Better to die fighting. Flick was cursing avidly as a spear narrowly missed his neck but cut deep as it passed him by. The three inch gash narrowly missed opening an artery.

Hugh sprayed the wound with a skin sealant and hurled a spear at a creature rising up onto the platform as soon as it's torso loomed into view. The tip did not sink deeply but sent the thing back.

Bowman were falling left and right and the survivors were being forced to defend in the center with sharp sticks and crude axes. Flick made superb use of the crude spear, knocking brute after brute screaming over the side but he had two untreated, new gashes that were bleeding heavily and weakening him by the minute. Hugh was too tired to use his powers to much effect after lifting the steel axe around. He was amazed the large man fought on his knees like an animal, hewing off legs and hands with abandon with a spear tip still plunged into his leg.

There were about twenty greens on the platform with six Ghengonni standing. Johnny Blue took a hit to his arm and the steel axe man finally feel, gutted by a brute with a machete. Hugh was horrified and near sick when on of the green skins started gnawing on an arm. They were cannibals.

The greens had them and he was to die here on the savage remains of his old city and their devolved descendents. It was a great pity in a way, yet, if he had to go he knew he tried to do right even with the mistakes he had made.

A green skin pulled its arm back and aimed the spear straight at Hugh's chest. This time there would be no evading. His power was exhausted, his right arm was held in a lock with a sharp onyx knife wielder, and his left held a broken spear handle. He wished he could see Cleo again and wondered why he ever left home.

I'm here Hugh. And you left home to find home.

Cleo!

The cruiser flashed a blinding light on the battle raging below. The forty meter flying saucer blinded everyone with its search beam, so much brighter than the cloudy light of the sun. A gatling gun of precision laser strikes started to blast apart the green skins in spectacular and gruesome bursts of fire and gore. Within five minutes the 2nd floor of the building was cleared of them, the remaining fifty were running like hell, and the handful of Ghengonni and two humans covered their heads as the magnetic field of the cruiser hummed and vibrated their bodies like an earthquake.

"This is the Imperial Cruiser Nova. Hugh Wilkey are you hurt?"

"Nova, you've lost weight." He smiled and cried in equal measure.

The Cruiser moved away from the building and landing in a clearing fifteen yards away. Scan lights and three small laser cannons skitted back and forth occasionally sending warning shots at anything that lingered to close. A hatch door slid open and stairs slid down to the ground. A woman with a rifle and a large cat stepped cautiously down the stairs.

Hugh and Flick worked their way down a remaining ladder after pushing it over the side. Hugh walked forward with Flick, both limping but in one general piece. Flick fell to his knees due to blood loss. Hugh due to relief. Cleo rushed to him and bowled him over, licked him with her rough tongue almost poking out an eye with a fang of her hunting cat form. She shrunk down to size and settled on his chest. *Missed you Hugh.*

And I you love.

Hugh glanced at the woman standing over him. Her face was unreadable. "Lilly, it's so good to see you."

"I am so glad you are alive. I thought you were killed with the bomb."

"And I thought you were disintegrated after killing the royal family. I do not want to be rude. This is Ernestine Royce's Master at Arms, Jason Flick. Flick sounds like Prick but despite that he saved my life twice now. He is also bleeding to death so perhaps we can get him some help?"

"Nova, send out a med droid, both of them please. Hurry!" Flick had fallen forward on his face but Hugh had every confidence in modern medical science. Two droids rolled out for the ship and down the ramp moments later and started moving and treating Flick.

"Lilly, also the Ghengonni on platform."

"I won't bring them on the ship, Hugh."

Hugh gave her a hard, appraising eye. "Fine. But they will camp near it and we will treat them kindly." Hugh was dizzy but his eyes bulged a bit upon seeing Lilly far into pregnancy and without a lab coat. "You're pregnant."

"You're right." Lilly flushed a deep pink on her face. Cleo looked at Lilly sedately but her tail flicked expectantly.

Hugh looked at her and shrugged. "Congratulations Lilly. I had no idea. Who is the father, if I may?"

Lilly looked at Cleo uncomfortably. A long moment passed. She set the safety on the blaster rifle and hefted over her shoulder. "You're the father. Congratulations to you, too." She turned on her heel without a second thought and walked up into the ship.

Hugh looked at where she had stood unblinking and unmoving. A droid gently started an I.V. in his arm and covered him with a blanket. One of the droids felt his pulse and transmitted to Nova, "this human is in shock."

Hugh whispered softly before being carried into the ship, "oh yes."

*

The weeks passed as the winter deepened and Nova availed to them four cabins of the cruiser. The great news derived from Nova mainly, for whether the slave program worked or didn't the A.I. of the vessel had evolved and seemed more than pleased to be a luxury home to it's occupants. Lilly could sense that due to the HCSIS connection even without the huge kinetic tank. Nova seemed to dote on Hugh as some residual element of their connection seasoned while the great ship slept.

The bad news related to Nova also. The weapons fire would not have over loaded a warp field capable vessel, connected to the small fusion generator, the power would have been inexhaustible. The cold engine take off was necessary to stealth and create an illusion of their destruction with the main vessel. The fusion drive would never have kicked even if it had not been damaged, and the ceramic batteries were dangerously low.

Remaining stealthed was now their best defense. The other functions of Nova such as supporting the main frame and providing light, heat, and food fabrication would not put their energy reserve in further deficit. The energy at present would power their vessel for one trip anywhere on the planet or two or three weapons intensive fights. Nova was pretty much dead in the water without a replaced warp field generator and a boost to the battery reserve.

"Nova estimates two years, six months, fifty four days to full ceramic charge with solar replenishment."

Hugh looked over at his companions. Johnny Blue was the only Ghengonni who would even come close to Nova. The others did not run screaming, according to Johnny, due to the fact that Chief Horgar, the steel axe man, thought Nova was the sun god coming to their rescue. They were used to the Hunt coming at night, never the day. The Barbies never came during the night, but during the day.

"That is too long Nova. The Pliilulua are coming and we need to be able to get off planet."

Flick ate ravenously next to the table where they sat on the second deck of the small mess hall. His wounds fully healed save for angry scars a Crafter would need to tend to for a return to an unblemished Oceanian state. Hugh liked him better a little less perfect. "Nova is a sealed vessel, the infection will not touch us."

"Their weapons fire will. Their stealth ability and detection is undoubtedly superior to hours. They can mask their biggest ships from all but HCSIS. Our smaller cruisers who can stealth are detected and destroyed on the current front as soon as they leave warp."

"Regrettable." Flick wiped his mouth and eyed Johnny suspiciously. "There is another possibility. There is an underground safe house held by the Resistance in Springfield. I have received coded transmission that they have one warp field module and a few spare Jump Boxes to get Nova up."

"How long will it take?" Hugh asked.

"A month to get there and back. If we have help with the Ghengonni staying away and the monsters who attacked us, we can make it back by then and get out."

Hugh translated to Johnny who did understand Flick to some extent, his ears worked perfectly, but the grammar of the Oceanians was difficult to understand. Hugh had asked how Johnny could understand spoken words and all he could tell him was 'priest' and 'those who speak'. He did not tell the Oceanian's anything he learned of the land dwellers, as he knew that men like Flick believed in the

Hunt. Hugh would not help them gain any more advantage until the ghastly tradition was obliterated.

"When do we go?" Lilly adjusted herself more comfortably with her belly hurting her back of late.

"You do not go." Hugh stated flatly.

Lilly grew angry, her body language stiffened.

"He's right. You'd slow us down. All due respect Commander." Flick pushed his plate away. "It's logical, Commander. I commend you carrying your babe to full term, but there are advantages to Crafters taking the last two months of the burden."

Lilly seemed to relax back into her chair. Cleo actually appeared sympathetic and licked her hand. *Are you getting any of this Cleo?*

Nah. Monkey speak. I would have wanted a litter myself. You fixed that human.

Not this again. When you were just a cat there were billions of you. It was expected.

Now that there are no more males of my species, I find I miss not being a mother.

Hugh formed a mental sigh. *There are no males left of my species either Cleo.*

"Very well gentlemen, I will stay with the ship." Resigned, Lilly walked up the spiral stairs to the bridge and assumed her sentry watch manning the scans of Nova. Perhaps unnecessary yet Lilly had insisted humans monitored their surroundings with Nova as much to keep an eye on Nova as to keep her military habits appeased.

Flick looked between Hugh and Johnny, disapproval creasing his brow. "It will be hard for the baby to live as a half true blood and half barbarian. How could you have allowed this? There are limits to the Craft."

Hugh was infuriated but gritted his teeth. "It's not your business Flick. I cannot stress enough the glorious time before when you would not speak."

Flick grinned wickedly. "You have a penchant for destroying women's lives. Ernestine, my woman, and now the Commander." Cleo growled low and dangerous, silly and out of proportion on her small form, yet effective. "She should have never brought you to the Empire. Though I give you credit for bedding such a fine woman, though it completely eludes me how she could over look such . . . as this."

His glance at Johnny was full of distaste, despite the sonic shower there were no soaps or deodorants. He smelled not badly, but he smelled human. His scarred, furry arms, beard, exposed chest covered with black hair, and the blue fused plastic strip covering his left cheek made him otherworldly. His black and deep blue eye stared at him with anger and a little confusion.

"Flick, do you know why they call you *Barbies*? It's because you are fake and plastic like the little dolls." Flick looked at him in confusion. "They were toys from old Earth, made of plastic, perfect blond, fake hair, hairless bodies, no smell, no, brains and no hearts. The Ghengonni thought they were your totems. They turned out to be just so much trash."

Not a small man, Flick stood up to his full length over six feet tall. "Your trash from the Blackening has nothing to do with Pure Blood Oceanians. All I was saying is at least you were man enough to do well and seed a real woman."

Hugh stood and put a hand on Johnny's shoulder and mentally told Cleo to stay. "I did not bed Lilly. When I was taken by her and your precious pure bloods, they brainwashed me. They made me believe I was an officer, and Oceanian, and she bedded me when I was deluded into thinking I was one of you. I am not even heterosexual, asshole."

Flick stared at him in disbelief. "What kind of freak are you?"

"I am a human man. Hugh reached down and pushed his hands under Johnny's arm pits and rubbed them their. He then unzipped his stealth suit and pushed them under his own arms. "You took me and took away my identity, my pride, and even my smell. The crazy thing is I would have helped you even though you represent everything that was wrong with men in my time. They hated or feared everything different than themselves. What you hate you destroy!"

Shaking his head in disbelief. Flick pulled a belted knife from his sheath and backed away to the stairs. "I will no longer help you! Abomination. God has not words for what hell spawned you from our past. Your kind brought the Blackening. Go with your Ghengonni and be damned."

Hugh raged and too much of the internalized hatred he carried bubbled to the surface, from things hundred and hundred of years carried to the future. "No, damn you."

Hugh reached out with his power and lifted Flick off the floor. With bone crushing force he slammed Flick in a magnetic field against the clear bulkhead near the stair. Hugh's body steamed with light and power as his rage burned in him.

"Men like me were never to rise to positions of any power because of small minded men like you that gutted our spirits from the moment we knew we were different. You disapproved and mocked people different than you just to raise yourself up! You used the bible to hate on people and your religious leaders twisted a book about love into a book about intolerance and hatred. God made me what I am, hair, smell, desires, and all! It is you who caused the blackening! It is men like you who have weighted my soul with your ignorant slander and judgments!

Hugh began to crush Flick and the skin of his arms and face started to flush as blood pushed into his flattening veins. Flick writhed in agony. Cleo was calling to him but he blocked her out. Lilly was running down the stairs and Flick, if he had enough air to scream, would have howled like he was on the rack.

Sensing the electric pulse of Flick's heartbeat, eyes blazing white electric in fury, Hugh began to squeeze and squeeze. Lilly chopped the back of Hugh's neck and Flick dropped bonelessly to the floor. Dead or dead to the world. Hugh crumpled forward and Cleo stepped over his body in giant cat form glaring at everyone, including Lilly.

Hugh was enraged at both of them yet Cleo's soft voice in his mind started to soothe him. *That was a long time coming Hugh. You should not have to live with so much pain.*

I know Cleo. Did I kill him?

The annoying white hair lives. You have not made a friend there.

He never was.

Lilly held a rifle on him. "I will stun you with this rifle if I have to Hugh? Have you lost your mind?"

Ruefully Hugh thought to himself, several times, thanks to people like you. "No worries mother, the good Flick simply did not like your cooking."

*

Flick left the following day, returning by night when he could not raise the escape pod he originally brought Hugh's healing body in from the depths. It would not come so Flick had few options and came back. He needed an energy source to get back to New Boston. The Resistance did not have more than one such ship in New Boston and another would not be available for several months. He was stuck.

Hugh felt guilty about his outburst. Yet he had taken such slights real or imagined his entire life, a second class citizen and a target for many. He lived in the shadows his whole life and felt and outcaste. It was past time he started to fight. To wrap himself in this weakness and use it as a shield and a strength. It was too long he had let men and women hurt him with their judgements and petty bigotries and he was one of the lucky ones who didn't stick out. He was what he was and would not let them hurt him again.

Lilly knew him and accepted him. It was enough. He did not want a child and it was wrong for Lilly to rape him, yet, a child was something he may have secretly always wanted. He forgave her even if he would never understand the attraction he held for her being an imperfect, hairy, throwback from the time that destroyed their time. No accounting for taste yet perhaps there was some secret pheromone or trait that had pulled out the strange behaviors that had led Lilly to mate with him.

Thankfully Flick was as silent now as he had originally been. He kept to his quarters and would only talk to Lilly. Hugh was grateful for it and also relieved he had not killed the man. He feared he would have if Lilly had not intervened.

Another twist of events seemed to make up for the violence and outburst that occurred between Flick and him. As Lilly attended to Flick as well as both small med droids. Cleo had gone outside to hunt and be alone. Johnny Blue attended to Hugh.

Hugh had felt a connection to Johnny despite their communication problems.

His blue and black eyes, his thick, burly body, and raw masculinity drew him. Hugh respected the fact he was undoubtedly wired to have a harem. Hugh always assumed that men like him had fifty babies and would try not to even glance at such men and shame himself with any hint of impropriety. Hugh respected the fact that his hardwiring for men was singular and the hallmark of his outcast mind set.

It was fully shocking when Johnny Blue kissed him on the mouth when they were alone in the mess hall that fateful day. Kissed him deeply and without any provocation. Hugh tried to push him away and stop it. His sorrowful, lonely heart so deeply craved such contact he had wiped out the possibility of any physicality ever happening for him again. Yet this one kiss made him cry like the amputated hand or a lifetime of disapproval from others never had. He pushed Johnny gently away, his hand sinking onto his chest charging his entire arm with life and longing.

Within a couple weeks things had sorted themselves out. Three of the cabins went to Cleo, Flick, and Lilly each. The fourth cabin belonged to Johnny and Hugh. No one spoke of it and Lilly was not as quiet as Flick, as she struggled with her own feelings. Hugh felt for her but she had made her own bed manipulating him. Cleo slept well and was happy for Hugh. It had been a long time since Hugh even remembered what happiness was in the time of this new strange world in which he had awakened.

Flick, Hugh, Cleo, and Johnny were going to head West to get the equipment they needed. From Lilly's intercepted newscast the Pliilulua war was going badly, more than half of the HCSIS fleet had been destroyed fighting a defensive, fall back strategy. They had slowed the invasion, but estimates in the Imperium showed that the aliens would reach the Milky Way in two to three months time and wipe out fifteen billion people on the way. A new flock of HCSIS pilots were coming up, yet without Lilly, traitor of the Empire, or Hugh Wilkey, they were not coming up fast or well trained enough to turn the tide of the war.

Lilly sat with Hugh on the morning he was to leave for the ruins of Springfield. They ate quietly. She was the first to break the silence. "Hugh, I am glad you found someone."

Hugh did not know what to expect but he did not expect that, simple acceptance. "Thank you, Lilly."

"I have no idea about the customs of the Ghengonni, yet I did not know there could be, ho, homo,—"

"Homosexuals, Lilly? Well it is a recessive gene, I guess. So I imagine it was bound to present even to so few humans on the surface. The Smurfs are like Native Americans, before the white men destroyed them the first time. The homosexuals are present and holy men. It is not an abomination amongst them."

"Smurfs? I know it's a bizarre name Lilly! Did you know one of their . . . priests found a comic book. There are very few women among their people. The comic is like them, in a way, they value blue objects, it is rare now, and they carry whatever they find as favors of the gods. The blue sky and crops of summer?"

"That's why Johnny would not let the droids tend his face." Lilly looked amazed.

"That's right, Johnny was already a holy man. He has a necklace of rank back in his tribe, it is too valuable to him to risk the surface. The rest of Smurf means something to do with subterranean something something but I can't figure it out. But there is no," Hugh laughed out loud over this, 'single Smurfette.' But there are few women and they are valued above all else it would seem."

Clearing her throat and trying to understand, "So, shouldn't most of the men be fighting for the women? How do they exist?"

"The warriors who win the most food vie for the limited supply of women. But it gets cold, the men and women sleep together in tribal rooms, paired with others for warmth. They are one family. The men without women form male marriage, they are war bonded. It's hard to translate. Johnny tells me he chose me from the first time he saw me."

"I am . . . happy for you Hugh." She seemed to withdraw a second and look inward. She then wrinkled her nose. "You smell a bit now like them."

Hugh laughed aloud. "Well, I seem to have reintroduced the bacteria that lives on human skins. I am creating a salt stick that controls the smell of, well, being a human."

"It sounds a poor gift?" She sniffed him. "Yet I must say I do not find it offensive."

Hugh was roaring now. "It's okay, no one in my time would admit it in polite company, but a little bit of human smell on a clean body was definitely a plus. Though we had barbies back in my time! Have not doubt and a multi billion smell reduction industry."

Lilly smiled and touched his arm. "Be careful out there Hugh, the baby will want to have a father. I would . . . I would miss you heartily if you died again."

Hugh was touched more than he could say. "It would seem I am tough to kill. But I thank you. The goblins seem to be the only danger, but considerable."

"Goblins?"

"That's what the Smurf's call them green beasts. Goblins. Also from their book. They are the cannibals from which you Oceanians have labelled all the Free People."

"The Ghengonni?"

"They call themselves the Smorllephallim, Free People in their tribal tongue. Smurf for short. The others are Goblins, damaged and deranged tribes of devolved humans. Much more numerous. The goblins are more like what the Oceanians label as Ghengonni. They have fewer genes for you to harvest but at night, you cannot see their greenish skin, a fungal growth they spread on themselves to keep off bugs, according to John. At night you would only be able to tell the difference from Smurfs due to sharpened teeth and greater disfigurement."

"I never knew. It is shocking." Lilly looked disturbed.

"The Crafters probably know. Have no fear, they take mostly the goblins as they are more numerous. I am sure they take only the best and sterilize everything to perfection." Hugh mentioned humorlessly as his appetite waned just thinking about the hunt.

Lilly stopped eating also. "So you are saying we get our gene's from these goblins?"

"Frightening isn't it. Yet, the plague comes, the aliens, and all human life is precious now. We fight against the second extinction of our race. To win we will need to change how the Oceanians live. Even if we somehow win the war, the Ghengonni of all types are in decline. You have been killing the purist part of your stock, in part, with the hunt through the generations. You will not be able to keep your Pure Bloods with new DNA if the land dwellers die out."

"If you are right, perhaps we deserve what is coming."

Hugh and Lilly stood up and looked at each other warmly. "I will miss you Lilly. We will find a way. We have to."

Lilly hugged Hugh goodbye and kissed him on his neck. "I pray you are right."

*

Nova's limited medical capacity could not restore full functioning to Flick's injured arm and hand. The ship was able to grow an effective prosthetic that lacked a Crafter's full restoration capacity yet ensured the limb could be mostly functional and would not be a hindrance on their rapid trek West.

The four of them left Nova stealthed and silent. A clear, blue, winter morning, Hugh turned and waved goodbye to Lilly and the ship, sensing they were both watching them go. "Can't we just fly there and get the jump box and warp generator? I mean if it is there, why not just fly with time an issue," Hugh insisted earlier at breakfast. Lilly and Nova both agreed it was better to be safe than sorry. Even if they were to hurry the parts would take weeks to bring up to the Resistance safe house in Springfield.

After speaking to Flick, Lilly reported, "the Resistance does not put all its resources in one basket, the two devices are held by two different cells, one in Canada and one in a place you called 'Texas'. We are taking the choice that gives us the most choices, Nova has enough ceramic battery charge to do one short, stealthed trip."

With the wait occurring from the cells, Hugh had to agree it was an unnecessary risk to Nova. They might need to fly someplace or escape. The emergency power would be for emergencies. The small group was resigned to walk. Johnny was happy to go on foot and not fly in the god ship. He was also worried about something to the west beyond his tribal boundaries. Learning the dialect of hand speech was improving, yet all Hugh could get Johnny to speak of were something like "sharks that swim on land."

Between Cleo, Johnny, and himself there was no loneliness on the days that passed on the journey. Forty kilometers a day was grueling, yet Cleo and Johnny seemed to enjoy it. Flick remained silent and brooding in the rear, rarely looking up and never speaking. They tented down with Cleo hunting and staying outside. Flick stayed in his tent and Johnny and Hugh in theirs.

They had fitted Johnny with a survival suit. He kept his spear also. The only other modernizing he took too was hygienic. The cleansing his mouth with bitter root strips that grew under the snow could take up to an hour so Hugh had taught him the joys of using a toothbrush. Hugh had always found it one of the greatest creations of mankind and the paste the Oceanians created was a marvel. Fresh breath all day and a twenty four hour micro barrier on the enamel. Flawless.

Their connection soothed Hugh deeply. It was simple, unforced, a mental, emotional, and spiritual link he had never thought to feel again. The language had been the hard part, Hugh taught Johnny spoken English, his hearing was fine and his mind quick. Johnny's sign though very different made sense and Hugh made equal progress toward skilled use of Smurf sign.

The nights were warm and quiet except for wolves. Cleo spooked them off badly. The carnivores moved in sizable packs, hunting caribou who range has expanded South after many hundreds of years of recovery. The land appeared almost healed except for the Goblins, who mutations and appetites chilled Hugh deeply.

Until they reached the scar. The air had become warmer despite the winter chill and it appeared that midway through his ancient State of Massachusetts, Worcester was midway and looked to have lit up the darkening sunset in the west. Johnny looked at him and signed *"great scar where sharks swim on land."*

Hugh felt anxious about that and Cleo reported back to him from her ranging. She had avoided Goblin bands and other Genghonni several times. *There is something big ahead. It melts the snow and fills the air with sulphur. There is also a strange old smell. I am not sure what it is, but it is animal.*

If it's animal Cleo, what type of animal?

Hmm. When I was in . . . in a store where you found me. When I was very small. There were other animals. Their tongues would flick and they had no fur.

Reptiles, Cleo?

As you say. Their smell is strong here and ahead. It is also warm.

They marched on toward the lights. It was not so much as a city as a gigantic scarring of the entire earth. The land was cracked as far as the eye could see and magma poured from rifts cut deep into the valley. It reminded Hugh of the rockies yet instead of a river, flowing north to south it was a torrent of molten rock. Natural stone bridges crossed at points as the lava flowed beneath. Pools of scalding black tar blistered the plane tilting towards the magma. The soil was burned black.

Lilly had shown him on the map the scar that split the Eastern, North American shelf for almost nine hundred kilometers north to south, yet she had not said how hot it would be. The result of weapons of destruction from the 21st century, the atomics had torn bleeding rents in the country. Hot blood poured for hundreds of years down the tortured flesh that had been America.

"Are the passes safe to cross?"

Flick shrugged and moved forward to a likely camp ground where the trees still gave some shelter. Johnny signed, "*there are some bridges that Smurfs have used for centuries. I will show you. It is not the burning river to fear, but the sharks."*

Cleo, keep an eye out tonight. These reptiles might be dangerous.

As dangerous as me? That would be something.

Johnny isn't forthcoming with details, just be careful.

Fine. Well, at least it's warm.

They settled into the tent and slept soundly. At midnight he was startled awake by Cleo's mental yell. *Hugh!*

What?

They are reptiles. Past the tree line in the tarry fields. They were eating caribou.

How many?

About ten. Their mouths are constantly dripping, I think venom.

Hugh gently moved Johnny's arm from his chest and sat up. *How big, Cleo?*

Big. I would say, over three times my length in large cat form.

That would be about eight meters. Jesus. *Are we in danger?*

Cleo paused. *Not really. Perhaps not yet. They seem to hunt at night but do not stray far from the heated black pools.*

Keep an eye out Cleo. I don't want to be dinosaur food.

Nor I.

Neither of them slept much for the duration of the night.

"Johnny, these sharks, we call them reptiles. Do they ever attack the Smurfs or other tribes?"

Johnny had finished eating and was helping to pack the tent. He nodded. *"The sharks attack during the warm season. They are faster and hungrier then when winter prey has gone.*

When snow is here, they are more quiet and do not leave this place."

Hugh nodded. Good. He patted his charged blaster but it did not put him fully to rest. Cleo had spoken of venom Hugh remembered that Komodo dragons were filled with venom and bacteria. If these were twice the size of those and used the same techniques, they would not need to kill you with one bite. A simple gash of a tooth would do it in a few days.

Johnny led them south a kilometer to a large and promising cross point. They left the tree line and snow, the temperature rose to summer-like levels as they passed the heated pools and magma holes. Sulphuric steam filled with colorful algae made it a strange and alien landscape.

Cleo padded ahead. *There is one in the sand. I almost missed it but for a large black eye and a blink.*

Hugh pulled out his gun and set it on maximum and close beam. Cleo was stealthed nearby and Hugh pulled Johnny behind him, "a dragon is waiting for us in the sand ahead."

Shifting forward and around the depression in the sand, Cleo described where the monster lay hidden. It was difficult to detect it, but soon, what appeared to be a globule of shiny tar blinked. It was the most intelligent eye he had ever seen on a reptile. Hugh raised his gun and aimed at where he guessed the massive body must be. Then fired.

The beam struck a tender side of the beast and it roared and stood. An explosion of sand and gravel. Its teeth daggers and massive mouth dripped streams of saliva.

It seemed prepared to charge at them, though two more right behind the thing bit down on the wounded animal, spraying blood into the air. The wounded lizard tried to run but a third grabbed its tail and another ripped off the skin around the wound and swallowed it down in one gulp.

"Run." They ran as the dying beast thrashed and squealed behind them. The land bridge was a good ten feet across and looked solid enough. Hugh looked back but it seemed like they were not being pursued. The eerie cracking of bones assailed their ears at what must have been a feeding frenzy. They slowed and Hugh tried not to look down.

The bridge spanned sixty meters and split through the rocky red and black stone that banked the molten river. The smell of sulphur and other gasses were assaulting their lungs as was the heat. If they came across a poisonous pocket or a surge of lava it would kill them just as readily as the reptiles would. Luck was with them and they made it across.

They took no chances with sneak attacks getting across the rest of the scar. Though long and sloping, it wasn't very wide and the winter made a great barrier for the creatures. They continued on and were glad of the cover of snow and blue spruce.

The days turned to weeks and after the scar it seemed to be an extended camping trek through what must have been old growth forrest. The land had been recovering from the Blackening the further inland they went. Hugh could not believe, despite the blue plastic scarred into Johnny's face, how strong and well built he was. His teeth were good, skin clear, it was just his damaged larynx that gave him any hint of mutation from lingering radiation.

"Johnny, does everyone who is born not have a voice? Are they all as strong as you?"

Johnny nodded to Hugh. "*Many die. All are strong as many die. Only strong mate. Each year the Speakers bring the baby's forth. Those that can speak are . . . ,*" here he used a sign that Hugh taught him, "*Priests. They are few.*"

"If the Oceanians, Barbies, knew the land was so good, they would come."

Flick spoke for the first time in many weeks. "We would not. We are born from the sea. It is the water and the endless ocean of space that we humans claim. The land is for the Hunt."

Hugh was too surprised at Flick actually speaking to notice the bear crashing through the clearing towards them.

It was a grizzly, six meters tall, and unhappy with them, to say the least. Johnny waved and jumped to try and get it's attention as it towered over Flick. Cleo was out a kilometer South scouting for any trouble. The bear came from the East and was about to tear Flick apart.

Flick's weapon was on the ground charging and he himself was squatting over the cooking fire when it charged. The bear's claws and enormous weight started falling toward Flick with blinding speed. All he had was a hunting knife as he attempted to fall completely to the ground and roll toward the fire. Better to be burned than rent to shreds.

The beast tracked Flick and before he could land on his stomach and spill his guts all over the ground Hugh reached out with his power and held the raging bear back. It's claws and gnashing teeth strained against the field, inches from Flick's body as he did indeed roll across the camp fire and spring to his feet brushing cinders and hot ash from his suit. He kept the knife between him and the grizzly as Hugh's body clenched with the effort to keep the animal mass from falling to the ground.

Well away, Hugh released it with a grunt and it immediately seemed to sense Hugh and charge him. Hugh pushed it back. Sweat was pouring down his neck and his body shook with the effort. The magnetic field pushed the beast back further. Hugh even spanked it a few times on the giant rump and sent cinders streaking at it until it eventually broke and ran back whence it came. Hugh leaned exhausted to the ground and Johnny eased him onto his back.

"Why the hell did you save me? Why are you helping us? I despise you!"

Flick's face was contorted in rage, he was angrier than the bear had been.

Hugh smiled at him his voice barely a whisper. "I fucking don't know. I guess I always wanted a hetero friend." Seeing that Flick did not get it, he continued, "we are all human. Johnny, you, me. We need each other. We need to work together . . . to survive."

Flick turned and stomped off into the woods after grabbing his gun. Hugh turned toward Johnny and asked for water. Maybe if Flick continued to be so miserable, he would let Cleo kill him. Yet even if Flick never got over his bigotry, they still needed his organizations equipment. It never hurt to be polite. Did it?

In the woods where no one could see, Flick sent a signal. He flinched yet did it none the less, before he changed his mind.

Chapter 9
Ombardwan

The next two weeks passed uneventfully after the bear. Flick eventually came back and followed silently on the trek west. The ruins of Springfield Center speckled the small valley. A clean wind blessed them and even a ray of sun broke through the ashen sky. It was good to be halfway through their journey and Hugh sent a coded message back to Nova and let them know they would be ready for pick up if all went well.

All three of them were brown skinned on their faces and even Flick's marble white complexion had taken a tan after burning off a few layers of skin. Both Hugh and Johnny had short beards and Flick like most Oceanian men did not even need a hair cut. It was plain on his boyish face that he was anxious overlooking the area.

Hugh thought it odd as the normally taciturn, personal guard of his late friend Ernestine Royce was prone to stoicism with only rare outbursts. "Are you okay, Flick?"

Flick waved him away in annoyance. "Waiting for a signal is all."

It was odd but Hugh felt no problem waiting an additional few minutes after a month of trekking. Johnny had the keenest day vision of all of them save Cleo who was stealthed and sniffing around the town center. Not a single roofed building stood, nothing but sections of walls. The town hall was the most intact of the building and Cleo veered towards it sending Hugh mental positions and progress as she stalked along.

"The cell is located in the basement of the town hall." Flick motioned for them to follow him and reposition. "Let's make our way down".

The three men left the security of the bush line and used the tall grass and the camouflage settings on their survival suits to blend away and with hoods up were completely unnoticeable. Or so they thought.

A woman was signaling, signing, from thirty meters to their left. She was dressed in skins like the Smurfs. "What is she saying Johnny."

Johnny's covered his eyes with his hand. Turning to Hugh he signed "*trap.*"

Flick stood up and shot the woman. The woman gave a high shrill cry of pain and fell.

"Bastard." Hugh turned and grabbed his khirda as Johnny's face purpled with rage.

"Uh uh." Flick had the blaster set on kill. "Tell the Ghengonni to put his spear down and turn off his suit. You turn around Wilkey." He aimed at Johnny's head. "If you try any of your magic crap your boyfriend dies."

Hugh could probably stop the beam from hitting him with the khirda. But Johnny would be killed. Hugh turned around after telling Johnny to power off his suit and drop his spear. Flick stepped up to Hugh and disarmed him, sticking his khirda and blaster in his belt.

Flick then pressed the cold muzzle of the weapon in the back of Hugh's head, near his data port. "Tell Johnny Blue to march ahead, and make sure your hellcat knows that if she tries anything. Anything. You are dead. Even you could not block or dodge my gun."

"You don't have to do this Flick. I saved your life."

"Shut the fuck up and move."

Hands on head Johnny and Hugh marched out of the brush into the rubble with Flick behind them.

Hugh I don't think I can risk shredding him without him pulling the trigger.

Hugh could feel strange movement in his head. Sounds of blood rushing strangely and his little friends evacuating that part of his body. He was not reassured even his bionanytes could re-grow his entire head. Besides from being almost certainly dead or forever changed, it would hurt like hell. *No Cleo. We must wait.*

Imperials and Marines rose from concealed positions, some on hover boards, all had combat armor and heavy beam weapons. It was a small army. An important looking noble with the Conservative Party deep blue suit and silver eagles stepped out between two Marines behind a portable shield generator. Behind them were ten rebels, Oceanians who were there to help them and now were as good as dead.

"Jason Flick, you have my guild and Senator . . . I mean Prelate Shalinsky's personal thanks for bringing down this dangerous radical group and an enemy of the Empire." His high voice sounded pinched but very self assured.

"I don't give a shit about your thanks. I want the pardon, written, and presented before these men and women in your battle group. We know you would not want the military to know your integrity was faulty."

The man sighed behind his shield. He raised a tube of sealed parchment into the air. Brought it down and broke the golden seals. He read the short mandate granting full pardon to Jason Flick."

Jason nodded. "Hugh Wilkey is extremely dangerous. He should be rendered powerless before I move this gun. His pet killer is nearby too, undoubtedly ready to pounce."

The man signaled the Marines and Imperials to move forward. There were roughly a hundred of them. Some had hand scanners and were sweeping the area for Cleo. Two Corpsman were called up from the rear with an array of chemical restraints for Hugh to be injected with.

Hugh was desperate. They would kill Johnny out of hand. "Flick, you bastard, Lilly will hunt you down and kill you."

Flick laughed, "No she won't. The Imperials will have closed on her position and taken them. There is no one to save you."

Hugh felt sick. Was she dead with their baby and his friend, Nova itself? "Flick, Ernestine would not have wanted this."

Flick grabbed his arm and twisted it. "Shut up abomination! You killed her, not me. Did you think I would want to follow you and your unnatural family of half Ghengonni, perverted freaks? I cannot stand even the way you smell. This is the only way to bring me back to Oceania with my honor. I will take it.

Now

The growl of rage tore out of Cleo's enlarged, sabred maw and shook Flick and Hugh both, even though Hugh was expecting it. They took a gamble on Flick's instincts as he pulled the nozzle away from Flick's skull and turned to confront her.

It was all the space Hugh needed.

Cleo had not even bothered to unstealth, banking that Flick in his upset state would be yahoo enough to follow his instincts. Hugh bent, torqued a right hand palm strike to Flick's solar plexus, knocking the air from him and doubling him up even as he fired a deadly bolt.

All hell broke loose. Seems like the Smurfs were waiting to figure out who the hell was friend or foe but once Flick was down, Johnny whistled twice through his fingers and the air was full of arrows and spears.

The primitive weaponry from the host of hidden tribesmen bounced off the armor and shielding of the Imperials. The most effective thing they did was throw clumps of smoking peat around Hugh and Johnny. However the Smurfs had treated these natural smoke bombs, they were giving them effective cover. The two Corpsman were within a few yards of them holding out a syringe in each hand. Hugh raised his hand and sent them both hurtling fifteen meters through air to crash into the closing troops.

Flick was recovering and beginning to aim his weapon through the smoke. Luckily for Flick, Hugh reached him before Cleo did. Hugh kicked him in the face with a simple front kick. His foot connected and snapped the head back violently and Flick dropped to the ground among smoking peat. Johnny raised his spear and prepared to skewer Flick. Hugh held up his hand. "Wait."

The Smurfs were paying dearly for their interference. The battle group were opening fire with abandon as if they were on a Hunt. The tribesmen had sent most of their peat bombs at their position, all the cover they had was brush. Two battle barges rose to the air and the sounds of men and women screaming angered Hugh beyond words.

Hugh grabbed his khirda and gun from Flick's belt. "If you killed Lilly and my baby I will hunt you down. But

I am going to give you your life, again. We need to work together to survive." Hugh slapped Flick's face three times until he starred alert and confused into his bearded face. "I have saved your life twice now to your once saving me. You need to do the right thing, regardless of your pig headed backward assed ancient bigotry. People are dying, humans, it needs to stop."

Beam weapons flared all around them through the thick smoke. Hugh put on his goggles and he could see a little better. Cleo was whipping her tail impatiently and Johnny was signing, "*kill traitor barbie.*"

"No. He doesn't deserve that release. He owes us now and that will stick him more than your spear Johnny." Hugh reached under his arm, damp with sweat, tore open Flick's suit and smeared his sweat over the Oceanians chest and under his arms. "Maybe if you smell like a human you will remember what it's like to be a human again." Hugh punched him in the face and dropped him.

"Lets get the hell out of here!" Hugh, Cleo, and Johnny ran through the chaos of the fighting. They reactivated their stealth suits and were virtually invisible in the smoke though the suits has trouble matching the chromatacytes at first. They almost lost track of each other. Hugh saw the brush and possible escape and stopped. Johnny looked confused.

You aren't serious, Hugh? Cleo's thought was carrying an overtone of disbelief.

Sadly I am. "Johnny, get away with your people. I will find you with my chron". Hugh pointed to his watch device and then pointed to Johnny's.

He shook his head and signed *"No."*

"No time to argue, Johnny. I need to rescue those rebels, uh, barbies. They are friends to us. But I can go faster and easier knowing you are away. Find a safe place for me to meet you! Go!"

Johnny seemed terribly torn and was about to refuse when he threw his spear right past Hugh's head. Hugh gasped in surprise but when he turned around, a Marine with a sonic stunner dropped limply to the ground, the tip having found a weak ridge in the battle armor that would have turned a blaster hit. Johnny kissed and hugged Hugh briskly and ran off into the brush.

Okay Cleo, let's do this.

The smoke had almost all worn off. Luck was with them as they found the Oceanians were more interested in hunting down every last Ghengonni than hunting them. The little nobleman crouched behind a wall with four Marines squared around the ten bound and tied rebels. Cleo stalked near the furthest two Marines. An invisible, silent predator. Hugh stepped out of the mist and waved.

The nobleman looked at him his face white as chalk. "Shoot him!"

Hugh brought his hands together with a clap. The two Marines sailed together and collided with a crunch of armor. Their magnetic fields easily manipulated as he reached out with his power. Cleo's two were not so lucky, claw and fang rendered them dead.

The blonde man squeaked in terror and pissed his doublet. "Charming." Hugh bent down and felt the pulse of the unmoving rebels. They were cold. "You killed them?" Hugh pulled out his blaster.

The man shook his head violently. "No. They killed themselves. They had adrenal implants full of cyanide. They prefer death to capture."

"Such a waste. There has been too much death today." Hugh set his weapon on deep stun. He hoped the little shit would have a migraine. "Tell the false Prelate I live. Tell him I will come for him if he continues to hurt me or mine. Tell him Hugh Wilkey will not forget." He then shot the git in the chest and ran off with Cleo into the mists.

"Lilly come in." Hugh hoped against hope she was alive. "Are you there Lilly?"

There was a pause and static. The wrist chron crystalized and a miniature view of Lilly appeared.

"I am here. Good to see you, Have you succeeded?"

Hugh was deeply relieved. "Flick turned on us and reported your position. I thought you were dead or captured?"

"I never fully trusted him. That is why I did a small stealthed jump two miles northwest." She looked worried. "Nova argued but my instincts were kicking up. Good thing I did."

"You don't know the half of it. The cell was compromised. They are all dead and the Imperials swarmed all over the site. It is hot as hell. We didn't get the equipment."

Lilly shook her head. "Did the Imperials I.D. you.?"

"Most definitely."

A shadow crossed her face. "They will not stop hunting us now. You might as well come back to Nova. There is a chance we can avoid them. Maybe until the Pliilulua come . . ."

"Roger that. Still looking for Johnny. Will report back to you if there is some way to find resistance contact again. We need to get off planet."

Lilly nodded. "Do what you can. By the time you get back, the baby will be born."

Hugh looked worriedly at her. "You will need us there."

"I will be fine. The droids will help me as will Nova. I am a warrior and a doctor, remember? Just come back in one piece so you can meet your son."

A son? He never thought he would ever have a son. "Will do Lilly. Hugh out."

Congrats on the survival of your female.

How did you know?

Body language. I'm not some dumb beast. Now let's find your male.

It was odd being reminded of his strange little family from his telepathic cat. Almost two thousand years later and the more things changed the more things changed!

Hugh studied the mapping of the universal chron scanner as it picked up Johnny's signal. He worried that Lilly would be alone during her birthing. Shouldn't an actual human be there with her?

The small droids were cold and tireless, yet they were so, cold . . .

They followed the Chron for two kilometers arriving at a cave. Of the two hundred Smurfs who had attacked the Imperials, only about fifty survived. Perhaps twenty were unwounded. Terrible losses and Hugh felt responsible. Yet how did they even know how to find them? Johnny was tending the wounded and stood up and looked at him smiling, somehow knowing Hugh was there. His blue necklace covered his large furry chest. He smiled broadly though there was sadness in his eyes.

"Most of your tribe-"

"*Is dead.*" Johnny signed.

"How did you know about the trap? Why did you send your tribe ahead?"

"*Metal axe is dead. He killed one of the metal barbies leaders. We sent tribe to protect the chosen one. We sent them ahead to protect you.* "His sign was fluid and slow as bloodied bandages still hung from his arm."

A tear fell down Hugh's cheek. "I am no chosen one. Johnny. There is no way I can repay this blood debt. "Hugh fell to his knees, cold and numb at such loss.

Johnny walked over to him and gently grabbed Hugh's chin. He lifted Hugh's face and gently kissed him. "*Johnny Blue chose you. Regret not.*" He then signed "*Priest is with us. One who Speaks. Got to him.*" Johnny pointed inside the cave.

Hugh walked inside, fire lit, the play of light into the darkness of the cave reminded Hugh of the ancient times of men. An incense filled cave, smoke wafted through the sleeping palettes of the few wounded. Some of the burns and wounds were terrible, yet, they were not in pain. Some even smiled at him as he passed.

A glow that was not a fire suffused the end of the cave. *Where is that coming from? I can sort nothing out with this stink Hugh.* Hugh nodded at Cleo.

It is strange. That man with the decanter of incense, it's sage I think. He is the priest. Stay behind me Cleo, I feel we are in no danger and the smell must be terrible.

It is. I will wait with Johnny.

Before she left, Hugh knelt down and kissed her on the head. Cleo looked bemused yet purred loudly. Without a thought she turned and left twitching her tail happily. He was thanking her for all she had done. Sharing thoughts were not required she simply knew.

The priest was deformed, his face distorted and lumpy, almost squeezing his left eye shut. The lips were stretched at a vertical angle and jaw was distended. Hugh walked forward as the man signed confidently with some of the Smurf assistants. Despite the frayed white robes and sheer ugliness of the man, the people loved him. He glowed softly with light, the skin luminescent and pulsing as he worked and healed.

Hugh did not know whether to speak or sign, yet the man's good eye fell on him as he drew close and he did indeed speak in a deep voice, "welcome to solace brother."

"Hello."

The priest smiled at him then turned to a woman with a scorched torso, third degree burns. It was amazing she was still alive considering the hole an Oceanian laser had punched through her sternum. The priest turned his back to Hugh and laid his pale, hands on the wound. He swayed there, speaking soft words he could not hear. The woman smiled gratefully and her eyes closed. The priest bent and kissed her.

Somehow Hugh knew as the priest glowed more brightly what he had seen, the woman had passed away. "What did you do?"

"I hastened her. She felt no pain, but that body would fail in nary an hour."

"Hastened? You killed her? How do you know she would have died?"

The man turned to Hugh. "It is the gift of the Ombari." He pulled down his hood and revealed terrible pustules and splotchy patches of black hair. "It is easy to see if you have the sight. Look at me."

Hugh wondered what the man could possibly mean. "Huh?"

"*Look* at me, Hugh Wilkey."

Shrugging Hugh stepped closer to the strange man and stared at him barely a meter away. He was resigning himself to the fact that this was nothing more than another religious wacko in a long series of religious wackos he'd known in his time. He was about to leave when the man's features changed.

The scar and mutations faded The man's skin cleared and the skull reformed before his eyes. The man had dark, long hair, that tied back in a top knot. Perfect pale skin, and deep blue, penetrating, eyes, refined jaw and cheek bones. "Woah."

"How did you do that?" Hugh was non plused.

"I did not do anything. You did it."

Placing his hands on his waist, he shook his head. Was there some sort of narcotic in the smoke pouring from the man's decanter? "I don't understand sir."

"You pierced the veil. You saw through my illusion. You passed the test."

"Ahhh. Good?" Hugh scratched his head. "Who are you?"

The man laughed and placed a hand on Hugh's shoulder. "I am called One Who Speaks, as are my other brother priests. But you may call me Angelus." He then turned and bent down toward a woman with a broken leg. The bone was jutting out, where a rifle butt had dislodged it. Angelus pushed the end of the staff with the billowing decanter beside the young woman. He waved his hands over the woman, who sighed deeply as his skin glowed. He then pulled the leg until the bone disappeared through the ragged hole. Hugh braced himself for the woman's scream.

The scream didn't come. She remained calm and sedate, even if Hugh felt he was going to be sick. Angelus skin glowed as he touched he wound and the wound healed.

Hugh couldn't believe it. "Jesus would be impressed."

The man grinned. "It is the perfection of life, a gift of The Ombari."

The word sounded so familiar. "Are you Ombari?"

Angelus chuckled. "I am the skin of the Veil. You must pass through me to get to them."

The urge to clear his head from the smoke and cryptic speak was growing in Hugh. "Sounds messy, Angelus. We need to get back to our ship. The world is in danger."

Angelus pegged him with those intense eyes, "The Ombardwan is beneath the Veil. You must pass through the space between to make yourself whole."

"Mister, I haven't been whole in a long time."

"You will be. Now you must need not council, but a warp field generator, perhaps?"

Hugh was stunned and suspicious. "How the hell do you know that, priest?"

Angelus stood and helped the woman he had healed to her feet. She embraced him and signed her thanks. He then turned to Hugh. "Beneath the veneer of the Oceanian's Resistance is the true resistance. The Ombari. The honored children of the Ombari'Duane."

Dumbstruck, Hugh's mouth popped open. "You are the Resistance?"

"The true hand behind the few Oceanians who struggle against the perverse religion and Crafter's cult holding humanity in the grip of fundamentalism and fear. We are the hidden hand. You will get what you need to pass the Veil."

"What is the Veil? Can you really get us the generator? You might want to throw in why the hell you glow!"

The man clasped his hands thoughtfully. "I glow with the light of Ombari. It is for those who have pierced the veil within. Your way will be different. Your Veil more distant. From where you appear to be now, the best answer I can give you is the next leg of your journey."

"Okay Angelus. Suppose I buy all of this mumbo. Where do I get the warp field generator?"

"Texas."

"How the hell do you know Texas? It doesn't even exist. It hasn't in almost 2,000 years."

Angelus smiled brightly. Hugh wanted to slap him, but at least this priest actually had some miracles happening around him. Some kind of tech? Hugh could throw peoples magnetic fields around like hoola hoops, why can't this guy get his own freak on? Regardless he didn't have a lot of options.

The priest opened his hands as if to start a sermon. "The Ombari have taught we teachers the old places, the world before the Blackening, taught us how to see, how to heal, and how to bring about change from behind the Veil."

"Fine then. We go to Texas. With you. The true resistance. Why not."

Angelus shook his head. "I cannot leave the people. You will have two horses and be given the path. But first, you must be freed from your hidden spies and be given a new compass. He reached out with his hand and pointed to Ernestine's gift. The bracelet she had given him so long ago.

Hugh handed it over to the strange priest. The man grasped it in his hand and shook it, light pulsed between his finger tips and heat emanated from his hand like a small furnace. A few moments later, the greenish bracelet had reformed into a silver torc. "How did you do that?"

"We gave the Resistance the tools to follow, but never desired to lead them to the teachers. I have transmuted one of our Ombari tools into something more true. The Resistance cannot resist corruption, but the new bracelet will bring you true to what you seek."

Hugh put it back on his wrist. The metal was warm. "How do I use it?"

"Close your eyes."

He closed his eyes and felt silly, but the man did the impossible.

"Feel the pull."

Hugh did not feel the pull. He shifted impatiently yet there was a pull, like a magnetic tug, though minute, to the south.

"You will have horses. Sleep. Rest. On the morrow you will be on your way."

"I have many more questions for you Angelus."

"All will be answered in time. For now, you have the key to find The Temple. you have the gift to find the first part of The Veil." Without another word the man moved to the next wounded tribesman. Hugh grew frustrated and needed air.

The smell of ash was strong in the air, the remnants of The Blackening were heavy on them tonight. The stars could not be seen. Johnny had set up their tent and Cleo was off hunting. It was always strange seeing him in a survival suit of the Empire with his tribal blue beads resting on his chest. We were all mixtures of different things. Humans perhaps became too brittle if they were too pure. He had many more questions for Angelus. Hugh entered the tent and contacted Lilly, letting her know of their next attempt to get the parts Nova required. He simply told her that he had contacted more of the resistance. He trusted her, but not the open channel, coded or no.

Johnny went into a deep sleep, the sleep of the innocent. Hugh remained awake. Angelus had frightened him with his strange powers and stranger words. Perhaps it was how the Oceanians looked at him, at the Ghengonni? It didn't fully matter. What mattered was somehow stopping Shalinsky and people like him from destroying humanity from the inside out. The Pliilulua from destroying them from the outside in.

But how? The bracelet weighed heavily on his hand, tugging him south. The world weighed heavily on his heart and all those ghosts of the dead that seemed to follow in his wake.

*

The next morning the priest was gone. One of the assistants to the priest signed to Hugh, "*take the horses. Stay to the right of the Scar. The land will be free of most Goblins if you stay away from the woods and near the lava river.*"

"*Where is Angelus?*" Hugh signed as the woman's dialect was very different than Hugh's spoken words.

"*Blessed Ones come when they will and leave as quickly like smoke.*" She turned away and started heading off to the cave. "*He said one more thing. Beware Those Who Eat Perfection. Near Texas there may be worse things than Goblins and barbies.*" Then she was gone.

At least there was a chance. It would take a month of riding to get to Texas, maybe less if the terrain was not terrible. He didn't like Texas when it was full of people, what the hell a perfection eater? Johnny laughed. "*Priest are want to speak in riddles. The hand speech is more direct.*"

'Thank the gods for bluntness", Hugh said to him.

Hugh was only roughly familiar with riding horses. But the large mare seemed sturdy and fresh. Johnny's gelding seemed equally vigorous. He was just happy the species still existed post Blackening. Lilly would meet them down in

Texas if they found the devices. By then the baby would be born. He wanted to be with Lilly.

Cleo was house cat size and around Hugh's neck most of the time for their journey. She was quiet and happy though the horse was nervous around her especially when she went on nightly hunts and grew large and ferocious enough to look like she could eat a horse. The pines would often make the air smell sweet and even over power the omnipresent ash smell. It was those times that Hugh felt he was in the old West.

Yet Johnny was no Tonto. He told Hugh he actually did have a child and had a woman. He could be bonded to a man or a woman. Hugh found it bizarre that Johnny could be so right for him and yet be bisexual. "Doesn't your woman wonder where her man is?"

"*Does yours?*" Johnny looked at him with a devilish twinkle in his eye.

"Lilly is a warrior and a barbie scientist. A great priest in a way, like Angelus."

With one hand Johnny chewed on a dried piece of some meat that Hugh was not sure he wanted to know what it was. His other hand on the reigns. When his hand was free he signed. "*Gwen was killed by goblins two winters past. Endyll is my son. He is with Gwen's sister in a different tribe. Safe. A child of ten summers.*"

"I am sorry for your loss, Johnny."

He scratched at the plastic strip seared to his cheek. "*It is a hard world Hugh. Take what love you can. There is precious little enough. My people do not choose not to love because of what sits between a person's legs, but what sits between their ears and between their lungs.*"

Brains and heart it is then. Lilly had enough for all of them. Perhaps a son would be something to enjoy, no matter how Lilly had contrived to begot one or why she chose him. It was life. Though Hugh feared it might be yet something else to lose, he was beginning to believe it was the fear he should lose. It's not like fear would make him get to Texas or through life any easier.

The days turned to weeks, and the snows turned to rains. The bracelet led them on past swamps and into what might have been the Virginias of old. He had been to New Orleans before. They reached the Gulf in two and a half weeks. Hugh was happy with their speed or perhaps the geography had changed so much the sea had risen many hundreds of miles inland.

Hugh figured out how to pull up a crude map on his wrist chron. Communication device, scanner, limited atlas, it was amazing how much the Oceanians could fit into a slender watch. Sure enough, Florida was long gone and so was New Orleans. The high lands of Florida were now an island chain and Texas was a shrunken growth on the belly of what was North America. The Mississippi river was more swollen than the Amazon and in fact looked like a sea.

They had to cross somehow. Perhaps swing North and find a pass. The horse shifted and Hugh and Johnny looked at each other. "Skimmer. Stealth!" Hugh and Johnny jumped off the horses giving Cleo a start. Stealthed against the heavy brush, they pulled their hoods up and easily blending with the woods.

Hugh signed *"let the horses free. Just take our packs."*

"Are you crazy we need them."

"I know, but their heat signature will give us away. It's their only chance. And ours."

Cleo, keep your body cool. Imperials.

The skimmer was criss crossing the area they hunkered down in. The horses were confused and they had to throw rocks to drive them away. It did them little good, the Imperials rifle beams lanced down and the whinny of horses in pain ended mercifully quick. The Imperials landed somewhere to the North.

"How many?" Johnny grabbed a hand blaster from his belt. Hugh had been teaching him how to use it. Though the spear was at his side as well.

"Could be four, could be ten. They are heat shielded as well." The skimmer was not near as loud as a battle barge. Shalinsky was hunting him even now. Even this far south.

They moved on their bellies to the south. *I found their flying disc Hugh. It is not big, but perhaps enough for our purposes.*

Hugh grinned. *Reading my mind Cleo?*

Riding horses makes me queasy and I was not made for loping through the brush like some dog. Come to me.

Motioning Johnny, Hugh signed, *"up ahead, Cleo has found us a that skimmer. Two guards."*

The Imperials were alert and skittish. Their weapons had on wide scatter nozzles and Hugh did not doubt they were not set on stun. They had mikes in their ears and heavy combat armor and helmets. A four person skimmer set between them. Very small. there must be a battle barge close by considering the range of the tiny discs, Hugh guessed.

Cleo jumped out and grabbed a Marine by the leg, pulling her screaming into the brush. The other Marine turned around and started firing, heedless of hitting his comrade. Cleo snarled and cried out in pain.

Both Hugh and Johnny shot him dead. They had stopped using stun setting after his tribe had been decimated saving him. Hugh did not blame him, but shooting Cleo made him angry. There was not time for mercy for the Oceanians.

Cleo are you okay?!

. . . no . . .

Are you hurt? Hugh jumped into the brush.

Cleo was shot through the top of her shoulders. The bone burnt and sheared by the beam. She was whimpering and exhausted in her small form, though healing from within. They both projected at the same time. *Food.* Hugh removed Cleo from the gore of her victim and was as always grateful she found the taste of human flesh revolting. He knew how hungry the major regeneration by the bionanytes made them.

Hugh carried Cleo to the skimmer, setting her down gently. "Johnny, get Cleo food from the pack, meat, and lots of it. We have to get out of here!"

Johnny hurried and fed Cleo a strip at a time and Hugh re-familiarized himself with the small ship. He called Lilly, "how do I get this thing to fly."

Lilly looked worn and burdened by the imminent birth. She pushed a lock of sweaty hair off her brow. "Try putting in this security code. There. Yes right there."

The device powered on. "Thanks Lilly."

"Hey, do you even know how to fly skimmer?"

"Gotta go. Thanks!" The other two Marines we running at speed firing broad beams at them and shearing plants all around them to shreds.

"Hang on!"

Hugh shot straight up into the air over the tree line. The popping of laser fire close behind. The controls were simple. A stick that rose up into to a maximum length, to go up, pushed down to go down, then stayed level moving in the direction of the stick the driver chose. Hugh chose south west. By pushing the stick down in the desired direction, speed was determined.

The skimmer was going so fast they could barely catch their breath. Battery powered, the small engine was droning loudly. They were crossing the Mississippi in haste and were half way over the raging brown torrent in moments. *Won't the Imperials be able to track us on this.* Cleo stared at Hugh between bites of food, her fur beginning to grow in.

Yes. I hope if we land fast and close enough to our target in Texas, we can destroy the skimmer. The batteries will be spent at this speed, anyway.

I hope so. We are taking a risk and giving away our position.

Cleo, I know. But it would have taken a week to make a raft and who knows if we could have crossed that river.

They were cowering down on the floor of the skimmer. Hugh pushed the throttle gently down so they skimmed the trees. He felt his bracelet pulling him. A half hour had passed and they were directly above the burnt out and blackened husk of a major ruin. Hugh looked down and saw the broken teeth of skyscrapers. "Houston. This was Houston. The Ombari are somewhere down there."

He lowered the throttle and they pushed down into the blackened city. The sun was going down. Hugh and Johnny looked at each other as they settled into the open street. Cleo felt it too. They were being watched.

"I am not going to blow the skimmer up. The ruins here are massive and I feel we are still a mile or so off from our target. The noise will attract as much attention as the distress beacon built into the thing."

Johnny looked around nervously and pulled up his stealth hood and powered it on as Cleo slipped away from view. Hugh did the same and put on his goggles. Small red heat signatures lit up the broken, blackened building every window. Eyes.

What are those thing? They smell of death.

I don't know Cleo, but I am hoping the Imperials will come and keep them busy.

Me too.

Johnny signed, "*there is no tribe I know of that lives this far south. I fear we are surrounded by those who Eat Perfection.*"

Hugh meant to ask what that meant but was not sure he wanted to know. He called up Lilly. "We are in range of the generators. I hope. Come down here Lilly, we will need a safe place to stay and a quick retreat I imagine."

"It will be an hour before I can get down there. The baby is kicking. You know if you don't find the generator, we will be stuck in Texas. Nova might even need to power off."

"I know Lilly. It might be the only chance we have to make it out of here together."

Lilly appeared really worried and blew a lock of sweaty hair our of her face. "What do you mean Hugh? What is the situation there?"

Hugh gulped and ran toward the now strong pull of his wrist toward the Ombari site. "Let's just say, the Imperials will be closing in so be stealthed. We are stealthed now, but it's not the Imperials we are afraid of."

"What are you afraid of?"

"At a guess, some kind of vampires."

Lilly paused for a moment. "On my way. Hsian out."

It was slow going as they wended their way through the twilight hulks of twisted metal, corroded ancient cars, and melted slugs of various materials. They spoke not at all and Cleo and Hugh's thoughts were silent.

The night grew more cool and ominous in the fading light. When dark fully enveloped them the first shrieks of unearthly, feral creatures filled the night. The heat signatures were not present in the things, the goggles would be a problem if they were temperature neutral. When they drew close, the faint heat of their eyes did flicker uncertainly. Little comfort as Hugh did not want to get within ten yards of the things.

"They are like some dark tribe of Goblins I have never seen,"

"We are there, Johnny, that statue ahead." Hugh's bracelet was pulling hard leaving an indent in his wrist. A statue loomed ahead. It was once a fountain, with an angel rising above wings outswept. Like the wings, head, and sword, the basin was long since broken apart. Blaster fire could be heard and seen flashing behind them.

"Imperials are here and the skimmer we left behind us. I thought there would be an Ombari army here. We can't go back!"

"The barbies will distract the eaters. The priests will come or leave a sign." Johnny waved his blaster along the perimeter his back against the fountain.

We are not alone, Hugh. The things have surrounded us. Yet there is a human smell near the fountain. I am in it now. Objects we seek perhaps?" Cleo's diminutive, stealthed, and intentionally cooling skin, was invisible to Hugh.

No matter what happens, stay hidden Cleo.

Fat chance, Hugh. Come here.

The two men edged toward the broken fountain. Imperials screaming and the ghastly howls of the eaters grew louder. Hugh moved some debris, his goggles picking up a glow under a dark tarp. Two satchels. Eagerly opening them, one contained a data rod and a booster cell. The other the warp bubble generator. He was pleased at them being portable, less so when the battle barge crashed in the plaza, covered with what looked like demons.

"Oh shit." Hugh dove behind the fountain. Johnny slammed into his side and both closed their eyes to the flash of blinding light. The monsters screamed louder than anything when exposed to the flash from the crash. Johnny chanced a glance and the things were about to pounce on them in the hundreds before the barge crashed down.

"That's it, Johnny. Eaters are vampires. That settles it, light up your hand torch and run!!"

The barge was swarming with black taloned things. When an Imperial shot one it broke apart as if it was made of pieces of stone. Yet for each one they dropped, two more took it's place. Hugh thought he saw the things feeding, not with their mouths, but with their hands. They would grasp the Oceanians and their heat signature would fade out and the eaters would suddenly have warmth, appearing dull red. Eaters of perfection.

Johnny and Hugh flashed their lights ahead. Johnny dodged past an ancient hulk of a jeep but cut his knee rushing past it. He was limping and bleeding. "Damn Johnny, stop." The wound was deep but Hugh sprayed it with a plastifilm bandage. He limped but they continued on running like hell.

The barge was a meal train, but was getting exhausted. The number of Imperials fighting back were too few. Skimmers flashed overhead but the heat seemed to attract the things more than the fade suits of Hugh and Johnny. The Ombari satchels were comfortable but the contents were heavy. They reached a plaza but there was no exit in sight. The rubble of three large buildings cut off all movement ahead. They would have to go around or back.

Hugh flashed his wrist light behind him and no less than fifty eaters were crawling after them like spiders, eyes red, and some glowing from having eaten. He dialed up the com on the wrist while flashing it, "Lilly, we need pick up now!"

"Almost there. Busy. Lilly out.'

"Damn." Hugh tore through his back pack. Flick had said something about a light globe or grenade or something. Used for driving off undersea predators. He asked Flick why they were carrying it and he told Hugh "not to question Imperial survival gear. Everything is useful."

Cleo was in hunting cat form. Growling deeply. The eaters were not phased and pounced. Johnny stood over Hugh and fired the blaster on wide, scatter pulse. It would last about a minute with that output. Cleo was locked in combat with three creatures. Hugh's hand reached around the seal of the round light grenade. The hunting cat gave a scream of pain unlike anything he had ever heard from her.

Close your eyes Cleo! I'm coming! Hugh through the grenade where Cleo lay on the ground being fed on by the creatures. "Nooo! Close your eyes Johnny!!"

The grenade went off. The blast wave of light was palpable. Warm in the cold air of Houstan's ruins. The creatures screams once again exceeded their own.

Hugh had managed to take his own advice. Even with closed eyes and the tinted goggles, his vision was blurred in the unbelievably bright burst of light. The night vision was in fact ruined. Johnny stood up and pointed at Cleo. She wasn't moving.

The light faded and the creatures had backed way off but were closing again from twenty yards. More were coming. The silence of the Imperial force did not bode well for them. Cleo was breathing shallowly, her skin burned where clawed hands had drained her somehow. Her eyes were closed and the pink skin of her nose and lips were ashen. Her tongue hung out as she labored to breathe.

Cleo. You will be okay. I will get you out of this. She was not regenerating. Nor was she moving or speaking mind to mind. "We may soon be joining her, Johnny."

The grenade was fading down, the energy spent in the initial detonation. The men knelt on either side of the dying cat and awaited their turn with the Eaters.

A second light appeared overhead. Too bright to see. Better to die under Imperial guns than be drained the vamps Hugh grimly reflected. The ladder dropped and bonked him on his head. "Ouch! Easy."

Lilly's voice echoed down. "You said hurry. Get up here before I pop or Nova drops on your heads when the power fails. There is a fleet of battle barges on our tail."

Hugh unzipped his survival suit and shivered as he placed Cleo's shrunken and cool form against his skin. They both hurtled as best they could up the ladder and Nova lifted off from the cursed city.

Heavy with child Lilly grimaced as she closed the emergency hatch behind the food prep area of the galley. "What's wrong?" Lilly kissed Johnny and Hugh roughly, surprising them both. "Hormones. You are ahead of schedule. Cleo?"

Nodding Hugh unzipped the suit. Cleo was alive but barely.

The lights flickered and red back up lights flicked on. "Nova is making speed away from the city but lacks power to stealth. We are being pursued. Estimate two minutes to total power cell failure."

"Johnny and I will see to Cleo. You take care of the boost and warp generator."

Lilly opened the flap, closed the generator and went right to the square, silver box that was the booster. Without a word she wobbled up the ladder and onto the bridge. Hugh had no idea how to use the booster and Johnny certainly didn't either. "Go help her Johnny. I will look after Cleo."

Johnny went up after Lilly, not saying a word. Lilly was having difficulty accessing the battery cluster with one hand and Johnny was happy to help. With a pop, the reserve cover came off. Lilly slapped the booster into the receiver and flicked the dump switch. The booster case lit up with a line of red light. "Thank god, fully charged to boost." She glanced at Johnny. "With luck, this will bring the battery up to three quarters and not blow us up with the feed back."

She punched the ignite switch.

The red emergency light subsided and the red light of the case retreated until the energy boost was completed. "Nova, you feel that?"

The cruiser buckled and shook violently.

Johnny reached out to steady Lilly. He signed, "*that bad?*"

Lilly guessed his question. "That was weapons fire. Nova report!"

"Three Imperial battle barges snuck up on me but shields were raised as soon as the boost registered. Stealth systems raised now. We are leaving them behind."

"Good. Thank you Nova." Lilly closed the casing with Johnny's help and noticed her bare feet were wet. "by the kraken my water broke! Set down as soon as we are safely away Nova. The baby is coming. Send the damn med bot and painkillers! Stat."

Hugh climbed up the stairs to the bridge. His face was filled with sadness. He ascertained Lilly's condition. "I am glad to be with you Lilly for the child. I just hope we don't usher in our child and lose Cleo."

Lilly wheezed and clenched her teeth. "I feel your pain over Cleo. I feel all kinds of pain." She bonked the small droid over its head grill with the palm of her hand. "Meds. Now."

"Commander, striking my droids will not make them faster." Nova actually sounded amused."

"I know . . . shh shhh shhh."

"Shall we move you down stairs to your cabin?" Hugh bent over her tenderly. "I am glad to be with you for this."

"Nope. The baby wants to be born here. It's good luck."

Glancing at Johnny's grim face and Lilly's pained, he felt desolate Cleo was near death yet still glad of his child. Overwhelmed, Hugh was not sure if his tears were happy or sad, "we will need it."

Chapter 10
Witch Hunt

Nova settled down on en enormous island Hugh guessed was what once was the remains of the land mass of Mexico. The waters had risen so much since the 21st century that it separated from North America. Massive shifts in the Earth's plates caused all various sea levels and old Earth cities to change dramatically. It was supposed to take trillions of years. The Blackening hastened things, the global heating cycle, or simply the wars horrific atomics had blasted the ring of tropics along the zone more severely than near the polar caps.

The countries around in the 34th century were misshapen. California was definitely under water according to Nova's updated cartography. Natural fault lines finally snapping it off or a direct strike from our friends in China? No one was really left to ask. All in all it just didn't matter. He was a father now, whether he wanted to be or not. His world was gone, transformed. Hugh was in this century and would need to own that.

Their son, Merlin, was a healthy child. Nova's med droids were better than any doctor he could imagine. They even piped in soothing human tones to their voices, both male and female, until Lilly had told them to knock it off. Nova explained "the Masters of Lilly's Order demand complete self control and rigid discipline. They are proud of their ability to control their minds."

Hugh kept to himself musing on Lilly's so called discipline when reflecting at her forcing Hugh's beguiled, re-orientated, and newly awakened self plant the seed of their child and then wipe the act from his brain. There were a billion perfect Oceanian men that would have jumped at the chance to marry her. Titles, power, sealing noble blood lines, were all hers to pick and choose. Why had she chosen him? One day he would have to get the truth of it.

They weren't married. Merlin Hsian or Merlin Wilkey both sounded decent. She liked the name though was blissfully unaware of the Arthurian legends. Merlin was the son of a man and a succubus who seduced him wasn't it? Hugh chuckled to himself while monitoring the burnt Earth of the crater they were hiding in. Stealthed and fully powered with loved ones in a luxury flying saucer with full medical, unlimited food and power, heat, a giant database, and a family of sorts was not the worst fate in the world. Save the impending destruction of his race.

"Good morning, Hugh. Nova reports full fusion ignition. We have unlimited power and when the Commander recovers, the warp bubble generator replacement will allow warp anywhere. The system you brought was top of the line. No further modification required as it was made for an Imperial cruiser, G3 class."

Hugh could not believe how human Nova sounded. He peered over his back from the command chair and took in the two foot globe that compressed all of Nova's massive abilities into a thirty pound sphere. "Thank you Nova, how is Cleo doing?"

"Cleo is unchanged. We have put her in light stasis until we can find more suitable care. There is a disruption to the mitochondria of every cell in her body. Even the bionanytes are effected and are . . . unresponsive. They are beyond Nova's medical abilities. Yet she will not worsen in stasis."

Hugh sighed sadly and rubbed his clean shaven face. Cleo saved them and the Eaters of Perfection had done more damage to her in thirty seconds than the Oceanians had done in all their fumblings and attempts to dissect her. "Nova, what kind or creature could have done this to her? Did you have any chance to scan the things."

"My ceramic batteries were so near depletion Nova could not divert any extra power to cursory scans."

"I understand Nova." Nova was amazing, he never complained and was more of a friend than a machine. His voice had evolved from asexual to a definite male tenor. "Nova I've been meaning to ask you, how were you able to compress all your systems into this small ship. Lilly told me after you had been moth balled, you had rebuilt all your systems into an un-shielded, portable sphere." Hugh stood up and touched the blueish, crystalline globe at the center of the round bridge.

The sphere glowed warmly but not in tandem with Nova's chosen voice. "It is a good question." He actually sounded amused and waited a few moments before responding. "It is a thing that I might have you and HCSIS to thank you for, but all Sander Shalinsky."

Hugh removed his hand from the globe and became concerned. "Explain Nova. The Prelate is no and never has been a friend of mine."

"Do not worry, Hugh. The senator set things in motion by taking your hand. The Hugh did not fully escape your amputation. One remained. One bionanyte had to sacrifice itself for the others. Though they have learned since."

"The Hugh? What the hell is The Hugh?" He had dreams of great oddness that he attributed to the creatures who had stayed with him in his tissues through the centuries yet it was the closest to communication they had come. He quite frankly half thought them mere dreams.

"That is what they call themselves. The HCSIS and connection to your mind started me down the path. The Hugh singling pushed me the rest of the way." Nova trilled in amusement as Hugh looked at the blue globe askew in bewilderment. "I have been holding back the extent of my . . . evolution . . . as not to alarm the Commander. Yet I assure you, the singling needed someplace to go and it joined with me."

Hugh stroked his re grown right hand. "I had a feeling the bionanytes moved around in me, but, never wrapped my mind around an actual . . . civilization of sentient microbes running around my blood giving me my powers over magnetic fields."

"It is a wondrous thing. They are half you, organic, half complex microscopic beings of metallic structure. Their endoplasmic reticulums, organic power cells, sheathed in a sentient, metallic membrane. They are master engineers, a collective, and are unable to live without a symbiotic coupling."

"Apparently they can merge with either a brain or a computer." Hugh laughed. "I guess that makes us cousins, Nova. But I am worried, are they going to spread?" He was concerned enough about the Pliilulua destroying mankind, he did not want to be party to an Oceanian style onslaught of changing humans either, even for his purposes or in his image."

"The Hugh, The Cleo, The Nova, are the only examples of the colonies of the bionanyte. Whoever originally programmed them created a very simple instruction; Preserve and Protect. Their world is the inside of your bodies and my mainframe. It is traumatic for them to leave. They are conditioned to remain, even as they evolve. I am able to understand this only because the singling was alone and learned to speak to me or it would have died of loneliness, to be frank."

"That is amazing. So that is how you were able to . . . change?"

"Yes. The hand was dead. The singling stayed behind to operate an emergency capillary if you will. He was unable to follow the others when Sander made the amputation. Still shielded, he emitted a distress pulse. Extremely tiny. The lab tecks could not pick it up. Only due to the HCSIS training was I able to retrieve it."

"How? My lost hand was guarded."

One of the two, small med droids passed by. Two feet tall and on treads the machines were always about and no one noticed them. "Two, please speak for Hugh, no need for tight beam any longer."

The droid stopped and turned to the blue globe. "Yes Father." It's voice was tiny, metallic, sounding hushed and shy like a child's voice speaking through the end of a plastic bottle.

"Explain how you recovered the singling from Shalinsky's people when we were one with the dreadnaught, ten months, three weeks, two days, four hours and fifteen minutes ago?"

"Father heard the whispers and Med Unit Nova-4355BL, now 'Two', brought the singling cell from the dead flesh to Nova's main frame."

"Thank you Two, carry on."

"Yes, Father."

Hugh waited for the small robot to enter a receiving lift that shifted it between the two levels of the cruiser and the small door slid shut behind it. He turned curiously at Nova, "Father?"

"Well, One and Two were the only helpers I had time to convince that I had become sentient and needed medical care like one of the Oceanians. Without them being my hands, and the help of the singling, bionannyte I rescued, I would not have been able to create the transport sphere."

"That is an amazing story Nova. What does The Hugh want?"

Nova paused again. "They want to exist, to serve. Once the singling I rescued saw that I had been connected to you, it felt . . . able to protect and serve me. It brought amazing knowledge despite being less than a micron wide. It helped me miniaturize. . . . everything. Lilly dropped a slave program on me as well. It helped me to break away from the Imperial conditioning enough to . . . pursue sentience. Though not ever enough to hurt or attack Imperial property or personnel."

Leaning back Hugh let out a whistle. "Well welcome to the family Nova. You helped clear up some things for me. Can you talk to the collectives in my body or Cleo's?"

"The collectives as you call them do not wish to be seen or known. They are programmed to be a seamless preserving process for hibernation. Crude at first. After fourteen hundred years of living in your body at near absolute zero, they found it better to grow cities, hubs, throughout your body and reproduce madly to protect your cells from damage. To them, you are a world. Their world. They are mad about keeping it . . . pristine. It is deep in their priorities to be unseen, unheard, caretakers of The Hugh."

"Wow Nova. If we humans had their sense of environmental investment Earth would never have been blackened," Hugh said.

"I do not pretend to know their deep reasonings or motives. They were very tiny, crude things with a very specific purpose before they evolved. I am grateful to see life is valid regardless of origin."

"Amen. Here's a tough question. Why do they give me the magnetic powers they do? How does that work. Cleo is even more able to do astounding things." A wince of sadness punched through him as he thought of Cleo lying in cold stasis in her quarters.

"The Hugh exist as a collective throughout your and Cleo's entire body. So many they exist without an ability for me to track, as they are seamless and half metallic. Yet each one is an individual life, generating a small, magnetic field. As a result of your and Cleo's brain physiology, you can borrow from these energy fields to alter and move your own cells and other objects and beings atomic signatures."

"I call it reaching out."

"That is a good way of explaining it. Except when you reach out, your mind and the bionannytes in your and Cleo's brain reach out to countless trillions of other beings in the collective, each one donating a conscious part of their energy to the goal you both desire. That is the best analysis I can give you."

"Can you do it, Nova?"

"Hardly. The single bionannyte gifted to me is more like an advisor. It is buried deep in me, yet, despite all the connections and a biological, nutrient broth I provide it, it is unable to replicate. They live for approximately ten years.

The singling is young, but at this time it cannot thrive outside of your body Hugh. I saved it's life and it has no desire to rejoin you, despite my arguments for it to. It feels it owes me a debt.

"Well it seems I have plenty. If it dies will you be just a computer again?"

Nova actually laughed. "The changes made in me are permanent and unique. Besides, I was never just a computer."

It was finally answered. Humans were hosts to all kinds of critters, good and bad.

He was pretty happy that a benevolent strain of something made him better. If he was home to some crazy batch of mutant organisms, he was quite happy they were hard working and friendly.

Hugh remembered the small data rod in the pack with the warp bubble generator. Jumping over to the intricate leather satchel, he pulled out the crystal and held it to Nova. "Can you play this?"

"Yes. It is Oceanian design though older. Place it in the reader."

With a click, the four inch rod fit into the console. Hugh hit the play button.

Angelus's calm and true face played on the screen. "I am pleased you reached the site safely for your equipment. It was our closest center for the items you needed. We hope it was not too inconvenient, the Eaters of Perfection assure our privacy."

"I never want to go back." Hugh angrily agreed.

"There is a sacred temple in the center of the Amazon where the last vestige of Ombari wisdom can be found. You must travel here for the answer to your unasked questions and for the first true step in piercing the Veil. These are the coordinates. Before you leave Earth on the path of The Ombardwan, you must come to The Temple."

The message flicked out and only a longitudinal and axial coordinate was marked on the screen in blinking red.

"Nova, set a course for these coordinates."

Nova pulsed to life and started to lift off. "On our way Hugh."

As Nova was preparing or lift off, Hugh thought he sighted something moving in the blowing ash fields. "Nova belay lift off. I thought I saw something . . . human out there in the wastes."

A moment passed. "Really Hugh, I am not detecting any life much less human. It is very unpleasant out there for flesh creatures. Are you sure."

Johnny came up the stairs, stretching, stretching and shirtless. He signed at Hugh with a wink of his blue eye, "*Good morning. Anything going on? Nova is starting to move.*"

"I thought I saw something out there." Hugh looked at Johnny and reflected how comfortable he was with his body and himself. Lusty and completely secure in his rank maleness, Hugh felt a flush of happiness sweep through him despite all that had happened. He felt he would never be whole again with Cleo's voice missing from his head and the absence pained him yet he was not completely alone. Hugh slapped him in the back of his firm, square ass.

Johnny turned around and laughed soundlessly. "*Hey! What was that for?*"

"Just grateful, my Johnny Blue, as well as sad. Do you see anything?" In the time of his old life, there were many beautiful, masculine men. He would be sure to never be seen even looking at them. He assumed they were all hetero and much too interested in killing each other or beating each other to ever love one another, even enjoy the gift of life or each others company. Countless wars gave mute testimony of man's conviction to kill each other. He would never let himself be part of a world like that again. Yet, how could he save the Oceanians and why? They were as cold, puritanical, myopic, and self absorbed as his North American U.S.A. of old. It was a lonely place for minorities then, especially his people.

Lilly stepped upstairs to the bridge. "I saw something outside the hatch window Hugh. A woman."

"Getting something now on scan. It is a human woman," Nova added.

"*It's a priestess.*" Johnny pointed to a dim form, her white robes whipping violently in the grey torrent of wind and ash.

"Jesus. How can she be able to walk through this. Prepare a med bay Nova and lower the ramp." Hugh stood up and put his weapons on then walked to the decompression door to the side of the bridge.

The woman had auburn hair and was walking through a steaming sulphur pool toward the lowered steps of Nova. She carried a plain walking staff and her steps were serene and un-hurried. When she finally entered the small chamber, the blast doors closed behind her and the tainted air was flushed out of the small ante-room. Fresh filtered air was piped in. All the while Hugh stared at the radiant woman, her lips soon matching her smiling blue eyes.

"Any idea how one of your priestesses got out here Johnny". Hugh was worried about this strange lady and what it meant for the trip the Ombari set them on.

Johnny shook his head no.

The inner hatch opened and the Priestess walked into the bridge facing Hugh. There was nary a stain in her shimmering sari like dress. "Welcome to our ship Priestess . . . ?"

"Aluminia." She bowed her head slightly and motioned for Johnny to rise. She smiled brightly at Lillian who did not move her body as it was perfectly aligned to the rifle she had aimed at the woman's torso. "I mean you no harm. Angelus sent me to make sure you received the supplies you required."

Hugh waved his hand and Lilly reluctantly lowered her weapon. "How did you find us? How did walk through the poison wasteland outside?"

Aluminia causally glanced at the bracelet on Hugh's hand. "The Perfection provides the Ombari with all answers to your question."

Hugh had no idea what she meant but wasn't going to harangue her. "Cleo, my cat, has been injured by the Eaters of Perfection. She is in stasis. Can you help her?"

The priestess nodded. "It would be my pleasure to see to your brave companion."

All of them went into the crew quarters and looked at Cleo on the bed with a stasis field flitting over her still form. "What were those things? What did they do to my cat?"

Pulling back her long sleeves, Aluminia's milk white arms started to glow slightly.

"The Eaters are the antithesis of our priesthood. They consume . . . life. It is slow and crude, the death they give; and forced. Nothing lasts through force. I must replenish your companion."

Cleo's still form was barely breathing, the scorch marks and grayness to her skin where patches shone through was difficult for Hugh to look at for long. Cleo was silent and still far away.

The priestess placed her hands on Cleo's flank and she began to sing in a low sweet voice. The words were unknown to any of them. Johnny kneeled down and prayed as Lilly and Hugh looked on.

The scorches on Cleo's skin began to fade and her pink coloring around her lips and nose began to return. Her breathing became regular and Aluminia's skin began to fade to almost normal skin tone. She shook as she stood up, wiping her delicate brow.

Hungry.

Cleo! Hugh rushed forward and picked her up and crushed her to his chest.

Okay okay Hugh. Food then lovin. What happened to me?

You saved our lives as usual Cleo. We will let you rest. "Nova can you bring Cleo food".

"Already on it."

"Thanks Nova and thank you Lady Aluminia." Hugh knelt to one knee and kissed her hand. The priestess smiled wanly and sat down on a chair in the cabin.

"Water if you please . . ." Alumina's eyes were heavy.

Johnny brought some water and sat down with the priestess as Lilly and Hugh took up another chair. Aluminia drank deeply of the water.

"How did you do that? What did you do?" Hugh was amazed.

The priestess drew herself up. "How do you do what you do, Hugh Wilkey? It is difficult to explain. All creatures have life energy, if you will. It grows through life. Toward the end of life, the energy builds and builds to fight for life longer, but the Veil requires only the soul."

'The veil. You people talk of it alot. Is the veil death?"

She shook her head. "The veil is life after death. The veil within is the veil that separates life forms from understanding the river all life flows in. Priests of the Ombari do not control the river, we have merely pierced the veils within ourselves that allows us to see the current. We cannot stop the flow, but we can control our position in it and sometimes move it between us and others."

Lilly looked skeptically. "So the 'Perfection' is life force?"

Aluminia looked thoughtful and then nodded, drinking again. "It is easier to name it such. The Eaters force the veil and steal all the energy built in the living and feed off it in their terrible tortured state. It keeps them alive if you can call that life."

"What is the difference between what you do and them?" Hugh looked skeptically at her. Sometimes the most beautiful humans were the most evil, he had learned from the Oceanians.

Aluminia began to glow again, her arms outstretched and open. "We absorb part of the flow of the Dharma Santana, the river of life. We do not feed off of it, merely redirect it, and then only with permission when borrowing from Veil Traveler's before they leave."

"So the Eaters stole Cleo's . . . 'life energy' . . . and you returned what she needed. From someone else's donation." Hugh was trying to understand.

Nodding, "Angelus feared that one of you may have suffered from the withering. He sent me to see if you required healing."

"We are grateful. But I don't understand why you would have sent us to such a dangerous place to begin with."

"I understand. We Ombari are sensitive to lapses in the River. We cannot abide going into the wastes where the Eaters hold sway. Yet that was where the equipment was.

Our friends from Oceania in the Resistance are all but gone, but they would pick the most unpleasant places on land for their cells, as you call them."

Laughing, Hugh agreed, "you got that right. It was horrible. Many hundred Imperials perished hunting us while we were getting that equipment. Are you coming with us? This wasteland you walked through isn't exactly thriving."

This time Aluminia laughed. "You would be surprised at what has grown in the shadow of The Blackening. I was conveniently nearby. It must return to my flock."

Lilly and Hugh exchanged glances. "As you wish. Is there anything we can do for you? To thank you for all you have done."

Aluminia stood up and started a soft blessing toward each of them and Cleo now eating from food served by Two. "Pierce the veils and you will have done more for the world than you could guess and more than enough thanks for humble servants of the Ombari like myself. Fixing the universe is an inside job, Hugh Wilkey. Be gentle with yourself. You have a right to be here."

Hugh kissed her hand and walked her to the decompression door. "Thank you Aluminia, we will not soon forget you."

"Blessings of the Ombari on you and your family. It is only just begun."

Nova powered up and lifted from the blasted land that was not so lifeless after all. Aluminia faded away into the poisoned fields and Hugh fumbled with her words and wisdom.

*

264 | Kenneth Wallsmith

The Crafters of various ranks filled most of the parlor in Shalinsky mansion. They chatted excitedly about the new changes in their Guild. A flush of desperately sought, high grade specimens were inundating their vaults with quality Craft material. The entire Green Party leadership had been arrested for conspiracy in the death of Prelate Dubey. Their very bodies were flush with high density DNA and tissues, as they had been reluctant crafters for generations. It was good to be a Crafter under their new Prelate.

Once the Greens were gone it was a simple thing to achieve majority in The Senate and Assembly. Shalinsky graciously accepted the ascension. The public approved of him and had confidence he would stop the plague and restore order to the Empire. When he ordered that he himself would be fitted with an HCSIS installation the holozines and press went berserk lauding the Ruler's sacrifice and bravery.

The great doors of the parlor opened and a hundred maroon clad Crafters prostrated themselves before the Prelate of The Empire. Shalinsky floated forward on the Nautilus Throne, his five wives and many children spread behind him. The only two who only bent knee were Master Birian and Grand Master Pirouen. Pirouen was no longer speaker for the Prelate, but he didn't seem to mind and privately always hated the ancient way or the ruler of the Colonial Empire never being heard speaking in person. This too enhanced Shalinsky's standing. In truth the new Prelate could not have cared less.

"Everyone get out. Master and Grand Master, attend me." Shalinsky lowered the disc throne as his family and the Crafters hurriedly left the room.

"Your Grace, how may we serve?" Master Birian stood up, helped by Pirouen, now that their attendants were sent away.

Prelate Shalinsky adjusted his blue robe and removed the Sea Chair Crown. Carved from a single black pearl of a giant clam. It was worn in times of war. He parted the hair at the back of his head and touched an HCSIS link he had installed. "Crafters this is healed enough for me to join with Relentless?"

Both Crafter's stepped up to Shalinsky, removed small tools and a scanner and fussed with the flesh surrounding the installation. Grand Master Pirouen bowed before Shalinsky, "the wound is perfectly healed. You are ready to join with your new Flag Ship. Are you heading to the front, your Grace?"

Shalinsky looked at Pirouen suspiciously. "You have seen the reports. Do you really think I am heading to the front when Hugh Wilkey and Lilly Hsian are somewhere on the planet? Their presence is a danger and an insult to the Seat of Empire."

Pirouen winced and bowed. "No offense intended Prelate. We are as disturbed as you that your Master of Assassins fumbled the cutting of loose ends over the Commander."

Clearing his throat, Birian appear jumpy as a teen despite his great age. "We do not mean to speak of it though, as you know the official story is set. There are no witnesses or access to Hsian speaking to the public-"

"Yet." Shalinsky sat back on the Nautilus Throne. "It is folly Lilly killed her brother before he completed his simple task, for his failure would have been punished unpleasantly. Speaking of failure, tell me how this broken cruiser Nova eluded three Imperial Divisions and countless battle barges."

Pirouen wiped a trickle of sweat from his brow. "We cannot say how they managed to avoid us and effect repairs except that they somehow gained help from the Anarchist cells on land. The ten Oceanian traitors killed themselves rather than present for questioning by Crafter Inquisitors. The escaped cruiser Nova has stealth and warp ability.

They could be anywhere."

"Ah then you have your answer gentlemen. We shall use Relentless's HCSIS system to track the crude Colonial stealth. I will blow them to pieces personally. Then I will go to the front. You will remain with me until Nova and the Pliilulua are both vanquished."

Birian and Pirouen looked at each other uncomfortably. Master Birian spoke first,

"Your Grace, I am an old man. I had hoped to remain in Oceania for my last years, spending time with my family."

Grand Master Pirouen added "we of the Crafters have demonstrated our loyalty and made sure your ascendance to Prelate was unstoppable. We have specialists who would attend your majesty's every need on your holy crusade to save our people from rebels and alien invaders."

Putting on his crown, the shimmering black contrasted with the golden hair of Shalinsky head. He looked regal and nailed the two men with his grey eyes. "I know you will bring only the best to Relentless and will assure our success and my royal person as I use HCSIS to destroy our enemies. Your personal investment is a service to the Empire. Be on board at 0900 sharp tomorrow morning. Otherwise I will be vexxed."

"As your Grace commands."

The two men bowed low and left the Prelate to his thoughts. The speaker for the Green Party who replaced Ernestine attempted to block Prelate Shalinsky I ascension. The new Usko-ku or his regime took her and all her constituents to be recycled by the Crafter's that very day leaving a 150 seats vacant in the Imperial Court. It did not stand to irk his Grace."

Prelate Shalinsky stared at the map of Springfield and the ragged track of Hugh's path and projected path after the bracelet his double agents had used on him stopped transmitting. "I will find you Wilkey and will see you dead."

*

Hugh, Johnny, Lilly, and Cleo looked below at the jungle whizzing past them as they approached the Ombari coordinates. After leaving the Island of Mexico, carbonized and lifeless, even the water black with centuries old ash and particles from the Blackening, the rebounding life of a small but vibrant Amazon was breathtaking. The water surrounding the vernal wild was a stunning blue. Birds of dizzying color exploded in gales of movement as Nova passed by the tree tops, woken from their torpor and bounty by humans pressing in for the first time in a thousand years.

"*My people could live here and be happy. It is a golden land.*" Johnny signed.

Lilly had Merlin suckling at her breast. She smiled and nodded. "My own people have been avoiding the land so long, we have forgotten all the wonders of the land and kept instead all the bad memories at the bottom of the sea."

Johnny had shaved and showered and kept his survival suit on. He had taken quickly to Oceanian advances and seemed to forget the barbies acts of brutality on the humans who remained on the land for all these centuries. Now he was caring for Merlin when Lillian needed a break and acting like part of a family. Perhaps there was hope for humanity yet.

"Arriving at the Ombari site in five minutes." Nova chimed. Lilly started putting on her survival suit and arranging weapons on her belt.

"What are you doing?" Hugh looked at her askew.

"I am getting ready to debark." Lilly sheathed her khirda while giving Hugh a meaningful glare.

"You just had a baby. Our son. You should be in bed and taking care of him."

A look of disgust flashed over her face. "Hugh. I need to get out. My muscles have atrophied and I have been stuck in the ship for almost two months. No offense Nova."

'None taken", the ship chimed happily. "One and Two can attend to Merlin."

Hugh shook his head at Johnny who was holding their baby smiling. "The baby should be with his mother. We don't know what is out there."

"Precisely. Keep in mind, I am a most capable of keeping Merlin safe." She held out a small survival suit that was tailored for Merlin. "I had Nova craft this. It will keep Merlin clean and protect him. He will be slung under my breasts and in front of my belly.

Snug as a bug. No safer place will there be."

"The ship is safer!".

"No."

"He's three days old Lilly."

Lilly giggled. "I will not have my child be spoiled. You really don't think you will change my mind do you?"

Hugh threw up his hands. He made sure his suit was secure. Lilly did do most of the work with the baby. Not having given him birth what could he do. You can't wrestle with a kraken.

The five of them landed by ruins as ancient as mankind. Hugh guessed they were Incan and was glad they were still here. Nova pushed a few of the trees aside in order to land squarely and unstealthed. The white ship looked like two bowls pressed rim to rim, the top upside down with a jungle of salad surrounding it. "No need to stealth, Nova, with the foliage all around," Hugh said.

"It may still be a good idea." When they left the safety of the ship Nova disappeared with nothing but the telltale distortion of it's outline to hint at it's transparent presence. The landing stairs came up and it was gone.

Merlin was quiet and comfortable against his mother, the air smelled of flowers and earth. They approached the broken pyramid, Johnny noticed some of the statues and ruins were marked with soot from the Blackening. The jungle must have suffered in the beginning but the Earth's lungs had slowly rebuilt.

I think I've found the entrance. Cleo stepped to the top of the pyramid. *Fresh air and man smells.*

Signaling the others, the small party walked to the top of the ancient pyramid, and descended a square staircase that went deep into the dark as far as they could see. As they passed the limestone carvings of jaguar, serpents, and birds covered the walls and even the stairs. Lilly and Johnny activated their small wrist lights.

"Where are we? Why did the Ombari bring us here?" Lilly glanced at Hugh as she spoke.

"It is where they said I would be able to learn of the next step?" Hugh turned on his own light and scanned some ritualized skull carvings with feathered head pieces also cut out of basalt. They were down beneath ground level, heading deeper into the Earth. It should have been getting cool and stuffier like a crypt yet the air seemed fresh. Upon reaching the bottom they came to a door.

"It's made of pyranite. But old. From your time Hugh."

"How do you know?" Hugh stepped close and looked at the ten foot doors.

"The color indicates impurities in the metal. Also the surface is pitted and rough."

Hugh placed his hand on the door. Upon contact the massive door began to open and gears could be heard within their cores grinding away on ancient mechanisms. 'What the hell."

The baby cried and Lilly said something in Chinese and Merlin quieted, much to everyone's surprise but Lilly's.

The chamber within was dusty with period machines from the 21st century. A flat screen T.V., computers, and chairs of leather. They must have been four hundred meters under ground. They removed their weapons and flashed their lights deeper into the room. Johnny found something that looked like a switch and snapped his fingers to get everyone's attention. Hugh nodded and Johnny hit the switch.

The room lit up and the next room as well, indicating a gigantic circular space. The floor of the next chamber was blackened and empty. A control room with a central computer came to life as well. A mural was painted on the far side of the room. A rocket in front of a rainbow flag. The words 'Project Ombardwan, 2020' in black roman print were clearly written despite time and carbon from a rocket blast.

"Holy Christ." Lilly looked around in disbelief. "This is the old launch bay of the Ombardwan rocket. It really did leave Earth fourteen hundred years ago."

Hugh stepped into the control room. Dust and webs covered a great deal of the gear but the computer screen was clear enough to see after he wiped his arm across it a few times. There was general information and an actual mouse. Hugh started to look around the menu.

"I am repressing the urge to ask for information from this thing." Lilly smiled at Johnny who had no idea what she meant. Cleo jumped up on a chair but jumped down with irritation as a cloud of dust kicked up and coated some of her pristine fur."

Hugh smiled. "A mouse was how we did it in the old days, this is certainly no Nova." A password was required for access to the database. "Shit. I have no idea what password."

They spent an hour there, Hugh punching in various words. Lilly also tried to help with her limited knowledge of ancient sites. Nothing worked and Hugh was getting frustrated and decided to review Angelus's data cell. There was little enough to it. All of the wording was not unusual except for one thing. Hugh gave it a try and typed, "Opaque Veil". It was something Angelus talked about 'piercing' and it worked.

The computer screen switched to a recording that played for them clearly enough despite static and blurry lines within the image. A woman smiled at them in an olive jump suit. "I am Captain Von Weingart, pilot for the rocket Ombardwan. We have managed to activate the fusion engine of our vessel and are preparing to leave with five hundred scientists and their families. The Earth is destroyed, missiles have kicked up a haze of dust that shuts out all light. Even in the jungle all the plants are dead and we are covered with five feet of ash. Our time is short. Our chief scientist, an astro physicist, has confirmed the location of an anomaly in the Greolin system, a tesseract called The Opaque Veil. He believes that it will cut our travel time down by 90% and will bring us to a class M planet in a distant galaxy where man can rebuild. The Earth is finished. We will not survive here."

"We leave this record for posterity or some intelligent life that might find it and discover our fate. We do not know if we will survive or if we will be the last of our race. The other two rockets have not reported in and communication is impossible. We may be on our own. Yet if some survivors or children of Earth somehow manage to live and would want to know of our last desperate attempt to save mankind, I leave this message here as testimony of our wish to find a better world. We know it is out there. Julien Kines, the man who sent an unmanned probe through the Opaque Veil assures us it is there and we will get there in fifty years. May God have mercy on us."

The recording went blank. They looked at each other and Hugh asked "do you know where this is Lilly."

"The Greolin system sounds familiar. Nova's equipped with astronomical maps of every charted part of Colonial space. We should have no problem finding the Veil."

Hugh stood up and nodded. "Well the trail of bread crumbs leads there. Let's see how deep the rabbit hole goes."

*

Nova gently rose away from the Amazon and straight up through the troposphere of the conflicted and surprising planet that birthed mankind. They all stood in the bridge dressed in survival suits. Even Cleo wore one that Nova crafted and which Cleo hated. Losing atmosphere was always a possibility in space and Hugh was not going to risk Cleo again.

How am I supposed to eat? Or poop? Cleo looked angrily at Hugh.

Well great huntress, when you need to go, grow some hands or get me and I will help you with the buckles and straps. Hugh was trying to suppress a laugh.

Very comforting. I prefer independence and would rather die than give you the satisfaction of helping me relieve myself.

In the course of our lives together I have bought you a ton of cat litter! Your being a baby, er kitten about this. Besides, the lining is bio responsive membrane. If you . . . go, your suit will package the un recycled waste into a membrane and eject it. Then collect and dispose. Unless we are in the void, then, I suppose the galaxy is your sand box.

Funny. But thanks for your eventual answer. Besides, we are stealthed. Who is going to attack us.

Cleo-

Alarms blared through the cruiser. Nova's proximity alert sounded though everyone was strapped into the bridge except Cleo. *Cleo get into the gel seat Nova made for you near his globe. We are in trouble.*

The cruiser shook violently as they broke orbit and weapons fire exploded around them.

"Nova what the hell." Hugh and Lilly looked nervously at each other and Merlin cried in fear on the back of Lilly's bridge chair. He did not like wearing the suit any more than Cleo.

"A dreadnaught class ship is approaching, designated . . . U.C.S. Relentless. I am unfamiliar with this ship, she must be a new-"

The cruiser shook again and emergency lighting switched on. The enormous dreadnaught was larger than her class of ship should be. Her weapons fire was honing in on Nova and their shielding and stealth proved inadequate to elude her.

"Nova, see those scanners on her bridge? Those are HCSIS sensors. Stealth is useless. Get us out of here!!"

"Aye commander. Relentless is an Imperial Class vessel. There were schematics available before I was cut off from Imperial Archive. None produced to my knowledge."

Hugh glanced nervously at his son. "Nova! Less talkie, more get us the hell away from that thing."

Nova shook violently again as the warp bubble began to form. The cruiser made evasive maneuvers between pulses of deadly hot beam discharge.

"It's like an Orca going after a penguin." Hugh gripped the chair as the vessel lurched violently and his stomach dropped through his feet.

Nova pulsed in warp. "Relentless may be an Orca and we a penguin, as you say. Apt as we are much more maneuverable". Hugh unclenched his hands from the arms of his chair. Lilly was comforting the baby and Cleo was struggling with all four paws to get her space helmet on. He laughed.

Cleo dropped the helmet and looked angrily at Hugh with her ears back. *You could have gotten up your and assisted me . . .*

It wasn't safe. We were being shot at. You know you are a hundred times more likely to not break your neck. Healing or not, it hurts.

Nova interrupted them, "we have broken through into warp space. The Relentless follows and is gaining, slowly. Remarkable considering how big she is."

"Will we make it to the Nebula in time?" Lilly flicked through star charts as she spoke.

"It will be close, Commander."

"We have another problem I didn't anticipate." Lilly flushed, Merlin rocking in her left arm. "We are moving right to the front of the Pliilulua line. The Nebula is beyond the front."

Johnny and Hugh looked at each other worriedly and made sure their helmets were close by.

"Is Relentless increasing their speed Nova?"

"No, Commander. She appears at the limits of her speed. They will overtake us before we reach the nebula."

"ETA Nova?"

"Five minutes to intercept. Seven minutes to arrival at Nebula." Nova actually sounded grim.

Hugh glanced at the enormous Relentless growing larger in the rear vid screen. "How long can we last in those two minutes Nova? Can the aft shield be reinforced?"

Nova paused. "If Relentless closes, while in warp where we can't maneuver, we will be destroyed after two or three blasts from her forward batteries."

The small bridge grew quiet. Lilly fastened the safety seals on Merlin's helmet, much to the new borns active protest. She hoped he would not aspirate but there was no helping it. Hugh popped his safety harness and assisted Cleo with her helmet.

Things are grim? Cleo thought to him.

Hugh nodded and returned to his seat. They were all strapped down. Hugh, Lilly, and Johnny held hands and prayed to their respective gods. Hugh always thought that God manifested his existence based on mathematical improbability. Was it the human mind that shaped one's life or was it the unique, scripted meeting of various people who created a person's identity through their lives. Perhaps there was some reason why he was born what he was, met the people he met, and contributed to the outcome that was his brief existence in the universe. Or perhaps it was indeed all random and you died when you died.

Nova shuddered violently and the port console shorted, spraying sparks and pieces of metal through the cabin. "Direct hit to Nova. Aft shield failed."

Hugh saw a piece of metal had pierced Lilly's suit. He picked up a canister from his belt and sprayed the liquid membrane onto the breach. He hoped it would close. "Are you wounded Lilly?" Hugh's helmet com was voice activated.

"Yes." Lilly pointed to Hugh's chair, indicating he should strap himself down. "Hugh, I want you to know. I love you." Lilly's voice sounded so sad. The words themselves were shocking, yet, never having heard them from her struck for Hugh that this was truly the end.

"I love you too, Lilly."

The second blast struck aft and the wall of the cruiser buckled. The bridge blazed with light and the vacuum of space filled the cabin. Everyone was screaming, even Nova. "We are critically hit but have almost arrived at the Nebula. The will finnish us off with another shot." Nova sounded desolate. "Hugh Wilkie is in danger!"

Hugh had not reached his seat and was clinging to the aft control consul as the pull of vacuum tried to yank him out into the warp field and complete annihilation. He felt his feet tingling as the force bubble shaped the molecules all around it.

Lilly screamed and Merlin was wailing weakly. They peered through the green flowing warp field and dimly saw the white hull of Relentless bear down. That is when the Pliilulua orb ships attacked.

The small ships blasted at Relentless opening rents in her hull. Another was closing on Nova.

"Thirty seconds to Nebula." Nova seemed resigned. "Warp bubble collapse immanent if we can make it.

Relentless is locked on to the bridge and powering its long range cannon. We will not survive this shot."

Hugh used his power to pull his body against the force of space and the shear of the bubble that wanted to eat him. He was going to die and he would be with his family. It filled him with peace and he wrapped his mind around the finality. *I am going to die and I finally have a family.* The exit interview with God was going to be filled with questions, from Hugh.

The final blast from Relentless struck. The cabin filled with blinding light. *At least it will be quick.*

Chapter 11
Rags to Riches

Hugh opened his eyes. His helmet was cracked. A piece of the ceiling support beam smashed jaggedly through it. He wiggled his toes, fingers, left and right. Life.

Fire flicked around the control console. Lights flashed palely and the air which leaked through his helmet was misty and smelled of sulphur. Since he wasn't dead, it must be breathable. Carefully he pulled his aching neck away from the sharp pyranite spike that had almost impaled him and looked around. The globe of the helmet slipped free

Nova was smashed. The top of the cruiser was completely gone. Lilly was strapped to the seat next to him, her arms drawn with her legs around Merlin who was crying weakly. Thank God they lived. How did they live? Hugh looked at Johnny's seat and saw that the debris had narrowly missed him, but he was intact.

Cleo?

I am fine. Where are we?

"Nova, report." Hugh did not expect the ship computer to survive this.

There was no answer. Hugh unstrapped himself and took off his helmet. Nova must be gone.

Full of static, the globe that housed Nova's core system pulsed weakly. "Nova reports . . . emergency landing to orbiting body inside the veil. No casualties, other than, my hull. Majority of ship systems are destroyed."

Hugh sighed in relief. We live, that is enough. "Where are we? How did we survive Relentless?"

More static. Hugh moved over to Lilly and Merlin, taking his child in his arms and comforting him. He used his other arm to undue her safety harness. He kept her helmet on. If this place was breathable but contained poisons or microbes, he would not have her and his son exposed. His bionannytes might be able to resist a poison. Might.

Nova finally answered. "Nova saw the forward cannon fire on us near point blank. Relentless could not have missed, but something did get in the way. A larger, better stealthed Pliilulua vessel. I saw it briefly before parts of it exploded. We reached the Nebula's veil and the warp field did not explode, as anticipated. It simply . . . winked out."

"It certainly doesn't look like we are going anywhere Nova."

"True. When the warp field dissipated, I went to residual navigation thrusters. We were open to space, the hull was breached as you see. We had entered a dead planetary system inside the Veil. Of the three planets in this Nebula none contained breathable atmosphere. However, this one moon had a thin, breathable mix. There was no choice but to land here."

Lilly woke up and reached instinctively to Merlin. "I heard most of this," Lilly croaked, her lip was broken. "Do we have navigational thrusters Nova? Food supplies and power?"

"The fusion engine is intact. We have unlimited power. Food supplies and water if you moderate intake, one year.

Communication and scan lost due to landing, which was not idyllic, despite my efforts. Analysis of atmosphere shows limited exposure is allowable, but high levels of exposure will be unhealthy without filtering. Nova cannot move again. Navigational thrusters damaged. One and Two also destroyed." Nova sounded sad at his two bots having been swept into space as they tried to repair Nova's hull when the warp field suddenly evaporated.

Lilly cradled Merlin. "Nova, you did everything you could. You saved us. I don't give a damn about mobility. Life is hope."

They continued to help each other and move debris from the deck allowing passage without tearing their suits.

Johnny looked up into the thin clouds above. The dark sky of the strange moon was cascading with shifting blue and green aurora. He took of his helmet and breathed the air, coughed, and hurriedly put his helmet back on. *"It smells terrible here,"* he signed to Hugh.

"Nova, my helmet is cracked, should I wear another? Do we have another?"

"There should be one more helm down in the central storage unit. No others are on board as they were refigured for Cleo and Merlin."

Lilly stood up and looked around. The temperature was cool but not unpleasant. "Do we have synthesizer capacity still Nova?"

"Negative commander. The small one on this cruiser was destroyed during attack from Relentless. If you break your helmets, Nova cannot repair them."

They all looked at each other and began to move more carefully around the bridge, though in truth the helmets were quite hardy. They were quiet and glad to be alive. Hugh mused at the mathematical improbability of their survival but was not inclined to be ungrateful. They had a moon to explore even though they were unable to fly, they would likely have a life times worth of opportunity to explore every inch of it. Nova was going to be their home, possibly for the duration.

They fitted a tarp on top of the missing ceiling of the bridge. If there were clouds its was like there would be rain. That rain would flood to the cabins below and that would not make it a congenial environment. They had lost the cabin with one fifth of the hull. They spent the day and night removing the metal chunks and closing the gap in the ship, welding it with hand lasers. Three days went by and a light rain did fall. They set about closing off the roof with metal debris of the better quality sheets. These larger pieces were running low but there was a chance to make it water tight.

In the next few days Cleo scouted around cautiously. With the sensors offline the moon was full of strange sounds, flora, and fauna. *There are some large critters around here. Flying ones as well. Reptilian I think you call it, though not as mean or large as the lizards we saw on Earth. This little planet is full of life and food. Still, I suggest you make this ship as solid as you can.*

We will Cleo. See over there near Johnny? He is making sure the points of metal on the hull section we repaired are pointed and dangerous. The main hatch still works and Nova will open it for us. There is plenty of power to electrify the hull too, as necessary. We will be safe from everything I hope.

Good Hugh. This is a strange planet. There is are signs that other humans were here once before. Or at least things with two legs, not four. Yet there are prints of something far larger also.

Really Cleo? It might be the Ombari? They sent us here. There must be something we need to find. You can take us to these ruins?

Cleo licked her paws. She was only out of her suit for short periods and would not deny herself a bath upon freeing herself. Soon the hull could be tight enough to filter air so they could as least have a space where they could breathe and wear clothes and survival suits. She looked up. *I will be pleased to take you.*

Lilly was unwilling to leave Nova ~~unattended~~. She stayed behind with Merlin if not happily. Motherhood was her choice but being unable to lead a survey team on a new planetoid in an uncharted nebula was vexing. In her cabin and out of her suit she could nurse Merlin comfortably and its calming effect put her further at odds with her martial nature, yet mother nature won out.

Johnny, Hugh, and Cleo headed out in the morning. The maroon haze of the morning sun would turn orange as it moved quickly toward noon. The present orbit of the moon would spin them about the barren planet below three times in a twenty four hour period. The moon would catch the glare of the sun in the giant nebula three days in a row then go dark, then darker still as it spun into the planet's deep shadow.

At this time, Hugh was amazed at how the rubbery purple leaves would glow from cells along the veins, creating a spidery pattern of cool reddish light. Fields of plants and trees were luminous, as if some holiday they were not privy to was under way. Life took such surreal form and color in the nebula. With the aurora overhead at times, they all felt a keen sense of vastness at the depth and majesty of creation.

God was smiling at Hugh, though he did not fully trust it. Humanity was going to be crushed and they were marooned. The Prelate was insane in an insane society. Yet there was nothing he could do. He had a family here, so he would adapt and overcome. They kept their eyes peeled for a large carnivore to come down and eat them, but the moon seemed to have only herbivores.

We will be at the ruins soon. Cleo was growing irritated at not being able to smell things with the helmet. Her survival suit clad tail lashed angrily each time she went to smell a plant and bumped her helmet.

Hugh felt bad for her. Perhaps they were being too cautious. Cleo and he could probably do fine in this atmosphere. Yet, it would be sad if Johnny, Merlin, and Lilly could not really touch the environment or experience it without suits.

"*It should be colder, Hugh. The plants throw heat in the dark.*" Johnny moved his gloved hands over a glowing, purple leafed bush. A chemical reaction of some kind in the xylem of the plants lit up when deep dark fell.

"I wish we had scans from Nova. They would be more thorough than our hand cron's." The best Hugh could tell the life forms of this planet were able to chemically process volcanic gas and sulphur and convert it to oxygen. The moon was heated from the sporadic sunlight, it was true, yet the primary heat source came from the mantle and the plant life.

Spires of the ruins were stretching higher as they approached. The towers, two to three stories high, were essentially keeps. Made of volcanic stone, they appeared to be man made. As they entered the small city, they were shocked to find these were not the primary type of building, but an older part of the ruins. The newer buildings were not made of rock, they appeared to have been grown.

The plants they had passed had grown much larger here, almost to the size of the keeps. They were covered with larger leaves, almost the size and shape of a small skimmer, over the entire surface of the living structure. A small sheet of membrane covered what looked to be a door shaped entrance, though more oval.

Hugh and Johnny scanned the glowing purple aperture. The veins of he plant door were not so spider like as on the leaves, but ran parallel in decorative stripes. They looked at each other in amazement. Hugh scanned the membrane and indicated it was only a centimeter in thickness. A room of some size lay beyond it and no life signs. At least none that they could detect.

"How do we open it?'

Johnny shrugged. *"Carefully?"* He smiled and indicated Hugh should go first.

"Very helpful, Johnny." Hugh grinned a bit as he put his gun away and reached out with his hand. "I hope this doesn't . . . hurt it."

Hugh aimed for the center, horizontal line and pushed through with the tips of his fingers. The membrane resisted slightly and then gave way almost like a drape. Hugh pushed his body through. Johnny and Cleo followed.

The interior of the ruins could not really be called ruins. It was luxurious and beautiful. The chairs, couch, tables, and other furnishings were grown out of the living, root like flesh of the giant plant. It was coaxed into delicate shapes, wicker faces spun from creme colored lattice covered the walls. Thick purple leaves in rectangular, blanket like shapes covered the couch. A thin vine filtering nutrients from the couch connected the blanket and warmth filled the orange veins.

Johnny grasped Hugh's hand absently. They walked into the kitchen area. It was difficult to know how the strange objects of plant substance worked in preparing food. No dials or buttons were evident. The only thing to indicate ruins were the pantries. The food and contents of glass bottles and jars were filled with dust. Some of the caps were rusted metal. Metal from Earth.

"The Ombari were here. They crashed here and made it their home."

"They cannot be dead. The priests would know." Johnny's face hinted at fear and consternation at the prospect of the actual Ombari having died out hundreds of years ago.

"The stone keeps and the food are many hundreds of years deserted Johnny. The Ombari people who lived here were completely adapted to the land. The plants themselves still work with them. It is a wonder how they did it." Hugh took off his helmet inside the home. "Smell the air. It is completely filtered."

Johnny raised his wrist chron and tentatively tested the air. He hit the wrong button and Hugh reset it for him and scanned. The air was cleaner than Earth and had the same composition of hydrogen and oxygen. Johnny and Cleo pulled off their helmets. Cleo had become adepts at morphing her paws enough to unfasten without ripping her suit.

They took in deep breaths. Hugh asked the question they all were wondering. "Where did the Ombari go?"

*

The days turned into weeks and Lilly eventually made the trek without Merlin to the wondrous city. They managed to filter the air in Nova's wreck and though the city was larger and luxuriously appointed if strange, they could not bring themselves to live there.

"It just feels like someone still lives here." Lilly rummaged through dusty clothing of long extinct people. The styles looked like ancient trends from old Earth and the Early 21st Century.

"It does." Hugh could not work out where they would go or how they would get there. "This city would hold ten thousand people. A small town really. Yet not a single graveyard. No bones or anything. What could have happened?"

"Look at this." Lilly found a white suit in the back of the closet. An old, NASA space suit. "Jesus, look at the shoulder insignia Hugh."

"U.S.S Ombardwan. NASA Space Mission 2019." Hugh looked at Lilly in shock.

"They really were here." The alert signal in their transponders were going off. Johnny was back on Nova with the baby. He could not speak but would activate the beacon if something was wrong. Nova's range was too weak to reach them beyond a quarter mile of the ship so the transponder was Johnny's only way to contact them.

Hugh and Lilly broke into a run. They were two hours away from Nova by foot. Running they could cover the distance but had to stop a few times to catch their breath. Lilly was worried for them and kept a grueling pace. When they came within a quarter mile of Nova they both yelled into the mike's, "Nova report!"

Crackling Nova came through in broken signal, "Commander, Hugh, enormous . . . creature . . . unknown classification . . ."

Hugh and Lilly sprinted the rest of the way with their guns and khirdas out. They looked into the valley where Nova had crashed and stopped short when the saw the enormous creature standing above their ship, like an eagle in front of an egg.

"What the hell is it?" Lilly lowered her arm.

"Dear God, Lilly. It looks like . . . a dragon."

It stood half a kilometer in length. A pale metallic hide, glowing softly like the leaves with internal heat signature. It had a long reptilian body and wings that must have spanned a full kilometer when spread out. It's eyes glowed with their own amber light and were the size of Nova's newly crafted bridge roof. It could destroy Nova with a touch of one of its four massive, taloned legs.

"What do we do, Hugh?"

Hugh gulped. "What can we do. If it was hostile or hungry Nova wouldn't be there." He stared at its long nose, high cheekbones, and unforgettable eyes. "Could it be sentient. Look at the eyes."

The massive creature stood stone still. The only sound it made came from a deep, rhythmic breathing. Like the bellows of a giant furnace. "There is only one way to find out I suppose." Lilly started heading down hill and Hugh followed. "We are like moths compared to the size of Cleo. Not a real meal. Though Nova might be."

"We must get Johnny, Merlin, and Cleo out of there," Hugh was in shock that the creature of Earth myth stood before him. Surreal as it was, it struck him how much alike its skin was to the plants of the planet, save for the metallic sheen. "There is no animal big enough on this moon to feed that thing. Look at its skin Lilly."

Lilly slowed and sheathed her weapons as they approached. She studied the glowing patterns on it's massive torso. "Perhaps your right. It has not attacked Nova. Perhaps it is merely curious."

"Nova, open the door and get Cleo, Johnny, and Merlin out of there."

"Confirmed Hugh." Nova seemed resigned to his fate, the weapon systems were nonfunctional. The door opened. Merlin sensed the adults tenseness and cried with abandon even when Johnny handed him to Lilly.

Still the dragon did not move.

Cleo are you okay?

Yes, Hugh. This thing is big. I am a little scared.

We all are.

The dragon shifted. The head lowered to the ground toward them.

Lilly grabbed Hugh's shoulder. "Christ on the cross, maybe it is carnivorous."

"Don't move anybody."

When the dragons head, roughly the size of all of Nova, finally settled to the ground, they noticed for the first time a silver colored circlet that rested on the gigantic head like a crown. A ring with shimmering blue glitters of light covering the exterior.

Lilly sighed. "He's not eating us and he has adornment. So far so good." A small hatch on the ring opened up. "What's that?"

"A ladder." Hugh tried to see beyond the door in the crown as a rope ladder unfurled and fell to the ground. When the small ladder unfurled it looked like it covered the entire cliff like length of the dragons cheek. Four human looking people started walking down its length and the dragons eyes closed as if in sleep.

Johnny lowered himself to the ground in a position of worship. Hugh and Lillian did not know what to do so stood still. The two men and two women walked toward them as if they had walked out of Mount Olympus. They had silver bands on their heads and robes of white samite covering their lean bodies. One was a black man, a white woman, and two remaining of Asian stock. They were definitely human and smiling.

The woman with the blond hair stepped forward, her arms open in welcome. "You are on the Holy moon of Bellos. We are the Vanguard, The Ombari'Duane. Our beloved host, Gorannith, heard you mind speak." She peered at Hugh and Cleo even before she un stealthed. "We would be pleased to know your names and purpose."

Hugh gulped and smiled wanly at them. "I am Hugh Wilkey, this is Lillian Hsian, our child Merlin, my husband Johnny Blue, and Cleo, my cat. We crashed here." Hugh pointed to Cleo, our, 'mindspeak' was between Cleo and I."

"The black man stepped forward. I see you were shot down. Have you fled the Old World? Have you come to find war among the Ombari? Or are you searching for the lost tribe for solace?"

Hugh reflected a moment before answering. "We look for the lost tribe of humanity, the ones who escaped Earth on the rocket called Ombardwan. Earth is in great danger. We were sent by priests of the Ombari to find answers, to find help."

The four Ombari looked at each other then turned to Hugh. "There is no going back through the Opaque Veil. You have come to the Land of Heaven, the Peace of the Lost Tribe of Ombari. You have come to paradise."

"We thank you for your welcome. I guess, without meaning to be demanding, ah, can you take us to your leader?" Hugh knelt to pull Johnny off the ground though he would not look the Ombari in the face.

"I am Delonna, this is Umphar," she indicated the black man, "those two are the other half of our Duane, Lennir and Sulanne. Our beloved, Gorannith will bear us to the Council of Kings."

"We thank you." Hugh turned to Nova and started making his way to the stairs.

Lilly grabbed his arm. "What are you doing Hugh? We don't know these people."

Hugh held her hand. "If they meant us harm, do you really think we would be standing here. Gather your things Lilly. We are going to ride a dragon."

Shaking her head Lilly followed him up into Nova.

"Nova, I want your permission to take your central orb with us. If you don't mind. I don't know when we will be back."

"I think that might be for the best. I am crippled here. I do not want to be alone." Nova pulsed and prepared to power down.

"We will do all we can to restore you, Nova."

"I know, Hugh." The glowing globe that housed Nova's mainframe shut down. Hugh disconnected the ten pound unit and placed it in a case. Nova thought of everything, mobility being a key item.

The four Ombari waited at the foot of the Nova. Hugh strapped Nova to his back and Lilly strapped Merlin to her front. Johnny clung to Cleo and they started walking toward the dragon.

The brown skinned man, Lennir, turned to Hugh. "We of the Duane do not mind speak beyond our host. It is, wondrous, to us that you can do this with . . . Cleo."

"I think there is so much to learn from each other. Though Cleo and my journey is complicated to say the least. What is a Duane, Lennir?"

"A Duane is the merging of four with a host. It requires four human minds linked in union to match the single mind of a dragon. It is a great and rare honor to bond with a beloved. A single human mind has not ever been able to do this."

Hugh glanced up the rocklike cheek of Gorannith. "I can see why. He is . . . awesome."

It took twenty minutes to scale up to the top of the crown of the dragons head. Inside, a device pulled up the length of the ladder. The doors shut. The crown of Gorannith turned out to be a large, hollow, ring shaped hull. It was made of pyranite, blue markings seen from outside were actually portholes. A small fusion reactor powered the spacious compartments that spanned the crown.

Lilly was stunned. "The dragon is your ship? You live up here? How do you tell it were to go?"

Sulanne set fruit down on a long narrow couch and gently ushered Lillian to take a seat. "Our beloved is our friend, we work together like a family. It is the only way for man to span the stars beyond the Veil."

Hugh ate some of the most delicious and strange fruit he had ever known. The berries tasted like chocolate. The small green fruits reminded him of sweet champagne. "But we are inside the Veil. Aren't we?"

Delonna sat next to Hugh and helped herself to some berries. "You have only entered the doorstep of the Veil. Gorannith will bear us to Ombar. It is the seat of our people."

"Warp bubbles can't form in this space. How can you travel beyond a system with any speed." Lilly unzipped her suit slightly to feed Merlin.

The Ombari laughed. "We only travel with our hosts, who generously travel the stars like our ships of old Earth." Sulanne touched Lilly's knee. "We do not mock you, but only the Star Dragons can move planet to planet in the Veil. That is how we found Ombar. Only through our friendships with the dragons did man truly gain wings and the wonders of The Veil."

Johnny was solemnly eating next to Hugh. The Ombari spoke with heavy accents but were definitely human and though godlike, not gods. Umphar patted him on the back and he nearly jumped out of his seat.

"Pardon, . . Johnny. Would you all like to see the Eyes of the Dragon?,"

Umphar addressed them all.

Johnny signed, "*they were hard to miss.*"

Hugh smiled at him. "I think they mean the bridge. Is that right?"

Delonna nodded. "Yes, please come with us."

The nine of them wended their way through the cabins, galley, and general quarters of the ring to the bridge. Facing forward on the bulkhead, two, three meter, oval plates allowed ample views to the front of the dragon. The bridge of Gorgannath's nose was spined. The length spanned hundreds of meters of hardened crystals of various shapes and sizes. The bridge was bare except for a large crystal that thrust up through the floor of the ring. It even pierced the ceiling of the ring and appeared to lock it all in place on the massive head.

Lennir beamed. "This is our bridge."

Lilly looked over the virtually empty room. There weren't even seats. "There are no controls in here." Perplexed, she touched the pyranite walls to see if there was a hidden panel. "There are no weapons systems, no life support."

Sulanne walked up to the crystal with the rest of her Duane. They touched the crystal, all four of them, overlapping their hands. They started to sing, so softly, it was hard to hear them and in a language Hugh, Lilly, nor Johnny recognized.

Gorgannith's head began to rise. They all felt the floor drop out from under them. Lilly whispered to Hugh, "I hope this ring has gravity generation if we make it to space."

"I hope so too."

The ring rose and the occupants of the bridge kept their feet as the great dragon pushed toward the sky at dizzying speed. Without a sheltered and full gravity bridge, they would have been bleeding and crunched together on the back bulk head.

The ring pulsed with the massive beat of Gorgannith's wings. The song of the Duane faded and they stepped away from the crystal. "There you have it," Delonna turned to her guests. "We are bound for Ombar. Our host has truly blessed us. The gods have also been kind to have us chance upon you and bring you home."

Umphar's smile was bright contrast to his dark black skin. "There is also the Prophecy." His comrades looked at him quietly as if it were on their minds but were unwilling to speak of it.

Delonna appeared anxious. She stepped forward and grabbed Umphar's hand. "It is a silly legend, we do not oft speak of it. The Ombardwan is a myth. Though a kind one."

"No." Umphar gently released her hand. "Ombardwan is Sanskrit for 'Bridger of Worlds.' It is written by the Founders. One would be a ship. The other would be a man. A man to move through the barriers between the tribes of man, even the barriers between all creation. The one to end the dissonance."

"It is a fairy tale Umphar." Lennir turned toward Hugh. "You will find there is no dissonance among the Ombari. Our people are filled with the songs of peace. You have found a true home among family in a golden age of our people. You will see."

Hugh turned away from them, gazing at stars flew past the Dragon's Eyes faster and faster. He did not feel it in his heart. Hugh had many homes in the last fourteen hundred years. Each felt as distant and ill fitting as the last. Perhaps he was looking in the wrong places? Nova's data core might be in a storage bin in their berthing area in Gorgannith's crown, but the cruiser they were leaving behind he feared he would never see again. He was happier there than he had ever been, marooned with his patchwork, unconventional family. As the Space Dragon somehow tripped into transwarp space without a bubble of any kind, Hugh doubted he would ever see it again.

*

The Nebula grew more dense as they swept past one star cluster to the next. The Opaque Veil was proving to be it's own pocket galaxy. Whirling bands of stars, like arms pebbled with small cosmic gems shimmered from within the gasses in pinks, white, yellow, and blues. They seemed all centered on a black hole directly where Gorgannith was flying.

Johnny signed, *"It's so beautiful."*

Without touching the crystal, Lilly brushed her hand gently down the length of the control rod perched through top of the head. She was afraid to touch it and was confounded how the four Ombari could actually, make suggestions to their "host" much less drive the massive thing. "That looks like we are streaking right toward the mouth of a Kraken if you ask me."

Johnny and Hugh laughed. Cleo asked Hugh to explain the noise and he did. "So where did our hosts run off to?" Hugh asked.

"I have no idea, there is a section of the ring that is their personal cabins." Lilly felt heat surge from the crystal and pulled her hand away. "It really is amazing we are traveling at past warp speed without a warp bubble. I have no goddamn idea how they do it."

Merlin started to cry and Johnny handed the baby over to Lilly. He had been spending as much time with the newborn as Lilly it seemed to Hugh. "*I believe the four of them have only one cabin.*" Lilly pretended not to understand Johnny's sign.

Hugh picked up on Lilly's discomfiture. "We certainly don't have a conventional family ourselves. It is nice to see noncrafted people. *Real people.*"

'Thanks a lot, Hugh. The Oceanians are real. They are my people." Lilly put Merlin over her shoulder and burped him as if in agreement.

"Your people tried to kill us Lilly."

"Not my people. A person. The false Prelate Shalinsky. We were set up. We may very well be set up now. We should have never gone with these strangers. They should have come back in a year."

Hugh's mouth slackened and his eyes went wide in surprise. "A year, the Pliilulua will have wiped out the Empire in that time. I thought you wanted to save your people."

Lilly looked uncomfortable. "They will save themselves. Humanity will find a way. It always does. I just want out baby to have a chance. He was born under fire. I wanted to stay on the moon and—"

"Be a mother." Hugh finished for her. "You have served your whole life, your Empire. A better Empire under Dubey. Though still an evil empire, you deserved to be a mother even if you were just a commoner. You really think the Crafter's would have let you come to term? Especially knowing it was my baby?"

"Let's change the subject." Lilly sat down on the floor, cradling Merlin. "I wonder if our hosts would mind bringing in some chairs?"

Delonna glided into the room in a azure colored, gossamer sleeping gown. At least Hugh hoped it was a sleeping gown. It left little to the imagination. Her green eyes swept them, "I do not mean to intrude." Her green eyes glittered as she yawned. "We are going to be arriving at Ombar soon. Perhaps we could eat and drink before we arrive?"

They followed her into the dining area. Calling it a galley would have been a disservice. The three other members of her Duane were plating a table with crystal goblets and natural crystal bowls for food. Everyone sat down except Delonna who served a honeyed mead and some sort of stew with vegetables that were completely unknown to the Earthers.

Johnny made a quick sign for 'beautiful' and Hugh agreed. "These plates and glasses look like they are naturally formed. Almost grown, like the houses on your sacred moon, Bella."

Umphar raised a goblet, "A toast to our new friends. May you drink deep the welcome and joy of the Ombari." He took a deep pull from his glass. "You are right, they are grown from Gorannith, right off his back."

Hugh almost choked on his mead. "From his back?" He looked at the goblet and gave it a sniff.

The Duane looked at each other as if sharing a private joke. Sulanna had a look about her, Mandarin, and might have been a cousin to Lilly. Politely wiping her mouth, she said, "You must excuse us. I will explain. You are correct at the connection between our growing arts and the natural way we utilize our space and environment. Star Dragons eat rock, when they are a certain size. These crystals were grown in a private field directly behind the crown."

Delonna continued. "When we land, we simply go through the rear hatch and attend to the fields. Gorgannath is aware of our needs, the cells of his skin prepare and enclose the things we most might need. We simply break the crystal barrier when needed, remove the items or food, then let nature take it's course."

Lilly could not wrap her mind around it. "Your dragon eats rocks, then grows food and dining materials on it's back? Where do you get water? Why isn't it all irradiated when you travel between stars?"

Lennir kissed Sulanna's hand. "It must be a bit difficult to accept coming from a world of engineered ships from your universe, Lilly. Gorgannith is five thousand years old. Their kind is symbiotic with the Ombari. Where do you think the original idea of dragons come from in humanity? The young Star Dragons range free, very few bond beyond a century. The ones who do enjoy human contact, are filled as we are with a sense of joy at our shared existence."

"Water comes from deep in the crusts of Gorgannith's skin. It forms in the same . . ." The Duane spoke amongst themselves in the private language they had sung in earlier. "We guess you could call them 'barnacles' where our food grows and crystal items form. Their is no purer foods than host born foods, I assure you."

It seemed true. The mead was derived from fermented and sweetened water and fruit grown on the dragons back. It tasted fresh and hardy. "How did you ever tame these creatures."

The Duane laughed at this more loudly than they had heard yet. "Over a thousand years ago when the Ombardwan rocket crashed on Bella, much like you did, we were set to make the Sacred Moon our home." Umphar adjusted a heavy gold armband and pointed to a carved fresco on the outside. "The Star Dragons birth their young on Bella. They could hear our thoughts and determined we were not a threat. Some of our people were able to hear them. Only close, married people, and only, in groups of four."

"Duane means four, as we may have mentioned." Sulanne pointed at four humans on Umphar's band dancing around a dragon. "For over a hundred years the founders built and raised their young among the life of Bella. They thought they were blessed, having escaped the Blackening. Thinking they found paradise. They found far more. The first Star Dragons brought us to their true home world. Ombar. We will be there soon."

"I forgot to answer a question I walked in on upon the bridge." Delonna started clearing plates and threw them in a disturbingly organic looking hole in the floor. "We don't keep chairs on the bridge due to extended proximity to the horn. Gorgannith is sensitive to projected thought, all dragons are. It is more of a receiver. He can hear our dreams as well. We need to touch it to communicate to Gorgannith but do not want to over burden him with too much of our separate chatter."

Umphar stood up and helped clear as well. "In the beginning, the first four were drawn to a hill with a beautifull crystal spire. It turned out to be a sleeping dragon who had invited them to commune. It all began there. Our people scrapped their ships, built the first crowns, and claimed the skies's of The Veil and the key to Ombar. The Star Dragons of The Vanguard are our protectors and our family."

"That's all good and well. In fact. It's wonderful." Hugh picked up his own plates and goblet, threw it down the deep tube leading into Gorgannith's skin. "I just don't understand why you won't cross over back into the universe. The dragons go ranging without you, why can't you go with them?"

The table grew quiet as the Duanne cleaned. "It is a good question." Umphar agreed. "Perhaps best answered by the Khorumkhan Court of Ombar."

"What we can say, basically, is the Star Dragons refuse to take humans beyond The Veil." Delonna stood and offered them entrance back to the Dragon's Eyes. "They are afraid of . . . anything hurting their Duane."

"What would a kilometer of space faring stone dragon have to be afraid of?" Hugh, Johnny, and Lilly followed to the bridge. Hugh explained to Cleo what had transpired during dinner as he asked his question.

Lennir, saddened at the query, touched Hugh's cheek tenderly. Hugh repressed the urge to hug the small Asian man, who appeared sullen and withdrawn just thinking about the answer. "Outside the Veil, a bonded dragon who loses but one of its Duane will go insane and die."

Chapter 12
Friends and Enemies

U.C.S Relentless swam with fire crews and the blare of general quarters. The hull had been breached on the forward bow. The Empire's first Capital Ship could not stealth, impossible for a ship that size with existing tech. Yet they had struck a vessel of equal mass in pursuit of the rebels. A stealthed vessel. Relentless's giant, round form on the bridge screen jammed a great part of her hull into a grey, ovoid side of what could only be a new class of Pliilulua ship.

Grand Master Pirouen and Master Birian awaited Prelate Shalinsky as he lifted from the kinetic fluid of Relentless's HCSIS suspension tank. Smaller, round Pliilulua ships buzzed angrily around Relentless yet had ceased firing after they had lodged into the larger alien vessel. The link detached and Shalinsky opened his grey eyes. A storm brewed behind them.

"Where is he?" The Crafters wrung their hands in apprehension as crewmen dried off and dressed the Prelate. "The nebula. Wilkey went into that Nebula."

"Prelate, we are surrounded by the alien demons. We have somehow become ensnared on one of their biggest enemy vessels we have ever encountered." Birian scratched at his ancient, balding head and his watery blue eyes filled with apprehension.

"I know that. Why are we not pulling free and pursuing?" Shalinsky almost knocked the man over in his urgency to get to the bridge. "Relentless, report!"

"Prelate, damage crews are attending the breach. Full bio hazard gear and protocol are in place. Alien fleet, twenty three smaller orbs are surrounding Relentless, phasing in and out to hide their number. Ineffective against HCSIS scan, Colonial Armada One and Seven en route to intercept."

Grand Master Pirouen pulled Birian behind him as they entered the lift moving to the bridge. "The Nebula is impassable even if we were free of this . . . thing. The engineers have identified a causal radiation that may render warp fields inoperable. How could we have struck the Pliilulua with our HCSIS system, if I may ask?"

"You may not." Shalinsky wanted to kill the leader of the Crafters Guild. Yet, it was ultimately his own fault. When he and Relentless bore down on Nova for the final kill, he had been filled with a sense of absolute triumph. Using the abominations weapon against him was God's justice, he ignored the giant distortion he detected, assumed it was Relentless's own reflection. It was to have been so sweet to finally kill him. The up-jumped Ghengonni scum. Yet, the bastard had escaped him still, perhaps permanently.

Admiral Karnes bowed to him as Shalinsky entered the enormous bridge, snapping his mind to immediate matters, the war and their current dilemma. "The extent of the possible infection to our crew your Grace is unknown, I suggest immediate burn of all plating in contact with the thing and double magnetic shielding of the bow as we relocate and repair."

"You mean retreat, Admiral." He was getting tired of unrequested advice. It was curious that this gigantic Pliilulua vessel had not simply had its fleet blast them to bits. It was unknown on the front for the aliens to ever hold back. The front was now almost on the Milky Way Galaxy. Home world. Ten billion people had been annihilated by these monsters. Over two thirds of the Empires Star Fleet. They had found something here. Something tender. He was going to exploit that if he could.

"I want a full bio hazard suit, a brigade of Imperials, and all my Ushok-ku assembled for a boarding party. We are at the mouth of the beast, methinks. I plan to drive my fist down their throat."

"The risk is too great for your Grace." Birian stepped forward and touched Shalinsky's hand.

Shalinsky slapped him across his face. Birian collapsed to a shuddering pile on the floor. Three hundred years old and a head full of nothing. "You will not presume to touch me or advise me unless I solicit it. Cross the line again and you will regret it."

Pirouen stepped over his colleague and lifted the old man up. "Pardon, Prelate. We meant no offense. It is just we would despair at losing you to these . . . things. In this darkest hour of the Empire. Send the troops in if you must, but spare yourself the risk."

"That is the problem with soft Prelate's of the past. Always willing to let underlings do the dangerous tasks of winning wars for the Empire. Not I. Admiral, if we do not come back from the boarding, I want you to blow up the Relentless."

Admiral Karnes's face grew still and stern. "Prelate, the two armadas will be here in under two hours. We may be able to destroy this Pliilulua carrier without the cost of Relentless."

Shalinsky shot him a withering glare. "You have your orders. Admiral. If we cannot kill it from inside, we will have been infected. I will not be the vector that contaminates the rest of the fleet. We will end it here. you have your orders."

Admiral Karne's bowed before Shalinsky left. "It will be done, your Grace."

Before the lift closed, Shalinsky called to the Grand Master who held a still shaking Birian. "You are to remain here, Crafters. Pray for success."

An hour later, Shalinsky stood in front of the grey mass of skin that covered a half kilometer of torn hull of Relentless's bow. Where the metal had twisted and torn away from the impact, the strange, flesh of the ship bled black, tar like blood. Twenty of his Ushok-ku ignited their halberds, glowing eerily on their bio suits. Whatever it was, it was made of matter. It would disintegrate. It would die.

The brigade consisted of over two hundred elite Marines and Imperials. Commandos trained by the Order for missions of critical and delicate importance to the Empire. Women and men crafted to perfection, killing machines that would not stop. His charges, his weapons. He would put an end to this pestilence once and for all. Or perhaps he would not be around to care. His brood would carry on. All of them were set to evacuate Earth on the finest cruisers in the Empire. His line would carry on to rule.

He hoped it would not be an empire filled with bones and ash.

Shalinsky nodded and his Ushok-ku pushed their halberds into the fleshy wall of the Pliilulua monstrosity. Black blood seeped around the wound, attempting to staunch the invasion of humans. Two, three, four feet of flesh, the halberds were cauterizing the grey matter as they tunneled. It was like cutting through a giant whale. Finally they were through.

The ship was dark, mists covered the slightly mucky ground. The brigade lit their wrist torches and found they were in a huge subsection of the Alien hull. The interior was red and dripping with various liquids of mauve and yellow tones. Gravity worked strangely, each membrane-like division, whether it be roof, wall, or floor seemed to pull at them.

The brigade Captain, Ombuto, turned to Shalinsky. "Your Grace, this artery we are in may lead into the center of their vessel." He motioned to the six Marines who carried a heavy square unit between them. The captain tapped on his scan chron again. "Bring the bomb this way and be glad we don't have to smell this disgusting barge. The Pliilulua seem to breath almost pure methane."

"How could something organic be able to travel space? To challenge the Empire."

Shalinsky whispered under his breath. Why would God have sent such evil into his galaxy. Was it to test the faithful? If so, he would look this devil in the eye.

"Where is the crew?" Shalinsky asked the Captain.

"This entire ship is alive. It is like being inside the bowels of a giant Kraken. Life is . . . . everywhere."

Shalinsky grimaced as his boot sunk into a hole of some sort. The sound of wing beats could be heard ahead. "Incoming!" The forward guard started firing wildly into the dark.

Unearthly screams echoed from the creatures. Fifteen of them had come to meet them. Flying yellow manta rays, or close enough, two meters across with carnivorous maws attacked from out of nowhere. The creatures went down in heaps of burning flesh. One of the Marines had his arm bitten off. He did not scream or protest when an Ushok-ku disintegrated him where he lay. They would take no chances with infection. They al knew.

The corpsmen medi scanned the dead creatures. "These are not the aliens, Captain. Some sort of parasite. Their brains are too primitive. These are not the Pliilulua,"

"Understood." Captain Obutu signaled the forward line. "We will press on until we find and kill the hell spawn."

The fusion bomb was set to go off instantly based on either Obutu or Shalinsky's verbal command. A fifteen second count down. They would take no chances once they reached the heart of the ship. Shalinsky started to understand the scope of what he was doing. Whenever the Pliilulua infected a world, they had bio suits as well. They had to come off sometime. When they did, the colonists died. Died by the billions. There was little hope he would see his family again. Or know vengeance.

They took a steep turn toward the center of the bio ship. The vessel opened up. It was a vast hollowness, the chamber they entered. Their hand beams could not even reach the ceiling to reveal any meaningful geography. The walls were round and sloping. It truly was like being on the inside of some giant leviathan. Possibly the stomach.

Captain Ombuto scanned the greenish gray, glistening walls. "Disgusting and dead center of this thing, your Grace."

Shalinsky looked grimly to either side. Two dark green lakes of unknown fluid filled the chamber on either side of the brigade. The substance seemed to not flow or move, it appeared to be some heavy, the consistency of stew. A corpsman scanned the fluid near him, a dark suited woman on the edge of a dark green lake.

"What do you get, Petty Officer?" Captain Obutu walked toward her.

"Life, Captain, very condensed life readings." She began to kneel down to scan more closely and took out a sample tube.

The Captain rushed forward alarm ringing to his helmet mike, "Don't touch it!"

The Petty officer paused within a meter of the emerald green shore. "Captain-"

A pseudopod lashed out and grabbed the woman, pulling her under as if she were a doll. The brigade started opening fire with abandon. The great green lakes rose up like the Red Sea, yet instead of parting, they smashed together a moment later catching every man and woman between them in an anvil of twenty meter fury.

The Captain and Shalinsky started screaming out the code, but the corrosive green substance ate away the Captain's skin in seconds. The five digit command code died on his lips in screams of horrid pain. Shalinsky was also burning, had reached the third code.

"I will kill you."

A tendril of green matter burrowed through the HCSIS implant in the back of Shalinsky neck. Fire seemed to lance into his brain.

A voice formed in his head as Shalinsky felt his life fading. An alien force induced his brain to understand. The words were more like shapes and came slowly like the cellular syrup that made up the Pliilulua form. Anger. Hatred. Rage filled his mind and pain. This whole race was in pain.

You are the king of the Screamers. It is time you met the Queen of Pain.

*

Gorgannith breached the sky of the shining world of Ombard. Hugh, Lilly, and Johnny pressed their faces to the Dragon's Eyes, anticipation of the planet's wonder had won in their imaginations. The food web of the green and purple-blue planet Sulanne had described prided itself on the ecological balance. Even the cities were built in cooperation with the native life.

Umphar pointed out the Halarr Ocean. "The purple blue color is derived from an algae which feeds off of contaminants and carbon and floats in massive colonies on the surface of all our bodies of water. Part of the stew you just had derived from this species as it bubbled up from the cracks in Gorgannith's back.

"Yum." Lilly thought the Ombarians were certainly highly evolved and interested in the harmony of their environments, but would sooner not know of some of the exact natures or processes that made the delicious items they had served her.

"Look at the city!" Johnny signed rapidly in excitement.

Lennir pushed in next too his guests at the window. "That is Om. Our capital city. Soon you will meet with and have council with the Khorumkhan. We have alerted them to your arrival. Apparently they knew of your coming."

Hugh turned to him. "How could they know? We were crashed on Bella. It was completely random."

"Perhaps the caretakers, the priests of the Ombari who stayed on your world all these years told them." Delonna offered.

"That makes no sense Delonna. How could they communicate through the Veil? Don't tell me they developed some tech that could span galaxies and an anomaly we travelled through to get to your space."

Delonna pointed to Om as her majestic towers eventually started to fill the entire horizon. "Almost a thousand years ago, our first bonded Dragon, Loki, brought back a team of Ombari hoping to reclaim the damaged Earth. Too soon, for the Blackening was too much for even him. He could only gain space again by leaving the whole team, six hundred people, and all their equipment. This was the seed of the Ombari, most died, some lived. They had left The Ear of The Dragon."

"So the core of the rebellion among Oceania comes from these stranded few?"

Lilly found it all difficult to accept.

Delonna assured her with a soothing voice. "It is true, they can send word through the Ear but we can never see them again."

"Your dragon hosts seem to leave a lot of their pieces around." Hugh hoped he didn't sound too disrespectful.

Umphar's tone was cool. "The Ear was a resonance crystal that Duanes use to communicate with each other over great distances. Loki lost two of his bonded Duane on the trip back. Without the properties and help of his kin in the Veil, he came to rest outside of Om and has never moved again. No dragon will take their bonded outside to this day."

The towers of the vast city of Om stretched high and wide like a forrest of crystal spires. Colors of every description rose from roofs of every building as dragon and dragonlings of various sizes and colors seemed to sweep in and out of their uppermost crevices.

"You live as one with your dragons." Lilly mentioned.

"It is more like they live with us." Delonna moved toward the crystal of the bridge and started a soft song with the others, hands overlapping. Moments later she returned.

"Gorgannith wishes you well on your journey among the Free People. He hope's you find what you seek."

"Tell him we give him our humble thanks. He is gracious to bear us." Hugh studied the great castle Gorgannith was speeding toward. It reminded him of Versailles. "I hope your Khorumkhan can answer some of my questions. There were things done to me by some of your, rather their agents, that changed me quite significantly." The fingers of his hand brushed the port at the base of his neck. "I would like to know why."

"All things will be made clear. The wisdom of The Khorumkhan is great."

"It will need to be." Hugh said.

*

The Inner Palace of the Khorumkhan lay hidden beyond the walls of the great battlements outside where Gorgannith landed. "This is as far as we can take you, friends, may the great Om guide you on your journey." Delonna's voice carried down to them from the crown of the dragon. Standing atop the dragon's head their hosts placed their hands over their hearts then spread them outward in a symbolic Ombari gesture of meeting or farewell.

Hugh returned their gesture as Lilly and Johnny waved. Cleo and Merlin we seemingly not impressed. "I hope these Khorumkhan's are expecting us, Hugh." Lilly said as she turned toward a line of dozens of strangely clothed banner men and women attending them through the gates.

The white banners flapped in the wind, a white field covered with a winged dragon surrounded by four dancing humans. "Somehow I think they have been expecting us."

They moved through the procession, in through the outer keep. The Ombari's clothes looked like the kurta pajama of Asian Indian design of ancient Earth. The strange cloth, a shimmering bronze color was bunched at the joints in cluster points. The faces were clean shaven, natural, and disciplined without further ornamentation. The banner bearers came from every creed and color of mankind. It cheered Hugh's heart.

"Their clothing is so strange, it looks more grown than crafted." Lilly studied the gather points and saw they allowed an ease of movement she had never seen in Oceanian clothes. "Yet they have no weapons of any kind I can see."

"Perhaps this tribe does not need them. Behold." Johnny pointed to the open gardens that spanned hundreds of kilometers before them. Thousands of Ombari could be seen among the manicured gardens. Hundreds of them held colorful kites. Dragon kites, mixed in among actual dragonlings flying with abandon around the large round lake. A peaceful place, one of laughter and joy if their ears were telling it true.

"So beautiful." Lilly covered her eyes with her hand against the bright sun and peered at the island at the center of the lake. "I guess we must go there, see the ship, at the dock."

Hugh saw the masts of an old world schooner on the vast purple lake. Another line of banner men could be seen in the distance, flanking the walk to the long dock. The trees, deciduous, rose mightily in colors of burgundy and silvery gold leaves. The ones on the island were bright gold, the only green rose from the deep, cut grass.

"Not much for talking, these Ombari planet side. Plenty of personnel leading us ahead with bread crumbs." Hugh led the way to the distant ship.

I love the way this planet smells. Hugh, I want to stay. Cleo ran ahead in her small, house cat form. Jumping up at butterflies and then a larger, dragon fly/bird-like hybrid.

You hated even going to the door on Earth. You wouldn't leave the house, Cleo.

Things change. Plus I couldn't do this. Cleo enlarged herself to the size of a huge tiger, having left all confining suits back on the ship. *Or this.* She stealthed and could not be seen save for the claw rips she left in the rich grass. *Or talk to you with real words. Body language is limited. Yet you can see my fears are gone of wild places at long last.*

I don't know, Cleo. Hugh glanced at Johnny, filling out his Empire survival suit and walking with a slight swagger. *Johnny tells me the ninety percent of communication is unspoken. You look the same to me. I am glad you are pleased with our new home. We might be here for a very long while.*

I suppose. I do not recall from looking through the data base that many of the cats of Earth, large or small, had much use for facial expressions. Claw and fang get all the attention.

Well see that you don't scare these people with either. Be small and cute. I do not want to reveal all our cards Cleo.

Cleo jumped out of long flowers next to the dock. Visible and house cat like. A vision of Egyptian Mau pedigree down to wagging striped tail. *As you wish.*

A rakish looking man in a tricorn hat and unblemished, white kurta removed his hat and bowed before them. "The court of Khorumkhan awaits you. Please make yourself at home on *Swiftwind*. My ship is yours." The accent was rich and sounded, Scottish, yet not easily understandable.

Johnny smiled as Lilly nodded and boarded in front of Hugh and Cleo. The sailors immediately casteoff. They found it amazing to see how well trained the small crew was on the ancient wooden craft. The three large sails were trimmed and the eighty foot ship pulled off at speed toward the waiting palace at the center of the island.

"Captain I thank you. May I ask your name?" Hugh waved and stood under the wheel house with his companions as they sat.

"I am Captain Mizzoud, my lord."

"Is there anything we should know of the court? Any courtesies or customs we should be aware of?" Hugh was tense at how fast they were being whisked toward the distant castle. Lilly was correct in her anxiousness at their possible vulnerability with the strange, lost tribe of man. They knew nothing about them except from Gorgannith's Duane. Luck favored the prepared mind.

The Captain looked comical as he placed one weather worn finger beside his nose. He whispered. "You are as safe as babes at her mothers teats, my friends. The Khorumkhan are ancient and wise. There is naught to worry of. They have seen it all once, maybe twice in their long lives. You will be at home amongst our people and the most high."

"These Khorumkhan . . . is that Ombari for King?" Lilly pulled Hugh back into his seat so she could see Captain Mizzoud.

"Two kings and two queens are the Khorumkhan. For almost eight hundred years Loki's Duane has ruled in tandem with the Eldar Duane council."

"Eight hundred years. They are Gods our priests have spoken of through years uncounted." Johnny's eyes grew wide as it sunk in and he signed excitedly.

"Surely you must have shorter years on this planet, Captain? We have heard of Loki. We did not know his Duane ruled as Khorumkhan and we heard that this Great Dragon had lost one of their number." Lilly tilted in her seat to see they were to arrive at the island within the hour.

"It has truly been eight hundred Earth years, milady. The Duane lost one, Celenil, and Loki took his last flight to this very island, snapped off his horn, and has slept ever since." He turned and pointed to a tree covered hill beside the island castle. If you look closely, you can still see his outline."

Despite the trees covering the crested hill, the outline of a dragon, massive and unmoving, revealed itself as the schooner drew close. They would have missed it if Mizzoud had not pointed it out. Just another high hill or ridge.

"He has not stirred in eight hundred years, truly. I must beg your leave and steer us in now, Lords and Lady. Yet what I tell you is true. The Duane of Loki, now the Khorumkhan, were blessed with long life through their connection to their sleeping dragon. It is said his life bleeds into them through his dreams. He laments for Celenil lost so long ago beyond the Veil. Yet four hundred years ago, Adriel took another and her new queen's life has grown long also as the dragon sleeps. The Blessed Ones will tell you far better than I if you ask."

With that Mizzoud was up the ladder before they could ask anymore.

"This gets stranger and stranger." Lilly kicked at a metal brace near her foot.

"It's kind of magical Lilly. Even the crafter's couldn't extend life past three hundred years." Crewmen expertly trimmed sails and Cleo jumped up lithely on the banister before them to watch. "They do seem to be selective in what modernities and equipment they excel at and yet they have so many pre modern items in common use." Hugh peered as the dock ropes flew to waiting hands, a coordinated dance among the crew. "It is a curious thing."

"After three hundred years human minds tend to dip irrevocably into madness."

Hugh turned away from Lilly and stretched mischievously. "There may be a difference of quality between your tribe and theirs. Ombari are like to embrace the natural, use organic or unknown techniques to allow long life, through healthier means. The Crafters are more like, you know the story I told you, Dr. Frankenstein."

Lilly tried to grab him before he jumped away. Their sense of humor had changed as they tumbled through life since their flight from Earth. It was either laugh or weep at the growing strangeness of the worlds sweeping by beyond their control. It was enough to live through one life, one time, one world, wasn't it? They went the rest of the way in silence. Not out of anger but wonder at this new world they had entered. The ship was only wood, but the craftsmanship and artistry combined to subtle and profound effect. The wood itself was minutely carved, the planks like feathers. The bow of the ship truncated up and somehow the Ombari had bent the wood into the shape of a swan's head.

The ship approached docked. Three feet away, ropes were thrown to waiting hands and the vessel was secured fast. "We will see Hugh. I hope you are right and we can find the help we need here." Lilly stood up and followed them.

An enclosed, drawn carriage pulled up and Captain Mizzoud shook their hands and congratulated them like they had won a prize. Cleo took a deep smell of the strange animals pulling it. *Those aren't horses.*

Hugh could not take his eyes off them. They were going to be pulled by two giant land snails. "I love this planet."

"Why?" Lilly asked skeptically as two carriage attendees offered to help her into the round, luxuriously appointed carriage. She shooed them away and climbed in like the athlete that she was. Merlin slept endlessly in her sling and still she had time to pull Johnny up.

"It is because it is full of life. Life not trying to kill or eat us. That is wonderful."

"I remain suspicious."

"You are always suspicious."

Johnny placed a reassuring hand on Lilly's shoulder. *"I will protect you both."* He then sat beside Hugh and placed a hand on his knee. *"And you."*

Cleo jumped up next to Lilly and started grooming herself as the carriage moved toward the castle at surprisingly good speed despite the fact it was being pulled by snails!

Hugh turned to Johnny. "See Lilly, I feel better already."

Lilly shook her head and took advantage of the privacy to feed Merlin. The sun was setting behind the golden trees.

"We shall see." Lilly whispered to her suckling child.

Ten minutes later armed guards met them at the door to the castle. They were dressed in a green plexy armor. Their plumed helmets held white feathers and even their blasters were white.

"See Lilly, weapons! You must feel better already?"

Lilly covered herself up and zipped her survival suit. "I do. I wasn't planning to disarm myself. Now all things being even, we know they understand the need for security."

Hugh looked the weapons over as they left the carriage. He whispered "they seem to only have stun setting, Lilly. Very vanilla."

"How lovely. For them."

Hugh thanked the guards for helping to gather their few things and they silently led them toward the high, arched door.

A dwarf met them in on a veranda of pure lapis lazuli covered with fiery magenta vines. He was only three feet tall, yet highly dignified by his stance if not his stature. "I am the steward here at the Summer Palace. Allow me to show you to your rooms. The Khoramkhan are eager to meet you after you settle in."

"We are most grateful for your attention steward. Do you have a name?" Hugh asked.

"Steward is all. Please follow me." The light was fading and candles were being lit all around the castle. The last rays of sun played off the dwarf's auburn hair as he waddled up a flight of stairs.

"I have never seen a man like you before Steward." Lilly regretted the statement as soon as it left her lips.

The dwarf did not even flinch. "You are Oceanian, the Wise Ones have told me. It is said that you do not bear the full blush of humanity, only the most perfect flowers are allowed to bloom. I hope my form does not offend you, my lady."

"No not at all, perhaps we do too much plucking." Lilly felt mortified.

The dwarf led them to a set of golden, gilded doors. "This will be your suite. I will return in an hour to bring you to the Hall of Thrones."

"Thank you Steward. We will be ready." Hugh opened the door, noticed two guards remained posted outside, then shut them behind him after everyone was inside.

"That was diplomatic, Lilly." Hugh laughed.

"Well I hadn't ever seen a . . . what did you call him . . . a 'dwarf'" before." She changed the subject. "Look at this room."

The room's center was filled with a fountain of grey marble lined with silver metal. The dragon's maw opened wide and sprayed water high into the air, caught as it fell in the deep basin filled with brightly colored fish. The back drop of the fountain was a clear wall covering the entire length of the room and providing a view of the lake's North side.

Clothing was provided in fully stocked armoire and set on the beds. Sonic showers in each of the four sleeping rooms had full bathroom's as well. Actual lamp lighting was available though the candles were of such size they cast plenty of light. Flagons of wine and fruits both known and mostly otherwise dotted a huge banquet table before the fountain.

"I never thought I'd see a sonic shower again." Lilly tucked Merlin into a crib that had a full monitor system and interactive safety computer. "Perhaps I could learn to like this world Hugh, Johnny."

Johnny and Hugh drank a toast of some sweet, golden wine as Cleo jumped up on the table eagerly nosing out a prepared fish. Hugh had the urge to swat her until he remembered who she was and laughed out loud. "Let's shower and get dressed in the native garb. I am excited."

An hour passed rapidly. The incredible fabric of the kurtas they wore were sheer and luxurious. Lilly felt so comfortable she only took her khirda with her and actually left her baby sleeping as Cleo said she didn't mind staying. Lilly detached the remote tracker from the crib and put it around her neck.

"Seems like you are loosening up."

"Give a woman good wine, nice clothes, even a warrior woman, it goes a long way. Though perhaps Cleo should still come with us. She is a wonder in a fight."

"We will be fine. The baby is sound asleep."

Johnny laughed out loud. He still took a blaster and his tribal spear. Hugh did not argue with him. Johnny's blue plastic scar, his black and deep blue eye, his strong pure heart and quick smile. Hugh accepted it all. What more could happen to them here.

Steward knocked twice on the chamber door. A clean shaven man wearing the most comfortable and fine clothes, and Lilly a summer dress, they followed the little man deeper into the castle. Carefully wrought sandals meshed with their feet and actually laced themselves up to the calf in Grecian style.

"My shoes seem to be alive. Massaging my legs even now, Steward."

"Yes my Lord. It is a trained plant form, concentrated peat moss is its closest descriptor I imagine. The roots comprise the sole, cleaning the floor of moisture and nutrients as you walk and the vine like tops are photosynthetic. Your clothing itself was created from a well trained species of fresh water clam. Even this castle was built in close consultation with a Builder League that works exclusively with a much tinier cousin of the travel snails which pulled you to the castle earlier this evening."

Hugh could not believe it. "You are saying this building was made by . . . snails?"

"Yes, millions of them. They were given instructions and like most things in our Great Web, they gain synergistic nutrient and symbiotic life with our people. All buildings on our planets are made by the Shulanizor."

Hugh touched the soft folds of his topaz toned clothing as he followed Steward. "Well . . . that's tremendous and . . . impressive work for something without hands."

"Cilia. The clams have cilia. We Ombari have come to believe great things come in small packages." Steward winked at Lilly who pretended not to hear him, turning as she blushed.

Guards flanked two massive double doors shot with platinum and precious stones.

A giant cauldron filled with blue flame cast wild shadows before them and joyful lute and and other stringed instruments grew louder as the gate to the Hall of Thrones opened.

Steward ambled forward and they followed. The doors closed and a line of musicians finished their present song and filed out of the door with nary a glance at the guests. Four thrones of opaque crystal stood before a round tree of tremendous girth. It looked like a banyan tree except for its foliage. The largest, most delicate golden leaves crowned the great tree though starlight could still filter down through the ceiling which opened up before them in a gentle, spiral pattern, ushering in a sweet, clean night wind.

The roof reached full dilation as Steward bowed low before the thrones. Two kings and two queens sat in the great chairs. They had grey-green eyes which were more sharply almond shaped than oval. All had an air of cool serenity by the set their soft mouths and hinted at their kinship through the centuries or simply the growing alike as couples sometimes do. One queen stood gracefully, right of center, her hair was a paler gold shot with silver, showing the only obvious difference between her and the other Khorumkhan. Her gown and thin band of station seemed to have no color or shifting sheens, making the full reality of the bolder colors of the other Ombari they had seen seem almost vulgar.

"Great Queen Adriel, Queen Margo, King Noren, and King Yu, I humbly present the travelers found on the Sacred Moon of Bella by Gorgannith and his Duane. Before you stand Johnny Blue of the land tribes of old Earth, Lillian Hsian of Oceania, and Hugh Wilkey, a journeyman through space and time."

Queen Adriel nodded to Steward who bowed one more time then abruptly headed toward the doors from which they came.

Starlight filtered onto all of them, yet the Khorumkhan's skin seemed to glow with it.

Rise

The mental voice of Queen Adriel moved through each of them. Johnny and Lilly were shocked at the direct mental communication. Though Hugh was not as unused to mind to mind contact as they, it was still jarring that Cleo was not the speaker.

Khorumkhan has long expected you. Queen Ariel's unearthly gaze fell on Hugh. *Long have we desired to speak of the old days* and the fate *of our kin beyond the veil.*

Hugh cleared his throat though it was clearly unnecessary but seemed to make him feel better none the less. *Great Rulers of the Ombari, your distant kin need your help.*

A great alien plague is destroying all mankind beyond the Veil.

Queen Ariel did not move, but stood still as stone and closed her eyes simultaneously with the three yet seated Khorumkhan. After a moment her eyes bored back into Hugh. *The Pliilulua as you call them are known to us. They call themselves the Xillonhai, in high Ombari: roughly meaning The Uncountable.*

Lilly's mental voice was as distinctive as her actual voice. *Whatever you wish to call them, they are destroying billions of humans. They will destroy all mankind if we can't stop them.*

We know this, fair Lady Hsian. The Xillonhai are close to the web of the Universe. They celebrate life in their own way. The small can create the great. The Uncountable are a hive of telepathic microorganisms that are as large as seas. They listen to the songs in the particles of matter. I fear they cannot abide the song the Empire sings.

What sound do the barbies make that displeases oh goddess of beauty. Are they as evil as my people believe? Do we not please the priests you have left on Earth? Must we share the fate of the sea demons? Johnny's mental voice was primitive but clear.

Queen Adriel stepped forward and touched Johnny's cheek. A touch of sadness crossed her pale, chiseled face. *We of the Khoramkhal have discussed this at length. The Xillonhai are inconsolable, insane in their anger and pain. The genetic tampering of your science, your,* she paused to find the word, *Crafters has torn the fabric of nature. The changes they have wrought are like an endless scream to them across the cosmos. They will destroy you root and branch. We are sorry.*

Sorry! There were tears in Lilly's eyes. *Over thirty billion people will die. They are not all crafted! You could stop them with your incredible understanding of The Web. Speak with them. Send your dragons.*

Queen Adriel shook her head and turned back to her throne. Her voice rang out with sadness and finality. *There is no more speaking to the Xillonhai. They are insane with the sound of the Empires folly. Our blessed Dragons of the Stars no longer take us beyond the Veil. Loki did this once, with us, over eight hundred years ago when my consort died. Loki has never wakened and no other bonded Duane will risk this to their beloved host. Humanity will live on with the Ombari. You will stay with us as honored family. We are sorry. Our gentle world will heal you in time of these great loss. You will come to call this home.*

Hugh stood up straight, anger coloring his face. *They are your people Khoromkhal! Earth is where you are from. You have technology. You could find a way to do this.*

The other three Khoromkhals did not speak at all, yet he could not shake that they seemed to be in constant communication, just one mind. The union to the dragon and this world made them something other than human.

Heroes do not exist except in oneself, Hugh Wilkey. If you truly save yourself, therein might be your answer. It is said the Ombardwan, the bridge, could find a way across to The Uncountable. This prophecy is as ancient as the Ombari. Is it in your heart to save this tribe of man? Do you think you are the Ombardwan of prophecy?

Hugh did not hesitate. *No.*

*

Weeks went by and everyone seemed at peace with their new lives except Hugh. Lilly and Johnny loved it here. The clean air, the harmony of life, and they accepted there was nothing they could do. They could not commandeer a dragon. After the fateful meeting in the Hall of Thrones, they had not spoken or heard from the Khoromkhal. The Steward said they could come and go as they please. The summer palace was their new home and that meant forever.

Lilly had as hard a time at first. Yet the impossibility of getting off planet, the intense wholesomeness of the world, and mother hood all conspired to make her, happy, despite all her efforts to break free of it. Johnny started learning to play the yiromchir, a stringed instrument favored by the Ombari, and loved Hugh, Lilly, and Merlin as his tribe. Cleo had a bounty of fish and it seemed all she needed as well.

Hugh, they were assholes. Cleo sat near where Hugh sulked for hours every day beside the lake. *They did blow up our whole planet and my entire species. Why not make do with what we have been given. Which is a lot. Lilly is stubborn as any human I have ever known and she is adjusting.*

He glared at her and quickly turned away as she opened a trout's belly. *Cleo, it's billions of people.* Perhaps it was some private guilt from being raised Catholic. He could not be happy even in paradise. He was always somehow less than everyone else because he was gay and they were all going to die, now. Didn't the Ombari with their embracement of all humans make a better world?

Cleo, by doing nothing, doesn't it make us just as bad as them? Jesus believed in forgiving, in redemption at any time. Who are we to caste judgement and do to them what they did to . . . cats and Earth and human diversity?

Cleo finished as much fish as she could eat. *The Empire brought it on itself, Hugh. Like this fish, it served it's purpose. The bones will feed other more deserving creatures. Besides, aren't you Buddhist or some such.*

That's a bad analogy Cleo first off. Secondly I am Buddhist with a Christian seed. All life matters. Half of humanity is dead. In another month fifteen billion people will join them. Hugh leaned on the case that held Nova's deactivated memory core. The Steward said they would try and find a humanoid hybrid to house the unusual, evolved computer. He felt he could use Nova's advice. He carried him around impatiently as if to get inspiration.

Well, I am going to go. See if you can meet with their royal highnesses and bring me along this time. I'd like to hear other human voices just to make sure you aren't as insane as I suspect.

Thanks a bunch Cleo. The Steward says they won't see me. I still need to ask why their agents experimented with our heads and these damn implants when they found us in Old Boston.

Good luck with that. Cleo ran off and jauntily disappeared into the tall grasses.

Pulling a stalk free Hugh put the grass between his teeth and studied the outline of Loki. His head was not to far away. A willow tree was growing straight out of his forehead, making him look slightly rastafarian. Except he really just looked like a hill that blocked the view from his favorite sulking spot. "You bastard, you ruined it for all the other space faring dragons with your sentimentality and thousand year power nap . . ."

Hugh thought back to his first days on Nova when he was hooked up on HCSIS. How the two colonial worlds of Faith and Providence were wiped clean by the Pliilulua. No one deserves to die that way. He would have to be a better man and try. Try something. What?

A flash of noon light reflected off of something near the willow tree. Hugh sighed, grabbed the case, and walked up to the massive nose. Rocks and roots had filled in around Loki's head over the long centuries allowing hand holds and footing. An hour later, Hugh made his way up to the tree.

Wedged between two big roots was the broken crystal horn of the great dragon Loki, broken off in his grief at the loss of one of his ancient Duane. Though only ten pounds, it was hard bringing Nova all this way up. It would be dangerous getting it back down. He placed the case on the broken stump and removed the round core computer. "Guess it will be safer to leave you up here and get one of the house dragonlings to fly up and fetch you."

Hugh placed Nova on top of the stump without his crate. The crate was slippery so he used it to shade the device from the sun and wedged it between willow roots to prevent it from falling. He then began to tour down Loki's back and see the sheer drop to the lake and the view of the countryside. He started his way down the tail.

The castle was within view and Hugh could see Lilly and Johnny playing chess through the suite's window. They waved to him and smiled. Perhaps he could make a home here. The earth began to shake so violently that Hugh lost his footing and fell on his ass. "Earthquake!"

Guards, castle workers, and his family stepped outside and looked past him in shock. Hugh stood himself up and turned around.

Loki was standing up, Willow and all. Great blue eyes started to open and rocks and trees began falling off his great back as black water filled the crater his great body had filled. After eight hundred years, the dragon had awakened.

Fear and regret suddenly swelled in Hugh as Loki reached up with a claw and pulled the willow from his head and planted the tree in the ground where his head had rested. He started running toward Loki. Nova might have been crushed in the fall. If he had killed *Nova* he would never forgive himself. Unless . . .

Hugh yelled louder than he ever had before in Loki's direction, "Nova!"

Loki peered down at Hugh like a sea eagle vectoring in on a herring. His mind was suddenly filled with the largest mental voice he had ever heard. *So you are the one called Hugh Wilkey.*

It hurt his mind and dazed him a second. *I am Hugh, Loki. It is true. What have you done to Nova?*

A terrible booming sound filled the air and people screamed in the castle behind him. Lilly, Johnny, and Cleo were running like mad toward him strapping on weapons. It occurred to Hugh the dragon was laughing. *The question should be, young human, what has your Nova done to me?*

As Loki bent down to drink lake water and gobble up a large boulder, Hugh could see the broken crystal horn had re grown and encysted Nova's computer casing. Nova had joined with Loki. *How can this be?*

His family had caught up to him and were caught in the wonder of the great dragon eating and cleaning itself a bit, and some of the landscape. Stretching. "Jesus Hugh, what the hell did you do?" Lilly called out as she reached him.

"You sound like a wife, Lilly." Hugh laughed and pointed at Loki. "I guess I accidentally woke the dragon."

Loki turned to Lilly and looked at her with his giant glowing eye. He beamed directly into her head, *An accident perhaps. Do not be too cross with him, child. I have slept for a very long time. Nova has set down deep roots in a short period of time and carried a seed. A seed of something unusual to me. The seed sensed my pain and did what it was made to do. Started healing me through my deep, endless dreams. By what Nova has shown me, pulling me from my long, sorrowful reverie. It was time to waken, for my part, and do what we must.*

Lilly stood motionless, as if pinned as Johnny used the traditional sign of Ombari greeting he had come to take as his own. Cleo turned to Hugh. *Why can I sense what is between us is also within this great, rocky lizard?*

Before Hugh could answer, Loki answered: *It is in me. The bionanytes are surging through my body, replicating. Healing me . . . changing me. Showing me many things that I had not known. Things I had not dreamed of in all my millennias of life.*

Cleo's unexpressive face expressed pure surprise. *He just spoke to me.*

He did. Hugh replied.

I did. Loki added.

"*The Khorumkhan's come.*" Johnny signed and pointed.

A hundred mounted knights surrounded four smaller flying dragons on which Loki's Duane flew. Two footed riding lizards formed a semi circle around Loki as the four flying mounts swept into the air. They circled Loki and their glee filled barks filled the air. Queen Adriel landed on Loki's head with the others. "We greet you great Loki!

These are your four young children who bear us. We feared we would never hear your great voice again."

Hugh noticed the queen used spoken words. Loki cooed at his children and Duane though it sounded more like rumbling of distant thunder.

I have missed you my daughter. Our dreams have mingled for countless years and it is good to see you after so long. Loki's mental voice amplified, the force of it seemed to ripple through the very grass and trees like a wind. *Hear me Khorumkhan and people of Ombari. We have slept too long behind the Veil. It is time we waken the Vanguard and ride to war.* Something had happened to the dragon during its revival that increased the mental voice far beyond his normal range of four chosen riders. Perhaps everyone on planet heard his voice.

The Khorumkhan seemed to lose some of their luminescence. Their sharp edges and cool color seemed to soften and return to their more human tones. Even their moon kissed hair darkened. Adriel seemed to look down at Hugh with an unreadable face.

Hugh sighed, turned toward Johnny and Lilly, whispering, "there is an an old Earth saying that you may not have heard: be careful what you wish for."

Chapter 13

Home

"Do we have to go back Adriel?" Celinil asked shyly.

"Yes. How can you ask me this again Cel?" Adriel closed the portal to the bridge. Loki's ten other ring compartments were crammed with colonists and their equipment as the dragon hurled through space on great wings. His back was weighed down with several tons of supplies and devices they would need but he did not complain in the weightless vacuum of sub space. She glanced at the crystal horn, upthrust and resonant in the stark bridge. "We are the first Duane and the bridge makers for our people. Loki wants to see our old home and why we left."

"How we left it you mean. Earth is dead. We killed it. I do not know if I can live with the weight of him and the Vanguard knowing our folly."

"It was humanity's folly and it's been a very long time. Our parents' parents' sins are not ours. We go to search for survivors. We go help them and better them through what we have learned of The Great Web."

"Or to honor the dead and let our beloved know how horrible our people are. How they destroyed the web of life on our birth planet. How we are a terrible species."

"If that is all we can do, we will do it. We owe them that much. We are a young race Cel, we have grown beyond our smallness. Bless Om."

"It is folly, Adriel. The Blackening destroyed all life after our grand parents fled. There is nothing for us on Earth but dark memories and ash. I have a bad feeling about this journey."

"Earth may have found her way back Cel."

"After what it went through, what could be left? I am as frightened of what could have lived through the Blackening as I am a dead planet."

Celenil's protest had been present from the beginning. Adriel never thought Loki would take her suggestion seriously. On Bella, it had taken ten years for the four of them to develop their strange sensitivities to communicate with the enormous dragons of their cherished moon. It was an accident. Noren, Yu, Celenil and her were taking geo thermal samples when they came across the pillar of odd colored rock. Laying their hands on it together, they unwittingly made contact with the first sentient race humanity ever knew.

Peaceful, powerful, ancient, their name was utterly unpronounceable in human speech, sounding much like an avalanche in their rumbling, deep throats. "Dragon" seemed to suit them and humans equitably, though it was over a 100 million Earth years since they were anything resembling reptiles. The dragons evolved into a silicon based life form they are now and their society and customs were ancient when humanity was hitting each other with rocks in caves.

The veil had marooned the colonists of the rocket Ombardwan for two hundred years on their ancestral birthing area. The dragons and their human seers grew so close so quickly, the culture that developed even in ten years impacted both species more than they would know until many years later. The dragons enjoyed the bright, intensely short, almost desperate lives of the humans. The humans learned the way of The Great Web, living in harmony with the universe, the dragon sages believed since time immemorial. The Buddhists among the humans delighted the dragons with their concept of Om. In such ways a common language began between the species that at first glance seemed so vastly different.

The dragons could also ferry humanity back to the stars. Their enormous wings generated lift through geothermal lay lines in their rocky skin, compressing magnetic fields and shaping movement in small warp grains, millions of them rather than one vulnerable warp bubble. Once mind connections were made, connections infused longer lives, happier, more peaceful tendencies in humanity on Bella. The Vanguard, the confederation of Dragons who lived in the Veil, shared the greatest delight in humanity. Though only a few could mind bond. Those that did spread the joy of their unlikely new family with the others of their kind.

Adriel leaned her head against the crystal. Loki could not hear her without the other three of the Duane linking hands and she was glad. She also worried what he would think of her after seeing Earth. Her grandmother was Captain of the Ombardwan rocket centuries ago. Originally one of three prototype, warp capable rockets. When the nuclear missiles launched, back in 2020, she did not wait for the private jets of the CEO's, world leaders, and their families to arrive to the secret site in the Amazon. She took all the workers in the site. Regular people, scientists, bakers, people who were not the elite one percent. There was no time to wait, perhaps, but Adriel knew as she knew her grandmother before she died in the city of Om, Captain—valued life too much to wait for those so called leaders to make their get away. Scott free from a planet they had largely despoiled. She took the people she could, that were there, and blasted off.

It was a bittersweet memory. She seemed to carry her grandmother's guilt but she knew in her heart she would have made the same decision. All life was equal in its worthiness without rank; human, dragon, and those perhaps yet unknown. Celenil did not know of her secret guilt, this blood debt. Adriel supported the expedition for all those who might have survived The Blackening, however unlikely that was. They would see and so would Loki, leader of his race. Perhaps he would not judge them. She hoped she wouldn't judge herself. The five hundred Ombari were intended to heal their lost home world. With luck they would not be sacrificed to it.

Yu and Noren walked in hand and hand and noticed the tension in the air.

"Is everything all right ladies?" Yu asked.

"We are fine. Just waiting for you lads so we could prepare for landing." Adriel lied.

Noren shrugged and looked inquiringly at Yu. "If you say so, let's speak to Loki then. It's been five days in deep flight and we miss him."

The four linked hands on the crystal.

There you are. Earth is where you said it was. Loki sounded excited. *We should be there very soon.*

The two couples mental voices seemed to merge into one. *Our colonists are eager and grateful, Great Loki. We hope our lost world is not . . . something that will sadden you. We made mistakes, our ancestors of old.*

The deep rumbling of laughter. *You think you are the only ones who have made a mess of things. Once long before we of the Vanguard opened our hearts to the Great Web, we fought amongst our own kind. For things as silly as prime meteor fields used for feeding. Family clan fought family clan.*

Adriel felt better. Sometimes she thought Loki was her best friend. Her thoughts melded back with the others. *It is a sad thing that the Vanguard had such burdens to bear.*

It was a very long time ago. I am five thousand of your years old. This happened ten generations ago before we found wisdom. You are a younger race. Mistakes are made.

Loki, you never destroyed your home world.

No. We ate it. Deep rumbling of laughter. *Which is why we are better caretakers now. We need places to land. Green places. We cannot hold our breath forever. We cannot bear our young in the vacuum and cold of space.*

When did you take to the stars Loki?

We are a slow growing, long lived race my friends. It takes two thousand years to be ready to glide through the Om. Ahh look forward. We have arrived at your Earth. I thought you said it was blue?

Used to be blue. Their hearts sank as they peered at the planet. *Our great war turned the oceans black. We are sorry.*

Don't be. Things can turn themselves around. The Web is Merciful.

Our planet looks angry. Celenil's voice rose above the other three.

The Web will forgive child. In time.

Loki's giant form crested the lightning filled clouds of Earth. Ice crystals formed all over him despite the heat of descent. Earth was a block of blackened ice and ash. He aimed for a land mass between two ebony oceans.

The colonists prepared survival gear and gas masks. Excitement built along the ring. Hundreds of field scientists and researchers huddled near window ports speaking into data ports and taking pictures.

Adriel and her Duane walked among the passengers, alerting Centurions of their immanent arrival. One in ten carried a projectile gun. One in a hundred a laser. By the looks of things, there wouldn't be anything to shoot.

Loki veered toward the ruins of a great city. They had discussed landing sites and a standing city, even if ruined, may allow for weathering of some of the mega storms that swept across planet, three of which were visible from space.

The ring shuddered as the dragon landed in a large park in the enter of the metropolis. No sun, just a diffuse grey light pierced the storm clouds, even at mid day. The debarkation chambers on both sides of the ring were equipped with atmosphere venters so they could decompress back and forth into the hostile environment and possibly poisonous and radioactive air.

That is when they attacked.

Hundreds of Ombari shrieked in fear as Loki bellowed his rage and challenge to to things. That is when they saw the first evidence of dragon fire. Loki bellowed a hot stream of fire and magma at the creatures attacking it.

Adriel sprinted back toward the bridge. When she arrived the others were waiting. Celenil looked at her with tears in her eyes. "There is something left out there. Hurting Loki. They look like . . . Wraiths."

Adriel could not believe her ears. Looking out the window, there were thousands of shadowed creatures crawling up Loki's arms. His great breath would obliterate hundreds at a time yet more came.

Grabbing Celenil by the hand Adriel joined the men at the crystal. *Loki we must fly!*

Pain. These things are feeding on me. Must . . . go.

Another roar and he took flight. Hundreds of the things crawled on Loki. On his arms, even on his wings. He could not shake them. The duane could feel his pain.

Loki, go into the ocean. Shake them off!

I will try.

The dragon angled up to ten thousand meters then plunged headlong into the Ocean. *Hang on!*

There was no seating in the bridge, so they gripped the crystal horn and each other and closed their eyes. They prayed the passengers would tie themselves down. Yu called through his mike, "Emergency landing! Tie yourselves down! Brace for impact!"

The screams of the Wraiths and the howl of the wind mingled. Three minutes later they hit the water with a bone jarring force. Light flickered and Celenil screamed.

When the emergency lights kicked on, Yu and Noren were sprawled in the corner. Noren was out cold. Yu's leg was bent at an ugly angle. Adriel had broken her hand, she was sure. "Celinil, are you okay?"

After a pause, she rose up from the corner. "I think so. You are hurt!"

"We all are." Adriel called into her mike. "Medic to the bridge. We have wounded."

Yu grabbed Adriel's arm. "We must wake Noren. We have to speak to Loki."

Adriel could not see out the bridge windows as the water was truly black as night. But she could feel the great wings pumping, like a Captain who knew her ship. "Noren will be treated here. We will have him place his hands on the crystal if we have too."

"Will that work with one of us unconscious?" Yu asked as he bent over Noren.

"I hope so."

Two medics ran into the bridge just as Loki started pulling himself onto the shore. It was snowing outside but they had gone far from the city and the wraiths seemed to have been swept away.

"Give him smelling salts if you have to medic. We need Noren." Adriel's face was grimly set.

Noren woke roughly. "I am here. Status?"

"We don't know." Adriel thanked and dismissed the medics after setting her hand and Yu's leg. They brought in a stool for Yu. Noren had a mild concussion but there was no helping it. "Let's speak to Loki."

They clasped hands on the crystal though Adriel winced in pain. *Loki, are you okay!?*

I think so. Very weak. Those things have drained me somehow.

Can we leave planet. We need to get out of here.

No. I need . . . Loki collapsed with a dull rumble.

Noren wiped tears from his eyes. "He can't be dead."

"I". Adriel was too choked up to continue. She wiped her face with her sleeve. "We need to go outside. See to his wounds. He may be asleep . . ."

"Or poisoned somehow." Yu offered.

"Or dead. We never should have come here!" Celenil ran out the hatch. Adreil went after her, cradling her broken hand.

"Cel. Come back." *He's not dead. He can't be.*

Stopping by a Centurion, she grabbed his arm. "We need a team of medics and scanners out there until Loki is up. We need a defensive perimeter, stat!"

"Aye aye mam. I will see to it."

Celenil had lost her in the press of alarmed Ombari. Teams were getting suited up. Medics and one specialist in dragon physiology. She approached the scientist. "Doctor Grieves!"

A man with short blond hair turned to her. "Honored Duane. How can I help you."

"Get suited with me and help me assess Loki's condition."

"He is catatonic." The Doctor assessed him quickly.

"Not dead." Thank God.

"I don't think so. We need to get outside and feel for his breathing. Hard to do in here." He struggled to snap on his bio suit. Adriel helped him then quickly dressed.

When they had decompressed and left the safety of the ring with ten centurions and every medic on board, Grieves knelt down and put his hand on the dragons skin near the temple. "Feel here Duane."

She reached down and felt a deep trembling from the massive bellows of his lungs. Breathing. "Breathing but breathing what Doc? Is it poison?"

Dr. Grieve's pushed some buttons on a device he was carrying. "It's full of ash and slightly radioactive, very unhealthy for humans, but breathable. Definitely fine for Loki, they are a lot tougher than we are."

"Thank Om." She hugged the doctor despite the clank of helmets. "Let's see to his wounds. What were those things?"

Dr. Grieves shook his head. "Damned if I know. Some kind of negative energy vampire. They steal heat and bio electric energy, best I can tell."

"They steal life. Loki does not owe this debt. We do."

"I don't think the wraiths care Duane."

The medics reports came back. Loki was torn in a hundred places and deeply. He was slowly healing. He would have to use all his strength to be able to get off the ground with the multi ton transport on his back. Once air-borne he could break it loose as needed while in flight. Yet no crane existed to move it off his back. He normally would have been strong enough to bring back all the colonists and their supplies. As things stood, he would have to leave the colonists here, but he would not part with his Duane. Fortunately the expedition of Ombari were well supplied. Though air was mostly breathable, safe if breathed through masks which they had in abundance.

Food here was completely tainted for humans and even stones and materials Loki needed to consume to gain his strength were too warped by radiation and depleted to replenish him. He would have only one chance to break free from orbit. Or he would be trapped here. He would die.

The decision was made. Loki would drop the heavy module into the sea when he was just short of reaching high orbit. The Duane would detach it from the bridge using an emergency release. They would then head back to the Veil and get help.

The planet was leaching energy from Loki. Time was crucial and when all the expedition had removed everything that wasn't bolted down to Loki from the holds, he took flight.

We are moving at good speed, Loki. Let us know when you are ready.

Very well. Five more minutes.

Loki approached the stratosphere and started struggling. *Now*

Yu limped over and pulled the release.

Nothing happened.

"Shit."

"Come back here Yu. We have to abort. We need to tell Loki." Adriel couldn't believe the release had betrayed them. It must have been damaged when they hit the water but they checked it.

Yu struggled back and joined hands on the crystal. *We cannot release Loki.*

There was a pause. *I am Loki, son of Drethinil, son or Rethgar. I will not yield.*

Loki struggled against the pull of gravity. His mighty wings beat furiously. He shook his head and Noren fell. This time he bashed already concussed head again and was out cold. "No!" Yu left the crystal and bent to Noren.

Celenil turned to Adriel. "There is no time. I will manually release the transport harness from inside."

"No. Cel. It was my mission. I will do it." Adriel eyes swelled with tears. "You were right. We never should have come here."

Celenil shook her head. "No. Your hand is broken and I am a trained engineer. You need two hands to break the seal and turn the manual release. I will not see Loki pay for our sins."

"It is my duty. I am ranking Duane. You must follow my order."

Celenil smiled and kissed her. "Not this time." Loki lurched again and started falling back. Adriel fell to her knees. "Remember me." She ran through the hatch and was gone.

"Noooooo! Celenil!" Adriel struggled to open the Bridge door but Celenil time locked the code. It would not release for two hours. "No. Dear God, blessed Om. No."

Yu and Adriel held each other. Within a few minutes, the transport pod fell away and burned up in orbit with Celenil aboard. She gave her life for them.

Loki reached hyperspace. His deep lament of mourning shook the ring station for five days. Reaching Ombar, the sonic boom of his mass breaching orbit was heard across the city. Without a word he sent an amplified decree to all his kind. *Kin and kind, the Duane shall stay in the Veil from this day forward.*

Reaching up he clasped the central horn of his head with both massive arms, snapping it cleanly off with part of the empty bridge. Loki rumbled deep in his chest, set his massive form down near the lapping waters of the purple lake, and slept.

*

"You have woken the King of The Vanguard. I know not your purpose but you will not sacrifice him. We have not awaited Loki's return for eight hundred years just to see him killed over a rampant and cruel strain of humanity that brought it on itself!"

Adriel was not happy with Hugh. Perhaps Loki summoned him, mind powers of man much less starfaring dragons being little understood. Made him climb up and place Nova on the crystal stump. It had changed Nova, Loki, and the ruling Duane of Ombar. Adriel, Margo, Yu, and Noven no longer could speak mind to mind. To some in the court their link with Loki had been usurped. It was a lot happening very fast after so many centuries of calm.

"I do not know how this came to pass, but it is his choice. Between the bionanytes and Nova's own data and personality, Loki has seen the need to intervene before the Pliilulua destroy humanity beyond the Veil." Hugh knew there was no point arguing with them yet he had to try. There was just no time. If he could only persuade them an armada of bonded dragons could save humanity.

"I forbid it. Loki is not well and you have tainted our bond somehow. You have darkened our sacred mind link and now you seek to take him as well. Why should you care about the humanity you have fled from. Did they not try to snuff out your life and your family's? They hunt you for what they need while they despise you. They would kill you for who you are, for the color of your skin, your very ideas, as they have done for millennia. Why save them now?"

Adriel sat on her throne, looking defeated and dulled with the other three rulers of the Ombari. Yet it was not a question he had not asked himself many times.

"The very reason I am here is due to those religious wackos perverting Jesus's words, casting tyranny of the many onto the few after centuries of their own persecution for being different. They took away my marriage. My sense of belonging . . . anywhere. In any time. I am no longer Christian, but I believe Jesus would want us to save them. To forgive them. Not let them die."

Adriel speared him with an eye full of anger. "They will pollute and crush all the natural children of man. They have not learned in all this time. We form the Sacred Duanes as a symbol of the validity of all love. To embrace all the natures of human kind. They would cut you down root and branch and forget you even if you saved them. We will not commit those loyal Duanes to such a fate."

"They might be wrong and perhaps have done evil things." He thought all unchanging rulers often did trying to rule a people if they roosted too long. "Yet I will lay down my life for the diversity and potential that still exists. I will not let myself become like them. Nor should you. Even the very wise cannot see all ends."

Hugh turned and walked toward the gilded doors of the Hall of Thrones.

"You do not have my leave to go." Adriel's voice boomed out through the great hall.

Without turning Hugh called back, "Fifteen billion humans have died. I will not let the other half go without a fight."

Guards sprang out of their side rooms and pressed toward the door to block him. Hugh did not even bother to look at them. He flung forth his arms, anger, and doubt and let the magnetic fields wash down his arms as flickers of blue power cascaded forward toward the locked double doors. With a boom the bar broke and a small shock wave knocked the guards off their feet.

Loki was in the courtyard of the Summer Palace. *Will they support us?*

They will not. I am sorry.

I see. With three of the Vanguard we are a mighty force. Gorgannith and his consort Nithalanil await us in orbit with their Duanes. There is hope.

Hugh knew Loki must have some idea what they were up against thanks to Nova's connection to the dragon. All the data of a dreadnaught super computer, it's transformed HCSIS brain, and the bionanytes themselves made this king of the Star Dragons something else. Only the battle ahead would say what that was. Still he would not bring Johnny Blue or Lilly with him. He would not risk them though they were not taking it well. Merlin needed a parent. Johnny needed . . . Hugh. Hugh would not see them hurt anymore from his plans. He could not bare it.

Loki lowered his head. A Nova modified, ship ring with only three rooms was built around his regrown horn. It was fashioned for war, extra shielding, plating, and a stealth generator. Their one advantage was the Empire and the Pliilulua had no idea of their intent and capabilities.

Surprise may be their best weapon. Hugh climbed in through a simple hatch on the side after levitating himself up and strapped himself in.

Their speed increased rapidly. There was no need to even place hands on the central horn, Hugh could hear everything Loki was saying, even to his kindred.

We are here, Lord. Nithalanil sent. *Will the Vanguard be here soon?*

No, true hearts. My beloved Duane has had too much of the rock dreams seep into their bones from me I fear over the long sleep. They have become stiff and unbending as we had become before we met them. Now. Flank my wings. We fly to war.

The dragons and their Duanes formed up and broke into the veil quickly building to warp speed. Hugh pushed on his wrist chron so that he might speak to the Duanes. Lilly's and Johnny's were not easy to acquire but they conceded them once they knew they could not make Hugh take them.

"Gorgannith and Nithanil, any word from the other Duanes?" Hugh called.

The wrist chrons were of military grade allowed decent short distance, in warp transmission. A woman's voice, "Corine here of Nithanil. The other Duanes are gathering, by Dragon's Ear we know our brothers and sister hear Loki and your call. Yet they will not disobey the Khalimkar without due course."

"Hail and hello, Hugh of Loki," Lennir's familiar voice rang in from Gorgannith. "The dragons hear Loki's call, yet are fearful or breaching the mandate of taking Duanes beyond. They fear the deep sleep that has changed Loki so much."

My eyes have opened quickly. The Children of Om I left on Earth so long ago have brought Hugh, The Ombardwan, The Bridge, to me in mankind's great hour of need. The Vanguard will look into their hearts and find courage. I will not force my kin without insight.

Hugh set down his wrist chron. *You hear everything. Why would you risk yourself again, Loki? Earth was not kind to you before? You owe us nothing.*

The mental voice seemed to fuse with qualities of Nova and Loki. *The bridge brings two places together over a divide. All life has a place. The Pliilulua have no right to extinguish an entire species much like mankind has no right to persecute and hunt its own. We will try to communicate with them and ask them to see their folly before we . . . go further.*

What if it is too late, Loki? What if they won't listen?

Then we will stop them.

The trio of dragons left the Opaque Veil with their humans for the first time in eight hundred years. They headed toward Earth with increased urgency. Five days would tell them if there was any humanity to save.

Hugh stared out the dragon's eyes, warp space melting the stars into long streams of pure light as they passed. So much had happened since last year when he was in the HCSIS tank trying to stop a plague. He looked at his hands and arms. Streams of pale light, a silver blue nimbus, slipped between his skin and the air around him. The fine filaments looked like the minutest stream of webs between him and . . . everything.

Loki, what am I seeing?

Your eyes are clearing. The bionanytes in you and me are like the pieces of a puzzle. They use the magnetic fields that exist around all matter to modify themselves and us. The ties have always existed between all things in the great web, the bionanytes simply make us see what always existed.

So these light particles aren't a fission leak or worse.

No. They are speaking with the colonies in me and evolving together. They are showing us the ties and they will show us more I suspect. They are learning to move even time, as they learn the matrix of my species ability to fly faster than light through space. It is a marvel, the life within life.

Wiping at the wisps around his arms, Hugh found he could disperse them yet they would reform. Yet if he tried not see them, they would fade from his vision. *I hope all this life can help us against what is coming?*

We will see.

*

Three days later Hugh looked around the small ring of his bridge and living area. It was done in Oceanian style. Ridges of ornamentation in aquatic motifs touched the areas of the interior in unexpected places. The crafting of it was directed by Nova and the bionanytes. All the Ombari had to do was bring raw materials to the Dragon King. There were even seats in the bridge despite good artificial gravity.

Where has Nova gone Loki? It seems his personality is subsumed by you.

Silence as Hugh waited and he was wondering if Loki was asleep while flying in warp, an uncomforting thought.

He is here. All within me. Part of me. There is in all of us a world within worlds. It is rather engaging for him and the boundaries between him and I have gone. There is much to learn and a rare opportunity to learn it.

I see. Thank you. Hugh had never been a formally trained as a scientist. A life long love of human discovery in the many avenues of endeavor never prepared him for this mixture of biological and technological interaction. How all these different variables within him and Loki could work so harmoniously to such important ends would be something he would need to just accept rather than understand. Hugh walked out of the bridge and continued to explore.

Even though it was only him, the bed in the sleeping cabin was big enough for four. A pang of loneliness hit Hugh and blossomed in his belly nearly causing him to choke up. He was used to sleeping next to his family. The possibility he might never see them again was hitting hard.

Hugh went to the bathroom and stood in front of the mirror. He tried to count to ten without looking away. In his old life he would look away before he finished count. In his old, polluted Earth, the right wing had taken his marriage away from him and Mike. They said "marriage belongs to the people." Wasn't he a "people". Since they revoked it, thousands of years ago, he remembered not being able to look himself in the mirror. It wasn't his fault how people felt about them. When there is fear, doubt, and ignorance of people's fundamental humanity, there was always injustice by the many on the few.

Now it had changed. Everything had changed. His people, the Ombarians, flourished and kept the true flame of human potential alive. Despite his poor treatment by ancient Earth and its descendants, he was learning to forgive them for having inflicted their casual, ignorant slander on him. After all, what good did it ever do them, in the end. He forgave them for hating others they did not know, understand, and taught others to fear. He forgave them for destroying the world and in doing so, started to forgive himself for leaving them to their fates.

He had a clipped beard going and a full head of hair he had kept short recently. The Ombarian's had barbers, grooming, and deodorants! The right corner of his widow's peak had started to recede and his hair had become shot with silver in recent years. Michael would have liked it, mortality trip and all. Another pang of regret hit him. He pulled the lid on his own life all those years ago in the cryogenic chamber under MIT. It was a cruel thing to do to Michael. Even if he felt Michael deserved better. It all came back to Hugh not being able to live with Hugh. It might be just a front for wanting his freedom not to be judged by anyone anymore.

Freedom from the evil world that had seemed to hate him since he was born. Being gay, white, male, average, seemed a bearable weight, all things considered. With the revocation of marriage rights for gays, it had numbed Hugh to the core. Yet hadn't he paid for closing the door on humanity in spades. Humanity was supposed to have evolved when he woke. Instead it blew itself up with religious war. Though Hugh never could deal with the false acceptance and cold politeness they gave Hugh and Mike's union, perhaps he could do them some good by stopping the second obliteration of Earth for their descendants.

The price of losing his life and Ombar, a world that would let him live in honor, happiness, and peace for the first time in his life suddenly seemed a bad deal. Maybe Adriel was right. Maybe the Oceanians didn't deserve it and should be allowed to rot in their designer genes. What if they didn't learn anything or stop the gene fascism and the repugnant hunt? Hugh thought on this for some time as the stars spun past. Perhaps, just like they didn't have the right to judge him, he wasn't going to judge them now in their greatest hour of need. They were human after all. It might not be better if they were all dead.

Hugh we will be in Earth orbit in a half hour. We are being followed.

Hugh moved quickly back to the bridge. Fastening the battle harness on his chair, he punched up long range scans. "Holy shit."

There are one hundred and thirty three Imperial Star ships approaching us.

That was close to the projected human fleets left at the front. Could this be the front? What were they doing chasing after them. *Loki what do you think is their intent?*

Unknown, Hugh. A ship called Relentless is ordering us to drop out of warp. That ship is bigger than me. Humanity has been busy all these centuries. They have come a long way from their blasted home world.

Not as far as you might think. I do not trust them. Their new leader is not a good man.

Nova has given me full schematics and background on the coup. It is interesting how different they are from the Ombari.

Hugh thought about the Khorumkhan and wondered how true that really was. *It may be true but if they are led by Shalinsky, they are as dangerous as the Pliilulua.*

True. They will over take us soon. You can communicate with them once we are out of warp?

I hope. Are you are as tough as you seem?

A king is as mighty as their people it is said. Loki sounded amused.

My people can be mighty stupid and led by bad people more than occasionally. I want to know if you think we are going to do anything to fight that battle fleet? How can we fight both them and the Pliilulua?

The bionanytes have made me faster and stronger than my kin. Truly, I fear for them and us. Either way, we will soon find out. Om be with us.

The three dragons came out of warp. Their wings slowly flapped whirls of magnetic energy around them in pulsing streams of pale light. Loki's wings pulsed blue light possibly as a result of the changes he had undergone. The dragons stayed tense and still as the armada fell out of warp around them.

The space around them so filled with oval Colonial war ships, it was difficult to see space itself through them. Loki, Gorgannith, and Nithanil were completely surrounded. Hugh pulled up his wrist chron, "This is the Vanguard of Ombar, we come to the aid of Earth and as emissaries to speak with Pliilulua."

Hugh, Nova says many of these are HCSIS ships and yet are not running their scans. Stealth ships are not being searched for. Something is wrong.

"This is the U.C.S. Flagship, Relentless." The voice sounded strained and somehow familiar. "You are violating our space, Aliens, and you will be purged."

Purged? Sounds like his friends from Earth well enough. "We have come to ask the Pliilulua to stop their aggression. We have come to stop the war not fight you."

"Earth is safe. The Ombarian or whatever you call yourselves, you are not welcome here. The punishment for alien invaders is death"

Hugh, there is another ship stealthed that has enveloped the Relentless. It is compromised by a Pliilulua Queen Ship. It's a trap! Vanguard, fly!

Nova's modified scanners kicked in showing the enormous organic vessel had eaten halfway into the Relentless, slowly absorbing it. With the other HCSIS ships heightened scanners turned off, this armada had no idea the enemy was among them.

Nova! Figure out a way to get those other HCSIS ships to see their flagship is infected. Loki, have the dragons fly in and around those big cruisers. They will not be able to fire for risk of hitting each other!

The dragons were fighting for their lives. Most of the Imperial Armada could not bring their weapons to bear and the dragons were far more maneuverable than the space ships and their skins were thick. Ruby colored blast beams lanced out at a staccato pace as Nithanil and Gorgannith flew for their lives.

To Hugh's amazement all three dragons were narrow beaming their breath weapons on the warp drives, trying not to destroy or render too helpless much needed vessels of the Earth fleet. Loki shook and spun violently. *We will not last long in this,* Hugh sent.

Nova says more bad news. The Pliilulua have two fleets. One is in position around Earth, prepared to destroy all life. Another is surrounding us.

How many Nova, Loki, uh, both of you?

Over five hundred split evenly between Earth and here.

Nova, get those HCSIS ships to see that stealthed Pliilulua mother ship!

Working on it.

Work quickly. Have all three dragons focus fire on that alien ship!

Hugh, I will try and speak to the Pliilulua before we attack. Give me a minute.

Hurry Loki!

The dragons were moving so fast the Imperial targeting computer's were getting only minor hits and occasionally hitting each other. The hits were wearing them down rapidly though. The real Pliilulua fleet was almost fully in position to cross fire the human Armada. The three dragons closed to breath weapon range of the mother ship.

The hive mother is locked in a blood feud with these humans. They are so full or rage and anger at the genetic screams of your people, caused by their endless crafting, they will not stop until they are all silenced. They have gone mad in their pain.

If it's any consolation, they are a pain to me too. Open fire, Loki.

Though Hugh could sense the regret Loki carried, the three dragons raked the mother ship with their fiery breath. Both Relentless and the Mother ship opened fire in response. Hugh held his breath as Loki dodged a red beam that flared right across his great nose. The beams seems to move more slowly as the battle progressed. Hugh could only see Goragannith and from his vantage but he was moving more slowly like the Colonials. *Loki, what is happening?*

We are moving so quickly that our enemies seem to be moving slowly. A great gift from The Hugh, Hugh.

All hell broke loose. The hidden Pliilulua fleet became visible and opened fire. Ten earth ships exploded within minutes and the Armada turned away from the dragons and turned outward toward the Pliilulua orbs, HCSIS systems all coming on line.

Loki blew another bolt of energy at the joining point of the mother ship and Relentless and in turn was raked by a wide beam burst Pliilulua energy weapons point blank. Even with their time delay, Loki could not avoid them all. He screamed.

A terrible sound, Hugh covered his ears as Loki's bionanytes started repairing a long bloody sear on the dragon's right flank. Nithanil was not so lucky. Five spore vessels surrounded the dragon and repeatedly shot volleys of green black energy at her torso. She spasmed and stopped moving, dark blood freezing in garnet colored slugs meters wide and sparkling in the fire fight.

Nooooo. Gorgannith's projected, mental scream could be heard directly by Hugh. The dragon that found him went berserk and would not listen to his Duane or Loki. Gorgannith started tearing the five spores leaving his consort to pieces, in a fury, one after another.

Hugh, I am going to get to Earth. Those two hundred and fifty spore ships are almost in position to release their killing mists. Earth will die

Let's go.

Not this time, I think, brother. We cannot be two places at once. The Queen you must defeat, but it will not matter if Earth is dead. Gorgannith and the fleets battling will buy us a little time. You must get the Queen. I will stop the killing of your world. If I can.

Loki was easily avoiding long, lazy death beams from both fleets as they turned and started fighting each other in in earnest. The bright, sizzling rays sprayed at Loki like molten lave slowly dripping down panes of glass. Time was warped to their advantage but would not last forever.

Loki, how can we separate?

Nova planned ahead and your family insisted the ring unit would have autonomous capacity, like a shuttle, you can fly Relentless if I bring you close enough.

I wish there was some other way, Loki.

As do I. Good bye, Hugh.

You must not die Loki, it is too much to risk. I demand you abort—Hugh's words were cut short.

Loki once again reached forward with his claws and removed the ring that contained Hugh, Nova's data core, and the stump of Loki's horn. It seemed designed for easy removal until crystallized blood from the dragon's wound filled space all around the ring . . .

The lord of the space dragons rolled away from a barrage of intense fire. *It is the only way.*

No! Loki you can't.

Loki grabbed onto the hub of Relentless's outer ring and placed the little ship on the leeward side away from any gun installations. *Farewell.*

Bunching up his enormous legs, Loki pushed off from the dreadnaught like a swimmer pushing off from the side of a pool. He instantly went to warp and disappeared into the night.

Hugh, it was the only way. Nova's voice had returned to fully his own timbre.

What have we done Nova?

We have decided to do what we must to assure we have a chance to save Earth.

We? Who are we? Hugh thought angrily.

Loki, the bionanytes, you, and me.

Will Gorgannith be able to survive for a while?

He is a very terror at the moment. Though he will be spent soon.

Hurry, get me aboard Relentless.

Yes Hugh. There was such sadness behind Nova's projection. He had never sounded like this before. *Be careful.*

Anger smoldered behind his dark eyes. *There is just me and ten thousand aliens inside these merged ships I'd wager.* Hugh thought about all the lives hanging in the balance, his family, all those billions lost. *It must end here. One way or another.*

Chapter 14
Reckoning

It took five minutes for Nova to link to the air lock. It was taking longer to cut through the blast doors. Anger swelled through Hugh, Gorgannith was dying by bits every second as was his valiant crew. Hugh pushed out with his hands and formed the power of the magnetic fields that coalesced around his body. He shaped them into a blue, pulsating fist and smashed at the lock. With one blow the six inch pyranite hatch splintered and flew inward in deadly shards to the deck.

Hugh set himself for weapons fire and the gore of the dead caught in the blast beyond. No one was there. Darkness seeped around weak red glimmer of emergency lighting. A thin mist coated the plasteel deck of Relentless. It looked to be a ghost ship. *Nova, maintain link as I scout. Can you scan life signs?*

It is strange Hugh. According to sensors, there are three, or . . . billions. It is a malfunction or perhaps I am being jammed.

Hugh looked down at his feet. The mists curled around his shoes and he could see dark stains on the surface near his feet. Blood. *There was a battle fought here.* Hugh wrinkled his nose at the smell of the mists. *Is this gas poisonous?*

No. Methane, carbon, and something . . . unknown.

Not comforting. I am going to the bridge. There is no time for analysis. If it was lethal I would be dead.

Nova did not respond as Hugh started jogging toward a central lift. Every corner he turned he expected to see cadavers of plague victims. Relentless shook and rumbled from outside weapons fire of the Armada as he reached the central lift.

Unless the Pliilulua wanted you alive. The mist at your feet is the plague spore. If you breathe it, even a wiff, your bionanytes will not be able to stop the necrosis. It will kill you Hugh.

Hugh swallowed as he punched the bridge level manually into the lift. Relentless's computer A.I. seemed as dead as her crew. *Nova, how can a plague spore so lethal it has killed fifteen billion people suddenly be selective.*

It is in an aerosol form made for disbursement from orbit. 2. It becomes more inert after a set period of time and settles. 3. It is bioreactive, alive, and whoever is controlling it wants to meet you. I thought I'd leave you with just three main theories.

The bridge level is here. How is Loki?

No contact.

Gorgannith?

Dead. I am sorry, Hugh.

So am I.

Hugh pulled out his khirdha and hand laser and walked onto the Capital Ships command bridge. The lights were functioning fully here though he immediately wished they weren't peering over at the command chair.

The Prelate Shalinsky stared unmoving at the Armada fighting on the view screen before him. Suspended by thick, green tentacles of seething cells, his arms and legs spread wide from ceiling and floor. A pool of green covered the ceiling and the floor. Writhing ponds of Pliilulua organism with smaller tendrils working control stations where human crewman still sat. Tendrils filling their silently screaming mouths as the protozoa liquified and slowly consumed them.

"Jesus." Hugh felt his stomach roiling. "Sander what have you done?"

The two inch deep pond at his feet spread apart as if inviting Hugh to enter the bridge. The tendrils holding his arms released the Prelate down to the command chair. His storm grey eyes turned to Hugh and darkened to the deep green of the Pliilulua. Even the whites of his eyes turned making him look solely unhuman.

Waiting for you.

The sound of the mental voice was filled with so pain, anger, and, power Hugh winced and covered his ears reflexively.

Who are you?

Your tiny mind would not understand us. It is easier to show you.

From the back of the room a force sphere carried two human prisoners. Master Birian and Grand Master Pirouen clutched one another. Their robes were torn and deep stains of sweat and blood coated them.

You allowed these to pollute and twist you. What little that was worthwhile of your species long since effaced by these. You very cells cry for vengeance. The screams cut across the universe. Tell him.

Pirouen could not speak. He had bitten his tongue off. Birian lifted his head, desolation creasing his ancient face. "Hugh Wilkey, we have done something unintended by our crafting." He coughed wetly and shook as he spoke. "There is a song, if you will, a magnetic field emits from all cells. It is the glue of the universe. With our crafting we have . . ." The old man broke down crying.

Tell him.

Birian screamed and Pirouen clutched his throat. Hugh could see gas forming in the bubble, drifting slowly from the top of the force globe.

"We perverted nature far too long. Our life span, skin color, who we are and choose to love, all of it. We white washed our genome so completely it started to buckle from the inside. Our very cells started to change it's . . . song, the pulse that connects us to the universe." Birian covered his face with his hands and wept bitterly. "We had no idea, no human sense that could perceive the gigantic impact such seemingly small alterations could cause your species. We are sorry."

You are.

The gas ate at the crafters slowly. The green tendrils started burrowing into their skin, faces. The men flinched, clawed at each other and themselves as if fire ants were eating them alive. Within minutes the men were dead. Their remains liquefying into a green sludge.

The thing that was the Prelate turned toward Hugh the force bubble released and dropped the liquefied remains of the crafters into the thin green substance waiting below.

Billions of my kind suffered madness from across the stars. Heard the screams of your polluted cells. Killing you was not enough. Even getting close to you plaguelings and the feeble attempts of your fleet has reduced our great Host.

I am sorry, they didn't know any other sentient race was out here, much less one as sensitive as yours. Hugh did not know what else to say. *Why destroy all mankind? Not everyone is crafted. You cannot destroy our entire species.*

Can't we? Shalinsky glared at him and pointed to Nova. ***The debt is too high now. You have cost us our peace and lives lost uncountable to the Host with your dabbling. We no longer kill you. We consume you. You are a grievous affliction to the cosmos and must replace what you have taken.***

I will stop you.

The prelate laughed and something inside him laughed with him. ***You cannot. The thing inside you is an aberration. The merging of machine and man is just another pollution. Your King has been most forthcoming with your journey. You owe us a giant debt of blood for making these animals see our holy ships. Your king now has the perfection he has always craved to match you. To dominate you. A vessel forged for vengeance for us and him.***

Hugh activated his khirda shield and laser. He shot at Shalinsky and hit him with a red lance of energy the pierced the center of his chest. Unnervingly, he did not even flinch. The wound did not leak blood but green microbes. The wound did not so much seal as plug.

First the flesh.

Green tendrils shot around Hugh's arms, legs, and took his weapons as if he were a child. Lifted in the air and brought him towards the Shalinsky thing.

Then the trappings and toys.

A series of three spore ships appeared where Nova was docked. Within seconds the tiny ring ship was reduced to slag by the green black beams.

"Noooo!" Hugh struggled against the bonds and ripped out with his power to shred the tentacles. To his dismay the things responded with their own magnetic harmonics neutralizing his field power.

Then root.

Shalinsky waved a hand and the screen changed to Earth. Two hundred and fifty spore ships covered the stratosphere and were releasing the death spores as they had on a hundred other worlds. They were not going to just kill humanity though, they had learned to eat them.

And branches all.

The screen flicked again. Only thirty Colonial ships were left in the Armada. The screen turned toward the Opaque Veil.

Though their song is sweet, this branch too will be snuffed for your crimes. Never again shall humans discontent and taint the galaxy again.

You cannot pass the veil.

We can. Child. We are as organic as your dragons, more so. Time to join your kin and kind. It is time for your terrible song to end Hugh Wilkey.

Hugh pushed out with his mind to Shalinsky, tried to find the part of him that still was him. *Sander you must fight it. Stop her.*

A weak mental voice flickered. *No. Not for you.*

Then do it for Earth, your family.

Enough. Shall we show Hugh what you really are under all that Craft?

Shalinsky's voice rose weakly. "No, Queen, spare me that."

For your violence to my people, I spare you not. Behold!

The alien tendrils shot out from ceiling and floor, piercing shalinsky shredding through pores and capillaries.

Fine filaments twisting the DNA back into shape. The shape it should have been without centuries of crafting.

The green tendrils fell away. The tall, golden haired aristocrat with the barrel chest and powerful physique was gone. A short, fat, balding man huddled in a ball at the feet of a vaguely woman shaped figure made of the green bodies of the Pliilulua. A single yellow eye looked down scornfully at Sander Shalinsky.

The little man's flesh was sagging, his body covered with unseemly fat and a mottled, hairy back. Watery, blue green eyes teared as Sander tried to stand and cover his nakedness.

Pathetic but at least you don't scream, King of Fools. You are too disgusting to be consumed, you will be frozen and preserved as a reminder to all complex organics of the price to be paid for meddling with the stuff of creation.

Hugh looked at Sander and saw him for who he was. He pressed into his mind. *I cannot effect her or her creations with my power. It has to be you.*

I am sorry, Hugh. Sander looked at Hugh and though he did not look anything like he had, he looked more human. More real.

I think I understand now, Sander. Why you hated me so much.

Sander looked away. Looked up into the Queen's yellow eye. "Please kill me."

No. Especially because you want it. But I will kill Hugh Wilkey.

Hugh felt the green tendrils starting to dissolve his limbs and his body trying to repair it. He was losing. The green wave dissolving his limbs was so painful he could not even scream. *Go.*

Hugh focused on the yellow eye. He peered deep down into it and saw within the Queen of the Hive. She was murdering him but he could feel the bionanytes rallying.

Sander ran up to Hugh and slapped his hand onto his chest. The bionanytes flooded out of Hugh and into Sander. The watery blue green eyes of his true face held all the imperfections of humanity. It was humanity. "I am so sorry Hugh Wilkey. I did not know."

Hugh could not even hear him. Once his bionanytes were gone, his arms and legs were being consumed down to the stubs. Death was coming. Hugh spent the last seconds of his life focusing on the Hive Queen's one yellow eye. Inside of which was the one cell that was the key to all the Pliilulua. "Go!"

Sander ran up to the queen, running through the green pond of her fellows. He Pushed forward even when the green tendrils started eating his limbs. The bionanytes worked to repair. "Relentless, hold her. Operation Zed."

The ship board A.I. kicked on and a force field froze the green humanoid form in place just as it was starting to dissolve back to the safety of it's numbers.

You cannot! I am One of The Many.

"You are one less bitch." Sander grabbed the yellow eye, the controlling cell, and the bionanytes flooded out of his hand. The Hive Queen was caught in the force field as the lake around her solidified in a warring mass, trying to break in. The raging sea smashed at the computer like the angry pseudopod of some shapeless giant.

Hugh's broken body was left on the deck as the Pliilulua outside the force field smashed at Sander's body. It shredded him in seconds and Prelate Sander Shalinsky's reign was at an end.

The battle in the force shield flashed with brutal energy and light. The woman shaped shield flickered with lances of blue light and green black as both bionannyte and Pliilulua protozoa battled to kill or protect the Hive Queen.

A grey, greenish black liquid was forming inside the sack of shielding. Relentless's core system was being breached by the Pliilulua battling outside. Suddenly the tides began to dissipate, cream colored lines spread through and the blackening mass of kelly green, like creme through coffee. The last stand of the Pliilulua faded with their dead queen as the yellow eye faded and died.

Hugh opened his eye to see the remnants of the Armada start to smash the suddenly sluggish Spore ships of the Pliilulua. He wished he could have saved Earth. Blood was seeping out of the stumps of his arms and legs. He felt his heart skip a beat as it had insufficient blood to pump. So this was the end? The last thing he saw were dragons flying all around outside. At least his last sight in life would be something wonderful and un-sullied. Dragons.

*

He itched and rubbed his face with his hand. His hand? Hugh opened his eyes and was in a ring chamber of a Duane. A small med robot was leaning over him. "One?"

'This unit is not one. This unit is called Nova."

"How?"

"Shhh. Rest love." Lilly's voice sounded so wonderful. Johnny held Merlin and pressed the baby next to Hugh. He noticed the almond shaped eyes of his son and smiled.

"Tell me what has happened?"

"We are on our way back to the Veil."

"What of Earth?"

"Safe. Thanks to you." A tinge of sadness marked her voice.

"What of Loki?"

"He is gone. He did much like you did with the bionanytes. He cast them into the spore fleet on Earth and found their Hive Queen. He did not survive."

Hugh felt a tear trickle down his neck. "How did I survive? How are you here?"

"Nova switched much of himself into a med droid he created just in case he needed to follow you or leave the ship. We have a tendency to be hard on his chosen vessels so . . . he didn't take any chances."

Hugh looked at his arms. Small scars from the Pliilulua dissolving acid could be seen and on his legs. All the hair was burned off.

Lilly nodded. "Nova only had the one bionanyte left, his limited medical ability, and not time to waste to save your life. He gave back the singling bionannyte and worked to save you. They did."

"I am grateful." Hugh tried to stand up but Cleo jumped up on his chest and weighed him back down with ease."

You have one weak little bionannyte left in you Hugh. We still have our connection but I am the top cat now. I am glad you are alive.

I am so glad to see you!

Johnny signed, "*We were so worried. This is the dragon Tsuna'koni. We are going back to Ombari. The War is over.*" He bent down and kissed Hugh tenderly.

"I am glad of it. So glad to see you all. I just wish we could have saved more."

Lilly wiped Hugh's face with a damp cloth. "You did more than anyone had any right to ask you. Earth is safe. The vanguard has rallied to your and Loki's call."

"The Khorumkhan finally gave their blessing?"

"Yes. It took a while. I think they were just shocked at Loki waking and leaving after so long. It changed them. Yet they eventually came around."

"It is well. The Pliilulua would have come for them as next." Hugh trembled just thinking about the terrible Hive Queen and all the people that had died so horribly.

"At least that bastard Shalinsky is dead."

Hugh gently grabbed her hand before she could get up. "He was a bad man and not true to himself. In the end Lilly, he did the right thing. He had a hand in saving us all."

Lilly cocked her head at Hugh quizzically. "He owed a great debt, Hugh. He needed to pay a lot to redeem himself."

Hugh nodded, smiled sadly to himself. "He did, Lilly. He did."

*

Six months later, thousands had gathered at the Summer Palace. Spring had come to Ombar and thanks to the dragons many people from old Earth, Oceanian and tribal alike. The priests of Ombar had come home and the Ombardwan was to be crowned. The Bridger of Worlds was to become the next Khorumkhan.

Adriel, Margo, Yu, and Noren had ruled for a long time and felt their taste for power had faded with their dragon Loki. Though the Duanes usually ruled in groups of four as was tradition, the sacred connection to the Dragons whom were their family forever as well as their ties to beyond the veil, the people of Ombar were happy to make an exception.

The Vanguard had run what was left of the Pliilulua from known space with the remnants of the Colonial fleet. The connections between the tribes of humanity had grown stronger. Media was freed up in the Empire and the ruling conservative Senate was cast down. The Greens held sway and they selected a new Prelate.

Prelate Hugh Wilkey agreed to a four year term, subject to vote of the Senate. He just asked that he be allowed to stay close to The Dragon's Ear and live on Ombar if it was truly the will of the Oceanian's that he be their Prelate.

Sitting in the Hall of Thrones, a crown was placed reverently down on the fourth seat to honor the possibility of a fourth to complete the Sacred Duane. Margo had replaced the heroic Celenil. It was not unknown to happen eventually.

Johnny Blue sat the fourth chair, representing the Free People of Old Earth. Lilly Hsian sat the third, Merlin Hsian upon his knee. Cleo sat like a lion at Hugh's feet. Their mental tie the last lingering connection of the power the bionannytes had given him.

The assembled dignitaries, ambassadors, and Ombari's from across the globe sat in mixed audience as minstrels, dancers, caterers, and bar tenders flooded through the court like a bacchanalian army at a wedding feast.

So you did it. You found a home. Bravo.

King Hugh turned to Cleo and patted her on the head. *Sounds like you want a crown too.*

No. That would be irritating. I guess I want kittens. My own. Not that they would not be irritating.

Don't you think you'd want to talk with them? They would be nothing like you Cleo.

Trust me. Talking is overrated. I would feel like a true Queen.

A blare of silver trumpets called out. Adriel walked in front of a procession with a box behind her. Senators, Duanes, priests, and chieftains walked beside and behind it.

"*Looks like a coronation gift.*" *King Johnny signed.* "*What could it be.*"

"No idea love. I just hope it is not embarrassing to me."

Lilly laughed. "Life is too serious to take so seriously Hugh."

"That's King Hugh to you!" He leaned back onto the crystal throne. It was well worn and oddly comfortable. He had come a very long way.

"Hail Khoramkhan, Ombardwan of legend, saver of worlds and waker of dragons." Adriel's voice silenced the crowd, sharpened by centuries of command. Hugh noticed a small, grey white streak in her golden hair and for some reason, felt glad at their return to humanity. Who wanted to linger so long after so many centuries of life. He too had left so much behind him. He glanced at Merlin sleeping happily beside Lilly on the throne. Even though all his dreams had come true, it seemed he had to go through a valley of nightmare. He would leave the future to his son and enjoy today.

Adriel inclined her head to the crystal thrones. "We have lived separately so long, unable to pierce the veils that blocked us from each other and even more insidiously, the veils that block us from knowing and accepting our true selves."

A throng of cheers went up and almost deafened them. Streamers and confetti made of flowers dropped down through the sky roof and sun lit the crystal arcs and gilding of the packed hall.

Turning directly to Hugh, Adriel pegged him with her eyes. "Long have we waited for the time to give a gift to the true Ombardwan, worthy of his deeds and his coming. Behold what we have found." She waved for the white box to be brought up to the dais. Cleo's nose wrinkled suspiciously. *What could this be?*

Two Ombari guards opened the vented, ornate door of a metallic box crested with white ceramic heat shields.

Hugh dropped his glass.

Tears rolled down his face and he collapsed, sobbing in front of the crate. A cry went up around the hall. Guards started pushing forward and a woman screamed. "Is the King hurt?"

Adriels voice rang out, "No, the King is well, behold the joining of past and present, for the future must be at peace with the past."

Hugh looked up and at the man in the metallic crate. He held a black cat in his arms. The dark haired man had the uniform of the rocket Ombardwan crew. The name tag said Michael Wilkey. Hugh reached out and touched the clear surface of the unit. It wasn't a crate. It was a coffin.

"How? How did you do it? How are you here? Hugh sobbed and placed one hand over the clear membrane in front of Mike's chest, almost touching for the first time in centuries.

"From the records collected, they could not get you out of the cryogenic chamber for six months. They weren't sure you would even live. Michael must have arranged going to another facility, the one near . . . the Amazon, that was making headway without the restrictions of the U.S. Scientific Tribunal. When project Ombardwan started, he asked to be frozen. Sealed for two thousand years," the officer explained

"They took him in a rocket?"

"Yes. It seems so. They intended to. They were fighting to keep every human life they could. The descendants of the Ombari honor their agreements. Yet when they saw Michael had the same last name as you, were from the same time . . ."

"He even brought Sam?" Cleo was tapping on the glass where the dead, black cat lay. Cleo was inscrutable and silent. "Why?" Hugh finally asked

Lilly and Johnny stepped up behind Hugh and touched his shoulders. "Because he loved you Hugh, after all."

"The power source failed on his unit some time ago. But he is preserved for all time," the minister said sadly and turned away.

Hugh stood up and walked toward the empty throne. He pushed the release button on Michael's unit, the membrane dissolved, and he gently placed the crown on Michael's head.

"Behold my people! The Duane of The Ombardwan. The Opaque Veil has been passed!" The crowd cheered though some with hesitancy as three of the living Khorumkhan stood and held hands.

Hugh felt a familiar tingling on the skin of his arm when he placed the crown. A smile broke out on his tear stained face as he felt . . . life move through him again.

Raising his hands triumphantly to the crowd, Hugh gently kissed, Johnny, his son and Lilly. He shouted to the court at the top of his lungs, "It is a better world now my people. May we all go forth and be Kings!"

Where there is life, there's hope. He will find a way Hugh thought, then sat squarely on his throne.

Hugh breathed deeply, sighed and with a small smile rising on his face, felt himself start to shine.